THE
LAST
EXIT

THE
LAST
EXIT
A JEN LU MYSTERY

Michael Kaufman

CROOKED
LANE

NEW YORK

Copyright © 2021 by Michael Kaufman

All rights reserved.

Published in the United States by Crooked Lane Books, an imprint of The Quick Brown Fox & Company LLC.

Crooked Lane Books and its logo are trademarks of The Quick Brown Fox & Company LLC.

Library of Congress Catalog-in-Publication data available upon request.

ISBN (hardcover): 978-1-64385-567-7
ISBN (ebook): 978-1-64385-568-4

Cover design by Melanie Sun

Printed in the United States.

www.crookedlanebooks.com

Crooked Lane Books
34 West 27th St., 10th Floor
New York, NY 10001

First Edition: January 2021

10 9 8 7 6 5 4 3 2 1

To Betty

1

It was only eight in the morning, but I could already feel sweat collecting under our breasts. Jen had been kicked in the butt for switching me off for five minutes while on duty last week, so for the third day in a row, we were back in regulation blues, trudging along the two-mile path circling the Tidal Basin.

It was boring work. Retrieve phones dropped in the water. Search for kids who eluded their parents' jail-guard gaze for two seconds. Tolerate the private US Park Police. Help the dumber tourists figure out which one was the Jefferson Monument. Keep an eye out for the saltwater crocs. This task seemed a particular waste of time since only one had been spotted so far this summer. But then again, it had eaten a jogger. When the croc was shot and sliced open, the running shoes still looked new.

I was young, two years and three months. Detective Jen Lu was thirty-eight and change. I'll be dead in three more years. She'll live to a hundred after her mother does her duty and exits, and Jen can snag the treatment. Good for her.

08:03:52. The sun was smudged by haze that hung around like a fart under a blanket. We heard a shout by the FDR Memorial. Then a scream. I tagged the time and our position. We ran.

A Caucasian man who looked like he'd been stewed in scarlet food coloring was screaming at a Black woman in yellow running gear. She was lying on her side, clutching her shoulder. I scanned the man and found a match.

"Watch out," I cautioned Jen. We ran harder.

The man saw us and shot off like he had a Roman candle up his butt. We reached the prone woman, yelled, "You alright?" We got a nod and took off after the man.

He was good. We were better. We tackled him at the Martin Luther King Jr. Memorial. Nonviolence has its place, but I whacked him across the face.

"You didn't have to do that," Jen said.

"Sure I did, and you know it."

James O'Neil. Twenty-seven. Follows the Klan and two neo-Nazi sites. Arrested once for battery. Dad is a Timeless, so James got off.

We cuffed him and I called it in. We waited for the car, handed him over, me sharing the data and time stamp with the officer's synth. We went back and called an ambulance for the jogger, although she said she was fine.

Any hope we'd be rewarded with a better gig for the day crashed when I received the order to get back on patrol.

Tuesday, July 3. 08:42:11. Washington, DC. Good times.

* * *

"Chandler," she said to me, in the didactic tone of a really bored teacher, "having the Fourth of July fall on a Wednesday is the biggest bitch there is."

There are things I am still learning.

"Why?" I said.

"Think about it for a second," she said. Too bored to tell me.

Jen pulled her N95 back on, masking her up like half the people we passed. Two months into the Great Shenandoah Blaze, and DC was at the mercy of the wind. We were on our twelfth circuit. Two lost kids. Forty-five Shadows—nineteen females and twenty-six males with ten children in tow—who we ordered to keep walking or get out. Thirteen sets of directions given to monuments, museums, or the Metro. One bad tumble and a call to paramedics. Four men stopped and IDed. One photo for a group of tourists who acted like they owned the show.

Winds shifted, mask came off. More days now with no smoke—the fire was finally running out of fuel.

I said, "People only get one day off instead of a three-day weekend. Ditto with Tuesday or Thursday."

"Chandler, you're not so dumb after all."

I let that pass. I know she likes me, sort of.

"Then again," she said, "half the people don't have real work, so what the hell."

"What the hell," I agreed.

A good-looking young man and woman stared at Jen as we passed. Even in uniform, Jen turns heads. Tall. Ebony hair gathered into a ponytail that tumbles down her back. Chinese American. High cheekbones and startling blue eyes with heavy lashes, apparently inherited from a father she couldn't remember and about whom her mother refused to tell her anything. They shouted at passersby to stare.

I said we should grab lunch.

"You hungry?" she said.

"Yuk, yuk." I'm a synth implant, tucked into a fold of Jennifer's neocortex. Ergo, I don't get hungry, but I'm whacked the millisecond her energy starts to flag.

Lunch was a hummus roll with kimchi.

"Shouldn't we be having a hot dog?"

"Mañana."

Speaking of mañana, word came through at 12:41:39 that Les had gone home sick and we'd have to work the next night, the Fourth of July.

"Call in," she said.

The 1940s ringtone sounded in her rostromedial prefrontal cortex.

"Chandler," she said, "let's go with something less jarring for a while."

"Headache?"

"My life's a headache."

Even I knew this wasn't completely true, but I complied.

Captain Brooks answered. Jen explained she was supposed to go to a fireworks party at her boyfriend's family home. Earlier, I had asked if she could turn me on for part of it and at first she had said, "Fat chance," but later softened that to, "We'll see."

Captain Brooks didn't even bother to say he was sorry.

"I love you too," she said after he snapped off the connection. Jennifer once told me that the hardest thing she had ever learned as a cop was how to talk over a phone that existed only in her imagination. But she was kidding, since that wasn't her hardest thing by a long shot.

Then she brightened. "At least it means I'm out of this damn uniform and back to the unit."

Regular duty, but another twenty-five days on probation.

Tuesday, July 3. 12:46:09.

* * *

"Why *did* you turn me off last week?" I asked.

She ignored me.

We lumbered across the Mall on our way back to the station. It was in the low hundreds again, and the soupy air stunk of sweat, dried piss, crumbling asphalt, dead grass, and distant charred trees.

I waited a respectful time before disrespectfully asking again.

"Chandler," she said, "it's nothing."

Translation: "It's everything." Jennifer did her job and normally followed the rules. She never defied authority. Turning me off didn't make sense. She'd been docked a week's pay and was now pounding the pavement. I wondered if it had to do with her current obsession: "Eden," a massive bee on her brain. "Eden." Buzzing in fat quotation marks, because it was a prize collection of silly rumors glued together with spit and gossip. Humans have this unbending fascination with things they don't know. The very quality of not knowing invests the thing with hypercharged reality. And when something can't possibly exist, then it positively glows in their imaginations. "Eden" burned in Jennifer's brain.

I asked her.

"What?"

"Eden," I repeated.

"You're kidding. I would never turn you off for any work thing. It was . . . Drop it, will you? I made a stupid mistake."

I dropped it right into my human puzzle box. Jennifer always plays it straight, so why had she turned me off?

In front of the National Gallery, a recruitment mini-fair was in full swing. "65 and out!" a banner proclaimed. "Exit now!"

Jen's feet were sore and her legs were slabs of dead meat, so I gave her a nibble of adrenalin. We were on the new six-to-two shift they were giving foot patrols. Three officers had plopped over dead from heat exhaustion in April, so the new hours divvied up the afternoon death zone more evenly between the day and evening shifts.

Chatty guy that I am, I asked Jen what she was doing that night. I knew, of course, but we like to preserve the fiction of mental independence.

"Meeting Zach for a drink."

"Boot me up for a bit?"

She had allowed me to be drunk twice and stoned once.

"Chandler, grow up."

Back at the station, she signed out and switched me off.

Tuesday, July 3. 14:02:09. Washington, DC.

2

Early in their relationship, Jen realized that Zach had many *althoughs* in his life. He had a moderately steady, although excruciatingly small, income. He had a PhD in environmental economics from the London School of Economics, although that didn't exactly mean he had a job. For the past two years, he had run a gardening business, although the word *business* was a bit of a stretch, since he worked from a bicycle that dragged a tiny trailer. In the winter, he shoveled snow, although snow in DC was now as rare as pregnant popes. And he had a nice place to live, although, like millions of others, it was at home with his parents, even though he was forty-one. He was expecting, although not hoping, that would come to an end in January. After all, his parents were both sixty-four.

If Jen had first seen him in close-up photographs of his face, she wouldn't have tagged him for a fashion model. His eyes were slightly too far apart, and his head one size too large, as if that big brain of his had pressed everything outward at some point. He had a boyish mop of hair that was forever flopping into his eyes and, by contrast, a long-ago-broken nose.

But in some unaccountable way, snap all the pieces together and add in his strong shoulders, and they gave him a rugged yet vulnerable appeal. Jennifer found him remarkably good looking. No, more than that: she was mesmerized by his looks.

They had met a year earlier after an accident she had on the trail along the Potomac. Afterward, she had phoned her best friend and her work partner, Les.

"His hairline is so low I think he's part Neanderthal."

"Yech," Les had said. "Did you hurt yourself?"

"Caught a piece of glass. Nothing serious."

"You're still wearing those stupid minimalist shoes?"

Jen didn't respond.

"And he rescued you?"

"You don't have to say it like I was a damsel in distress."

"Did he?"

"Kind of. He was riding his bike and saw me fall. He stopped and asked if I was okay. I said I was fine. He got off his bike about ten feet away and had a sip of water, but it was obvious he was making sure I wasn't going to die. I repeated, 'I'm fine,' to try to get him to scram. I examined the bottom of my shoe. There was a nasty shard of glass sticking through the rubber."

"Through the thin rubber."

"Glass that somehow dug through the *extremely tough* rubber. I pulled it out. Started to stand, but, well . . . he pulled out a small first aid kit, came over to me, and said, 'Let's have a look.'

"I asked if he was a doctor and he laughed. I wriggled out of my shoe and there was blood everywhere. He said, 'You tested?' just like it was an everyday question. And when I said I was fine, he replied, 'Okay, then, let's have a look.' He cupped my foot in one hand—did I tell you he has nice hands?—"

"Nice hands are definitely a turn on," Les said.

"—and carefully wiped off the blood with a piece of gauze. The cut was on the ball of my foot, near my toes. He peered at it. He wiggled the two closest toes and looked up at me. I shook my head, saying it didn't hurt. He said, 'Scream if this does.' He pressed gently around the perimeter of the wound, checking for another piece inside. At each point, he glanced up at my face. Halfway around, I swore, and he suggested we go to a hospital. Les, you really want to hear all this?"

"Yeah, why not?"

"At first, I tried to walk, and he pushed his bike alongside. But it hurt like hell. So he said, 'Why don't you borrow my bike.' It wasn't fancy but I could tell it had decent parts and I said, 'What if I steal it?'"

"You tell him you're a cop?"

"Nope. He said, 'Well, you wouldn't take it, would you.' It wasn't a question or a command, just like he'd known me forever and trusted me. But the bike didn't have real pedals, just these clip-on knobs that I knew would kill my foot. So he said, 'Then hop on.' I pulled myself up sidesaddle on his bike frame, and off we went."

"Are you nuts? You took off with a total stranger?"

"He didn't give off any sketchy vibes."

"Classic psychopath."

"I'm not an idiot. There was nothing creepy. Totally the opposite. And anyway, I knew I could handle him."

"Okay." Les's voice was still tentative, but he always was a sucker for a good love story.

"I was trying to hold myself upright so I wouldn't touch him. I mean, I trusted him, but I didn't know the guy from Adam, and I was soaked from my run."

"Where did all this happen?"

"I told you, along the river."

"No, I mean how far out?"

"Maybe three miles. So he had his arms around me, holding the handlebar, and he has beautiful shoulders, and I guess I sort of let myself lean against him little by little and before long, I just about had my head against him, and he was telling me about how much he loved it out there, and I was saying I used to escape there when I was a kid. Before I knew it, he said, 'We're here,' and I'd barely noticed we'd come back into the city."

"But you say he's not exactly movie star material."

"I'm not so sure." She paused to think about this. "He has this rugged body and these really cute dimples when he smiles—"

"God, I love dimples."

"And his smile kind of pops out at you. Although I guess it did make his eyes kind of disappear under his hairline."

"Sounds hot. Does he have a brother?"

"I won't tell Christopher you said that."

"It was a joke. Anyway, you've already exchanged bodily fluids."

"Sweat and blood."

"Two out of three ain't bad."

"Three?"

"Blood, sweat, and tears. There are always those goddam tears."

After their second get-together, this time for a coffee, she reported back to Les.

"I saw him again."

"Your shining armor guy? Does he have a name?"

"Zach."

"Okay. I like Zachs."

"We were doing the usual, asking what we did, where we went to school, all that."

"Finally tell him you're a cop?"

"Of course."

"And?"

"Nothing. I guess he kind of looked surprised."

"Surprised?"

"I mean, none of the retrograde shit I still hear from some guys."

Les threw up a pair of air quotes. "'Pretty dykey'?"

"Or, 'Aren't you afraid of getting hurt?'"

"Classic."

"Although . . ." She gazed off as if picturing the scene. "I kinda got a feeling he was wondering about being with a cop. Sounds like he had some bad experiences with the police when he was living in Jamaica."

"Living in Jamaica?"

"For five years, after he did his PhD. He was working on a big climate change project."

"And now he shovels snow."

"What d'ya have against snow?"

*　*　*

On their third date, Jennifer and Zach had slept together—well, had sex.

"Apparently," Jennifer told Les, "there is no correlation between a low hairline and lack of ability in bed."

"His place?"

"Yeah, lives with his parents. Sort of an extended family vibe."

She never brought men home. Not that Ava and Taylor would mind. Just that it was their apartment, and they were giving her a deal, and she wanted to keep her private life just that—private.

"You can always bring him over." Both of Les's parents had exited, and now he and Christopher co-owned their condo. "You know, if you need a place."

"The Love Hotel," Jennifer had said.

"You're saying he was good?"

"Transcendent."

"Transcendent? Seriously?"

"If you only saw his hands."

3

It was barely dark, and damn if Washington, DC, wasn't exploding around us. Zach's parents lived in Columbia Heights, 1.92 miles from the White House. A lower-middle-class neighborhood twenty or thirty years back, before the lower middle class got lowered out of existence. I was switched on because Jen was signed in for duty. Their joint is the second and third floors of a tiny condo. Nice place, but skinny. So skinny that Jen once said she needed to suck in her breath before slipping through the front door, but she never actually did, so I knew she was exaggerating.

Crazy place, though. Zach's dad, Raffi, collected weird stuff. I mean *stuffed* stuff: stuffed real animals, stuffed fake animals, different brands of dried turkey stuffing, an old couch with stuffed cushions so plush you wouldn't want to set a baby down or you might lose it. Raffi once claimed that he might switch to snuff boxes because he was sick of the *stuff* items, and this new hobby would require only a one-letter change; now it was pretty much too late for even that.

Raffi and Leah had built an illegal deck on their flat roof. It was my first time up there as more than a switched-off lump of programmed biological matter wedged into Jen's brain. There must have been twenty of us up there. Plus the rooftop veggie garden Zach had put in. I did a quick calculation to see if the roof would support the planters, all that wet soil, plus all of us. When you only live to five, you don't want to mess around with premature death.

11

Anyway, it wouldn't be building collapse that got us tonight. Turns out that Columbia Heights is the pyromaniac capital of America. This place was going so nuts that no one on the roof seemed to notice the whump-whump-booms coming from the fireworks display two miles away on the Mall. Here, fireworks exploded overhead, sizzlers whistled in the alleyways, huge spectacles of light phumped in the sky in all directions. I felt the sound vibrate through her whole body. Clouds of gunpowder drifted under the streetlights down below. Extraordinary.

"Raffi," Jennifer said to Zach's dad, "did you know we invented fireworks?"

"Clever people, you Chinese." Raffi smiled. "Tang Dynasty, I believe it was."

Jennifer says that Zach inherited his curiosity from his father.

"But," Leah chimed in, "there is some speculation it was earlier, in the Sui Dynasty."

And his brains from his mother.

Jen said, "I didn't know any of that."

Leah waved her away. "Oh, it's just one of those silly things you pick up."

Jen wandered over to Zach. "What's the matter?" she said.

"No rain for three weeks. I'm worried about fires."

*   *   *

The call came in at 21:38:59: Domestic on V Street NW.

By the time we made it downstairs, I had one of the spanking new, deep purple cop motorcycles waiting for us. As we drove, I got the feed: African American. No arrests, no felony convictions, no warrants. Father had driven a taxi when he was young and had odd jobs as a night watchman and day laborer since then. Mother was a nurse, now unemployed, looks after a neighbor's young child some nights. Taxes up to date. Grown son lives with them, works when he can.

Siren on, we raced, Jen's adrenaline pumping into me like a fire engine running red lights through her veins. Good times.

We're members of the Elder Abuse Unit. Some old-school stuff—vulnerable parents getting abused by no-good kids—but, these days, a lot of parents abusing kids by not wanting to exit. Jen says it's sad news that we're needed, but I say, with humans being what they are, I'm not surprised.

A large, three-story house converted into apartments. Rose bushes with delicate yellow flowers out front, gunpowder heavy in the air. A crowd had gathered outside the open front door. How they had heard the screaming over the war-zone explosions was anyone's guess. One of the neighbors pointed over his shoulder with his thumb and yelled, "Second floor."

We walked in, Jen's hand on her holstered firearm. The stairs were clean; the hall smelled newly washed and polished. The only door on the second floor was ajar. We called out. It was quiet inside. That always makes you worried in domestics. Dead quiet equals dead people.

Jennifer called out again. Nothing.

Jen drew her gun, her forefinger lined up along the frame, ready to drop onto the trigger. We went inside.

They were in the kitchen, thankfully alive, but posed like a Norman Rockwell painting gone bad. Delmar Johnson Sr. and Delmar Johnson Jr., frozen at opposite ends of a once blue Formica table carefully set with cherry-red placemats, steel utensils, and china plates with tiny lavender flowers around their perimeter. The food was untouched. Facing us was Odette Johnson, Delmar Senior's wife, and on a high chair next to her, a toddler was contentedly eating dry Cheerios, one by one. Senior and Junior were pointing handguns at each other.

Jen said, "Police. Put down your weapons."

Neither man budged, and only Odette Johnson and the toddler looked up at us.

Junior said, "Mom, don't you go movin'."

I was formulating a strategy when Jen said, "Don't do anything stupid." I told her she'd just jumped ahead four steps. She grunted. We plastered on a calm voice and said, "Tell me what's going on, will you?"

Junior said, "Nothing's going on. That's the problem, isn't it?"

Senior said, "We never shoulda had you."

Ms. Johnson said to Junior, "Baby, he don't mean that."

Senior said, "Like hell."

Junior didn't take his eyes off his father, but it was clear he was talking to us. "You see? You see what I put up with?"

"Mr. Johnson." Jen meant Senior. "Sir, I need to ask you to put down your weapon."

"And him finally get his way?"

Jen said, "This isn't about that."

"You stupid?" Junior said. "Of course that what it's about. They don't sign up. They ain't gonna exit. What the hell's in it for me? You tell me that. You tell me."

We couldn't, and we didn't.

"Mr. Johnson, sir." We were addressing the father again. "You shouldn't have let it come to this. Don't you think it's natural for your boy to want a life?"

"He can do whatever the hell he wants."

"That right?" Junior said, and shot him.

Senior fell back, firing his own gun as he toppled, the bullet hitting his wife in the chest. Jennifer shot Junior through the hand holding the gun. She's a hell of a good shot under pressure.

Mr. Johnson Sr. was dead. Ms. Johnson mumbled one thing before she died: "We were gettin' to Eden."

4

From Wikipedia, the free encyclopedia:

"65 and out" is the slogan created by the so-called Ice Floe Movement. At the time, a whole generation was threatened by (i) skyrocketing unemployment caused by artificial intelligence, although high unemployment was partially lowered by the epidemic of rapid onset spongiform encephalitis (ROSE); (ii) massive social unrest because of ever-worsening inequality and the availability of the longevity treatment to the very few who could afford it; (iii) the growing economic impact of climate change; and (iv) increasingly unaffordable housing prices. Faced with this generational threat, economists at the University of Chicago suggested in 2028 that the source of the problem was an oversupply of the elderly.

In order to reestablish economic and population equilibrium, they successfully pressed for a voluntary policy of permanent retirement, or "exit." If a single parent or a couple, by the age of sixty-five, volunteers for euthanasia, any of their children under fifty years of age has access to a modified version of the longevity treatment (known colloquially as "the treatment"). Unlike the longevity treatment available to the super-rich, who become Timeless, the modified treatment doesn't stop recipients from aging, but it does protect them from ROSE and allows them to live in a fairly healthy state until well into their nineties, as long as they keep up with booster shots. In order to make the program sustainable, only those children with no children themselves are eligible. This modified version also sterilizes them.

5

"**B**ut, sir, she said they were going to Eden."

Captain Brooks stared at us. His smooth dark skin was marred by a thick keloid scar where his left eyebrow should have been. His old-school beard made him look like a baseball player from the teens or maybe one of the old hipsters, but without the good coffee or a baby on his shoulders.

09:22:41.

Jennifer swiped the back of her wrist across our forehead. "It's going to be a hot one again, sir." She smiled.

Captain Brooks did not smile back. He was third in the hierarchy of the MPD's First District. Particularly since the district boundaries changed a decade ago, it is the most prestigious of them all.

A few months ago, Jennifer had told Les that she had heard a rumor that Captain Brooks had once laughed at a joke.

Les had said, "Not in my time."

"Smiled?"

"Let me think." Before he could take another breath, he added, "Nope. Not that either."

"Act nice?"

Les said, "Forget it, Jen. He's a badass hard ass."

"I swear, he's putting it on."

"Yeah and I'm . . ."

"What?"

16

"Fuck if I know." Les had looked around as if he was going to discover his missing metaphor, but shook his head and returned his gaze to her. "Listen, Jen. Just quit sucking up to him."

"I'm not—"

"Jen, you're my friend."

"I hate when people start a sentence that way."

"Your problem is you never stand up for yourself."

"Thank you, Doctor."

"I mean it. Don't forget, you're Cobalt Blue."

He sometimes called her Cobalt. He said *Jen* was too pedestrian. As with any good nickname, it played on her name and physical features. Jen B. Lu, Chinese woman with extraordinary blue eyes, became Jen Blue. And at some point, Les decided she needed some playful ramping up and rechristened her Cobalt Blue. Superhero stuff. She said, "My eyes aren't actually cobalt blue. And even if they were, that nickname is absurd." But damn if she didn't smile inside.

"Stop letting everyone push you around," Les had said.

"Screw him. That better?"

"Much," Les had replied.

Nevertheless, she did keep trying, or at least it seemed that way to me. Nothing too gushy. No boxes of chocolates. I couldn't figure it out, though: both her oxytocin and cortisol levels spiked when she was around the Captain. Love and fear, comfort and anxiety, all mixed together in a voodoo stew. He's a gruff sort of man, but every last one of the officers, Les included, trusts him and respects him, even if most of them don't like him.

Jen is one of the few who likes him and wants him to like her. It's one more human mystery that wasn't programmed into my lines of code.

Anyway, I reminded her once again what Les had said. A fresh surge of cortisol gushed from her adrenal gland. But damn if it wasn't aimed at me. *Fuck off,* she said to me, but I felt her vocal cords loosen to a lower register right before she spoke again.

"Sir," she continued, this time more businesslike. Dropped the pleading tone and small talk about the weather. "This is the first outright confirmation I've had."

"What kind of confirmation you got? She going to give you an address for Eden? Directions?"

"I told you, she died."

He shot her a hard stare.

"Sir." Defiance waning.

"Then I suppose, Jen, you still don't have a thing. And you know—"

"I have a lead."

"—why you don't?" He stared her down in the way he must have done back when he was busting kids for shoplifting. "Because Eden's all made up. A nutbar fantasy."

"I don't think so." Weakly said.

"I don't pay you to think."

Jennifer thought, *He's watched too many tough-cop movies.*

"Of course you pay me to think . . . sir."

"What do you want?"

"To look into this Eden business."

"No. And let me tell you again what I want." He rubbed the knuckle of his thumb over the thick scar. "I want you to do your job and stop bothering me with this Eden crap."

Even right then, I knew there wasn't a chance in hell the captain was going to get what he wanted.

* * *

Lunch break. Keep her mitochondria chugging. We met up with Zach. Jen told me to shut up.

I listen. I learn.

I wondered if he even knew about me.

No, I heard back.

You know, I'll be living with him, too, in a few months.

Clam up.

She and I are part of a trial run. They've selected eighty cops in DC for a three-year trial. As secret as they can make it inside the police department, which is kind of like saying as clothed as they can keep a strip joint. Absolutely no publicity outside, though; some rumors, but that's about it. No one is allowed to tell spouses or friends. Hence, Zach doesn't have a clue I'm eavesdropping on every sweet thing he says when I'm turned on and we're together.

Only the beginning of the month and Jen's lunch budget was already toast—burnt to a crisp because of the docked pay. She unwrapped a sandwich of pink tub-meat that tasted of seagull and a flap of lettuce with the consistency of wet toilet paper. We ate, then headed down an alley at 12:22:01.

Zach reached for her hand. "You allowed to hold hands on duty?"

"Lunch time." Jen laughed.

"I can't wait for you to see their store."

"You sure these guys are legit?"

Zach said, "Hey, would I want to get you in trouble?"

"I'm already in trouble up to my ass."

"Your gorgeous ass."

"Bad guys spot us a mile away."

"I told you—" But we'd already reached the door.

Old brick building, a tall one-story. Sunflower solar panels decked the roof—building permit was in order—but the rest of the place seemed to date from when Lincoln was president.

Jen said, "God, it looks like they made buggy whips here."

I said to her, *No, they made*—

But she snapped at me, *I told you to keep quiet.*

Zach ushered us inside.

It was a high-ceilinged room. Except for a few windows way up and shelves at the back, three walls were totally covered by a display of tools and machines arrayed in amazing patterns and colors: typewriters of every vintage, sewing machines, transistor radios, hand-cranked adding machines, abacuses, electric mixers, toasters, a gizmo for milking cows, vibrators, electric drills and handsaws, wood-handled chisels, hammers, screwdrivers, clunky plastic telephones, colored pencils, paintbrushes, can openers, and wire whisks. As we watched, objects moved up or down, left or right, as if the walls were giant Rubik's cubes. Shapes created patterns, patterns split apart and reshaped by object, color, or size, and then fell apart to form others linked by theme. Good times.

Never before had I felt Jen's mind go completely still. We were gawking, drinking in the whole thing, but it was as if her mind was so flooded that she couldn't register a thing.

She whispered to Zach, "You said this was a computer store."

"Look," said Zach, pointing straight up. Square Japanese paper lanterns, made of thin white rice paper mounted on balsa wood frames, covered the whole ceiling. Each glowed pastel shades from a light tucked inside: warm yellows, a robin's-egg blue (not that we had many robins left this far south), a flamingo pink.

Right behind us, a woman's voice said, "Repurposed OLED phone displays."

We hadn't even noticed any people, but now we looked around. Sitting at workbenches were maybe twelve or fourteen people assembling or repairing computers and phones.

A gray-haired woman came over to us, and Zach introduced Jen to Mary Sue. "Watch," she said, and then, "Ceiling, do starry night for Zach and his friend."

The windows turned opaque. What had been yellow and blue became a nighttime sky like I'd only seen pictures of: a quarter moon and the Milky Way sweeping across the heavens.

"Damn it, Mary Sue," someone screamed in the half-dark. "I just about soldered my fingers."

With a command, she returned the sky to those Degas shades of yellow, pink, and pale blue.

While Zach talked to Mary Sue about buying a used tablet, we gazed at the changing patterns of machinery and gadgets on the walls. Jen silently picked out objects and guessed which way they were going to shift. I was certain I detected a code that used the colors of the machinery and positions on the grid to signify letters of the alphabet. But it was gibberish in every language I knew, and I concluded my secret code was coincidence.

We wandered along the aisles of the workspaces. No one objected and some folks smiled and said hi. Except one woman over to the side, speaking softly on the phone. She had thick black hair pulled into a long braid that snaked down her back like a sleeping python. No emotion flickered on her face as she studied Jen, but she turned off the tablet she'd been scribbling on.

* * *

"What the hell was that?" Jen asked. We were back outside, standing against sun-warmed brick.

Odd vibes coming from Jen, as if she was suddenly off balance.

"Cool, huh?" Zach said.

"Maybe."

"Just maybe?"

"It was all, I don't know . . ."

"They're smart, creative, and work incredibly hard."

I caught the pulses zapping back and forth as she formulated a joke in response, but these stopped. It was clear she was feeling uncomfortable, as if Zach was yanking her further into a world she was simultaneously fascinated by and suspicious of.

Boss, it's 12:55:03.

"Got to run."

We weren't back on a scooter for even a minute before she asked me who those people were.

"Zombies," I said.

"Oh, funny."

"No, that's what they named themselves. They love all that dead technology on their walls."

"Why?"

"No idea."

Zach had already explained and Jen had already bristled at the weirdness of it. It was a co-operative; members owned it together. They shared work, decision-making, and profits. They were linked up with other co-ops, each with a specialty. Korea and China: screens. Chicago: motherboards. One in the Basque region made nano fans and electrical connectors. Ones in Toronto, Stockholm, and Oakland focused on software. Some co-ops had hundreds of members; the Basque ones had thousands. Many were tiny. They shared and traded among themselves and then sold to the public. Their hardware was always a year behind the international giants, but they bragged their software was equal or superior. No advertising, no bloated salaries, no private jets, no payoffs to shareholders, no lobbying, so their machines sold for half the price.

"When you buy one," Zach had said, "they quote you a range of prices for each computer or phone and let you decide how much to pay."

"And?" Jen had said.

"Apparently most people opt for the higher end of the range."

"Jesus."

She hadn't asked Zach how much he was going to pay for a reconditioned tablet. I didn't think she wanted to find out.

We spent the rest of the day slogging through a ton of paperwork from the previous night's shooting of Delmar and Odette Johnson. Funny that humans keep expressions like that. *Paperwork.* Maybe they are all nostalgic, like the Zombies. Or maybe stuck on words. Or maybe lazy, and hadn't found time to come up with a new one. Anyway, Delmar Junior was downstairs in a cell, cooling his heels and complaining about his bandaged hand. It was fifty–fifty whether the charges would be dropped because of the elder abuse he'd suffered from his parents refusal to exit.

Right before she left for the day and switched me off, Jen opened the top right drawer of her shared desk. One of the entry cards to the Johnsons' apartment was tucked inside a plastic bag—not evidence of anything, just kept in case we needed to go back in. I saw the word *Eden* float into her head before she could block me. She picked up the bag and slowly rubbed the slippery plastic over the card. I knew what she was thinking, and I didn't like it one bit.

She didn't seem to like it much either. A lifetime of obedience kicked in.

She dropped the plastic bag back into the drawer, pushed it shut with the side of her leg, and headed for the exit, where she turned me off for the night.

*   *   *

At 13:19:05 the next day, Captain Brooks appeared at the squad door and tossed nine words into the room: "Joint briefing with drug squad. Top of the hour."

22

Our unit mate Amanda rolled her eyes at Jen and Les and popped a small bubble of pink gum. As Brooks turned to leave, Hammerhead called to him. "Why we're meeting them again so soon?"

Jen tensed.

Brooks turned slowly around and glared at him. "Because I said we are."

Lots of good opportunities for me to learn social graces when I work with these folks.

The drug squad—officially the Narcotics and Illegal Pharmaceuticals Enforcement Unit, but even Brooks isn't a big enough dick to say that each time—focused on the usual illegals, plus street metaopioids and other meds. It was the latter two that led to meetings with us twice a year. The Elder Abuse Unit wouldn't be mistaken for social workers, but busting people for possession of a heart medication wasn't exactly our thing.

We settled back into work. My people here: Jen, Les, Hammerhead, Amanda, and their synths. Les, full of caution and a sprinkling of camp humor. Hammerhead on the thick side: big thick fingers and a big thick skull that left little room for intellectual wattage, but he's as soft as a puppy with the old folks. Amanda had been a star in every high school sport ever invented, even if all that was left of those days was the bubblegum she incessantly smacked away on like a first baseman.

Oh, yeah, there was Brittany. That is, until she got her test results a month ago and took medical leave. She has rapid onset spongiform encephalitis, which is ripping through fifty-year-olds. No explanation of the cause, but heaps of speculation. The chemical soup humans are bathing in? Wi-Fi pumping from every device into every cell? God's revenge for whatever God should be revenging? Regardless, ROSE is nasty, fast, and slicing away an astounding sixteen percent of fifty- and sixty-year-olds and three and a half percent of folks in their forties. The ones whose parents didn't exit and so didn't get the modified treatment, that is. I hope Brittany will make it back.

At 13:55:48, I reminded Jen we needed to hoof it downstairs to the meeting room. She told the others. Hammerhead said, "Thanks, Mom."

Boyden, Gendra, Murph, and the Card were already there when we showed up. Gendra—whom we all call the Starlet—said, "This your idea to waste our time?" She flicked her head to toss a stream of blonde hair away from her face. The Starlet was always flicking her blonde hair this way and then glancing around to see if a casting director had caught her Hollywood moment.

Les said, "Nah, I just wanted to score some coke from you for the weekend."

The Card cleaned his nails with an evil-looking, black-bladed knife and said, "And what? Pay for it with contraband Depends?"

Amanda blew a pink bubble that expanded until it popped like a firecracker.

Murph said to Jen, "How're you enjoying probation?"

Jen said, "How're you enjoying being an asshole?"

Murph said, "Make nice, Jenny. You wouldn't want any of us complaining about you, would you now?"

There's this thing humans do that reminds me of dogs baring their big yellow teeth at each other to show how fearless they are, and then sniffing each other's asses to show they're cool with whatever goes down. Mainly men, but women in places like this are in the game too.

Brooks came in, tailed by a uniformed woman with lieutenant stripes and hair so flaming red I thought Brooks had set her on fire. Next came two men decked out in suits, one seersucker blue, one gray—the suits, not the men. Gray Suit must have been in his fifties, Seersucker younger.

Catch that, Jen said. These days, few men seemed ready to sweat it out in a suit jacket, although Seersucker's had the more ordinary short-sleeve jacket. *And ties.* Just about never see that.

They sat down without introducing themselves.

Captain Brooks tried to sound at the top of his game. He gestured toward the woman. "Lieutenant McNair is from headquarters. Our colleagues here are from the DEA. They want to—"

Seersucker Suit cut him off. "I wouldn't quite put it that way."

Brooks hadn't yet put it any way.

"We're hoping to have an informal chat," Seersucker continued. "We're doing the same with key people like you in all the stations. Uh, I wonder if you folks wouldn't mind turning off your phones."

I'd once met a synth who worked with a guy like this. He was the type who wore fluffy blue mittens with a couple of steel-gray crowbars tucked inside. It never took long before the mittens came off. Seersucker's aw-shucks request was delivered with a certainty that this wasn't negotiable. Everyone took out their phones and switched them off.

"And I understand all of you here have AI."

How does this guy know? Jen said to me.

We all looked at once to Brooks, who seemed equally surprised.

Brooks said, "Can't do. They're punched in. On the job."

Lieutenant McNair spoke for the first time. "Then turn off their comm function. Think your boys and girls can handle that, Captain?"

I've never heard a lieutenant put down a captain. A new damn thing every day around here.

She turned to us and said, "That's an order from my inspector." And she shot her gaze back at Captain Brooks. Boss dog had barked.

Captain Brooks looked away. He ran his thumb over his scar.

Then Seersucker Suit got all warm and fuzzy again and uttered a few more hush-hush words about what's said in this room stays in this room—"That sound alright with you?"—and turned to Gray Suit.

Gray Suit was rather extraordinary. Where Seersucker had the regulation clipped hair and McNair's had edges that could slice your hand off, Gray's hair—the same color as the matte-gray gun we'd snatched off this Italian guy thirty-four days ago—was fashioned into a short, intricate braid that reached his suit jacket. His face was completely tattooed with black geometric patterns. He seemed completely at ease. He was a big man, not particularly tall, but about as wide as an industrial refrigerator. He had surprisingly well-kept hands, manicured nails and all. They rested on the table, folded like he was a mortician at a Thanksgiving dinner and ready to lead us in prayer.

How old? Jen asked me.

Hard to tell with the tattoos. I studied his eyes, but his irises were so dark and deep it was like trying to spot a black rattlesnake on a moonless night.

How old? Jen asked again.

Not sure. Mid-fifties.

He spoke.

Where's he from?

Maori. New Zealand. South Island. With a whisper of a Swiss-German accent.

As he talked, his calm gaze rested on each man and woman for one short sentence before moving on to the next, like he was an automatic *shooga-shooga-shooga* lawn sprinkler that dispensed quiet authority instead of mere water.

"Thank you for taking time to meet with us." His eyes moved to the next person. "Something new is hitting the streets." Next person. "We need to stop it before it gets a foothold. In fact, we need to stop it before any more people hear about it."

There was no drama in his delivery. His very presence assured you he was expressing an undebatable truth.

"It appears that someone is producing a highly restricted pharmaceutical."

His calm eyes met those of each woman and each man.

We waited.

"We've had reports that someone is manufacturing and distributing a counterfeit version of the treatment," he said.

Even his calm authority couldn't stop the room from blowing up. For the Big Pharma consortium that produced it, the longevity treatment in both its original and stripped-down forms was a business worth hundreds of billions of dollars. It was also enormously complex to produce. This wasn't a drug you fried up in your basement—a hundred university chemistry labs couldn't come anywhere close. Knowledge and expertise were compartmentalized among the companies, giants like GPRA and Xeno/Roberts/Chu. Each was responsible for separate compounds and parts of the process. Technical secrets were also compartmentalized, and closely guarded. The steps carried out in the United States or France, China or England, India or Switzerland, were a complete mystery to the other partners. Each batch had an individual protein marker and could be traced. Raw materials, machinery, compounds, and the finished product were handled by a secret and frequently rotated fleet of planes and trucks. Only three clinics in all of the US dispensed the full treatment, and even the modified treatment was administered in heavily guarded clinics. To imagine someone having the knowledge or ability to replicate the treatment was impossible. Even imagining someone busting into the distribution process in anything but a one-off seemed impossible.

Gray Suit listened to the volley of questions. He didn't interrupt anyone even as everyone interrupted each other. But when he said, "Let me try to answer," a hush blanketed the room.

"No, we have no samples. The rumors point to an abbreviated version of the treatment, like the one that goes with exit, but we cannot be certain. The first report came from Richmond three weeks ago. The second report was from here two weeks ago.

"We have no leads. So far, nothing has popped up on social media. No telephone echoes. Nothing but rumors.

"We're moving quickly. As of last Wednesday, we've had an interagency task force. As you can see, I've been liaising with DEA—"

He's not drug enforcement.

"—and many others. We mean to stop this."

Jen raised her hand like she was a school kid.

"Yes?"

"I've heard stories not really about this, but someplace called Eden. Is there any chance this is connected?" Jen forced herself not to look at the captain, certain he'd be glaring at her.

Gray Suit said, "We've heard those stories too. Anything is possible, but those are fairy tales. This just might be real."

He looked around the room, his eyes targeting each person in turn.

"And please remember, we don't want you mentioning this to anyone. Not your mother, husband, wife, fellow officer, barber, or priest."

The Starlet said, "Why not?" She didn't even bother flicking her blonde hair away.

He smiled slyly. "Because I don't ask questions like that to the person who gave me the order."

The Starlet persisted. "We're shooting ourselves in the foot. How will we hear anything?"

Lieutenant McNair spoke. "You will listen. You will watch. You on the drug squad will ask your snitches if they're hearing about anything new. You abuse people will watch for unusual behavior."

She turned to Gray Suit.

He looked at his watch.

Meeting over.

Ten minutes later, Jen and I went upstairs to Captain Brooks's office, didn't find him there, and returned to the meeting room. We were just around the corner when we heard the door open. She stopped.

We heard Gray Suit speaking, his voice not loud, as if he'd turned back into the room. But it was distinct enough to hear.

"Do we have to worry about the woman?"

Captain Brooks's response was louder, as if he was facing the door. "Which one?"

We couldn't clearly make out Gray Suit's reply, but it seemed to be, "Who asked about Eden."

Captain Brooks dropped his voice. "Jen Lu? She's nothing. Absolutely fucking zero."

My boss tumbled into a black hole.

6

It was nighttime in Washington, DC, and here are some of the things that were happening.

Zach was leafing through a greenhouse catalog while sketching a garden plan for one of his clients. He pushed his thick hair out of his eyes. His sketch was neat, his work meticulous, in a way that spoke of care rather than obsession. But his mind kept wandering. He set down the catalogue and picked up a bestseller about quantum physics, something he knew nothing about but figured he should learn. It was in German, one of three languages he learned for the hell of it back when he was an undergrad. But focusing on this was even more hopeless than his gardening, for although his eyes followed the text down the page, he took in absolutely *nichts*. His mind was stuck on his parents.

*   *   *

Raffi and Leah were on their rooftop under a string of glowing white lightbulbs, snuggled side by side on vastly overstuffed cushions, reading and drinking iced tea. Leah said, "This is lovely, isn't it?"

Raffi tucked a finger inside his book to hold his page and sat up so he could look at her.

"I'll miss this," she said. Then she laughed. "Except I'll be dead, so I won't actually miss anything." A solitary tear slid down her face.

Raffi reached out and took her hand in his.

She attempted a smile, but it only flickered at the corners of her mouth and came off as a grimace. "To know the day of your death. It isn't very good, is it?"

"Would you like to do something? Go somewhere?"

A whole service industry catered to people like them. Exit trips. Exit ceremonies. Exit parties. Exit counseling.

"Why?"

"See something we've always wanted to see?"

"And spend the money Zach will need?"

"He wouldn't mind, not one bit."

"But we have all this." She gestured at their rooftop deck and the house below. She waved at the night. "We have each other. Anyhow, what would it matter if we were to finally see the Grand Canyon? We'll be dead in six months and five days. We have a hundred and eighty-five nights left. We'll take out the trash twenty-four more times. I might read a couple dozen books. I'm on my final toothbrush. We will never have grandchildren. We—"

"Leah, don't. We have our home and we have our son. We have each other. And we have life."

"For now."

"We can change our minds."

"And Zach?"

"He and Jennifer can live with us. It would be crowded, but there are worse things."

"You know that's not what I mean."

She meant Zach's health—so many people in their fifties, dying from ROSE.

All this was a pretend conversation. They had agonized, they had differed, they had ranted and raved, but they had made their final decision months ago. This time, it was Raffi who pulled them back to reality.

"Leah, I'll love you forever."

"You'll love me for a hundred and eighty-five days."

"Then that will be our forever."

* * *

A mile or so away and over on 14th, Les and Christopher were watching a movie and eating chocolate chip cookies that Les had just baked. "Slightly overdone," Les said.

"No, they're perfect," Christopher replied.

"I meant the plot of this movie."

Christopher, though, had seen it twice before and disagreed.

* * *

A mile from there, Jen sat up in bed, eyes fixed on a show but her mind replaying every second of the afternoon meeting with the Maori man in the gray suit. Every time she rewound, it ended with the captain saying the exact same words: *"Jen Lu? She's nothing. Absolutely fucking zero."*

Waves of emotion pounded at her, and she considered turning on Chandler to help regulate herself. But she wanted to suffer alone. One minute she was seething with anger, running monologues about spending her whole life crushed by shits. The next minute she was close to tears. She screamed silently at her mother for being a garbage parent and at Brooks for calling her a fucking zero. In her mind, she told Les to stop badgering her to be more assertive: enough Cobalt Blue already.

She heard a siren wail. She heard little Ezra crying in the apartment next door. She heard the incessant oompa-thud of polka-thrash coming from her neighbors up above.

The sounds jerked her away from her self-torturing loop. For the first time, she thought not about Brook's answer to Gray Suit's question, but about the question itself. Why had Gray Suit singled her out? All she'd done was ask one question about Eden. He'd answered her respectfully and calmly. What was he worried about?

It had only been a month since she'd begun hearing rumors about Eden. Not much at first. The word. The word once again. She had overheard a man at a store checkout talking about it, but when she asked him what it was, he'd stared at her with suspicion and walked away. Once while getting her hair cut, she'd listened to two women talking quietly to each other: "We're going." "You know how to find it?" "Not yet, but Benny's the best at figuring things out."

Little clues, crazy rumors. Eden was a new underground railroad that would sneak you across Canada's electronic barriers. Eden was in Africa. Eden was hidden in the mountains of Wyoming. Eden was a vast network of bunkers, a virtual underground city. Eden was on the far side of the moon. It seemed, as Captain Brooks had said, a load of crap; Gray Suit had called it a fairy tale. And yet the whisperers kept whispering, and their whispers kept working their way into her head.

She had heard one rumor that in Eden they gave you the treatment without anyone having to exit. It was salvation for children and rescue for parents. And that thought, as she lay in bed, wrenched her mother into her mind. Her nasty mother, four months shy of exit.

"We were getting to Eden," the dying woman had said.

She pinged Zach to see if he was still awake. No answer. She thought about their visit to the strange store. Why had it been unsettling? It wasn't the place. It was . . . Zach's enthusiasm . . . their differences . . . politics, police, the world . . . her life versus his.

She tried Les. Got a message back: *Go to sleep!*

At two in the morning, Jen still had her eyes open. The movie in her head started again.

"She's nothing. Absolutely fucking zero."

She snapped on the light, squinted as she fumbled into her clothes, and tiptoed to the apartment door so she wouldn't wake up Ava or Taylor. She thought of catching a rental to the station, thought again, and unlocked her bicycle.

She passed an encampment of Shadows. A group of men and women huddled around a small fire with some type of animal, likely a squirrel, roasting on a makeshift spit. A baby angrily cried, and she thought of little Ezra, by now happily asleep in his crib next door. Shadows. A generation or more without a job or social support. Didn't exist in anyone's reckoning of anything. Ignored, shoved around, and pushed away whenever they became too big a nuisance or whenever some politician needed a populist boost. Large migrating camps descending on fields and parks like locusts. Non-people. Mere shadows.

She arrived at the station.

The duty officer said, "What the hell you doin' here?"

"Nothing. Couldn't sleep."

She saw him shake his head at the sheer stupidity of this.

She went to the Elder Abuse Unit. Sat at her shared desk. Didn't turn on her computer. Didn't turn on Chandler. Sat there for ten minutes.

Slipped the plastic bag with the Johnsons' door card into her pocket. Headed out.

The duty officer commented, "That was fast."

"You were right. It was stupid to come in."

* * *

The lights in the vestibule flicked on when she opened the front door of the Johnsons' building. The hallway and stairs were spotless; they still smelled of polish. She tiptoed to the second floor. She was shaking so badly she had to brace her arms against the wall before she could slip on a pair of latex gloves. She removed the crime scene tape and let herself in. She was relieved when the lights didn't go on automatically, and drew out her light, but then realized that a neighbor seeing a light moving around was more likely to be suspicious than if all the lights were on.

It was hot and stuffy inside. It stank of uneaten food, unwashed dinner dishes, and frying pans. It stank of dirty diapers and blood. She was spooked at the thought of going into the kitchen, so she started in the living room. The curtains were drawn back, and her face in a window against the blackness beyond kept startling her. Childhood. Alone in her room after her mother said that bad men came after girls like her in the night. The dare game she'd played. Dared herself to look at the yawning blackness of the window, perhaps to see a stranger's face hovering in the night outside. And if she didn't look, she'd be even more conscious of what she wasn't looking at, and soon the windows would become all she could think about, as if they were growing by the second, swallowing up the room and the house and her life.

Now, as then, she made herself look at the window. She held her gaze and stared out the panes and counted. One. Two. Three.

She could not stop shaking. *Be Cobalt*, she told herself with a laugh. *Do what Cobalt would do.*

But her hands still trembled as she closed the curtains. At least no one would see her as she rifled through the meager bookcase, as she lifted cushions off the sofa, as she sorted through a stack of battered library books, as she patted the bottoms of chairs. At least no one would see her shaking.

What was she looking for? She had no idea, but it would be a clue. A map to Eden? A button chip? A description? A URL and password? A name?

Forty-five minutes later, she had finished with all but the kitchen. Searched every pocket in every coat and pair of slacks, flipped through every book in their small bookcase, stuck her hand inside every sock, rummaged in every drawer and cupboard. Each room, lights on, then lights off. She checked the time. She'd been there much too long. She needed to get out. Maybe she should leave this very second.

But instead, her stomach cramping with dread, she entered the kitchen. She tapped on the lights and, as she expected, saw the plates with food still on the table and a greasy frying pan on the stove. The plates seemed to be alive; they heaved with motion. Then froze. Fifty cockroaches had raised their heads as if guided by one mind. They stared at her, every last one of them, the big suckers that had migrated up from the Amazon. And then they skittered away, disappearing as quickly as taxis in a rainstorm.

Jen let out the breath she hadn't known she was holding. She took another breath. Damn if she didn't hate these big-ass roaches. She examined the room from the doorway. Brown splotches of blood stained the tablecloth and chairs where Mr. and Ms. Johnson had sat. Blood colored the old wooden floor. She entered the room and slid open every drawer, doing so carefully, but the cockroaches seemed to have vanished entirely. Odette Johnson had run a tight kitchen. Jen poked a spoon into bags of sugar and flour and carefully replaced them exactly as they had been. She stirred a fork into a jar of mustard. She removed the filter in the ancient range hood, finding it remarkably clean.

Finally, she tidied up after herself, then sat where Delmar Junior had. "Where are you?" she said. "Eden, where are you?"

Her focus snapped. Footsteps, climbing the wooden stairs. It couldn't be anyone coming here, she thought; it couldn't be, but she jumped up and clicked off the kitchen lights. The apartment plunged into darkness, and she slipped into a space next to the fridge.

She waited. Hearing things, the rustling of the roaches as they returned. She imagined she heard the wood splinter around the lock and the faint squeak of the hinges—then knew that was precisely what she'd heard. Footsteps. A flashlight beam shot into the kitchen, and she held her breath as the beam rested on the table, which started to come alive again with roaches. The light rested on the chairs one by one, then whipped quickly around the room and was gone. Footsteps down the short hallway to the living room. She counted, not knowing why, fifteen steps, and then heard them in the hall again. It had only been seconds. This person knew what he or she was looking for.

Jen rushed out the kitchen door, ready to grab whoever it was. The flashlight shot at her face, blinded her, and a darkened figure, more a presence than a person, rushed at her like a defensive tackle. He slammed into her, and Jen tumbled backward onto the kitchen floor. She landed flat on her back, the impact knocking the wind out of her. She heard footsteps running away.

One minute passed—two? The apartment was dead quiet. Jen staggered to her feet. Her head spun, and she braced herself on the table. She dropped into a chair. Even when she realized there were roaches skittering up her arm, she was too spent to worry about them. "Fuck off," she said, and brushed them away.

She stood up, snapped on the kitchen lights, and stumbled into the front hall. The door was open, the wood in the jamb pried ajar. She went into the living room. It was exactly how she had left it. Of course it was. The person only took fifteen seconds to find whatever it was they were looking for. Where had it been? *What* had it been? None of the cushions seemed disturbed. The drawer under the coffee table was still shut. The ancient picture album rested, closed, on top. The books in the small bookcase seemed in order.

Except that between two books, there was one conspicuous space she could swear hadn't been there before. A thick space for a thick book. She closed her eyes and saw the Bible resting right there.

Of course.

Eden.

But she had flipped through every book, shaken each one to see if something would fall out. Some had contained receipts—actual paper receipts, some handwritten and a few printed out from old machines, because the law said if someone asked, stores still had to provide them. And now it seemed as if the Johnsons had used books as a filing system, but none seemed significant. A fan. A used refrigerator. A phone. A high-chair. A stroller.

The Bible, though, had been stolen. Worth breaking into a crime scene for. Worth assaulting someone for. Worth going to jail for.

And it had slipped right through her shaking hands.

7

Sunday, July 8—16:59:00

Once a month, the boss visited her old lady. "Twelve times a year too many," Jen had once told me. Tough words to say to a guy who doesn't get to have a mom.

"Leave me on so I can meet her," I said. It was the butt-end of a long Sunday shift, and Jen was about to sign out, pop me off, and go for her visit.

"Why would I want to do that?"

"So I can understand why you go on about her like you do."

"You'll never understand."

But she did leave me on. We grabbed the Metro and then an auto-rickshaw. She phoned Zach, but he was still at his meeting. Community Action for Sustainable Prosperity, CASP, a group Zach was helping set up. He shot her a text back: *Meet you in an hour.*

The winds were now coming from the north and the temperature had leveled at a hundred. It was a remarkably clear day, the sky like the Tahitian sea. We arrived at a three-story building with yellowed vinyl siding and landscaping done by someone who hated plants. Probably just as well, since those few plants now looked like kindling for a campfire. We walked up the potholed driveway. They might as well have hung a sign out front that said, "Old people locked up here to die."

We stepped inside. *Four more visits to go,* Jen thought. *Four more payments. Four more months until I'm done with her forever.* I pretended not to hear any of it.

She waved her ID over the pad and passed through the metal detectors. I don't want to sound mean, but the first thing I noticed was a smell I didn't like. *Dying skin,* Jen said.

No, I replied. *That's only four percent of the smell, along with medicines and foul food and floor cleaner and smelly lotions and cheap perfumes and antiseptic soaps and diapers and accidents.*

Aren't you full of interesting information, Jen said.

We went into the administrator's office, where we were greeted by a bubbly white woman with thick makeup and hair so stiff I thought she was wearing a football helmet.

Jen said, "There's a problem with my June payment."

"Oh my," said the administrator, "that won't do now, will it?"

I figure you'd have to either be a saint or working off an overdose of uppers to stick with a job here. I didn't have the administrator pegged for a saint, but who knows. Look what Mother Teresa had gotten away with that didn't leak out until thirty years after her death.

I checked the administrator's chestnut-colored hair for cracks while she checked her records on an old-fashioned opaque computer screen on her desk. "No, it adds up like a charm."

Jen asked to see the screen. Math genius that she is, it didn't take her long to spot the problem. She tapped the glass. "There, that's it. She gets her hair done twice a month. You've repeated it every day."

"Oh, but in June she went each and every afternoon. And doesn't she look the charm?"

A few thoughts rammed through Jen's brain: *I can't possibly afford this. I won't pay.* But no words came out. Instead, her brain flooded with a long-familiar feeling of utter defeat.

The administrator agreed to spread the extra payment over the final four months and to make sure Jen's mother didn't go every day.

We took the stairs to the second floor two at a time, Jen's mood worsening with every step. By the time we reached the door to the activities room, I was shattered and wished I'd never been born.

You're dramatizing, Jen said to me.

Empathizing.

You never had to live with her.

I knew it all, though. She was a monster. She had scared away Jen's father when Jen was only five, but that made him a total fuckup too. She had absolutely destroyed every single day of Jen's life until Jen had finally moved out, and even then she'd done her level best to keep on spoiling it ever since.

We went into the activities room. Windows so dirty I thought there'd been an unscheduled eclipse of the sun. A potted ficus, dead on all fronts. A couch that must have had more organisms living in one square nanometer than the whole human population of the world—I swear I could see the cushions wriggling.

The place seemed to specialize in activities that made no sound. A man and three women played cards, one of them trying to sneak looks at her neighbor's hand. A man whose ears had been hijacked by a squadron of bristly hair was doing a mildly pornographic jigsaw puzzle. Another man was parked in front of a huge screen, ancient, oversized Beats headphones on his bald head, eyes shut in sleep, controls clutched in his shriveled hands, and *World of Warcraft* frozen in his avatar's death agony. Two women—alert and neatly dressed—played chess at a small table dragged as far away from the others as possible.

Wandering between them all was a Chinese woman, tall like Jen, with a great smile on her face. A gentle face, but slightly vacant. She saw us. "Oh, look who's here!" she said with excitement. She came toward us briskly, her hands reaching out in greeting. "Oh, my," she said as she grabbed Jen's hand. "Now tell me, who are you?"

And with a metaphorical click, Jen shut me down.

* * *

Next morning. 07:00.28. Back at the office and born again. I exist in shifts. But I'm not one to complain. It simply isn't part of the program.

Monday morning meeting. Jen, Les, Hammerhead, Amanda, and Captain Brooks.

Item One: A moment of silence for Brittany, who succumbed last night to ROSE. Fifty-one years old. Her brain had rapidly turned into a three-pound hunk of Swiss cheese left out in the sun too long.

39

Item Two: Amanda was going on a two-week holiday, starting Wednesday. No temp replacement. Hammerhead said, "That makes us down to, uh, three people." Captain Brooks congratulated him on his arithmetic.

Item Three: Air-quality update. Winds had shifted, Great Shenandoah just about out, particulates dropping, but we still needed to keep our eyes on our seniors.

Item Four: Jokes about Les's black eye coloring his white face, even though everyone knew it had happened at his weekly basketball game.

Item Five: Run-through of trial dates. James O'Neil, rich punk. Preliminary hearing coming up in a week for July 3 assault on the Tidal Basin path. Jen to meet with district attorney.

Item Six: One of the Johnsons' neighbors reported their apartment had been broken into. Les volunteered to take a look, but Jen said, "I might notice if anything was taken." Les said, "Good call. I'm too dumb to spot a television missing from the wall," but Captain Brooks told Jen to go. Adrenalin spiked and I calmed it down for her.

* * *

"Jesus," Jen said, "someone smashed it in."

I caught a strange vibe from Jen and a burst of fluttering thoughts that told me there were things she knew that neither she nor Jesus was about to reveal to me. I didn't share her off-duty memories. I didn't even get to know all she was thinking.

We went in.

"It stinks in here," I said.

"Not surprised," she said, and it was clear she wasn't.

We went into the kitchen and peered around. I heard her think *cockroaches*, but there were none to be seen. To the bedroom. The living room.

"Nothing big seems to be missing," Jen said. "Maybe it was a body bagger." The teens who collect small mementoes from murder scenes.

We returned to the bedroom. Jen searched through some drawers.

I asked what we were looking for.

"Maybe see if any jewelry's missing."

"How will we know if any is missing?"

"We won't."

40

"Then—"

"Do you have anything better to do today?"

Fearlessly fight crime? Stop kids from killing their parents or parents from killing their kids? Help old men cross the street?

We went into the living room. Shuffled through some drawers. Peered at the bookcase. Pulled out a book and rifled through the pages. A receipt dropped out. Jen acted surprised, but she didn't feel it, at least not to me. One by one, she shook books and more receipts dropped onto the floor.

Damn, I'm stupid sometimes.

"He told us not to waste time trying to find out about Eden," I said.

"He told *me* not to."

"Well, you are, aren't you?"

"I'm just curious."

"About what?"

"Don't know."

She piled up the receipts. Slipped them into her pocket.

And out we went.

*　*　*

12:16:03: DA Celeste Delong phoned. Asked if we could pop by that afternoon to talk about the James O'Neil assault case.

Here's how it works. I'm an objective set of eyes and ears, smell, taste, and touch. I'm Jen's comm link hooked into a mini-transmitter. I'm a database to supplement her underachieving human brain. In emergencies, arrests, fighting, or danger, I can take independent action—so *she* truly becomes *us*. I'm a minute-by-minute record of what we do. I can testify in court. I'm absolutely unable to lie. I don't have access to her memories, and I don't have access to all that she is thinking unless it has to do with an immediate situation that I'm also dealing with or she decides to share something with me. If she's caught turning me off while on duty, she gets fined, demoted, or fired. I don't voluntarily rat on her unless a superior officer demands that I do so.

There you have it. *National Geographic* presents "Life of a Synth Implant."

So earlier, although I figured she was sticking her nose where noses don't belong, I didn't ask about the receipts. I liked Jen and I didn't want to get her into trouble. She either would have told me, which would likely be a bad thing for her, or she would have lied, which would have been a bad thing for us. Case closed.

Jen and Celeste had worked together on several cases. Celeste was a big woman. Broad face, meaty arms, big breasts, big butt, big brains, big ambitions, big heart. Jen liked her.

They caught up: Celeste showed Jen snaps of her twins, one decked out in chartreuse, the other in cotton-candy pink. Cute, but the first thing you think these days is that because she has children herself, Celeste isn't eligible for the treatment. You choose your poison, she had once said to Jen. Perfect motto for all human action. You don't get out of here without losing something along the way.

Celeste briefed her on the case. The victim was thirty-one, Black father, Latinx mother. Living with a boyfriend, no children, employed. Victim was lucid about what happened, and her account corresponded with our report. She was university educated and worked at the Smithsonian, which would sound good to either a judge or a jury. Celeste, a Black woman, didn't have to explain what she meant by that.

Celeste ran through a series of questions with Jen, pretty much what she'd be asking in court. At a few points, she interrupted and dug a bit deeper. She said, "Good," and Jen felt nice and relaxed. Ready for the ring.

"Prelim trial is canceled," Celeste said.

Justice was swift in DC. AI reviewed the evidence and set a trial date. Defense could request an old-fashioned preliminary hearing, but they got dinged for the cost and it usually didn't get them anywhere. Few bothered anymore. I wasn't surprised this one was canceled, only that there ever was going to be one.

Celeste, though, said, "That blindsided me."

"Why's that?"

"You got the money his dad has, and you're either going to delay the trial or pull the case apart as quickly as you can."

"Maybe he wants to get it over with."

"Maybe." Then Celeste said, "I understand you have a synth."

Christ, Jen thought, *does everyone know?*

"Would you mind if I ask it—"

"Chandler."

Celeste smiled.

"—Chandler a direct question."

Jen stiffened but agreed.

Oh yeah, *National Geographic* left this out: If my host agrees or if I'm ordered by a higher-up, I can be asked a direct question. "Jen" answers, of course, and not in some possessed Linda Blair voice—old movies are a bit of a personal interest of mine—just her normal everything. But once she agrees, it's coming on a pipeline directly from me.

"Chandler," Celeste said, "does Jen's account conform exactly to your memory of the events?"

I answered that it did. Then Celeste led me through the exact same questions she had asked Jen, and I gave pretty much the same answers, although I was much more to the point.

After, Jen said to Celeste, "Did you really need to do that? It's, you know, pretty creepy."

"Ever hear of David Samuels?"

I slipped Jen the data.

"Big-deal lawyer."

"Very expensive and very good at what he does. I expect he'll request permission to ask if you have a synth and then question Chandler directly."

"I'm not worried."

"Well, I definitely am. James O'Neil's dad is a Timeless. Samuels isn't going to fool around. He'll rake you over coals so hot you'll wish to God you were in hell instead."

Shit, Jen thought. *Shit on a stick.*

8

It was a scalding night in DC, but Ava and Taylor didn't like using the air conditioner. Too expensive. Plus Ava had once confided they preferred sex when it was sweaty hot. Jen, single at the time, had smiled patiently but wanted to kill her.

Jen sat on her bed, on her white cotton sheets, wearing nothing. She liked those moments. Utterly free. No one telling her what to do. No mother about to barge in and call her a slut if she saw her sitting there undressed. Just her and her body.

Zach phoned.

"Watcha up to?" he asked.

"Nothing. Just sitting here."

"Oh."

"Without my clothes on."

He groaned.

"Did you just groan?" she said.

"Of course not."

"You did. I heard you."

"I mean, I can't think of anything in the world I'd rather see than you sitting there. Where are you?"

"In bed."

"I think my heart's palpitating."

"I don't believe you."

"Here, listen." The phone made a muffled, scrunching sound. "Hear that?"

She laughed. That niggling unease she had felt after visiting the computer store had totally vanished. She said she wanted to go to a movie

44

sometime. They made plans for an early morning bike ride and said goodnight.

She picked up the small stack of receipts. Older folks, cautious folks, still asked for receipts. The Johnsons had been cautious, although apparently not cautious enough. Jen had glanced at the receipts on Wednesday night when she snuck into the apartment. Although she'd been looking for handwritten notes and not studying the receipts themselves, she had casually noticed what they were for. But could she recall enough of them to figure out which one or ones were missing—which ones had been in the Bible?

She laid the ones she had on the white sheets. They formed a story of the Johnsons' lives: A second-hand stroller. A fan. A high chair. A hair dryer. A set of dishes. A used refrigerator. A Sunday suit for Delmar.

Was anything missing . . . ? Was it . . . ?

There had been a phone receipt.

Are you sure? she asked herself. For the first time, she wished she had turned Chandler on during her search. She would have an indelible memory of the receipts. Then again, she might also be without a job for bucking orders if Chandler was ever grilled.

Yes, she thought. *I'm certain.*

She closed her eyes.

She smelled the cotton sheets and the pleasant scent of a light sweat rising from her body. Almost inevitably, she heard her mother scolding her.

She focused on the missing receipt. On a Bible revealing its secret. *Used phone. Very cheap. Name on the receipt, Z-something. Zach? Zebra? Zoink?*

Jesus, what if?

She picked up her phone.

"Zach, I—"

"I can't get my mind off—"

"Zach, what was the name of that weird store we went to? The co-op thing?"

He laughed.

"Their name would be on your transaction," she said.

45

"I did a trade."

"For what?"

"I'm putting in a rooftop garden for them."

"Come on, Zach. They—"

"Anyway, it's Zombies. Officially, Zombie-something. I think Zombie Industrial Co-operative."

She was dressed and out the door in two minutes flat.

She pumped her pedals hard as she rode into the wind along the midnight streets.

She was four blocks away from the co-op when she first caught the smoke in the air—not the distant smell of the burning forest, but close by and harsh. By the time she was two blocks away and turning down an alley, the smell had morphed into the acrid scent of an extinguished blaze. It clawed into her nose and throat.

She arrived to see firefighters winding up hoses under their floating light bubbles. Here and there, the brick was charred black. The sunflower solar panels and the roof underneath them were gone, as were the high-up windows and the door. A drone with its own set of lights buzzed overhead and dipped through the space where there had once been an illuminated array of OLED displays. She wondered if they'd ever displayed a picture of a ceiling on fire.

"Anyone hurt?" Jen asked the firefighter who seemed to be in charge. She was a tall, olive-skinned woman wearing a short hijab under her helmet, and had the sorrowful look of someone who'd seen one too many of these.

The woman hesitated. Jen flashed her ID.

"Don't think so. We haven't found any remains."

"What happened?"

"Your guess is as good as mine. It's an old building. Plus heaps of electronics, solvents, and a biblical amount of junk. Likely an accident, but we'll have a couple of inspectors out here in the morning."

The drone buzzed out from the gutted building and returned to its pilot like a well-trained falcon.

Jen jutted her head toward the building. "Can I have a look?"

The firefighter shook her head. "Better not. You never know with these old places. Sorry, but I gotta . . ." She walked away.

Jennifer stood alone. She surveyed the scene. Firetrucks, firefighters, the floating lights. The strange and beautiful store in ruins. Then she noticed an unmarked car blocking the far end of the alley. Jennifer turned away and rode home.

* * *

She had pulled a crappy schedule this month. Tuesday was a single day off. Zach's call woke her at seven.

"You're still in bed?" He didn't sound pleased.

"What time . . . ?"

"You were going to be here at six for our ride."

Bicycle along the Potomac to Great Falls. Park bikes and scramble along the Billy Goat Trail. Picnic lunch. Sneak into the spot they'd found to make love.

"Your store burned down."

He laughed. "You were dreaming."

"The computer co-op. Zombies."

"Oh, shit."

She explained what little she knew. He started asking her questions, but she cut him off. "Honey, I've had"—she glanced at her phone—"four hours of sleep." They decided she'd come by his place in the mid-afternoon.

But before she hung up, she said, "Zach, could you do one thing for me? Find out how to reach one of the owners or people who worked there?"

"They all own it. That's what a co-op is."

"Can you?"

Before he could ask why, she mumbled goodbye.

As she drifted toward sleep, she thought how nice it would be to have Zach lying next to her. Her thoughts floated pleasantly, but before sleep completely drew her away, her mind tumbled for a second back to Eden and Gray Suit and the Johnsons and the Bible. Her last thought was that she really needed to talk to Les about it all.

* * *

47

"You could have checked with me," Zach said when she arrived that afternoon. "I mean, we had it planned."

She had invited Les to go on the ride and hike with them as soon as he got off work at three.

"I needed to . . ."

"What?"

"Talk to him."

"Then call him. Spend the whole day tomorrow at work with him. Do sleepovers at their place. This was supposed to be our time."

"You're jealous of Les."

"That's ridiculous. I barely get to see you, that's all."

Jen, too, had been feeling this. They had met almost a year ago. The sex was great; they loved being outdoors; they both loved the antique merry-go-round at the Smithsonian. But there was never enough time together, and they didn't always see eye to eye on politics and her job. Still, so what? They had decided to live together after his parents exited. He couldn't afford much for rent, and until her mom was out of the picture, she couldn't either. Cop pay wasn't what it used to be, not with so much public funding siphoned off by the private security firms.

Jen said, "We spent half the weekend together." She playfully touched his long-ago broken nose. "You just wanted to have sex in the woods."

"Well, yeah," he said, and turned his eyes away as if he felt childish to have raised a fuss.

Jen rode to the rescue. "Les isn't arriving for"—she checked the time—"about eight minutes." She gave him her most mischievous smile. "Quickie?"

He grabbed her hand and they raced inside.

* * *

The water level was so far down that the roar of the falls was half of what Jen remembered from a year before. Jen and Les watched kayakers approach what was left of the rapids and then tumble down the river between the exposed rocks. Hikers and picnickers dotted the area. Les pointed to the figure of Zach scrambling over some distant boulders. "That boy has got energy to spare."

Jen said, "Let's find a quieter place."

They walked away from the falls and found a small clearing hidden in the bushes. The roaring water was still audible but muffled by the trees. Cicadas zizzed in the stifling afternoon. They plunked down onto a scraggly patch of parched grass.

"Les, I've always told you everything, haven't I?"

"This about why you turned Chandler off?"

"No, why would you think that?"

He shrugged. "Ah, Cobalt." He slipped off his shirt and wiped his face with it.

She looked at him. His body was still ripped, even though he was in his forties. Bruises here and there from basketball and work.

"Screw male privilege," she said, and she pulled off the running bra she'd been wearing for her top.

"Go for it, Cobalt!"

She swatted at him.

"I need to ask you about a work thing."

"Why *did* you turn him off?"

"It was . . . I don't know. All of a sudden, I didn't want anyone in my head but me."

"They could have fired you."

"Don't you ever want to turn her off?"

"Christopher calls P.D. my girlfriend."

"What? You told him?"

"Don't worry, he's cool."

She took a breath. "You know when those guys came in last week? Afterward, I went back to ask Brooks about something else. They were just leaving the meeting room, and I was still around the corner and I, uh . . ."

"You eavesdropped."

"No, not on purpose. I didn't want to see the Maori guy again, so I stood there, sort of frozen."

"And you overheard him hit on Brooks."

"Les, I'm being serious."

They heard a rustle in the bushes, and Jen reached for her sports bra. But instead of a person, a copper-colored doe pushed through the foliage,

49

saw them, and bolted away with an angular jerk. Jen dropped her top back to the ground. She told him what she'd overheard.

Les said, "I keep telling you, don't worry about what Brooks says."

"But why would that guy want to know about me anyway?"

"Who knows."

"Remember, I asked about Eden? Those rumors I've been hearing. I—"

But just as Jen was about to say she thought Gray Suit was reacting to her question, just as she was about to tell Les about breaking into the Johnsons' apartment, getting attacked there, returning for the receipts, Zombie burning down, he interrupted her.

"Of course!"

"What?"

"It must have been the Starlet. Your names are almost the same: Gendra, Jen. And she was peppering him with those questions. Not just asking, but disagreeing with him."

"I don't know. I . . ."

"It's got to be her. Anyhow, Brooks would never say that about you."

"What do you mean?"

"Are you kidding? He likes you."

"How do you—?"

"Come on Jen. Everyone knows he likes you."

A flicker of doubt crept into Jennifer's mind. Maybe she had heard wrong. Maybe it was her own stupid insecurities grabbing her again.

He said, "Don't let those guys into your head. One extra voice is more than enough." He reached over and playfully wrapped an arm around her shoulder.

"Hey," she said, "I'm half undressed."

"Yeah, and I'm gay! Anyhow, I'm your buddy."

"Well buddy," she said, and felt herself relaxing, "you're pretty great."

"That is so true. Find Zach?"

"Let's go climbing."

9

Young creature that I am, I learned a new word this morning. *Apophenia*. It means seeing a pattern where there is none. Others call it patternicity, but that makes it sound mundane, doesn't it? Either way, people make patterns and links out of random or unrelated events. It's one more star in the infinite firmament of human weaknesses.

As always, Jen had switched me on and signed in. That is an actual pattern designated by the rule book. Switch on, then sign in. She said hello to the officers and staff we encountered as we walked to the task force office, where she gave Hammerhead a quick rundown of her day off and then endured his clumsy attempt to dramatize his visit to one particularly nasty family. The parents had been charged with first-degree murder of their forty-two-year-old daughter. The mother asked how was she supposed to know you shouldn't wash vegetables with lighter fluid? Even Hammerhead knew the answer to that one.

So, apophenia.

We sat at her shared desk. She told me that in the wee hours yesterday morning there'd been a fire at the computer store we visited with Zach. The co-op. She wanted to know if there were preliminary findings from the fire investigators. I asked why this concerned us. She said she wanted to know. She's the boss. I did a quick check. Zip.

She said that the day before, Zach had attempted to reach his one phone contact, the person he was in touch with about the rooftop garden.

51

Her phone was turned off all day. Even I knew this was kind of strange. But strange doesn't make a pattern, does it?

She asked me to find a number for the investigator. I asked again why this concerned us, and although she didn't tell me, I caught a glimpse of the stack of receipts she'd pocketed at the Johnsons'. I groaned—figuratively speaking, since I'm only a sliver of programmed organic matter that doesn't make actual sounds. She ignored me.

I said, "Jen, you shouldn't be doing this."

She said, "Tell me in one word why not."

I gave her two: "Captain Brooks."

"I'm investigating a murder I witnessed."

"How's that?"

She said, "I think they bought a phone at that co-op store."

"That doesn't answer my question," I said. "If they had bought a loaf of bread, would you be investigating all the bakeries? What's the connection with the murder?"

She said, "That's what I'm trying to find out."

She'd probably get off on a technicality.

She phoned Inspector Striowski. 08:46:32. On a regular phone, that is. I do comms for her and will phone when she needs her hands free, but she sometimes likes to do normal calls herself because she's an old-fashioned girl at heart.

She introduced herself, said she was hoping he could give her his preliminary findings. When he spoke, his vocal cords twanged loosely with age, like he'd spent years screaming over the wail of sirens and there wasn't much spring left in the meat. But he seemed sharp and obviously loved to talk about his work.

"This is absolutely OTR," he said.

"OTR?"

"Off the bleeding record."

"Shouldn't that be OTBR?"

"That's good."

"I'm only hoping to get your impressions."

"Missy, we try not to do impressions around here. Maybe eighty years ago, but now we do science."

I swatted away that damn cortisol that pops up in her brain in moments like this and released a hit of oxytocin.

"Then I'd love to hear your scientific observations."

"Now you're preaching my bible. You know anything about fire investigations?"

"You make them after a fire."

"That's good. I like you. We're looking for burn patterns."

He launched into a short training session about witness marks, ghosting patterns, differential chemical analysis, and other interesting things I'm going to read up on later. Jen's brain was sinking into quicksand, so I suggested she drop in a question.

"And what did all this point to—your, uh, ghosting patterns?"

"None of those. We didn't have any."

"Is that good?"

"We figured it started in a closet where they kept solvents for cleaning electronic parts. If I was an arsonist who didn't want to get caught, that's where I'd have revved 'er up."

She sucked in her breath. Held it. Waited.

"But then we took a gander at the stove. They had a little kitchen area. The evidence points strongly to this as the source. I'm pretty convinced, but I'll wait for our test results to make the final determination."

"So, you're saying . . ."

"It was bad wiring. An accident pure and simple."

"You're sure?"

"Well, like the Good Book says, 'The fire itself will test the quality of each man's work.'"

Damn, she thought, *the Bible again.*

Jen phoned Zach.

"Any luck reaching your person?"

"It's Mary Sue, who you met. Her phone is still turned off. Devin too—another guy there. I called a friend who knows them, but he has no idea where they've gone. It's like they're all hiding."

"The fire inspector says it was an accident."

"Then why have they all disappeared?"

"That's exactly what I'd like to know."

So, apophenia: Jen happens to visit this store. Sometime last year, an oldish couple bought a secondhand phone from said store. Last week, that couple got murdered, but before dying, the woman mentioned they were planning on going to Eden. Two days later, some bigwig with his face covered in tattoos dismisses Jen's question about Eden. Then the store burns down. Next day, the owners are nowhere to be found. Dang, says the human, if that's not a pattern, I don't know what is.

Doesn't matter that the store was in the couple's neighborhood and that thousands of people must have visited. Doesn't matter that "Eden" is a silly rumor. Doesn't matter that the fire was an accident. It obviously all fits together.

Apophenia.

*   *   *

DA Celeste Delong called the next morning.

"I need to ask you to do something."

"No problem."

"Best if you drop over."

When we arrived twenty-three minutes later, 10:05:04, DA Delong's confident disposition of the week before had taken the day off. She looked like a dog that had gotten a bad scolding for flunking obedience school. She barely met Jen's eyes.

"Jen, I best get right to the point. Richard O'Neil, James O'Neil's father, has asked to speak to you."

"Right before the trial?"

"You're the arresting officer."

"So?"

"He wants to meet you."

"That's ridiculous."

"I know."

"It's not done."

"I know."

"But he told you he wants to speak to me?"

"No." She still wasn't meeting our eyes. "I haven't talked to him myself. My boss was told by *his* boss you're to meet O'Neil."

"Really."

"Yes, really." Her embarrassment had turned to anger. Even a synth wouldn't want to do the dirty work for those above her.

"You're saying I'm not being asked."

"Oh, come on, sister. You know how they do things. He's a Timeless. What else do you really need to know?"

"When?"

"This afternoon. Three PM."

"Where?"

* * *

The club was in a mansion west of Dupont Circle, overlooking Rock Creek. Jen had never heard of the place, nor had Les or Hammerhead. I googled it and found absolutely nada. I checked the city database. Nada squared. When we reached the address, there was no signage that indicated it was anything but a normal residence for the tsar of Russia. As we arrived, a jet car landed on the roof, the only sound being the buzz of rotors and the whoosh of air. Hot damn, don't see many of these babies.

We've previously been called into three of these clubs of the rich, of the movers and shakers, of the well-placed, well-born, or well-heeled. One had stolen its décor from an English movie set: liveried staff, hushed library where the scent of crinkly old leather chairs and bound volumes fills the air, and a dining room where you were dragged out and shot if you picked up the wrong fork. The second was modern everything. Sleek furniture, stark lighting, flint-edged surfaces. The third was so colonial that I kept expecting to bump into George Washington. What they had in common, though, was staff so obsequious that if a member told them to lick dog shit from the soles of their shoes, they would not only comply, but say "Thank you, sir," or "Well done, ma'am" once they had.

At the door, a woman and a man greeted Jen by name. They were both perfect human beings—perfect faces, perfect smiles, perfect mid-twenties bodies dressed in perfectly matching uniforms: crisp black polo shirt, tight beige slacks, and deck shoes without socks. Perhaps their last job had been on a superyacht.

In a voice like silk the woman said, "Richard is expecting you."

Richard?

We followed them along a hallway.

I waited for Jen to notice.

The man turned to Jen. "I hope you've been having a good day."

Jen said she was.

Shit! They're—

Service units usually stand out a mile away. The tech is pretty good, but humans are a long way off from creating anyone you'd confuse with your best friend.

These two SUs were a different class altogether.

I wondered about this. Wouldn't the very rich want to have servile humans answering to their every whim? To which Jen said, *Robots don't gossip.* And, I thought, after *California v. Romano*, a personal service robot cannot be asked to testify against its owner.

Down another hall and through a set of glass doors, we entered paradise. It reminded me of pictures of the Crystal Palace in London, from the Great Exhibition of 1851. A soaring glass structure, teeming with trees and tropical plants, the scent so primordial, the air so heavy that even I wanted to live there forever.

Outside, the thermometers were busting and the air was bone dry from lack of rain. Here, the air was moist, and it was only 76.2 degrees, so to Jen the humidity felt soothing rather than oppressive. I expected our guides to pull out pith helmets and machetes as we wound along a pathway through the jungle, their deck shoes making a soft crunching sound on the tiny pebbles. We smelled the water and heard the falls before we reached the pond. Through the forest of leaves we caught flashes of Caribbean-blue water. The pond was a pool, of course, but it looked like the whole building had been built around water that had been there since the dinosaurs. To the right, a small waterfall splashed over the rocks. On the far side of the pond, there was a small beach.

We stopped twenty feet from the edge of the pond, on grass as perfect as the greens at Augusta National. The two SUs flanked us but did not speak.

There were two females and two males swimming and another eight people—five females and three males—lounging around the pond on couches and teak chairs that seemed to grow out of the rocks and plants.

Standing immobile with a waiting towel or ferrying a tray of drink or food, giving a massage or quietly reading a book out loud, were another ten robots of different ages and races and with some variation in size, but all in identical beige and black clothing.

Four of the members wore minimalist bathing suits, and eight were naked. Revised estimate for those outside the pool: four appeared to be female, three male, and one was anyone's guess. Good times.

Give me some names, Jen said to me. *Whoever you can identify.*

I scanned the humans, but the millisecond I started a search, I had the distressing feeling I'd had only once before in my life, and that had been in training. I was completely offline. Shut out of the broad universe that was my normal home. I don't have the ability to panic, but if I did, Jen would have been flying to the front door whether she wanted to or not.

Jen caught my reaction.

I'm jammed, I explained.

Impossible. Illegal.

She makes me laugh sometimes.

I said, *Should we seek egress?* Fancy talk for running on our scared asses. That would be correct protocol.

Distress is different from panic, and I was tottering at the edge of the Grand Canyon on the last day of the Earth. I felt utterly alone.

Stay cool, Jen said. *You've got me. We'll be fine.*

My mantra for the day: Stay cool. I turned on her oxytocin tap and felt goodness flood over me.

Near us, a man pulled himself up from the edge of the pond.

White. Five foot eleven and change. Looked mid-thirties. A surfer's mash of sun-bleached blond hair. Naked—no tan lines. Well-muscled. Teeth so white you needed sunglasses. Not circumcised and remarkably well endowed.

Jesus H, Jen whispered to herself.

The male SU next to us said, "Richard O'Neil."

We had googled the crap out of this guy both after our first meeting with DA Delong and again earlier today. But even if you've seen his picture, nothing quite prepares you for the firsthand sight of a 112-year-old man who looked like this.

"Detective Lu! Hey, thanks for dropping by our little Garden of Eden."

The timbre of his voice matched his youthful appearance. He reached out his hand and shook ours, firmly but not aggressively. He lingered a breath longer than necessary.

"Hey, if you'd like to cool down . . ." He pointed with a thumb over his shoulder.

"That's okay. I wouldn't want to get my gun wet."

He broke into the most pleasant laughter I have ever heard.

He swiveled to the SU beside him—"Jaisha, grab my clothes, quick"—and turned back to us. "Sorry, this must be embarrassing the hell out of you. What an idiot I am. Hang on."

With the stride of an athlete, he met the returning SU and quickly started pulling on his clothes. As he slipped into his underwear, Jen looked away, as if the sight of this gorgeous man dressing was far more intimate than seeing him totally naked.

He returned decked out in lightweight jeans of pale green denim, a matching green T-shirt, and suede loafers. The pale green was a stunning shade I'd only seen once before, in a photograph of a suit made for the twentieth-century rock star David Bowie.

O'Neil touched Jen's elbow and guided us gently away from the pond. "Come on," he said. "Let's get the hell out of here."

We walked in silence except for Jen's heart, which was thumping like a teenage girl's on her first date.

He's trying to seduce you.

Give me a break. He's old enough to be my great-granddad.

Sure, those were the words she said, but they were entirely out of whack with the pheromones oozing in and out of her.

The SUs walked several steps behind us as O'Neil led us to a door. When he opened it, he lightly touched Jen's back, as if she needed to be guided inside. His touch tingled on her back even after he moved his hand away.

He had brought us into a 1950s farmhouse kitchen. The smell of bread baking. Bulbous, round-edged refrigerator. Big gas-burning stove. Table with tubular steel legs and speckled blue Formica top. Pink plastic radio on the countertop. Shelves with jars of preserves: green pickles, red beets, and yellow beans. Homemade blue curtains.

"Jaisha, crack that window, will you?"

She slid open the window—the motion was like silk on glass—and Jen stared out in amazement, although exactly where or what "out" meant was anyone's guess. There was a small yard with a line of clothes fluttering in a gentle breeze and beyond that a field of corn that stretched out of sight. The tassels on the corn stalks rustled in the breeze. We heard crickets and birds and smelled fresh-cut hay.

"It's . . ." started Jen.

"I'm real happy you like it too," O'Neil said. "It's so beautiful and solid, it leaves you speechless, doesn't it?"

It was only then that he seemed to really look at us. He stared and seemed to struggle to turn his gaze away. "Wow. Your eyes. They're—"

"Blue."

"I was going to say extraordinary." He moved his head slightly one way and the other, as if checking for contacts.

She said, "They're real."

"I can't say I've ever . . ."

"I guess that makes us even. Your extraordinary cornfield and my blue eyes."

He finally broke his gaze. "Anywho, something to wet your whistle?"

The male SU opened the fridge. Soda, beer, and a pitcher of iced tea.

"Tea," Jen said.

"You're going to love it. It's from this one particular village in China. We split their annual production with the Politburo guys."

The SU poured a glass of iced tea, then O'Neil took it from him and carefully gave it to Jen, the fingers of his hand grazing the back of hers. He watched her take a sip as if all that mattered to him in the world was her happiness.

"Jennifer—do you mind if I call you that?" He went on without a pause. "You know what my son is? He's a messed-up, violent racist. What do you think of the tea? Amazing, isn't it?"

We had spent a half hour this morning with the DA, running through what might come up at this meeting. We had talked to Les. We had concluded that James O'Neil was probably a chip off his father's block. Richard O'Neil would probably badger Jen into staying silent, maybe threaten her, maybe try to bribe her, maybe both.

59

The female SU set a plate of freshly baked chocolate chip cookies on the table. Richard said, "They're homemade, Jennifer, and absolutely amazing." Jen took one but didn't yet bite into it.

Little was known about O'Neil's personal life except that he had two children from his first marriage, one who was rumored to have killed himself—all the news reports had been wiped away—and a second who had died before the treatment was perfected. Neo-Nazi James was the product of his third marriage.

Although he was born two decades or more before some of the original big names in the tech world, Richard O'Neil hadn't been quite as stellar an empire builder as Gates, Jobs, Bezos, and Zuckerberg, and it had taken him until the ripe old age of sixty-four before he passed the billion-dollar mark. He didn't focus on flashy consumer products, and so tended to run beneath the radar. One of his companies was solely responsible for the AI substructure used by almost a quarter of Fortune 500 companies and the US Navy. As a result, he had incredible influence, from Wall Street to the White House, and he courted politicians in both parties, or rather they courted him.

But here he was, cute as any guy on the planet could possibly be, trying to charm the pants off my boss and calling his own son a violent racist.

"You look surprised," O'Neil said.

"It's the tea."

He laughed his beautiful laugh, and his eyes sparkled at her. "I find that hard to believe."

Jen took a bite of the cookie.

"Good?"

She nodded and didn't speak until she had swallowed.

"You see, Mr. O'Neil—"

"Jennifer, it'll ruin my day if you don't call me Richard."

And to my total surprise, she said, "Richard . . . I was kind of guessing that since you got him off his first charge of assault, you countenanced his behavior and his views."

Richard looked stunned. "You're kidding. Racism is repugnant to me. I mean, why would I be flirting with you if I was a Nazi like my son?"

Bold move, that. Even I know that admitting you're flirting with the person you've just met and most definitely shouldn't be flirting with is like clearing out a pawn and then leading your chess game with the king. Guess it can be done, but you're probably going to go down hard and fast.

But instead of a rebuke, Jen smiled. "That's sweet, Richard."

"Jennifer, I got him off that charge because he's my son, and that's what you do for your kids. He promised to get his shit together."

I could feel a gleam coming into Jen's eyes. "Your strategy didn't quite grab you Olympic gold, did it?"

He looked at us thoughtfully and raised one eyebrow. "No, it didn't."

He smiled and his eyes warmed Jen right to her heart and made me cringe. He looked at the side of her mouth. "Oops," he said, "you have a crumb stuck here," and with two fingers brushed it away, then studied her to make sure he'd done his job. "Perfect."

Without missing a beat, he went on, "I tell you what I'd like right now, Jennifer. I'd like to see my son get sentenced to prison. I'd like to see him stuck face to face with the consequences of his despicable actions. I'd like to see him, for once, shaking in those storm-trooper boots of his."

"Then why am I here?"

"Because that's not what's going to happen. I can't let it happen, simple as that. It would hurt my reputation, lessen my clout, and hurt me personally. And it would kill his mother."

"You two still together?"

"No, not really. I wouldn't be flirting with you if I was. But I don't want to see her getting hurt. She's a really decent person."

"There's nothing I can do. It's up to the DA to drop the charges."

"If I had wanted that, it would have happened already. No, I want to see him scared, but I don't want him convicted."

"Then bribe the judge."

"You're suggesting I bribe a judge."

"You know I didn't mean it."

"Jaisha."

A recording of Jen saying, "Then bribe the judge," came through the pink radio on the counter.

"Don't worry. I know you didn't mean it." Without even looking at them, O'Neil said, "Jaisha, Rob, erase that line, will you?" He smiled his biggest smile.

He paused as if this nano-second task still required rewinding magnetic tape, finding the exact spot, and mashing down hard on two switches to record over it.

"But there is one other problem I want to avoid," O'Neil said. "If you testify against him, we'll have to demand a charge against you for beating up my son."

Jen started to speak, but he cut her off. "Jennifer, I don't want that at all, especially now that I've met you. But my son says you slapped him hard in the face."

Damn you, Chandler.

"He was resisting arrest." *Don't,* I screamed at her, *you're admitting we hit him.* But it was too late. "I needed to subdue him."

O'Neil didn't seem to notice her admission. "That's not what James says."

"It'll be his word against mine."

"I'm looking forward to what your synth unit has to say about this in court. I believe you do have one, don't you?" His eyes had lost any glimmer of warmth. "There you have it."

"Fuck you, *Richard.*" She lurched to her feet, and I worried she was going to smack him.

He didn't flinch, but his eyes held hers. His voice, his whole bearing, seemed at once to be kindly, entreating, and utterly sure of himself when he said, "Please, Jennifer. Detective Lu. Please, sit down."

Leave, I said.

She didn't budge. But damn if those years of humiliation and humbling and obedience didn't kick in once again. No, she didn't plunk back onto the chair, but then again, she didn't walk out like she should have.

O'Neil said, "I thought I was being clever with that recording bit, but it was inappropriate, probably illegal, and just plain stupid. And I'm too damn used to threatening people to get what I want. You don't have to accept it, but I give you my unconditional apology."

Jen glared at him but still did not move.

And then, out of the blue, Richard O'Neil started going all Sigmund Freud on us.

"Fuck. My son killed himself because I cared more about money than him. That's what his note said. 'You care about money more than you do about me, more than Mom, more than Jill, more than anyone.'"

Why the hell's he doing this? Jen said to me.

"Jill didn't live nearly long enough," O'Neil continued. "I've had three disastrous marriages. I've got a fuckup son. I'm rich beyond belief, and I have this." He gestured down at his body. "I've learned to buy my way into whatever the hell I want. But that isn't me, Jennifer." Then he waved his arms at the old farm kitchen around us. "This is me. This place is me."

If this skinny-dip into psychoanalysis was some sort of performance or another weird chess move, it was certainly not in any psych book I'd ever read. I looked at the robots. Both seemed unconcerned.

"I'm a fucking old man, Jennifer. I don't look it, I don't sound it, but, please, just let my boy off. I'll put him on such a short leash he'll need my permission to brush his teeth. You can do it. Testify you may have been mistaken, that you assumed he committed the assault because you saw him running, but you're now uncertain he was the assailant."

"And then I catch shit."

"You won't. In fact, it'll be the opposite. That much I can promise. Please, Detective Lu."

And only then did I notice his eyes. I suddenly saw eyes that were 112 years old. Not rheumy or clouded. They were, like the rest of him, young and clear. Perfect. But I saw through it all. One hundred and twelve years had been enough. His eyes weren't flirty, they weren't warm, they weren't cold. They were dead.

* * *

With the SUs trailing, O'Neil escorted us to the front foyer of the club. A small group of men and women were coming in as we arrived. Jen asked if she could use the restroom before she left. Rob, the other SU, guided her.

When we returned, a smiling O'Neil was holding court with the group. He seemed back to his old self—that is, his young self. He smiled right and left and straight ahead and then reached forward and patted the shoulder of one woman—we could only see her from behind—who, judging by her gray hair, slightly rounded shoulders, and wrinkly white hands, seemed old enough to be O'Neil's mother, although she was probably young enough to be his granddaughter.

The older woman spread her hands, palms up, and said, "People want it. People get it." She gave them a life's-a-bitch-but-it's-all-pretty-simple shrug and said, "And then people pay for it."

Everyone laughed. O'Neil noticed us and came over to say goodbye, polite and proper as could be, but he once again lightly cupped Jen's elbow as they shook hands.

I called up a squad car. Nothing available. No motorcycles, no scooters. I called a regular civilian car and it arrived in one minute, the windows still blacked out from the previous passengers. The seats were folded down like a bed, and it smelled of recent sex. God, humans can be gross.

As we drove, I could feel Jen buzzing, as if she had stuck her fingers into an electric socket. I tried to talk to her about O'Neil and our strange visit, but she said, "I need some peace and quiet," and dropped a blanket over her thoughts.

Only when we reached the station did she speak to me. "Chandler, is there data, research, even stories about erratic behavior among Timeless who've gotten the treatment?"

When I said there was, she asked me to make sense of it all and let her know tomorrow. Two minutes later, she signed out and sent me into oblivion.

10

"I had the weirdest hour of my life this afternoon."

Jennifer and Zach were walking down 14th, not far from Les and Christopher's place, heading for ice cream.

He smiled indulgently. "I've heard that one before."

"Well, this time really was. a 112-year-old billionaire hit on me, big time."

Zach laughed, "Go for it!"

They reached the ice cream shop and joined the line.

She added, "He looks about thirty-five. Nicest laugh you can imagine. He was naked."

"Uh, mind if I ask what you were doing naked with this guy?"

"*I* wasn't naked, silly."

A woman and two men, lined up in front of them, turned and shot not-at-all-surreptitious looks at Jen.

Much more quietly, Jen briefly told Zach what had happened, ending with, "I have to say, though, he was pretty impressive."

Jen watched Zach sample three flavors, but all the while she was thinking about Richard. In spite of his arrogance, his obvious attempt to charm her, and his bullying, she hadn't been able to exile him from her mind.

They sat outside at one of the small tables, and she watched him eat quickly before his ice cream melted.

He held out the cone. "Want a taste?"

She shook her head.

He said, "You're the only person in the world who doesn't like ice cream."

"I worry I'll freak out."

He laughed. And then saw she was not laughing.

She said, "Something my mother did when I was a kid."

"Wh—"

She shook her head. "Another time."

Jen wiped the memory from her thoughts, just the way she had been doing all her life.

"So," she said when enough time had passed, "what weird or not-weird things happened to you today?"

"Absolutely no one of any age or financial bracket hit on me."

"Poor baby. I could check if my pal Richard is interested in guys."

"But I am thinking of turning my business into a co-op."

"A co-op. Like . . ."

"Yeah, kind of. I'd have partners who'd own it with me. We'd share the work. And we'd look after each other. What do you think?"

"I think you should take out some good fire insurance."

After finishing at the ice cream shop, they went next door to the supermarket.

"What do you think of this cauliflower?" he said.

"I would say it has three florets too many."

Jen rarely went into a grocery store, and if she did, she was in and out in four minutes. Zach could fritter away an hour in there.

"I'm so glad you're getting into this," he said. He continued to poke through the stack of cauliflower. "You've never really told me what's wrong with your mom."

"Of course I have. Early onset dementia."

"No, I mean when you were a kid."

She became absorbed, Zach-like, in the green beans.

"She was awful, cruel, judgmental, and controlling," Jen replied.

He stopped fondling vegetables. "Those are just adjectives."

"Aren't you clever today. *Just adjectives*. Zach, we're in a damn grocery store and you're asking about the most traumatic stuff in my life."

And so Zach abandoned the nearly fully cart of his carefully chosen everything, grabbed her hand, and said, "Then let's find a place where you can tell me."

11

oddam it to hell! she screeched at me.
I love you, too, sweetheart.
Thursday, July 11, 20:48:21.

We were on the crumbling and crowded sidewalk outside the super-market on P Street, just west of 14th. She was gushing feelings: anger, clearly directed at yours truly, and a flood of love, directed I presumed at Zach, whose hand I felt in ours and who was now in our sights and look-ing a bit mystified, presumably at her sudden distraction. And underneath it all was a core of fear that seemed strange given that all was calm around us.

They tried to reach you.

Normal protocol. She's off duty, they need her, they get on the phone. If they don't get through, they activate me, and I'm on it.

She dug into the pocket of her shorts, pulled out her phone, saw the missed call.

She signaled Zach with her index finger. "One second," she said to him. Into the phone she said, "Dispatch," and then whispered, "Cancel" as she walked away from him to talk to me while speaking into the phone. Humans make so much work for themselves.

"What is it?" she said.

"Les needs you. Two of our regular families involved in an altercation."

"Can't he—"

"It's serious. He needs you."

She wedged the phone into the pocket of her khaki shorts as she walked back to Zach.

"They need me."

"Shit, no." He took a breath and swapped a more accommodating voice for his momentary disappointment. "No prob, honey. I'll wait up."

"It might be late."

"I'll be up. This is important."

Some big drama there. I called a car, and three minutes later we were tearing up the town. Good times.

* * *

Parents: Olive Ortega and Pancho Porter. Children: Manuel Porter, forty-one, and Archibald Ortega, forty-two. This family knew how to do names.

Two-story house, vegetable patch in the front yard. Tattered lawn sign on a stick: "We Support the DC18." The eighteen women and men—Black, Latino, Asian and white—ten of them cops and eight civil rights, trade union, environmental, and feminist activists who led the mini-uprising in the police department nine years back. The focus was against police racism and police coming down on protestors like enthusiastic storm troopers. The protest got crushed, the rebel police officers lost their jobs, and all were tossed in jail. Didn't reach the rotting in prison stage, though, because massive peaceful protests shut down the city until they were reinstated, the old bosses dumped, and the rules changed.

We'd been called here three times before. Hence, they're officially one of our regular families. Tons of friction, no violence; we even brought in a social worker since our own talents only go so far. We threaten and soothe, chastise and sympathize. But, apparently, our finest police-slash-social-work efforts hadn't panned out.

Neighbor from three doors down: Child's Play. That's his given name. Man, I wish I could be around when academics look back at the name thing that happened in the first decades of the twenty-first century. Could be a hobby for me. My scholarly articles: "Subversion and Restoration: Given Names, 1995–2033," and "Interrogating the Human/Natural Divide: Vegetable and Fruit Personal Names in Suburban DC."

Anyway, Child's Play definitely wasn't. He was built like a weasel and acted like a snake. But the report was that, this time, it was the snake who'd gotten bitten.

Out front, two cherry tops. Another unmarked. Just as we arrived, an ambulance pulled away from the curb and shot down the street, its siren splitting the night.

One uniform guarded the front door. She looked down at Jen's bare legs, gave an amused wink at Jen and waved us in. A second uniform was in the hallway, taking up space. He notched his head toward the back, paused as if formulating his thoughts and said, "Garage." A regular Hemingway.

We'd been out here before. Every tool had its specialized holder or rack. Identical jars with color-coded tops—in eye-popping, no-nonsense primaries—showed off Pancho Porter's carefully sorted nails and screws. Ladders gleamed. Garden tools looked like they'd come straight from the hardware store. I'd seen pictures of operating rooms dirtier than this joint.

The first thing I spotted was Pancho's impressive face. The man had the biggest cheeks I'd ever seen, like he was either a professional trumpet player or was storing a couple of cantaloupes for safekeeping.

The second thing I saw was a burgundy puddle of blood glistening on the polished concrete floor. Pancho stared at it, obviously upset, although I couldn't tell whether it was because his wife had spilled his neighbor's blood or because said blood was now staining his pristine gray floor.

One of the officers was gripping Olive Ortega by the biceps, her hands cuffed behind her. Her leathery face was so deeply wrinkled it was collapsing in on itself. And those orange contact lenses were not only five years out of style but made her face look like the remnants of a carved pumpkin a week after Halloween. She was tearing a strip off her husband. "I told you not to trust that stupid man. Didn't I tell you that? Didn't I?"

Pancho, his hands also cuffed behind him, was pleading with Les and two uniforms. "Come on, guys, let me wipe it up. Have some compassion here. You gotta give me that."

Jen and I couldn't take her eyes off those cantaloupes in his cheeks.

Les briefed us. There'd been a big screaming match. Neighbors phoned police. Right before police arrived, Olive had taken a hammer to Child's Play, who went down for the count.

"And?" Jen asked.

"You mean," said Les, "why did I bother calling you in?"

"Something like that."

"Because—"

Pancho and Olive amped up the volume.

She said, "I told you not to trust him."

"He said there was no risk. No risk."

"That was our savings."

"We agreed it was a good idea."

"Yeah, to get it. But we didn't agree to give him money in advance."

"He told me not to tell you."

"I married an idiot. A complete, stupid idiot."

As the argument waged, Jen turned back to Les. "Please, give me a hand here, Les. Zach's waiting for me."

"It's what they're arguing over. It seems that Child's Play promised to get them the treatment."

"Jesus."

"They claim they have no idea how he was getting it. Just that he promised to have it today."

"And?"

"Not certain. Maybe he got ripped off himself. Or maybe he's just scamming them."

"You got that from Child's Play?"

"He's unconscious."

"Will he survive?"

"No idea. I got it from these two, once I pieced together their incoherent bursts."

"Tattoo Man is going to be pleased as punch. Maybe you'll get a day off for being a good boy."

Actually, Les was always a good boy. As much as he encouraged Jen to kick a bit of ass, his own interest in ass, so he often told her, had nothing to do with kicking. He did his job, bent rules like everyone else, talked back at times, but he always followed orders. He liked his job well enough, but his main career goal was an eventual pension.

"You could have told me all this tomorrow," Jen continued.

"But that's not it, Cobalt."

She waited.

"They were saying things like, 'We were gonna live forever' and 'What's gonna happen to us now?' They were talking about 'getting it' or 'scoring some of the treatment.'"

"Okay."

"But then once, just once, he didn't call it the treatment." Les held her eyes, making sure he had her full attention. "Pancho Porter said, 'He promised to get us Eden.'"

*   *   *

Pancho and Olive were loaded into separate cruisers.

Jen lingered at the open door of the car that had just arrived to take us home, her foot resting on the rocker panel. She volleyed questions at Les, none of which he was able to return.

He said, "You don't sound anxious to get going anymore."

"I promised to tell Zach about my mother."

"Oh. Want to come to the station and question these two?"

"Yeah, maybe a good idea."

At the station, though, the suspects said they didn't know anything. No, they had no idea where Child's Play would get the treatment. And when asked about Eden, they glanced at each other, and then Pancho said they didn't know anything about it other than what the Bible taught them. He demanded they each see a lawyer, and that was that.

Les walked Jen to the front door. "You want to tell me what's going on?" he said. "This Eden thing you were asking about?"

I could tell Jen wanted to speak. But she had already crossed some uncrossable lines: disobeyed Brooks and broken into a crime scene one day, and removed evidence on another. She didn't want to involve Les.

Boss, you're gonna have to.

She stepped outside and with a metaphorical click, I disappeared.

12

A half hour later, Jen and Zach were on his rooftop with a bottle of vinho verde. No longer available from Portugal, this one came from one of the new vineyards in North Dakota, its green color diluted to the verge of nothingness.

Back when they were still getting to know each other, Jennifer had told Zach the basics about her mother—the adjectives, as he had said. But when Zach met her mother, the two of them had hit it off, although she didn't remember Zach from one monthly visit to the next.

Jen took Zach's hand, tilted her head, and stared up at the sky. There was too much ambient light to properly see the stars, but one thing was infinitely better than in her childhood: the air was no longer full of smog from car, truck, and bus engines.

Some things do get better, she thought.

"My dad left us when I was five," she began. "Mother deleted or tore up every photo. He's only a blurry image in my head."

Zach was watching her carefully. He had heard this part before.

"Maybe he needed to leave her, I don't know, but to abandon me like that, it's . . . Until then, she was tough to live with, but from that moment on, she dragged me deep into her personal hell. I could never do right. Scolding me. Slapping me. Locking me in the pitch-black bathroom and telling me she was never coming back . . . Zach, I was only a little girl."

She held out her glass, and Zach steadied her shaking hand so he could pour her more wine.

"The ice cream thing. I . . . I've never told anyone."

He gave a kind nod.

"It's really nothing."

He waited.

"I don't mean nothing. Just one of many things she did. The life I lived."

She started to bring the wine glass to her lips but stopped.

"I was seven years old. We were in a park with her older cousin and her cousin's husband, Reverend Chin. I was wearing the dress they brought me. It was the most beautiful thing ever, pink and full of lace and frills."

She caught Zach's look. "Yes, even I went through a pink stage. They bought me a soft ice cream cone. Chocolate. Mother stooped down, wagged her scary index finger, and hissed, 'You'll be sorry, miss, if I catch you getting so much as one drop on your new dress.'"

Jennifer's wineglass was quivering in her hand. Zach took it from her and set it down on the patio deck.

"I was trying to be so careful, but I was only seven. A huge plop of ice cream fell onto the dress. I tried to wipe it away with my little hand, but that only made it worse.

"Mother noticed and slapped the rest of the cone away and yelled, 'Look what you've done!' Her cousin tried to speak, but Mother would have none of it. I was bawling by then, and Reverend Chin picked me up to console me, but Mother snatched me away." She paused. "You heard enough?"

Zach started to answer, but she could not stop.

"We went home, just us two. Mother dragged me into the kitchen. She pointed at the table and barked at me to sit down. She pulled a tub of chocolate ice cream from the freezer, threw it into the sink, and ran hot water over it. I was terrified. I tried to imagine what was coming next. I could feel craziness pouring off her.

"She grabbed the tub, ripped off the lid, and said, 'You want ice cream? Well, here's ice cream for you.' She grabbed a handful of melting ice cream from the tub and crammed it into my mouth. Right away, she grabbed another handful and smeared it onto my mouth and nose. Another hand-ful, she wiped all over my dress.

"I was desperately trying to swallow, but the ice cream was so cold and there was so much. She started to tear at my dress—I mean, just tear it right off me. She was screaming, 'See what you've done! See what you've done!' She stuffed more ice cream into my mouth, and my nose was clogged with it, and I couldn't breathe. I was suffocating. For seconds, hours, I couldn't breathe and she was screaming, and I knew I was going to die."

Zach reached out, but she didn't even seem to notice that his hand was on her arm.

"Then I hit puberty and the true shaming began. I was too fat, I was too thin. The hair on my body was disgusting. My smell was disgusting. My nipples showed. I was a slut, I was a whore. I . . ."

Jen tried to keep the tears from coming, but when Zach moved his hand to hers, she gripped it so tightly his fingers bleached white. She started sobbing.

"I . . . I want to . . ." She grabbed a soft cushion, crammed it against her mouth, and screamed. Terror collided with anger and she cried, yelled, sweated, and shook as Zach held her tightly.

And then it ended.

She dropped the cushion, pushed him away, hard, and gasped for air. She slipped from her seat and collapsed onto the deck, panting like a spent athlete. With the bottom of her T-shirt, she wiped tears and snot from her face. She snatched up the pillow again and screamed some more, but this time, by the end she was laughing with tremendous joy. Eighteen years of that abuse until she left home; eighteen years, but she had survived.

She reached out to Zach, pulled him back to her, pushed him away, tugged off his clothes and wrestled off her own, wet with sweat, snot, and tears. They threw cushions and pillows onto the deck and made love, feverish love turned gentle and then wild again, until they finally fell asleep, tangled together in the night.

13

It was Friday the twelfth, which meant it was Friday the thirteenth minus one day, and so bad things were pretty close to happening. How did I know that? Preemptive apophenia. I was feeling more human by the second.

07:42:34. First stop, the three-year-old Washington Charity Hospital Complex. Crowded. Smelly. Already shabby. Dangerous. Staffed exclusively with doctors and nurses here on temporary work permits. Most could get by in English or Spanish, but some could not. Some were exceptionally well trained; others held the equivalent of a Boy Scout first aid merit badge.

Around town, the place was known as the Abattoir. One story has it that a guy was getting brain surgery when a shift ended. Hospital admin refused to pay overtime. Doctors signed out, man had to finish the brain surgery on himself. Why do I know this is BS? Because there's no way they'd try to pull off brain surgery in this place.

Which made it a pretty crappy place for Child's Play to be bunking down with a head injury.

With Les leading the way, we slalomed through the crowded lobby, waited too long at the sorry bank of elevators, decided to take the filthy stairs, raced each other laughing up to the fourth floor—Jen easily won—and trekked down a vomit-brown corridor lined with gurneys holding soiled patients who moaned, screamed, retched, and begged for a swift death.

75

We had been told on the phone what to expect, but Les insisted we double-check for ourselves. He was convinced the nurse he spoke to hadn't understood what he was asking, and he was certain that another was keeping us away because he came from a country where the cops' main job was to extort money and kill people.

Sure enough, Child's Play was still unconscious, with so many tubes and wires coming in and out of him that he looked like a miniature oil refinery. We talked to a nice Lebanese doctor who spoke English better than Hammerhead, whose ancestors had come from England 150 years ago. But to be fair, all Hammerhead had under his belt was the gutted US public school system, while the doctor had the unfair advantage of living in a war zone and refugee camps. The doctor promised to contact us the minute Child's Play woke up.

As soon as we left the hospital, Les took off to bid farewell to one of our old folks he had dealt with. "Fabulous woman, incredible community builder," he said. "Exiting tomorrow."

Jen and I ambled back to the station, me talking and then shutting up whenever Jen said she needed to think. "Mind if I follow along?" I asked.

It was Eden, of course, and the Bible thing that had been pinging in and out of her brain for days.

Her mind was drifting back and forth. Then she focused again on the receipt tucked inside the Bible, the receipt for the phone. In her mind's eye, I saw it in her hand. A tingle of energy flashed through her brain, and I felt her excitement as she turned it over and saw a series of words and numbers scribbled on the back. But they were blurry—in the memory, that is. There and not there at the same time. *What words, what numbers?* she thought. *And what do they mean?*

* * *

10:18:35. Jen was yawning. And yawning.

"What's up, sleepyhead?" I said.

"Sleepyhead? Aren't you the regular guy."

"Good late night?"

"Amazing late night." Jen sighed, then slapped the table. "So?" she said.

Clairvoyant that I am, I gave her a quick rundown on the research she had requested. Turned out that the articles on mental health issues among the Timeless were all anecdotal—stories of specialized clinics in California, Florida, and Connecticut, but nothing more. Any serious research had been suppressed by the drug companies under the Improving Pharmaceutical Research Act of 2030.

"Estimates are that fifteen to twenty Timeless popped themselves off in the US last year."

Jen said, "That's not so many."

"Are you kidding? No one knows how many Timeless there are here, but I'd put my money on four to six hundred."

"You have money now?"

"It's an expression."

"So I've heard."

"Anyhow, the program is still new, it's staggeringly expensive, and only people getting old would be willing to experiment with this."

"Still, twenty suicides aren't many."

"Boss, leave the math to me, will you? It's three hundred and eighty-five times the national average."

After that display of computational brilliance, it was a bit of this and that until Jen and Les were summoned to Captain Brooks's office. At his door, an unfriendly plainclothes guy glanced at our badges before letting us in. Never seen anything like that before. I figured it was because the tattooed man in the gray suit had returned to our station.

I was hoping the captain would offer us a coffee because I liked the buzz. He didn't even offer us a seat. We stood but didn't exactly snap to attention. I mean we're cops, not jarheads.

Gray Suit was once again in a gray suit, but this one had almost invisible ferns woven into it. With his first question, he quietly took charge. "Why are you two still standing?" He looked at the two extra chairs, which, as usual, were stacked with reports. "Captain," he said, "think we can make these two a bit more comfortable?"

Brooks didn't seem happy getting orders on his own turf, but he cleared off the papers and grunted that we should sit down. The martinis and hors d'oeuvres would be arriving any second.

Les recounted what Olive Ortega and Pancho Porter had said. He said that the victim and alleged dealer was still unconscious, a fact of which Gray Suit was obviously aware. Jen added her own recollections.

Gray Suit listened, never once interrupting. He wasn't a fidgety listener. He never took his eyes off the person speaking, and only when Les or Jen ran out of things to say did he add another question or ask for a clarification.

He asked why Les had called Jen in. "I understand from your captain that it was her night off."

"It was," Les said. "But this was a family we'd dealt with several times before. Jen was good at talking them down. Anything could happen with those two, and I wanted her there."

Gray Suit studied Les. He brushed the back of his fingers over the tattoos on his cheek, perhaps checking whether he'd done a decent job shaving that morning. It's a strange thing talking to someone whose face is given over to geometric patterns—it's damn hard to see beyond the tattoos, to look them in the eyes.

It also made him a formidable enemy, which I kind of figured was the whole point. As he watched Les, I felt adrenalin flooding from Jen's adrenal medulla. Her heart rate increased and she fought to control her breathing. As if sensing this, Gray Suit turned his attention to her.

"Anything else to add?" he asked her.

She said no.

He observed her for an uncomfortably long 9.42 seconds. And then thanked the two of them for taking time to speak to him.

We left, passing by the man at the door.

Secret Service, I said to her.

As soon as we returned to our office, Les shut the door—something we rarely did—and turned to Jen.

"You better tell me what's going on here," Les said.

"I don't want to get you in trouble."

"You're kind of late for that. I just lied for you."

"*More* trouble, then."

"I swear, that guy outside was Secret Service."

"I know," Jen said.

"It doesn't make sense."

"The president and VP are both Timeless."

"So?"

"Secret Service does the Executive branch," Jen said. "The top woman and man are Timeless. Timeless don't want everyone getting the treatment."

"Seems a stretch."

"Just maybe it's true."

"Anything just may be true."

Jen walked to the window, and we stared out. The leaves on the beautiful sycamore tree were a dusty brown, curling up on themselves.

"Do you think," she said, "it will ever rain again?"

"Cobalt, I've always trusted you. You've got to trust me."

"I will. I promise."

"When?"

"I don't know."

"When?"

She turned back to the window.

"Tonight," she said.

Code word for when P.D. and I are switched off.

Bad move, I said.

She didn't even bother to reply.

*   *   *

An hour later, we were downstairs in an interview room with Olive Ortega. We had already wasted fourteen minutes with her husband. Pancho Porter had obviously seen his share of TV cop shows and refused to say anything without a lawyer present. Couldn't say I blamed him, but damn him anyway. We stared at his trumpeter's face while he stared at his fingernails. At one point, I suggested to Jen that we ask where he bought the cantaloupes.

Olive was a different kettle of orange-eyed fish. She was so pissed at her stupid husband for stupidly giving all their money to that stupid neighbor that I bet she'd have sworn Pancho had shot Lincoln if we had asked.

Les said, "What did Child's Play promise to get you?"

"Have you ever heard such a stupid name? I mean . . . stupid."

"No. So what was it?"

"Just what we said. The treatment."

"The full treatment that the Timeless get? Or the treatment that people get when their parents exit?"

"What do you mean?"

Who's stupid now? I said to Jen.

Les explained what he meant.

Olive seemed dumbfounded. "It never occurred to me to ask. He said he'd get us Eden and we said hell yes."

"Eden," Jen said, jumping in.

"You were very nice when you visited those times."

"Thank you."

"Things got better. Between Pancho and our boy. For a while."

Jen smiled.

"The truth is, though, we don't want to exit. Know what I mean?"

Jen nodded.

Apparently that wasn't enough. Olive was waiting for her to speak.

Jen said, "I know it must be hard."

Olive said, "No, it's not *hard*. It's stupid. Who says that humans should have, you know, those dates on groceries?"

Jen said, "Expiration dates."

"Exactly. That's stupid."

"So Eden."

"Exactly."

"What's Eden?"

"I just told you."

Jen said, "Tell me again, will you please, just so I'm clear."

Olive shook her head. Everyone was obviously so stupid nowadays.

"It's what he called it. The treatment."

"Have you heard others call it that?"

Olive said "Probably. Here and there, like."

"Do you have a Bible?"

Olive looked offended. "Of course we have a Bible. Two. One Spanish and one in the original English. I go to the Assembly Hall each and every week."

"Did Child's Play give you a new Bible? Or look at yours?"

"Why would he do that? Officer, are you feeling okay? You're sounding, I don't know . . . "

Les said, "Stupid?"

And Olive laughed.

* * *

13:31.08. Nice Lebanese doc phoned. Child's Play was awake, but groggy.

Jen and I, Les and P.D. reached the Washington Charity Hospital Complex so quickly you'd think we had superpowers. Raced up to four.

But nice doctor unnicely turned his back when he saw us, like Les and Jen had some sort of disease he wasn't fond of. *What's that about?* I asked, and Jen shrugged.

There was a sign on the door: "Entry Prohibited." We went into the room. Child's Play was sitting up in bed, a whopping bandage around his head. Half the wires and tubes had been pulled out. One of his arms was cuffed to the bed.

Les said, "Seems she didn't kill you."

"Orange-eyed bitch."

"Child's Play," Jen said, "we've always been good to you."

"I got no beef with you."

"So, we need your help. Just a word or two. Between us. It's this Eden thing—"

But just as Jen said the word *thing*, a woman—white, late-twenties, chunked up like an MMA fighter, khaki fatigues, and with an Uzi dangling like a cocktail purse on a strap over her shoulder—pounded into the room, yelling, "Who the hell gave you permission to be here?"

Jen went for her badge. Woman went for her gun. Jen threw her hands in the air. "Whoa, there, we're police. Who the hell are you?"

"That door has a sign. No one comes in without my say-so."

"We're not 'no one.'"

Woman still hadn't lowered her gun. "Let's see some badges. Slowly," she said.

Les and Jen produced their badges. Woman said, "Outside," like she ran the show, which she apparently did.

Once back in the hallway, Les said we were the officers who had arrested the alleged perpetrators. The woman looked like she didn't care. Jen said we were in charge of the assault investigation, and the woman said that wasn't exactly true any longer.

Les asked if she was a cop.

Woman said, "Yes and no."

"DC?"

"No."

"FBI?"

"Before you lose your voice spouting initials, let's just say that I'm a private contractor."

"Working for . . . ?"

"Who I work for."

Jen said, "We need to talk to him. Child's Play"

Now the woman looked bored and restless. She studied her fingers like she was contemplating a manicure, but I had the impression she was actually thinking about techniques for pulling out someone's fingernails.

"It's not going to happen in a million years."

Not having that much time to wait, we turned away without a word. As we left the ward, Les muttered, "Fucking mercenaries. Makes you wonder what the hell's going on."

14

Zach's father, Raffi, wasn't a recipe man. More of a staring-into-the-refrigerator-and-running-some-mental-algorithm-and-producing-magic sort of cook. That night, so he claimed and no one could dispute, he made a Madagascar chicken dish. They had splurged and bought a real chicken. It was organic and had been well treated. It tasted very good.

Leah asked Jen about work.

"Ever been to the Charity Hospital?"

Leah said, "They say it's out of the nineteenth century."

Raffi said, "Imagine, living in a country where health care is seen as charity."

Jen sensed this was closing in on dangerous territory—health care . . . the treatment . . . exit—so she quickly described Pancho Porter's amazingly huge cheeks, which led to Raffi talking about getting dumped by a trumpet-playing girlfriend in high school, who, because of long hours of disciplined practice and equally disciplined kissing, had severely cracked lips.

"I got the short end of the stick," he said.

Leah said, "And you ended up with me."

"Which proves I didn't get the short end of the stick after all."

Leah brought out a peach pie. Befitting her college minor in chemistry, she approached her pies like she was putting together a bomb: one false move and it was all over. Exacting measurements, homemade crust, fresh fruit.

Raffi and Leah went out to visit a friend who was exiting in two weeks; Zach and Jen cleaned up, his hands in a sink of suds.

"He's a great cook, but man does he make a mess," Zach said.

Jen wiped the countertop and swept the floor. Broom in hand, she stopped. Her eyes rested on Zach's figure from behind.

"I can feel your beautiful eyes on me," he said without turning.

"I've never felt so at home as right here."

He half-turned, his hands still in the sudsy water, and smiled, his dimples perfect. She kissed him tenderly on the lips.

He said, "I've never been so happy as I am with you."

As he continued to scrub the baking dish, she hugged him from behind, resting her cheek against his back. She said, "Thank you," and then yawned noisily.

"I'm that exciting?" Zach said.

"Chandler was teasing me too."

"Who's Chandler? A new guy?"

"Oh, ah, no one. Someone I work with."

She knew her stumbling made it sound like she was having an affair. She knew she had to tell this wonderful man who had attentively listened to her childhood story and didn't tell her to get over it. Who made her feel so safe.

"I should tell you," she said, and climbed onto the counter.

"What's that?"

His tone told her he hadn't even imagined she was having an affair. But she took a deep breath and said, "You may have caught rumors of this, but DC and some of the other police departments are trying out an experimental program."

"Stop being racist?"

"Yuk yuk. We've done a pretty good job since the DC18. No, they're doing a test run of synthetic implants."

"Implants of what?"

"Well, these little organic computers."

"Sounds creepy."

"It's to give us quick access to data. An instant comm link. A second set of eyes to keep us safe. And pretty much a photographic record of what happens during our shift."

"It's alive?"

"Well, sort of. I mean it's not like it could live on its own."

"Where does it live?"

"You know. They, uh, put it in your brain."

"This is totally creepy."

He handed her the now-clean baking dish to dry.

"It's just that . . ."

He looked at her with alarm. "God, tell me you're not getting one of those. I mean, it's crazily invasive. Maybe dangerous. And you and everyone around you will be under constant surveillance."

She didn't respond.

"Please, honey. Please tell you're not going to get one of those."

Ten seconds passed, but to Jen it was an hour. She dismissed the impulse to change the subject. She owed it to him. To them.

"I already have one."

He looked stricken. "Since when?"

"Since two years and three months ago."

He stared at her, dumbfounded.

"You've had this—this *thing* all the time I've known you!"

"It's not—"

"So last night, when we made love, it was there too. Right now—"

"No, it isn't like that. I can turn him off."

"Whenever you want?"

"No. Not when I'm signed in."

"Wait, did you just say turn *him* off? Not *it*? This is getting creepier by the second."

"He—it's just an expression, silly." *Not exactly,* she thought. Chandler, like P.D. and some of the others, had for some experimental reason been gender coded, although many were non-binary. She didn't know if others kept changing, but Chandler certainly had been growing into his role, including his tough-guy talk.

"You're telling me that anytime I've ever seen you or we've talked when you're working, like that day at Zombies, everything we said, everything we did was being recorded and shared with others?"

"I don't think they share it."

"Really? And how do you know that?"

"I don't, but—"

"God, I can't believe you're telling me this. I feel so . . ."

"We were ordered to keep it quiet."

He put on a crappy German accent. "I was just following orders."

"Zach, that's a disgusting thing to say."

"Is it on right now?"

"I told you, only when I'm working."

"I feel so—I don't know—spied on. Violated."

"That seems a bit—"

"Jen, don't tell me what I'm feeling. Okay?"

They were silent. One of those noisy silences where every physical motion feels awkward, like your joints need oiling and even your breathing feels put on. They finished cleaning up.

Jen left. They didn't even pretend to discuss plans for that weekend.

It would be weeks before Jen would find out what Zach hadn't told her. That, while he was washing dishes, he had decided to tell her he had lied to her. It was true that he hadn't reached Mary Sue from the co-op, but he had managed to contact Devin. Not right away, but Zach had gotten a message to him, and Devin had phoned back from some other number and kept the call very short. They'd gone into hiding. They were scared that the fire had been set. Maybe as a warning. Maybe to destroy their business. But also, just maybe to kill them.

*   *   *

Les waved Jen in. "Wasn't actually expecting to see you tonight, but you're just in time for dessert." He glanced out the door, at the hallway, to see if Zach was coming. "Alone?"

"All," Jen said.

Christopher came into their small foyer and kissed her hello.

Jen said, "I'm so glad to see a normal, happy couple."

Christopher winced sympathetically. "This sounds bad. Want me to scram?"

"No, but I could use one of your caipirinhas." She grabbed Christopher's hand and dragged him into the kitchen, Les trailing behind.

Christopher fetched a bottle of cachaça from under the counter, a lime from a basket of fruit, some sugar, and ice and went to work. Meanwhile, Les pulled a tiramisu from the refrigerator and served it in shallow glass bowls.

Christopher and Les were physical opposites. Although Les had a great body, he wasn't particularly good-looking. He moved in a chunky, muscular way, and if he had been a boxer, he would have been a slugger, not an out-boxer who dances elegantly around opponents. Christopher was Brazilian and Black, and had a boring but stable job in the Department of Transportation. He was utterly normal in build, but he moved gracefully and seemed entirely at home in his body. He also had the most beautiful face she could imagine, serene and strong all at once.

I wish I could marry these two, she thought. Except she occasionally sensed that Christopher was, deep down, jealous of her relationship with Les, so it probably wouldn't work.

They went into the living room. Jen curled up at one end of the couch, Christopher at the other. Les took his usual spot, cross-legged on the rug on the other side of their coffee table. The two men started with the dessert, but Jen went right for the drink.

Christopher said, "I hear you guys had an awful day."

"Beginning," Jen said, "at a truly disgusting hospital."

"But," Christopher said, "don't you think it's good to have a charity hospital? I mean, people need it."

Les nodded to Christopher and turned to Jen. "So?"

Great interrogator that he was, Jen immediately spilled the beans that she had told Zach about Chandler.

"And on the freak-out meter?"

She pointed to the ceiling. "Christopher, did you react like a crazy person when you found out?"

"Are you kidding? P.D. keeps him safe. Why would I object? God, even with P.D, I still worry about him every time he steps out the door."

She was envious. Their life was so simple. You did your jobs, you exercised, you cooked and ate, you watched some shows or went out. You had sex, you slept. None of the drama at Zach's. No discussions about how screwed up the world was or the latest war or how everyone should start co-ops.

With the confession over, they all sank into a quiet evening. They watched a short movie. Ate popcorn. Talked about this and that.

About 10:30, Christopher said, "I've gotta crash."

Jen started to get up, but Les said to Christopher, "Hon, you mind if I talk to Jen for a while?"

"Praise the Lord! I can actually go to sleep without getting mauled by you."

He kissed Jen and then Les. "Good night, Tiger," he called as he left the room.

"You too," Les said.

"I was talking to Jennifer."

Once Christopher had gone, Jen said, "You really maul him?"

"I'd say we stack up pretty equitably on that one. Another drink?"

"Two was more than enough."

"Brazil's great contribution to inebriation. Now, come on. 'Fess up."

She circled around the topic of Eden for a minute, getting no further than Brooks telling her to stop wasting time on it. Les pretended to fall asleep.

"Okay, okay," she said. "Remember the report about someone breaking into the Johnsons' apartment?"

"You're shitting me. That was you?"

A sheepish grin came over her face.

"While on duty?"

"No."

"That was an amazingly dumb thing to do."

"You're the one always telling me to stand up to Brooks."

"Yeah, but I didn't tell you to openly disobey him, break into a crime scene when you're off duty, and cover it up by going back in. Good thing you didn't say any of this in front of Christopher; I'd never hear the end of it. Or even in front of P.D."

"Yeah, she is a bit of a suck," Jen said. It wasn't the first time Jen thought about how different Chandler and P.D. were, and wondered how much was from their original programming and how much was something akin to personality, whatever that might mean for a blob of organic computer.

"I'm serious, Jen. What the hell were you thinking?" But then, seeing her grin turn to alarm, he softened. "Well, at least your days of sucking up to Brooks are over, Cobalt."

"Les, Eden has been niggling at me since I first heard these rumors."

"Don't forget that. They're *rumors*."

"But now we hear about a counterfeit treatment."

"Maybe. Or maybe another rumor. Remember, Child's Play didn't deliver. I'm guessing he was scamming them." Out of the blue, he said, "Why the hell are you asking everyone about reading the Bible?"

"Not *reading* the Bible." She told him about the Bible getting stolen, the receipt from the co-op, and the co-op getting burned down.

He shook his head. "You're stitching together cobwebs. It's nothing . . . Probably nothing, anyway."

"Then why's there a mercenary outside of Child's Play's hospital room? And why was that Secret Service guy at the station?"

"Dunno. But, Jen, I have to tell you. You're my partner. You're my friend." He paused, looked at her with anguish, then said, "Jen, we do our work, but it's got to be by the book. I don't want you to lose your job. And I don't want to lose mine. Even if there's something going on, I don't want it screwing up everything Christopher and I have planned."

*   *   *

Jen trudged home. Took her an hour. It was late and the streets were quiet save for two or three small Shadow camps and the occasional bus or empty car going to its garage for the night. Everyone else was home with their lovers, their families. Everyone sleeping, content. It was a good time for self-pity.

She woke up the next morning feeling distant from the whole world. The weekend off. Nothing to do. She was alone.

She tried to go back to sleep, but her mind kept tumbling through the previous evening. She sat up and reached for her phone to check her messages. Nothing. She desperately wanted Zach to call her. She thought of phoning him but figured he should make the first move. She knew she could talk to Les about Zach, but she felt Les had hit the pause button. They were partners, would risk their lives for each other, and they were friends, but she couldn't expect the world from him.

She dressed, ate, and biked a third of the way to Harper's Ferry and back as fast as she could force herself to go. But the trip unsettled her. There seemed to be great bunches of litter alongside the pathway. She smelled death and, seconds later, spotted the carcass of a dead deer, its body teeming with flies. She caught a flash of broken glass, and before she could help it, she imagined stepping on it and Zach once again coming to her rescue.

Sunday, she was already tossing and fretting by 5:00 AM. She dragged herself out of bed, dressed, ate a banana, drank a cup of coffee, and ran fourteen miles. It was the only good time to run anymore—early morning or evening, that is, so you wouldn't fry.

No rigors, no exhaustion, though, could quiet her mind. She was pummeled by a looping playlist: Zach. Eden. Bibles. Les. Gray Suit. Child's Play. Mercenaries. Zach Eden Bibles Zach.

As she ran, she tried to focus on one thing, what she actually knew about Eden. Was that all it was, the street name for a counterfeit version of the treatment? Or could it be more than that? She replayed every time she had heard the word. First time couldn't have been more than six weeks earlier, perhaps two months. Where had she been? Not the women at the hairdresser's, not the man who wouldn't talk to her. She couldn't remember, likely because the first time it was simply a word, not yet part of a pattern, real or imagined. She cast around. She had an image of the district station, but that probably wasn't right. The image of a park. No, not that either.

For a while, she managed to crowbar Eden out of her mind and pressed herself to pump her legs harder. She tried to bludgeon herself into numbness.

As she pushed herself toward an exhaustion that just wouldn't come quickly enough, she kept returning to the blowup with Zach. She wondered if she should have told him about Chandler back when they'd met. God, there were so many differences between them. *And why the hell hasn't he phoned me?* Her mind drifted back to Richard O'Neil hitting on her, and she was caught off guard by a rush of disconcertingly delicious feelings. *Fantastic-looking. Rich beyond belief. Mesmerizing. Smart.* She punched away the thought that he was 112 years old. *Don't think he charmed me simply so I'd lie in court. He was interested in me. He was cool, definitely cool.* And these thoughts quickly morphed into a fantasy of the life they could have together. *Why not? I'll never worry about anything again. I'll have the full treatment. Screw Zach.*

She commanded herself to stop thinking such things, but Richard O'Neil started looping himself into her playlist.

By the end of the weekend, she not only realized but accepted that Zach deserved to be upset. She should have told him long ago. And now she should be phoning him to apologize and say she loved him.

But she just couldn't bring herself to pick up the phone.

15

Captain Brooks said, "What did I tell you two weeks ago? Forget about Eden."

Only eleven days, I said to her, and she told me to lock it.

Jen said, "But it's all changed since then, sir. Child's Play said he was going to sell them Eden."

"He told you this?"

"He was unconscious when we first visited."

"So you psychically connected?"

"When we visited him again, there was this private security woman who stopped us right when we were starting to question him."

"When?" He looked concerned, maybe even a bit pissed.

"Friday. End of the day."

He rubbed his scar. I was starting to worry he'd expose bone if he didn't lay off.

"Who was she working for?"

"Wouldn't say."

"Then you didn't talk to him."

"Not exactly."

"Inexactly?"

"We heard it from Olive Ortega. She said that Child's Play was going to sell her the treatment. Later in the interview, she called it Eden."

"Did you ask her what she meant by this?"

"She didn't have much to say."

92

"Playing dumb?"

"I don't think she needs to play at it, sir," Jen said. "She told us she didn't know anything about Eden. We—Les and me—asked if it was the full or modified treatment. They apparently hadn't even asked that."

"Why didn't you tell this to Teko Teko Mea?"

"That's his name?"

"I asked you a question."

"It only came out when we questioned Ortega again after we met on Friday."

No, it didn't, I corrected her. *Les told you. Thursday night. Pancho Porter's garage. 21:22.45.*

Jen ignored me. Damn, she was going to get all of us in trouble.

"You should have come and told me."

"You said not to bother you with Eden gossip."

"Then why are you telling me now?"

"Maybe it's more than gossip."

"So you Sherlocked it and concluded Eden is the street name for the black-market treatment."

"Something like that."

"Brilliant deduction."

"Thanks."

"Jen, I was being sarcastic. It's pretty obvious."

"But it's good to know, isn't it?"

"Only because now you can forget all the rumors and get back to your job."

"But it means they can listen for it. Scan for 'Eden' and see who's using it in conversations and texts."

"Happy to hear you've been hired by the NSA."

"Sir, I think you're being unnecessarily hard on me."

Go Cobalt!

"Do you now?" He turned up the voltage on his stare. I felt Cobalt Blue shrink back to Jen B. Lu. But then his look softened. He shook his head. "Jen, how many more weeks on your probation?"

"Two, sir. Just under."

We watched him scribble the number *2* on his pad, make a circle around it and then scratch it out.

She said, "Do you want me to contact—"

"Teko Teko Mea?"

"—and tell him what we heard?"

"No. I'll let him know. But you can—"

"Do my damn job?"

He almost smiled.

*   *   *

10:37:52, Jen's phone text-dinged.

I eavesdropped. I mean, what's a guy to do? Her eyes are my eyes.

From Zach: *Hey, J. I'm trying to figure out how I'm feeling about all this. Mind if we take a couple of days. Maybe see each other Wednesday night?*

Jen wrote out a long reply. Apologizing. Scolding. Saying she was hurt by his response. Saying she was sorry. But in the end, she deleted it all and typed, *K.*

She spoke to Hammerhead. She drank a coffee. She checked the notice board in the staff room. She was a ton of fun today.

Pinned to the notice board was a flyer for a weekly prayer meeting at a nearby fundamentalist church. It had a quote from the Bible, one of the usual "God's gonna whup your sorry ass if you don't be nice and give more money to your minister's private airplane fund." Jen ripped it down, but as she was about to bunch it up, her eyes fixed on the numbers attached to the quote. The usual format—I mean, I've studied this stuff. Book name chapter: verse.

"Chandler," she said, "I wonder if you could help me focus on something I saw when you were switched off."

Now we're talking.

It wasn't easy. With her help, I accessed her memories of her break-in at the Johnsons', the Bible, and the receipts, and as before, all I saw was a blur of numbers and letters, as if someone has erased a bunch of pencil markings. But human memory is a pretty fascinating thing. For me, all I need to do is think about something and I've got it. For them, it seems they sometimes need to *not* think about it, and it pops into their head hours or days later. I'm calling it their memory, but it's clear it isn't the same as true computer memory.

Thus I sailed her mind this way and that, like I was a captain on a pitching ship on the high seas, and before long, there it was, rising clear to the surface like three neon-colored fish:

John 9:16
Acts 12:19
Spesians 4:11

"What've we got, Chandler?"
"Bad Bible studies. The first one doesn't exist. There's no John 9:16."
"Either she jotted it down wrong, or my memory scrambled it."
Not wanting to offend the boss, I kept quiet.

The second verse was one of those Biblical history bits. King Herod had decided to kill Peter, Peter escapes, Herod decides to put to death those who protected him.

We pondered that one a bit, but other than stretching it into a reference to exit, it didn't seem to do much.

Moving on, I said, "*Spesians* might be her shorthand for Ephesians. And—sorry, Jen—this one is even more nothing than the last: 'And he gave some, apostles; and some, prophets; and some, evangelists; and some, pastors and teachers.'"

Bible studies over for now, Jen and I returned to the Washington Charity Hospital Complex to check on Child's Play. Maybe sneak in this time to see him and detect some crimes.

No guard outside his room. Good news.

No one inside his room. Not such good news.

At the nursing station, we flashed her badge at three nurses or nursing assistants or doctors or patient care assistants or custodians. Everyone dresses the same, and my programming always fails me: I never have a clue whether we're talking to someone who transplants hearts or changes dirty sheets. The badge-flashing routine always impresses me, although it didn't seem to do the trick on them. It was one nurse's first day, and he'd never heard of Child's Play except when used as an expression. A second spoke very poor English and said, "He gone," and made a whooshing motion of her arms that either signified he had been discharged or had learned how to fly. A third tried to check Child's Play's file but found no record he'd ever been there.

We were about to leave when the nice Lebanese doctor arrived. We asked about Child's Play. He blushed. "I, um . . ."

We waited.

"I can't really . . . it's . . ." His eyes looked very sad.

"You can't say where he's gone," Jen said.

"I can't even say someone was here who has gone."

"But—"

"Listen, they can boot me out of the country faster than . . ."

We waited to hear what it would be faster than, but instead he shook his head sorrowfully, turned, and walked away.

We headed over to V Street NW on a white and silver cop bicycle to pay a surprise visit to Delmar Johnson Jr.

"Delmar Johnson Jr. is a bit of an oaf." Jen likes to school me on the subtitles of human character.

"I thought," I said, "that oafs had to live in the country."

"No. We have urban oafs. And this one is a damn lucky oaf."

Delmar Junior was out on bail, facing only a charge of possession of an illegal firearm. The DA had decided a jury would rule that he acted in self-defense.

"Do you agree with that decision?" I said.

"That's not my job."

"I didn't ask you that."

"Dunno," Jen said. "His father might have shot him first. It was a standoff. And his dad was the one who shot his mother. And they were refusing to exit. Sounds like self-defense to me."

I didn't say anything.

"What?" she eventually said. "You don't agree?"

I said, "I'm not so sure."

Here's the strange thing. If she had asked me the same question two years ago, I would barely have known what she was getting at. A year ago, I would have understood but wouldn't have ventured an opinion. Six months ago, I would have toed the line. But I seem to be changing my mind. Well, that's only an expression. Or is it? Could I be developing a mind? I wonder what that feels like, to have a mind and not merely organic circuits? I wonder if Jen will notice. I wonder if anyone will notice. I wonder what will happen to my mind when I die in three years.

We locked the bike in front of their apartment.

"Before we go up, I need to get one thing straight," I said.

"What's that?"

"Is this the third or the fourth time you've been here? In other words, I want to know if you were the one who broke in."

"Where did you get that idea?"

"It's mapped all over your brain."

"Then, yes, I did. You knew anyway."

"I wanted to know if you trusted me."

"Chandler, of course I do."

"And?"

"Of course I don't."

Betrayed by your own partner.

"Don't take it the wrong way. But the question is, would you lie for me? I mean, I'd cover for Les any day of the—" She froze and I caught a whiff of an argument they had had. She quickly recovered. "There might even be a circumstance when I'd lie for Hammerhead, although nothing comes to mind."

"You never said whether you'd lie for me," I said.

"What's that supposed to mean?"

"Say I screw up, and I get you in trouble. Would you take the blame and cover for me like you'd probably do for Les? Or would you lay it on me?"

"Jesus. I don't even know what *you* means, in your case."

"Me. Yo. Moi. Ahau."

"What was that last one?"

"Maori. I've been boning up on it since we met Gray Suit."

"Let's go see the oaf, okay?"

The stairs again smelled freshly washed. Up on the second floor, the yellow police tape was gone, and the door had been crudely repaired. We knocked. No answer. We knocked again.

Delmar Junior came to the door in his boxers. Can't say I blamed him. It was damn hot in there. But these had black and white kittens all over them.

We had arrested him. We had questioned him twice. But he gawked at Jen like he'd never set eyes on us before.

"Mr. Johnson, I'm Detective Lu. We met at the police station."

We 'met'?

I'm trying to make him comfortable.

He's going to think you were in the next cell.

"Oh, yeah," he said. "Thought I catch you before. You the Chinese chick who busted me. Am I right?"

"No hard feelings?"

"For what?"

"Listen, I wonder if I could come in and talk to you for a moment."

"Do I gotta put on clothes?"

"No, that's cool."

He turned and walked back to the kitchen without giving us a second glance. It still smelled of dirty dishes, and except for the floor where the blood had been scrubbed off, it didn't look like Delmar had an advanced degree in home economics. We looked at the empty high chair. The toddler was back with the neighbor. Delmar plopped down in his old seat. He didn't invite us to sit down but Jen did so anyway.

"You not here to give me grief?"

"Nope. Your time of grief is almost over."

"I'm not saying I wanted to shoot him. It just happened. And I 'specially didn't want to see Ma killed. She was special."

"I'm sure you didn't. Just one of those things that happen."

When you've pointed a loaded pistol at your dad.

"Say," said Jen trying to sound offhand, "I wonder about something your Ma said."

"You be talkin' to her?"

"No, I mean right before she died. I was here, right?"

"Oh, yeah. Keep forgettin'."

He lifted a joint from an ashtray on the table and lit it, taking a big pull. He offered it to Jen, but she said no.

"She said they were getting to Eden."

"She always go sayin' that."

"Not going to heaven? You sure that's not what she was saying?"

"Well, of course she be sayin' that too. She sittin' up there right now, watchin' down on me." He looked up at the ceiling and gave a little wave. "But she got that Eden bug in her head so bad. He did too, and that's why they wasn't goin' near exit." He put on a falsetto. "'We don't need to exit. Don't you see, Junior? We go to Eden and you be taken care of.' I had three months, four months of that shit before I decided to pop him."

"Delmar, if I could give you a bit of advice. I'm a police officer and you probably don't want to go saying things like that."

He shrugged.

"I'd like to hear more about Eden. Do you know how they were going to get there?"

"She go on forever 'bout Eden. But they hardly had no money to take a car, and I never saw no bus ticket."

"Did they tell you where it was?"

"She always wavin' her Bible and goin' on 'bout John this and 'Spesians that."

You got that, boss? Spesians.

Got it, but it doesn't get us anywhere. I think that was a dead end.

Meanwhile, Delmar was again mimicking his mother. "'Don't you feel it, son?'"

"Any idea—"

But he was now rising to a full preaching voice. "'Let yourself feel it, son. It's all 'round us.'"

"Yeah, great. Any idea where she first heard about it?"

"Idea? . . . No."

Jen's heart sank.

"Hell, no *idea* at all. I can tell you exactly where and when," Junior said.

"You can?"

"Well . . . where, anyways."

"Okay."

"It was that weirdo store."

Jen's heartbeat mashed the accelerator from zero to sixty in one second flat.

Stay cool, sister.

With as close as she could get to a neutral voice, she said, "Which store?"

"Makes computers and phones. Crazy place. Crazy people."

"Did they tell your mom something?"

"They always be tellin' her somethin'."

"Always?"

"Ever since she started workin' there."

16

For over an hour and a half, Delmar Johnson Jr. stumbled through answers to Jen's questions, often missing the point entirely or finding amazingly obscure ways to say yes or no. Jen never once had the impression he was lying, dissembling, or trying to obscure the facts. He wasn't a bright guy, but neither she nor Chandler ever doubted he was telling the truth.

When the conversation finally wrapped up, Jen rushed back to the station, where she was pleased to find the office empty. Chandler brought up government and employment records on her computer and she filled in Delmar's story.

Odette Johnson was sixty-three, her husband sixty-four. Odette had been a nurse at Medstar Washington Hospital Center until arthritis in her right hand made some tasks very difficult and, rather than accommodate her disability, the hospital fired her under the provisions of the 2029 Great Jobs for All Act. She was unable to find a new job, and so as best she could, she cared for people in their homes for bad pay, often under lousy working conditions, and with eventual dismissal when she couldn't handle many of the physical tasks—some days merely opening a bottle of pills was excruciating, if not impossible. She supplemented her income by helping a friend clean homes, although that job also proved difficult.

Approximately a year earlier, Odette had gone to Zombies to buy a reconditioned phone—it was the cheapest place in the neighborhood and trusted by the local folks. There, she got to talking about her work. Another co-op member may have overheard this conversation and asked her about a medical problem or mentioned that few of them had proper health care coverage. Whatever it was, Odette started visiting the store every couple of weeks as an impromptu visiting nurse. ("They wasn't even paying her nothin' at first," Delmar said. "She said they was young and needed her.") Folks from other stores or services in their network started to come around.

"Who?" Jen had asked, and Delmar had looked at her like she'd asked for the middle name of the man on the moon.

Both Odette and some co-op members had approached doctors they knew, and before long, she was working three nights a week at an informal clinic held at the Zombie co-op for members of various co-ops in the city. The pay was modest, but it was better than what she earned house cleaning or doing home nursing care, and they added in-kind goods and services: food, clothes, transportation, and repairs. "The food sure got better around this place," reported Delmar, "I got to say that." That was also why they had a decent screen—a sixty-fourth birthday gift from her to her husband. "She said she got it saving credits from her work," Delmar said, but he had no idea what "credits" were.

Odette was an avid reader. Delmar said: "She always come home with a heap of books from the library. Real books. You never see no one read like her."

And Eden?

That seemed to have started more recently. "Hold on. Maybe when the cherry blossoms was doing."

That made it late February or early March these days. More than four months before she died.

"That's when she starts talking 'bout it. Saying that's where she's goin'. Saying that's where we all was goin'."

"Did she ever tell you where it was? Or not even exactly where, but whereabouts?"

He scratched his stomach.

"Or *what* it was," Jen pressed, "or how to get there?"

He said, "Got to have been then."

"What?"

"With the trees all out."

"Why's that?"

"We have two of them out front. You see them?"

"You probably wouldn't call me a tree person."

"Well, they was out and Mom, she says to me, 'I imagine this just what Eden gotta look like.'"

"She said that?"

"Ain't that what I'm tellin' you?"

"But no idea where it is?"

This time he rolled his eyes.

"Okay, let me ask you this . . . Delmar, you still with me? Delmar, is there any chance it was some sort of medicine?"

"You mean like cough medicine?"

"I was thinking a bit more serious. Like the treatment."

"Oh, that's a good one. If it was, then they coulda got it for me and I wouldn'ta needed to shoot them, would I?"

* * *

Six PM. Hours left of sunlight, but sun no longer throbbing. Jen zapped up a small smoothie, slipped into her running clothes, and headed toward Rock Creek Park.

She ran, her mind buzzing and darting: Her interview with Delmar Junior. Threats from Captain Brooks. Teko Teko Mea. The disappearance of Child's Play. All of it racing in circles.

She passed the restaurant where she and Zach had had their first date. As she ran, conversations with him and conversations with herself about him swarmed her mind, ambushing her with anxiety, anger, and dread. She was annoyed with Zach, annoyed with the things that had seemed hard and now seemed insurmountable in their relationship, annoyed that it wasn't effortless to be with him, annoyed with his politics and social concerns. But then she thought, *No, that's not totally true,* for lately she had found herself agreeing more and more with him on these things. But, God, why did they always have to talk about this stuff? What difference could any of them make?

Differences or not, she'd done him wrong. She hadn't trusted him in the simple way that Les trusted Christopher. How could she *not* have told him about Chandler? Yes, she had obediently followed the rules, but the real reason she'd stayed quiet was because she knew he'd be devastated.

She almost changed course so she could go to him that very minute to apologize. But somewhere along the wooded trails, up and down hillsides, beautiful even with the leaves drying up on the trees and the creeks down to a trickle, she blocked her thoughts about Zach long enough to think about work. She followed one thread and then another to piece together what she knew about Eden.

By the time she made it home, it was clear that four things didn't add up.

One: Odette Johnson had said, and Delmar Junior had confirmed, that she talked about getting *to* Eden. She never spoke of getting hold of the treatment; she never said she was going to "get some Eden." But it seemed, according to what Olive Ortega had told them, that this was the street name for the counterfeit, black-market treatment.

Two: Gray Suit's hostility toward her. Les had said the guy probably hadn't been talking about her, but a day later, she'd had Chandler repeat the conversation. Although he heard only what she heard, it was pretty clear Gray Suit had been speaking about her.

Three: the disappearance of Child's Play might've had a simple explanation. If Eden was an illegal drug and Child's Play knew about it, then Gray Suit's guys probably wanted to question him while also keeping the lid on the drug's existence. It was possible whoever was in charge might have spirited him away. But, no, that didn't explain how thoroughly he'd disappeared. She had tried to bring up his sheet and discovered that everything but his most basic ID was now sealed tight.

Finally: the timeline. According to Delmar Junior, his mother had started talking about Eden four or four and a half months earlier, after she began working with the co-op people. The cherry blossom memory was one of the few concrete things Delmar had said. It rang true. Yet Gray Suit said the first report they'd received came in the middle of the summer, only a month before he met with them at the station. You'd think that with all their phone, text, email, and internet surveillance, plus their snitches, if something as important as a counterfeit treatment had been out there since at least the early spring, they would have gotten wind of it.

She badly needed to speak to someone from the co-op.

Her mind lurched back to Zach. It was important for her investigation to call him, to press him on contacting a co-op member. But it was important for her relationship, she supposed, to let him have his space. Then again, also important for her to apologize for not telling him sooner.

She dialed his number.

"Oh," he said when he heard her voice.

Yep, she thought, *wrong choice to call.*

But they could get over this hump, move on, be happy again. She wanted to stay with him, and so she would apologize. Talking to him was not the wrong choice.

"I know you don't want to talk yet, but I need to ask you something. I could drop by wherever you are," she said hurriedly, not letting him sneak in a word edgewise.

"I, um—"

One minute later, she was on her bike and flying.

Zach was working late on a lovely street in Mt. Pleasant. It was one of his regular clients, and Jen had visited there before. In recent years, the unusually heavy rains would turn the backyard into a jungle, but now, what Jen saw when she arrived resembled a burnt-out sheep pasture in Greece.

Zach looked tired. Dead leaves were tangled in his hair, and dirt and sweat were smeared across his bare chest. But when his beautiful hands brushed away a thatch of hair that had tumbled into his eyes, the familiar gesture aroused Jen's feelings of tenderness and desire. She wanted to hold him. To feel her face against his chest, dirty or not. Tell him how sorry she was that she hadn't told him. Reassure him about Chandler in the way she'd been reassured before the implant procedure. Make this better.

And yet, she hesitated. He looked wary, he seemed unsure.

They did not kiss. They did not touch.

"Hey," he said.

"Hey back."

"This is . . ." he said.

"Yeah." She added, "We should . . ."

"I don't think I'm ready to talk."

"I was going to say, talk *sometime*."

"Yeah."

Start with the apology, she thought. But she realized that as soon as she apologized, and if he accepted the apology for not telling him, the logical question was whether she'd have it removed. She could not imagine doing so; she could not imagine *not* having Chandler with her when she worked. Still, she must apologize. She would do so before she left. But first . . .

"Zach, can you try again to reach the people from the co-op?" she asked.

"Why's it so important?"

"Remember the Fourth of July? When those two people were killed?"

"Of course I do." His tone was harsh. He sucked in his breath, as if he hadn't meant it. But Jen knew how much he hated the horrors she saw each day.

Time to show some trust, she thought. She said, "I need to tell you something I'm not supposed to. I feel silly saying this, but I need you to promise not to tell anyone."

He waited to hear what she would say. She waited for him to promise not to tell. She blinked first. "Well, do you?"

"Jesus. If you tell me not to tell anyone, then of course I won't."

"Fine," she said. "There've been reports of an illegal street version of the treatment. We arrested someone for assault who said they were trying to buy it. She referred to it as Eden."

"I still don't see a connection to the co-op."

"Right before she died, Odette Johnson—one of the people who got shot—said they were planning on getting to Eden. And it turns out she worked sometimes at the co-op. She was a nurse and did a clinic there. Her son says she started talking about Eden after she started working there."

He stared at her, anger written on his face. "You think they're drug dealers?"

"I'm not saying that. I'm trying to figure out how or even if it fits together. I need to talk to them. Find out about her, about her work there, and ask if they know anything about Eden."

"And if they're connected?"

"No harm, as long as they're not scamming people."

"They don't scam. They don't rip off. And they don't push drugs."

"Then can you try again to contact them?"

She could see his mind wrestling. And knowing what she did about him, she was guessing he was still hurt, still angry, but that he also realized he was being petulant and that she was showing him trust. And, sure enough, the Zach she loved won out.

"I guess I better 'fess up," he said.

"What?"

"I did reach them."

"What! You said to my face that you couldn't."

"They asked me not to tell anyone."

"Meanwhile, you're on my case about Chandler."

"There's no comparison. One is a friend—"

"And more important than me?"

"—who asked me to keep a personal secret. Another is the news that you have a living thing inside you, doing—I don't even know what this thing is doing."

"But you lied to me," Jen argued.

"They know you're a cop."

"How would they know that?"

"I told them. What's wrong with that? Suddenly ashamed of your job?"

Her phone rang. The nursing home. Her first thought was *she's finally dead.*

But the bubbly administrator bubbled an over-the-top greeting.

"Not now!" Jen barked, and hung up.

She knew that now she was being the petulant one but, unable to stop herself, she turned and walked away without another word.

17

We sat on a bench in the crowded waiting area. Jen said it was uncomfortable; I took her word for it. Next to us, a man waited for his own court appearance. He was scared. I knew this because his skin was popping off micro-explosions of fear gas like a new war was gearing up.

08:48:07.

A lithe Black woman arrived in the waiting area and cautiously looked around. "Victim," I said. Jen is okay at recognizing people, but last time we saw Makela Franklin, she'd been decked out in yellow running gear. Now she wore a crisp white shirt and metallic slacks that matched the aluminum lunchbox purse that every other professional seems to be toting this year.

DA Celeste Delong burst in, panting, and came to us first. "Damn elevator's out again. You ready?"

Jen said she was. Celeste huffed her way across the crowded room and started talking to Ms. Franklin. We watched the two of them. Celeste asked her something, Ms. Franklin shook her head no. Celeste spoke. Ms. Franklin shook her head again.

"Chandler, what are they saying?" She stared at their lips for me. Strictly speaking—well, any speaking—we shouldn't be listening in on a conversation between a DA and the victim and chief witness, but I translated.

"'I'm not sure anymore.'"

"'When we talked, you were certain what happened. How's this possible?'"

108

"'Just is.'

"'Ms. Franklin, this is really important. This guy's a Nazi. He wants to kill people like us. He attacked you. I want him in jail.'

"'I wasn't really harmed.'"

Jen said, "Shit."

At 09:00:00 on the dot, an entourage paraded in. As a sea of anxious people parted, I thought Moses and the Israelites had landed. The short procession headed to the courtroom door, glancing neither left nor right. Lawyer David Samuels was in the lead, followed by defendant James O'Neil, dressed like a preppy Yale undergrad in a brochure photo. Richard O'Neil, clothes on, was serious, but calm. Two women and a man carried briefcases and a file box.

"Trying to intimidate everyone," Jen muttered to me. Part of Jen's job was to educate me about the quirks of human behavior. But this time I thought she had it wrong.

"No," I said. "I don't think these types need to try at all. You're looking at power on legs."

If Jen could have stared at me in surprise, I would have felt those eyes of hers bearing down. Damn if I wasn't getting smarter by the day.

They stopped in front of the guard at the door. Samuels whispered to James, who smoothed down his hair and hid his smirk under a winning collegiate smile. Richard looked around as if he'd just sailed into an expensive restaurant and was checking for friends.

The guard announced our case and opened the doors.

Unless you're a lawyer or the defendant in a murder case who might be wearing normal clothes for the last time in your life, courtrooms are astoundingly boring places. Forget everything you've seen on TV. This place makes watching a bowl of oatmeal cool down seem exhilarating.

The first item was a defense request to empty the room of the public and the media. Don't even ask me to repeat the arguments, and anyway, much was said in hushed tones directly to the bench. Apparently they were persuasive. The judge booted out forty-one people.

Procedural matters dragged on for two hours. Jen was just about dozing off when her name rang out. Samuels was saying, "As we mentioned to Your Honor, we requested a closed trial because Detective Lu has a synthetic implant. We would like permission to question this implant directly."

Back and forth arguments. Celeste lost. "Damn," said Jen. But I was going to have my day in the sun.

I'll spare you the details. Makela Franklin said she didn't recognize the defendant. Yes, perhaps he was the one who yelled at her and then ran away, but she couldn't be certain. And it might have been an entirely different person who pushed her down the minute before.

Celeste called Jen to the stand. Jen made the mistake of looking away from Celeste, and for a second our eyes rested on Richard O'Neil. A hint of a smile raised the corners of his mouth. He nodded at her—an infinitesimally small nod, but he might as well have shouted instructions.

I felt it; I sensed it. A micro-battle flashed like lightning through Jen's brain. Richard O'Neil burned bright. For a second, I wondered who was going to win out: Jen, dazzled by this man, or Cobalt Blue, the cop keeping her oath.

Cobalt Blue stood her ground. She recounted what we'd seen and done. Under cross-examination, she admitted she hadn't actually seen the defendant strike or push Ms. Franklin, but it seemed Ms. Franklin had been pushed down a moment before. It seemed obvious who had done it, especially when the defendant ran away.

I was put under oath, although I said that wasn't necessary since I cannot lie. I repeated pretty much what Jen had said.

Samuels called James O'Neil to the stand.

"Mr. O'Neil, did you yell at Ms. Franklin?" the lawyer asked.

"Yes."

"Why?"

"Some guy attacked her, and I was frantic to make sure she was okay."

"What race was he?"

"I don't notice things like that. Hispanic or light Black."

"What happened next?"

"He took off. I ran up and asked if I could help her."

"You asked her?"

"I was pretty freaked out, seeing that type of thing. My adrenaline must have been pumping, and I may have been yelling at her."

"But then you ran away."

"I saw this police officer charging at me. When I was younger, I fell into a bad crowd and had some altercations with police that I'm deeply ashamed of. I figured she'd peg me for the attacker. It's stupid, but I got real scared and took off."

"And then?"

"She ran me down and tackled me."

"Did you resist arrest?"

"No. I was really scared."

"What happened next?"

"She slapped me hard across the face."

"Are you referring to Detective Lu?"

"Yes." He pointed at Jen. "Her."

Jen was called back. She admitted she had hit the defendant but said he'd been resisting arrest, and she was trying to subdue him with as little force as possible. She was lying for me, but I guess trying to save her ass too.

I was questioned again.

I really wish I knew how to lie.

"It felt good to hit him," I said.

*   *   *

Makela Franklin beelined for the exit, her shoulders slouching in humiliation and her eyes clinging to the ground like she was hunting for a spot to dig a hole.

Jen said to me, "Threatened? Paid off?" I said I'd put my money on threatened, but it could have been a bit of each.

The parade of bad guys headed for the door. Richard veered off for a second and paused next to us. "Too bad," he said with what seemed genuine sadness. "It could have been fun." And then left.

Celeste came over and sighed. "Justice in fucking action," she said.

18

In any given week, Jen usually enjoyed spending a few nights sleeping on her own. She would cook dinner or hang with Ava and Taylor in the apartment, watch a program, or read a book and tumble off to sleep. And yet, with the clammy feeling that the differences with Zach were irreconcilable, she felt lonely. Unwanted. Crappy.

It was the late afternoon. She did her laundry. She stewed over the trial that day. She drank a beer while Ava ironed a shirt for work—tonight, a candlelight tour of the White House.

"Real candles?"

"Yep, real candles all over the place."

Ava had a PhD in American history but now found herself doing DC tours for the infinitely rich. The company she gigged for had preferential access to the Capitol, the White House, the National Gallery, the National Archives, and—one of Ava's favorites—the Dwight D. Eisenhower Executive Office Building, which was closed to the public. She led groups of two, five, or six through these sites. It was gig work, which meant everything about it sucked, including some of the rich men and women who figured her body came with the price of the tour.

Jen went for a run. Couldn't get her mind off the trial that morning. She found herself near Les and Christopher's. They buzzed her up, and she told them about the miserable day in court.

Les said, "They got to her?"

"One way or another. Brooks wasn't happy."

"Don't blame him."

"I mean, with me."

"Not your fault."

"He had already scanned a transcript before I made it back to the station. Turns out, I hit the suspect."

Christopher looked appalled. He glared at Jen.

"It was, well . . . it was Chandler."

Les explained to Christopher that in emergencies, the implants could direct instantaneous reactions. This was meant as a lifesaving measure.

Christopher said, "Was this guy threatening you?"

"No. It was strange. Like Chandler was flexing his muscles."

Christopher stared at Les. The unspoken question: Could this happen to you?

"Hon, don't worry. P.D. is a gentler soul than Chandler."

Maybe, thought Jen, *the synth implants reflect their hosts.* Les definitely was an uncomplicated and gentle soul. Whenever he'd encouraged Jen to stand up for herself, whenever he said his Cobalt thing, Jen always knew he was taking a toke of vicarious pleasure. She, on the other hand? Submissive and eager to please, angry at herself for being so, and starting to figure out all this was tissue papering over some fucking deep rage. Overreacting to Zach. Or having a surrogate like Chandler act out for her.

"Well," said Les, "screw Brooks. Screw them all."

They shared a small joint. Christopher told them stories from the exciting world of interstate transportation. They giggled. Les whipped up some Thai fried bananas. But all the while, Jen felt the tension in the room, like Christopher was just waiting for her to leave so he could tell Les in no uncertain terms that he'd better not let Jen get him into trouble. Les had once confided to her that Christopher freaked out after he, Les, had come home smashed up from a fight; going rogue at work would be grounds for divorce.

* * *

Jen lay in bed, the buzz worn off, her mind racing through it all once again. Her insomnia-producing list now included what she hadn't bothered telling Les. When Brooks yelled at her that day, it had not only been for the botched trial but for again bringing up Eden only days after he warned her to drop it.

"Sir," she had said, "I think there may be a link between Eden and a computer co-op."

"You're now worried about computer stores."

"A co-op. They're—"

"I know what a co-op is, Detective."

"I really think it would be good if I—"

He grabbed his head with both hands. "I'm coming down with a bad case of déjà vu. I told you to drop it, remember?"

Jen didn't say anything.

"Detective, I asked you a question."

"Yes, sir. I remember."

"Something you don't understand about 'drop it'?"

"No sir."

"No Eden crap. No co-op crap. No computer store crap. You start poking around crap, and I'm gonna smell it a mile away."

19

We were a block away and easily beat the ambulance to the house on Irving Street NW, across from the Tubman Elementary School. Harriet Tubman, escaped slave, hero of the Underground Railroad, spy for the Union Army during the Civil War, and later suffragette.

We reached the home of Enrique and Miguel Estevan, father and son. The old man, very old, lay motionless on the indigo living room couch. His ash-gray face sagged as if his skin was five sizes too big. Skin puddled below his eyes like deflated balloons, and wattles of the stuff drooped beneath his jaw. His lipless mouth gaped open, but it showed surprisingly white teeth. And an incongruous full head of hair was so black it was almost blue—it had to be dyed but looked convincingly real.

His breaths were shallow. We found his pulse.

The younger man—he seemed to be in his sixties—was frantic.

We reassured him the ambulance would be here any second.

He pointed toward framed photographs on a side table. He grabbed one. A photo of a man in his sixties with his arm slung around the shoulder of a handsome young man.

"That's us."

Jen nodded in sympathy. Father and son when both were much younger.

"You don't understand . . . Where are they?"

"Almost here."

"Look closer," he said.

115

Jen glanced at the old man lying on the couch.

"No, look here." He tapped the younger man in the photo. "That's him. That's my son." He pointed to the couch. "That's him on the couch."

"But—"

He stretched a helpless hand toward the man on the couch. "I'm the older one in the picture." He stabbed a finger at the young man in the photo. "This was taken six weeks ago."

I don't want you to think I'm a heartless lump of clever cells, but binary programming didn't prepare me for people being nuts. Sorry, there I go. Prepare me for people with mental illness. I study it; we've attended courses. Jen corrects me when I say jerky things like that. But it just isn't logical. Dementia I kind of get, because I'm used to dealing with inferior human memories, so an impairment on that front never seems like a stretch. This one didn't feel like dementia, so I figured this man in his sixties required help.

The ambulance conveyed us to the hospital. We waited. Jen and I don't always see eye to eye, but she agreed that Enrique Estevan—the younger-looking one who claimed he was the father—didn't have a firm grasp on reality. I tried to impress her with a clever line: "Maybe reality doesn't have a firm grasp on itself." But it didn't entirely make sense, although a half hour later I turned out to be a prophet.

We checked Jen's messages. Shot the shit with other officers who had dragged people into the ER. Wandered back and sat next to Enrique, who squirmed on the plastic chair like he was sitting on top of an ant hill.

Thirty-three minutes later, a doctor came out and looked around like he needed to find someone and yet was hoping that person might not be there. He called out, "Mr. Estevan?" and when Enrique looked up, he came over to him.

"I'm so sorry, but your son has died of liver failure."

Your son? Jen said to me. *Doesn't he mean your father?*

"He was only forty-six," Enrique Estevan said.

And looked ninety-six.

We tagged along while Mr. Estevan filled out forms. We stepped away when he spoke to the hospital chaplain and rushed forward to hold him when we thought he was going to hit the deck. We rested a hand on his back while he met again with the doctor.

Mr. Estevan said, "He was completely normal until a week ago."

"There is a condition called"—the doctor glanced at his tablet— "Berardinelli-Seip lipodystrophy. I never heard of it until today. Maybe thirty Americans have it, maybe a thousand in the entire world. It's extremely rare."

It was caused by a gene mutation. Subcutaneous fat disappears in parts of the body, hence the sagging skin. It normally manifests in early childhood, progresses slowly, and has a variety of symptoms. There have been reports of cases where it starts later and progresses fairly quickly. But nothing that raced so quickly to death. The doctor could not explain it, but he did a decent enough job summarizing the same Wikipedia articles I was pulling up.

I buzzed for a car, and as we drove Mr. Estevan home, it felt like a hearse.

For a while he cried. Then he moaned and rocked himself back and forth. "This can't be happening," he said. I felt bad for the guy.

We phoned his sister in Baltimore and delivered the blues.

Jen asked Mr. Estevan if he'd be alright on his own until his sister arrived, but even I knew it was a dumb question. What could *alright* possibly mean when you'd just lost your child? The one who suddenly looked old enough to be your father. Or grandfather.

Cruel me did wonder why Enrique hadn't exited. Maybe this could have been prevented.

As we headed out the front door, he was still crying and moaning, "Poor Miguel. My beautiful, beautiful boy."

I called for a car. I didn't want to make a deal about my smart line, but I guess I did a bit, so I said, "Weird, huh?"

At first Jen didn't answer, but just as the car arrived, she said, "Damn if you weren't right again, Chandler. Something is fucking up reality."

20

"**I** needed to talk to someone."

Not exactly a catchy refrain from a top-forty love song, but that's what Jennifer said to Zach a couple of hours after she made it back from the hospital.

"Okay."

Dead silence on the phone line. Cross-legged on her bed. A chili-red T-shirt. A pair of Zach's cotton boxer shorts, white and cozy.

"Kind of crappy way for me to start, wasn't it?"

"It was a start, though."

She could hear him smiling as he said this. And this image of him smiling at her made her smile, and this made her relax, and this made her feel her love for him.

"Zach, not telling me you contacted the co-op folks, well, I felt untrusted, like I didn't meet your standards." She looked down at her legs, at her feet, at the sheets. "It wasn't a big thing, it . . . Next time, just tell me."

"I'm—"

But Jen didn't even wait for him to finish his apology. "Oh, screw it all. I love you. I'm sorry I didn't tell you about Chandler. It's important and weird, and I should have. And I know you're going to ask me whether I'll get him taken out, but I can't talk about that right now." Her tone became pleading. "But what's the deal with the co-op?"

"They're kind of in hiding."

"What, like they've gone underground?"

"Being careful. They think it was arson. They think they're being targeted."

"It wasn't. And why would they be targeted by anyone?"

"I'm telling you what they said."

Drama queens, she thought.

He said, "Do you still need to reach them?"

She thought of Captain Brooks warning her repeatedly to do her job and forget about these rumors. "I guess not," she said. "But I'll tell you what I do need."

*   *   *

They cuddled naked in his bed, the soft reading light pointed away from them. The duvet had been pushed onto the floor. Her hair was a mess, his face was red, and there was a wet spot on the sheets.

She told him about the middle-aged man who had looked as old as time. She told him about the father's grief.

Zach told her about a conversation he'd had with Mary Sue about exit. About how so many parents were willing to sacrifice more than a quarter of their lives just so their children could do what they had chosen to give up.

"It's kind of like the game we used to play, of who you'd run into a fire to save," Jen said.

"It seems that for most parents, the answer would be pretty simple," Zach said. "I guess exit is like that."

"So your new best friends—"

"Don't be snarky."

"Your friends"—this time she mimicked an emotionless robot voice from old sci-fi movies—"aren't exit fans?"

"They agree with what I've been saying: it's the wrong solution to real problems."

She regretted she had mentioned exit. "God, can we talk about—I don't know—anything else?"

They made weekend plans. They caught up.

But all the while, she grew ever more certain that he wasn't going to let his parents die just so he could live.

And all the while Jen was thinking: *My mother wouldn't have run into a house where there was even a candle burning to save me.*

21

On Monday, near the end of the workday, Les returned to the office. He cupped his hand behind his ear. "I hear a cold beer calling out to me." He slung himself onto an empty chair. "What a complete bitch of a day."

I said howdy to P.D. I do that sometimes, although she says I'm improperly using our comms link. P.D. is okay, but she's a tad on the cold side. She's brilliant at describing places and suspects, but she doesn't show much emotion. I do have to say, though, her written reports are the best in the business.

Les looked around. "Hammerhead and Amanda not in?"

On cue, Amanda stepped through the doorway with her usual athletic verve and a big pink bubble forming on her lips; Hammerhead lumbered in right behind. Amanda was pleasantly pale from her vacation spent indoors somewhere. They seemed startled to see us, and Hammerhead blushed.

Jen's phone rang. One of our regular customers—a couple in their early sixties who were already getting pestered by their two kids to start thinking about exit. Seems the kids just organized a farewell party to try to nudge them along. We piled on the reasonable and calm tones so thickly the phone line started sagging under the weight of platitudes. After ascertaining that everyone was going to be fine, Jen hung up.

Les was staring out the window.

"When did that tree start looking so bad?"

"Les, where have you been for the past two months?"

"Anyway, want to go for a beer?"

"Maybe."

Les turned to Hammerhead and Amanda. "Either of you game?"

And damn if they didn't first look to each other before they simultaneously answered no. A minute later, Amanda left, followed by Hammerhead, who, with his usual clumsiness, was simultaneously acting much too casual and much too elaborate as he explained why he had to leave.

Jen, are they . . .

God, Chandler, you're so thick. Of course they are.

Les said to Jen, "Last week you had that weird case, right? The young guy who died of old age." He waited for her to nod. "Well, I had the same thing today."

Jen asked me for the odds. I said that without knowing what caused these strange deaths, the question of odds was meaningless.

Les was talking. "I've never seen anything like it. It was disgusting."

"Did he die?"

"She. No, not yet. But the hospital says they'll be surprised if she lasts through the night. I thought she was an incredibly old lady, but she was only thirty-five."

"Chandler says the frequency is one person in ten million. We've got a million people in DC, and this is our second case."

"In a week."

"Weird," Jen said.

"Obviously," said Les, "God's revenge against homosexuality."

"Let's grab that beer."

"God's revenge against thirst."

Jen's shift was over. We walked over to have a brew and, swell boss that she is—*No,* she corrected me, *to stop your whining*—she left me turned on. Good times.

"Nice weekend?" Les asked.

"Yeah. Kind of like old times."

"Kind of?"

"Zach doesn't want his parents to exit."

"I told you to watch out for men with low hairlines."

"Remember, though, nice hands."

Jen was expecting a comeback laden with sexual innuendo. Instead, Les was silent. And then his voice was somber as he said, "I miss my folks more than you can imagine. They were the greatest."

"Me, though, I'm counting the days."

"You're a harsh woman, Cobalt Blue."

We went back to the station, Jen and I. It's got a different vibe at night. The offices are quiet, but the place feels rawer, more on edge. Drunks and druggies, shooters and Shadows, getting dragged in and booked. Frantic parents reporting runaway teens to the desk cops, who seem to work more slowly than in the daytime. All the lights on, but it's so dark.

"Chandler, let's find someone we can speak to. About that condition."

"A geneticist." I produced ten names and phone numbers from across the country.

"Start at the top."

Fourth one down and we connected.

Jen introduced herself to Dr. Benjamin Kaplanski, MD, PhD, Stanford Medical School, Department of Genetics. Jen, cop, DC, felt a bit outgunned.

She explained we'd had two cases of Berardinelli-Seip lipodystrophy in the past week. Dr. Kaplanski said how unusual that was. He sounded like he had his eye on a specialized clock where every tick took him one second further away from winning the Nobel Prize.

"Most clinical geneticists go their whole career without seeing a single case of congenital generalized lipodystrophy—that's how most of us refer to it."

"What causes it?"

"Do you have a strong background in genetics?" It was a nasty question.

"Do you have a strong background in being nice?"

Whoa! Cobalt Blue pops out again from her shell.

Nor did I expect his response.

"Good one. It's been a long day, wasted in meeting after meeting." And so he gave us a five-minute class in genetics. He explained there were different types of the disorder, each caused by the mutation of a different gene, and he named each one. I remembered them; they went in and out of Jen's brain without touching solid ground.

"Because it's so rare," Dr. Kaplanski said, "it isn't routinely screened for."

"Could this suddenly be increasing?"

"Two cases is two cases. Were these people related?"

"Not at all."

"Two cases is unusual, but occurrence figures aren't predictive of geographic distribution."

"But both cases came on suddenly."

"That is unusual, but not unheard of."

"For someone this old?"

"How old did you say they were?"

"One was thirty-five, the other was forty-eight."

"Now that is extremely unusual."

"That's a lot of unusuals stacked on top of each other. Can you treat it?"

"No, not really."

I like when humans say that. Can't just admit they're stumped, so got to add "not really," as if they're saying, "I could if I really wanted to."

"Because it's so rare," he said, "a therapeutic gene protocol like the ones we use for many disorders hasn't been developed. It simply isn't on anyone's priority list."

"What would it take to get there?"

"One more case and you give me a shout."

We phoned Les.

"We're baking a pie for a party tomorrow."

I felt Jen giving off sparks of jealousy—I could almost smell the burning circuits: Les, happily settled in his uncomplicated domestic life.

"We're back at the office."

"Oh, god."

"It'll just take a second."

"What?"

"My question."

"It's an apricot tart. They're finicky."

"Les!"

The sound was muffled, presumably by his thumb. And then he came back on.

"You know, when you sign out, that means you're allowed to go home. In fact, you're allowed to do whatever you want."

"And I wanted to come back to the office."

"Fine. What's up?"

"Your case today, the woman who was aging so quickly. What was her family situation?"

"This can't wait?"

She didn't bother to answer.

"Like I said, early thirties," Les explained.

"Working?"

"A waiter in a chichi restaurant."

"Race?"

"Name seems Middle Eastern or South Asian. Mariam Zhariri."

"Family?"

"Appears to be living with two partners, a man and a woman. Is that it?"

"Wait. Her health. What's her state of health?"

"Uh, she's dying?"

"No, I mean before that."

"How the hell would I know? They said she was fine. Which is more than I can say for me if I don't get back to Christopher and our pie."

*　*　*

This definitely was not the Washington Charity Hospital Complex. Nor, at the other extreme, one of the rich people's hospitals that doubled as luxury spas. But nevertheless, bright and clean and bustling with visitors carrying pink and purple flowers, efficient-looking nurses carrying tablets, doctors carrying world-weary expertise, and first-year residents carrying nerves and attitude. Welcome to the spanking new George Washington University–GlaxoSmithKlineWong Medical Center.

We hit the elevators, punched five, and landed in intensive care. Jen waved her ID and asked if Mariam Zhariri had made any progress. The nurse shook her head. Jen asked if she could see her. Jen thought maybe we could sneak a peek at her chart. The nurse shook her head. Jen mumbled a fake-o "Thanks," and we drooped away to the waiting room.

I'd pulled up Mariam's data and got pics of her two partners. Trans man, Daniel, and biologically assigned woman, Cari. I spotted the two of them, holding hands and looking distraught out of their minds. We approached them; Daniel stood up. He was five foot seven and pregnant. What the hippies long ago called a mind-fuck, but there you have it. Things change.

Jen, for all her mother's punishing religious injunctions, was pretty cool. She charts high on the Toronto Empathy Scale. She introduced herself and put a sympathetic hand on Daniel's shoulder, and I could feel pain ripple through Jen's body.

We sat down. Daniel did the talking. Same as we already heard, but worse. Mariam was continuing to deteriorate. Liver and heart. Nothing they could do unless they could stabilize her first, and so far, so bad.

"How quickly did this come on?"

"Six days ago," Daniel said. "She said she was feeling out of sorts. She couldn't describe it. Within a day—I mean it, *one* day— all this stuff started happening."

"Was she in good shape before?"

"She's always tired from work. Cari and I keep bugging her to exercise but . . . Other than that, she was in pretty good shape."

Daniel glanced at Cari.

Cari scowled at him. "What does it matter now if we tell her?" She turned to us. "Mariam got her test result a month ago. She has a ninety percent chance of getting ROSE."

"Why'd she get tested so young?" Like most people, Jen first got tested in her late thirties. Others wait until their late forties, hoping to delay their death sentence. Many wait until their parents neared sixty-five and the exit cutoff.

"She had a premonition," Cari replied.

"Do you believe in premonitions?"

"Of course not. But she was right, wasn't she?"

"How did she react?"

Cari shot Jen an are-you-kidding-me look.

"Anything else you can tell me?"

"What's it to you?" Cari said. Daniel put his hand on Cari's leg in an obvious attempt to cool her down, but Cari persisted. "We haven't done anything wrong."

We repeated what Dr. Kaplanski told us. We said this was the second case in a week. We were curious, that was all. Anything that might help us put together the pieces would be great.

Cari looked at Daniel, a big question mark in her eyes.

Jen would have missed it, but damn if I didn't spot it. His head moved sideways a zillionth of an inch, but it was enough.

Cari returned her gaze to us.

"No," she said, "Nothing I can think of."

Next morning, 09:32:48. It was blisteringly hot, already popping old thermometers that only went to 100. We were leisurely pumping up 16th on a police bicycle, heading to Enrique Estevan's house, when I spotted Child's Play at the bottom of Meridian Hill Park. A second later, the information was thrumming in Jen's brain. How humans ever did this alone is beyond me. She scuttled the bike on the sidewalk; screamed, "Lock" at the bike; clambered over the stone wall; and off we shot.

Child's Play noticed Jen and took off like a weasel. Many of the shrubs had lost their leaves in the drought, and so we were able to keep our eyes on him. He dashed across the gray spillway for the shut-off waterfall, through the trees, and up the path toward the hardpan that had once been a lawn. As we ran out from under the trees and back into the sun, we slammed into a wall of scorching air, but Jen accelerated rather than slowing down. We were closing the gap, but he still had eighty-seven yards on us.

"Damn," Jen said. He was leading us straight into the Shadow camp that had taken over the whole top third of the park. There were Shadow camps that had a good rep. Neat, clean, orderly, people doing what they could to support each other. And then there were some like this one.

I think we might have caught him, but Jen's reflexes unfortunately kicked in, and as Child's Play entered the nasty crowd, she yanked out her ID and held it in front of us, then started yelling, "Stop, police!" and

"Child's Play!" We watched in disgust as a path opened for him through the swarm of men and women, children and stray dogs, and just as quickly sealed up behind him.

We tried to push our way through. Men and women wearing only underwear or cutoffs, children in rags, men in greasy winter coats, women in layers of shabby dresses, naked women, naked men, naked children; matted hair, greasy hair, scalps that looked like hair had been ripped off in handfuls; scratches and rashes and sores oozing pus on faces, hands, and chests. The hot stench was overwhelming—pus, piss, feces, and sweat stewing in the sun.

We screamed, "Police! Back off." At first, people moved away, but too slowly. And then we ran smack into a group of children. We tried to dodge around them, but Jen bowled one over. The girl couldn't have been more than ten, but her face was blistered with dirty sores. Jen looked down at her, and I felt her surging mix of sadness, disgust, and horror. Jen glanced over the heads of the kids to see if we could even spot Child's Play anymore, and when she couldn't, crouched down to make sure the girl was okay.

Children, ten years old, twelve, fourteen, scrawny and dirty, swarmed over us in a wave of stink and disease.

22

"Zach, there's something terrible going on."

"Well, there's always something terrible going on, isn't there?"

"Yeah, but this is a whole other order-of-magnitude terrible. Science-fiction, apocalyptic terrible."

They had biked down to the Wharf to have a beer and to cool down in the evening air coming off the Potomac. But just as Jen was about to tell him about people turning old and dying, she flashed on the Shadow camp. It had seemed to take forever to extricate herself from the pile of filthy children and diseased adolescents. The smells had been hot, close, and raw. Skin dry and cracked, slimy and oozing. Jen had wiggled, pushed, and cursed, desperately trying to escape but equally desperate not to hurt anyone or to be seen as hurting anyone. Someone bit her. Someone licked her. Someone peed on her. Finally—after thirty seconds or thirty hours—a man yelled, and the kids clambered off and scurried behind a wall of adults.

Jen had wrenched herself onto her feet, her eyes flashing like a mad-woman, and found herself surrounded by Shadows. None showed any expression or made any move. Until, after more excruciatingly long seconds, the crowd parted, showing an exit path back in the direction she had come. She had bicycled home and taken the longest shower of her life.

"What?" he said.

"Nothing . . . I had to go into a disgusting Shadow camp today. One of the really bad ones. It's unimaginable, people living that way."

Zach nodded. "You degrade people enough and some of them take on the degradation themselves."

She needed to change the subject. "But that's not what I was starting to tell you about. It's this weird thing. People turning old—I mean, really old—overnight." She described what Miguel Estevan looked like, lying on the couch. "I've never seen such an old man. But he wasn't. He became ancient in just a few days, and soon after we got him to the hospital, he died. Of old age. Now we have a second case." And she talked about Mariam Zhariri.

"Well," said Zach, "I'll make one prediction. If a new disease is spreading, there's gonna be a whole bunch of new apocalyptic cults springing up. They'll find some quote in the Bible that absolutely predicted this was going to happen."

Over the past week, Jen had pretty much put the stolen Bible and the receipt out of her thoughts. But with the mention of the Bible, she now told Zach about Odette's copy with the co-op receipt inside. How she thought it might be significant, but the Bible quotes didn't lead to anything.

"What quotes?" he said.

She gave him chapter and verse. "But the first one doesn't even exist. None lead anywhere."

He took her hand. "Ye of little faith. I say we smoke a joint and read that most sexy of all Bible passages, the Song of Solomon, and see where *that* leads us."

23

"Fuck," Jen said.

Captain Brooks had sent for us.

Jen plodded up the stairs, one at a time. If she hadn't had any self-respect, she probably would have planted first one then the other foot on each stair, like a three-year old. Only Jen's brain was working fast, racing through the possibilities of what she'd done wrong this time. Me, I dug deep to calm her down.

Brooks didn't ask Jen to sit. So this wasn't going to be a heartwarming, father–daughter sort of moment.

"Detective Lu." He rubbed his keloid scar with the knuckle of his thumb.

Bad start.

"We are being sued. You. Me. And the DC police. For excessive force. Deprivation of rights." He waved at words on his overdesk display and read off a list, each item feeling like a blow to the top of Jen's head, as if we were a stake being hammered into the ground.

"Sir, this is for . . . ?"

He stared at her in mock disbelief. "Have you beat up anyone else lately? James O'Neil. His father is suing. Damn it, you're already under probation. You gotta be extra careful."

"Three more days, sir."

A rather pathetic five-minute discussion ensued. Jen attempted to defend herself.

"This gets me in shit." Brooks took another turn at his scar. "Looks like I can't control my own officers."

"But it happens all the time, sir. Criminal charges, suits."

"Not by a Timeless." He let that sink in. "Richard O'Neil is out to screw you."

Jen's face got so hot I thought I'd need to pull out a fire extinguisher. Escape from all her troubles. And the raw sexual beauty of this 112-year-old billionaire.

*   *   *

Right after the meeting, I thanked her.

"For what, asshole?"

"You didn't put the blame on me."

"I damn well should have. Asshole."

But she hadn't, had she?

Shortly after Brooks pounded us into the ground, she took a call about a family in full self-destruct mode, and that nailed us down for hours. Or I should say it kept *her* nailed down. She called up her own car, did her own comms, ignored my suggestions, searched records old style, and whenever she found a free moment, called me an asshole. I tried to tell myself I didn't have feelings, but I swear it hurt. Jen didn't speak to me for the rest of the day.

*   *   *

Thursday, July 26—09:04:18

Overnight, Jen had either settled down or decided to get on with things, and was treating me like everything was cool between us.

Back on Tuesday, once we'd escaped from the Shadow camp, we'd bicycled to her place, where she took such a long shower that reservoirs as far away as Wyoming dried up. She threw away the half-used cake of soap like it was a rat carrying the bubonic plague. She doused isopropyl alcohol on the spot where some kid had bitten her, even though the skin wasn't broken. She then poured so much bleach into the washing machine that her blue jeans came out blotched with reverse Rorschach spots and her underwear was so white you could only look at it through welder's glasses.

I had to ask her to explain why she felt, as she put it several times, so "oddly guilty" for doing all this. To me, it just made sense, but then again, all humans seem a bit filthy. She didn't answer, but flashes of gray skin, green snot, open sores, and ragged scabs ambushed her for the rest of the day.

Finally cleansed, we had continued on to Mr. Estevan's, only to find he wasn't home. I dug up his phone number. No answer, no message. Neighbors didn't know or wouldn't tell us anything. We wrote a note and wedged it under his door.

We finally reached him this morning, Thursday, and were at his place twenty minutes later.

The boss went in easy: "Sorry again about your loss. I can't imagine what you're going through. From your photo, he seemed a wonderful son. Are you getting help from your family?"

Mr. Estevan produced short answers—one word, two—as if words had lost their capacity to do any good. Jen kept saying, "Yes," and, "I understand," although she was thinking, *I don't understand any of this*.

Jen explained that she'd spoken to a doctor who specialized in genetic diseases, and said how unusual it was that Miguel's symptoms had showed up at his age. She said there'd been a second case on Monday.

She asked if she could ask him a few questions; it wouldn't take long.

His mouth said, "Yes"; his eyes said *Why?*; and his shoulders said, *What does any of this matter?*

"Mr. Estevan, before this started, how was your son's health?"

"I told them. No problems."

"Nothing you can think of?"

No answer.

"Had he been tested?"

"For what?"

"Rapid Onset Spongiform Encephalitis. ROSE."

"No. I don't know. He would have told me."

"Did he, I don't know, seem different before this happened?"

"How?"

"I don't know. Anything."

Mr. Estevan gazed toward the framed photographs.

"Mr. Estevan, you are . . ."

Sixty-four, I said.

"Sixty-four?"

He nodded in agreement.

"Were you planning on exiting?"

For the first time, Mr. Estevan became animated. "What are you saying about me? I was a good father. Carlotta was the best mother. What are you saying?"

"I've no doubt you both were wonderful parents. I assumed you'd be exiting, but I needed to check. Mr. Estevan, would you like a glass of water before we continue?"

For a second, Mr. Estevan stared hard at her, as if ready to take on the world. And then his shoulders slumped.

Jen said, "I know this is a difficult question, but please let me ask it. How did Miguel feel about it? Was he in agreement with your decision?"

"It made no difference what he thought. It was Carlotta's decision, and now it was my turn."

"I'm sure that's true, but people have feelings."

Mr. Estevan looked utterly lost. Jen continued, "Like my boyfriend. He doesn't want his parents to exit. It's natural that children might have feelings about this."

"So?"

"Did your son ever express such feelings to you? Was he opposed?"

"He said he heard of a different way."

"For what?"

"To get the treatment. And I wouldn't have to exit."

"How?"

"He wouldn't tell me. He said he didn't want to get me in trouble."

"Did he say he was going to get the treatment?"

And now we finally had Mr. Estevan's full attention.

"I don't want to get in trouble," he said.

"You won't . . . I'm sure you won't."

"Yes."

"Yes, he was getting the treatment?"

"Isn't that what I said?"

"Was he going to get it for you too?"

"He said he would take it first."

Mr. Estevan broke down into sobs that wracked his body for fifty-four seconds.

"Mr. Estevan, you had a brave son."

"It's what killed him, isn't it? I know it's what killed him."

* * *

13:27:48. There were more cases of Berardinelli-Seip lipodystrophy. Three in Newark. Two in Richmond. Two in Philly. Nothing in the rest of the country.

Enough to make the news this morning.

Enough for the first monster scratchings of panic to hit social media feeds.

Enough to get Gray Suit back to our station.

Right after completing her report on the Estevans, Jen readied herself to go up and speak to Captain Brooks. But instead, the summons came through to hit the conference room.

Posted outside the door was a cop with a drill-sergeant flat top. He was short, with the build of a light welterweight boxer. His fists were the size of Virginia hams, and his nose was mashed in, as if one day he'd decided he looked much too pretty for the job and smashed one of those ham hocks right into his own face. He checked out Jen, as she later said to Les, "from tits to toes and back again." Her words, not mine.

In we went. Gray Suit had the same two people with him. Seersucker suit from the DEA and Lieutenant McNair with her razor-sharp red hair.

The Drug Squad was there and seemed to have already been scolded for bad behavior. For once, the Card wasn't cleaning his nails with his knife, and even the Starlet looked serious.

We sat down. The briefing began. No warnings this time about turning off phones or comms.

Damn, I thought, *they're just about begging us to leak it.*

"Thank you for taking a moment to meet with me," Gray Suit said. His tattooed face ratcheted to the next person. "I'm sure you've all heard the strange news about this outbreak that causes rapid aging, and I understand you've had two cases yourselves." Again, with each sentence, he was on to the next person. His voice lacked drama, and there was no expression in his tattooed face. "There has already been a lot of speculation about the causes. A new virus or retrovirus. A scientific experiment gone bad. Chemical warfare from China, India, or Russia. And, naturally, the CIA makes the list." He did not smile, but this drew muted laughs.

"Our people"—whoever his people were—"think we've got it figured out. Don't ask me to try to explain the science, but they believe it's caused by a counterfeit treatment getting distributed by some underground network. Turns out it's one bad fake."

Tell him what Mr. Estevan said. But Jen held her tongue.

"People want it and pay big dollars to get it. Thousands and thousands. And then they pay for it with their lives. We've got to stop it."

Les said, "How is it administered?"

"It would have to be a doctor or a nurse, most likely in multiple treatments. This stuff isn't a hit of smack."

Murph from the drug squad said, "You think it's them, the doctors, selling it?"

"Maybe. But more likely organized crime."

"They're not going to have many more buyers if this keeps turning people into cadavers."

"It could be a bad batch, but I suspect the whole thing is a scam. We won't know until we catch them."

The Starlet flicked her hair and said, "This time, we're allowed to tell people?"

"Definitely. Like before, I'm meeting with officers in all the districts. My colleagues are doing the same in major cities. This time, though, there are no secrets. We need to catch these bastards fast. And there's one other thing. It's small, but it might help track them down. Yesterday, we received a report for the first time that this stuff is being called Eden."

Yesterday? Jen said to me. *I told Brooks a week ago.*

Our eyes flicked to Brooks, who calmly picked up his phone and typed. A second later, I received a text. *Keep it shut.*

"So," Gray Suit was saying, "I owe an apology to Detective—" Gray Suit jumped ahead four people and his eyes landed on Jen.

"Lu, sir."

"To Detective Lu. At our initial meeting, you asked if this drug might be related to the rumors of Eden. It turns out your hunch was right. It was a hunch, wasn't it?"

"It wasn't even a hunch. Just a question, sir."

"In that case, smart question."

His teeth smiled, his mouth smiled, his jaw smiled. But his calm, switchblade eyes could slice a stone in half.

* * *

"Captain Brooks, I—"

"Do this," he said. He placed his mobile onto his desk and put his index finger to his lips.

Jen stared at him. Like the maître d' at a fashionable restaurant, he waved his hand in silent invitation. She put her phone next to his.

He headed for the door and into the hallway. We followed him up the flight of stairs to the scorching rooftop. I felt like an ant who'd stepped under a magnifying glass and would burst into flames at any second.

"Diagnostic mode. Your implant."

"Sir?"

"That's an order."

Sorry, Chandler.

24

"**H**e's down?"

　　　"Sir, it's—"

"Is he down?"

She'd only flipped Chandler into diagnostic mode four times before, twice in their first months working together, then twice more for his annual checkup. Chandler was minimally aware and Jen felt him—foggy, dreamlike, but present—but his memory, speech, and communication functions were disabled.

"Yes, sir."

"Why did you want to see me?" Brooks asked. "If this is about the lawsuit, I'm not interested in talking about it."

"I have a report to show you."

"Relevant to that meeting?"

"Yes, sir. I interviewed Enrique Estevan. He's the father of the man who died last week. He said his son got hold of a counterfeit version of the treatment. He thinks that's what caused him to die that way."

"What do you think?"

"I'm not exactly a scientist."

"I asked what you thought, not what you know."

"Maybe it's the same as what Olive Ortega thought Child's Play was getting her. And it's the same as that guy—"

"For the last time, he's Teko Teko Mea."

"It's the same as what he said. That maybe Eden's the street name for the treatment."

"Didn't you have a responsibility to report this at the meeting?"

"Yes, sir. I suspect I did."

"Then . . . ?"

"I don't know, sir." There was something Gray Suit had said that had troubled her. A shiver of déjà vu. *What did he say?* Her mind stumbled onto Brooks's text to her, and this pushed away the thought of Gray Suit. She said, "Why did you tell me to keep my mouth shut?"

"What do you mean?"

"When he said he'd heard the rumor about Eden only yesterday, you messaged me to shut up. I told you a week ago, sir. You said you would tell him."

"Detective Lu, questioning your superior officer isn't in the cards. Particularly someone in your present position."

"Sir, I—"

"Here's what you will do. Keep looking into all this with the others. But if you find out anything that doesn't make sense, something that doesn't seem right, you come straight to me."

"Like what?"

He seemed to give this some thought, then shook his head. "You'll know if you see it. And come straight to me if you get a solid lead about who's distributing it. You do not write a report. You do not tell anyone over the phone. You do not tell your fellow officers. You come straight to me. Understand?"

This all seemed rather strange, but his reluctance for her to follow up the leads around Eden had seemed strange from the start. Still, she had always trusted him, and anyway, it was an order.

"Yes, sir," she said.

"And when you do, you leave your phone behind, you walk into my office, you point to my ceiling, and we come up here."

"Isn't that a bit dramatic, sir?"

"No shit. But that's what you're going to do."

*　*　*

It had only been three weeks since her last visit, but Jen was back in the bosom of the retirement and nursing home. The frothy administrator seemed to be having a new problem with her mother but was too embarrassed to say what it was on the telephone.

A note taped to the administrator's door said, *Back in 5!!!* followed by six hearts. Jen plunked herself down on the single chair in the waiting area.

A man supported by a walker painted fire-engine red pushed himself in.

He said hello to Jen and read the note. "Ms. Sunshine's out, is she?"

"Seems to be."

He kept standing.

"Would you like my chair?" Jen asked.

"No, that's fine. You're young."

It didn't quite make sense, but he said it with such certainty that somehow it did.

He waved at the building around them. "Are you thinking of taking very early retirement?"

"Might be a good idea, the way things are going at work. But I suspect I wouldn't move in here right away."

"You a cop, by any chance?" he said.

"The only people who spot that right away are cops and criminals. You a retired criminal? By any chance?"

He thought this was funny. "No, but it would have paid better. I wrote for the *Post*. Investigation. Politics."

He asked what district she was with. And then, when she said she was with the Elder Abuse Unit, he said, "I'm not a huge fan of exit. But that seems to put me in a minority these days."

She didn't want to talk about this. "Were you writing back during the DC18 stuff?" she asked.

He smiled. "Stuff? Did you know that the Russian Revolution back in 1917 was fueled by troops refusing to fire on demonstrators? That was one of the issues for the Eighteen."

"The Russian Revolution?"

"I'm being serious and you should too. No offense, but those were some brave women and men. Not only the eighteen who became the figureheads, but dozens of others whose names we'll never know." He then softened. "No, what I meant is that one of the big issues was how police responded to protest and demonstrations."

"Our job is to maintain law and order."

The man groaned.

"What's the matter with that?"

"In one sense, nothing at all. We need laws, we need order. But what if some laws work against the common person?"

"You're making a speech."

"Okay, here's an example. Climate change is killing us, right?"

"Obviously."

"Did you know that for years, oil and gas companies made sure laws were passed that effectively stifled protest about climate change and protecting the environment? And if a protest took place, you guys ended up doing the dirty work for them."

"That's not what we do."

The man smiled tolerantly. "Of course it's what police sometimes do. Ever bust a Shadow for vagrancy?"

The very mention of Shadows made her shudder. "I thought we were talking about climate change."

"Well, how many of those people were left homeless by the Great Storms? How many of them used to live in Miami before it was wiped off the face of the earth? Ever think of that? And, anyway, forget about climate change. Do those people have an alternative? There isn't enough work anymore, and we don't look after our poorer folks. We punish them."

She'd heard this sort of thing before. In fact, far too often at Zach's. He and his parents swore they weren't attacking her personally, but she sure felt they were.

Then he laughed. "Sorry, I don't get much chance any more to climb onto my soap box."

"As a friend of mine likes saying, 'What the hell.'"

"What I really wanted to do was congratulate you guys. That's what the DC18 were about. Not only against the racism built into the laws and police practices, and racist cops in your ranks. It had a much broader agenda. Your fellow officers did really well. I was proud of the DC Police and still am, at least for some of the changes you made. We sure haven't seen that as much in New York or Chicago."

At that moment, Ms. Sunshine appeared and welcomed Jen inside.

The administrator patted her helmet of hair. She forced such a big smile that Jen worried her makeup would crack. Then her smile faded. Red shone though the makeup. "My, this is difficult to discuss."

"Ma'am," Jen said, "I discuss some pretty difficult things every day at work, so you don't have to worry."

The administrator tittered. "I guess you must, but . . ."

It took some coaxing, but finally the administrator said, "It seems that—mind you, I'm not making any accusations—but there have been reports that your mother, well, she's—well, they say, flirting awfully aggressively."

Jen laughed. "You must be confusing my mother with someone else."

The administrator consulted a note on her desk as if making certain. "No, it seems it is her."

"Is that a problem?"

"Well, she keeps telling men that she wants to, well, f-f- . . . she wants to have sexual relations with them."

Jen didn't know whether to laugh or scream. She did neither, discussed the situation briefly, thanked the administrator and, as she left the office, mumbled over and over again, "Two months. Just two more months."

The man was still in the waiting area, leaning on his red walker. He handed Jen a scrap of paper. "If you're interested, here's a link to the series I wrote about the trial."

She stuffed the paper in her pocket, intending to throw it away when she got outside.

Instead it ended up on top of Zach's dresser after she emptied her pockets that evening.

* * *

Raffi and Leah were making raspberry jam. Each year, they made a large batch of one or two types of jam or jelly—raspberry, strawberry, peach, apricot, pear, apple, or grape—as they came into season, and that batch would last about three years.

No one said the obvious: they were now cooking for posterity.

Raffi said, "Raspberry jam is the queen of jams."

Leah said, "Apricot."

Jen said, "Any of your jams."

Then she felt embarrassed because she thought of the shelves of jam in the basement storage space that would last Zach and her until long after Raffi and Leah were gone.

Leah said, "Zach told us about your new interest."

"My what?"

"Gabriel Cohen's work."

She scrunched up her face in a look of incomprehension.

"But you were reading about the DC18, weren't you?"

Just then, Zach came into the kitchen. "That's not what I said. I said you left a piece of paper on my dresser with a URL and his name."

"Oh, that!" Jen said. "He's some old guy at the retirement home. Says he was a journalist."

Leah said, "That's kind of like saying, 'Albert Einstein says he was a scientist.'"

Raffi said, "He was a local hero, at least in our circles. Won two Pulitzers."

"He figured out I was a cop and wanted me to read what he wrote back then," Jen said. "That's all."

"It's been several years," Leah said, "but I'm guessing he's still worth reading, especially for a woman in the police force. Dear," she said turning to Raffi, "I think that's at a full boil."

The next minutes were the ones needing maximum concentration. Raffi stirred the boiling jam so it didn't burn, and when he turned off the stove, he skimmed off white foam. Jen pulled trays of sterilized jars from the oven. Leah ladled jam into the jars. Zach pulled lids out of the boiling water and plopped them on top. Jen screwed the tops down.

They cleaned splattered jam from the counter, the stove, and the floor.

Leah counted. "Fourteen jars! Fantastic."

At one jar of raspberry jam every four months, they'd finish the last of them about three years after Raffi and Leah were dead.

25

Jen was feeling pretty damn good. I figure I'm usually the first to know. "Nice weekend?"

"On Friday night, Zach and I went dancing to celebrate the end of my probation. On Saturday, we made jam."

I guess humans find that exciting. But when she feels good, I feel good.

Got buzzed by P.D. and Les. "Mariam Zhariri died yesterday. We're going to interview her spouses."

Jen didn't feel so good anymore.

It was the part of her job she hated the most. I told her she was doing important work. She knew this was my program speaking—garbage I seem to automatically trot out at moments like this, even though I know it's gratuitous and superficial.

Daniel and Cari were inconsolable. Jen and Les apologized over and over for bothering them, but Les said he knew that Mariam had obtained an illegal version of the treatment—neither Daniel nor Cari denied this—and that Mariam wasn't the only one who had been harmed. We needed to catch whoever was pushing this stuff before more people were killed.

Daniel's right hand gently rubbed his pregnant belly, and I wondered if they were worried he was going to lose the baby. Cari had her arm around his shoulders, as if she could protect him from our intrusive questions.

But our invasion of their mourning was all for naught. Neither had any idea where Mariam had obtained the fake treatment or who had administered it. They said Mariam had gone for two treatments, one week apart. This was new information.

Jen was thinking about this and missed Les's next question, but it was clear from their answer that he had asked them how she had gotten the treatment and who had administered it. Cari said they didn't know. Mariam hadn't wanted either of them getting in trouble if she got caught.

Then Jen asked whether they owned a Bible or had ever been to the computer co-op. They'd heard of the first, but the answer was no; double no to the second.

In the end, it was simple. Mariam was terrified of getting ROSE. She knew the only way she could receive the treatment was if her parents exited and if Daniel were to give up the baby. She wasn't going to let either of those things happen, and she paid with her life.

* * *

Police HQ. A new building that was supposed to echo the police stations of old, with sunset-orange bricks and offices with transom windows. Add a few spittoons, fat black telephones, and segregated washrooms, and you'd have it made.

Grumps Barfield was one of the department lawyers and damn if he didn't fit right in. He was a white guy with slicked-back brown hair, a baby-blue pinstripe shirt with the sleeves rolled up, and baggy white linen trousers held up by suspenders that he tucked his thumbs into when he spoke. He had a gold pocket watch attached to a fine chain—I didn't even know what the damn thing was until Jen told me. I figured that Barfield had memorized *To Kill a Mockingbird* as a child and was now living the dream, soft Southern drawl and all.

"Well, Detective," Barfield said. It came out as "whale, duh-tayek-tive." And really, really slow. "It looks to me we're havin' a heck of a showdown here with one . . . very . . . rich customer."

Jen jumped in with a rat-a-tat-tat paragraph about the assault charges. Her strategy for the rest of the meeting was to anticipate his next slow homily and fill in a lot of blanks.

But the conversation was inevitably recaptured by Barfield. "You can see, Detective, the upshot is that y'all are in trouble up to that fine little neck of yours." He bent back his baby finger. Then did the same with his ring finger. "The second upshot is it makes the whole department appear like a gang of thugs. Y'all can appreciate that, can't you now?" More fingers, more upshots: bad for her captain. And bad if the implant program got exposed.

"I'd hate to see y'all lose your job over this." He picked up his tablet with her personnel file. "Y'all've already been disciplined once this year."

And on it went. A slow, relentless discussion about the case, what Jen had actually done, what I'd actually done.

"And I see you met up with Mr. O'Neil before his son's trial," Barfield said.

"I was ordered to do that."

"Maybe so. Maybe so. But y'all see, don't you, how this sort of thing looks to the general public. Let me tell you this, young lady: whatever you do, don't you go speakin' to him again until this is resolved. You hear me now?"

She said, "Loud and clear."

After we left, all I could do was apologize to Jen. I liked how she replied: "Chandler, you screwed up. You've apologized. We're partners. We're not going to let this get us down."

*　*　*

Jen, Les, me, and P.D. went cruising for Child's Play. We probably should have taken bikes, but Les had pulled something on the weekend (which led to an avalanche of sexual innuendos from Jen, two of which I needed her to explain to me, and a third I explained to P.D., who doesn't like talking to Les—well, anyone, really—about sex).

We were checking out Michigan Park. There wasn't a park worth the name anywhere, although there were a couple of dead-grass fields where kids were playing ball. The whole neighborhood felt like someone had dug up a square mile of suburbia and dropped it on DC—the street landscape, detached houses, bored kids, and all. City boy that I am, I instinctively hated it.

Les was talking to Jen. "Things better with you and Zach?"

"Another hump we needed to get over."

"Love's a long line of humps."

More sexual innuendoes ensued.

"Love," said Les, getting the final word in on humps, "is a caravan of camels."

"Zach and I are so different from each other," Jen said.

"We're all different. That's what makes it a relationship."

"Oh, wise one, tell me all."

"That's easy. Life—"

"Shit! Over there!"

Jen lunged out of the car. It was Child's Play, wearing a shiny purple jacket. He spotted Jen and took off along the dead-tree-lined street. Les raced ahead in the car to cut him off. Child's Play slipped between two houses and we followed. Les zoomed up the street to make it around to Puerto Rico Avenue.

Child's Play crashed open a metal gate, startled a German shepherd, and scrambled over the back fence, which freed the dog to vent his full fury on us. Saliva flew, deep barks broke the air, and malice blazed in dark eyes that distilled ten millennia of dog resentment against humans for treating them like pets. I sent Jen's hand to her belt, grabbed her pepper spray, and as the hysterical creature lunged with dreams of tearing lunch from Jen's face, we shot it into the poor creature's eyes. *Sorry, kid.* But the beast got his revenge, because momentum carried his body forward and his teeth cut a gash into Jen's cheek.

Jen vaulted the fence, and we were going for the two-hundred-meter record across a vacant lot. *Bad choice for the bad guy,* Jen thought. Les would arrive from the north in sixteen seconds. South was an exposed road, and west was the barbed-wire-topped chain-link fence barring access to the Metro tracks.

We had lost time dealing with the dog, but we were gaining again on Child's Play. Cars were tearing up and down Puerto Rico, and when he ran into the street, one car screeched to a stop and another swerved around him, horn blaring. I thought Child's Play might be planning on hijacking a car, but instead he yanked off his purple jacket, flung it over the barbed wire, and with surprising agility climbed the fence. As we ran into the roadway, he glanced back at us and with two tugs, ripped his jacket free. He scrambled up the gravel embankment and started crossing the tracks. A train horn blared, a train shot past, and he disappeared from sight.

By then, we'd also run into the street, where a car slammed on its brakes and skidded to a stop. Jen slapped her hands on its hood and kept running. She wrestled into her gloves, and we were soon over the rusty fence, but as we started up the embankment, a Red Line train blasted out of nowhere—damn, they're fast— and the combination of her surprise and the hurricane wind sent us tumbling back down, landing us with a thud against the fence. We pulled ourselves up and blazed across the tracks and over the second fence. We looked down the road and saw Les holding Child's Play by the biceps.

We reached them and slumped against the side of the car. Les was looking awfully relaxed. "Phew," he said, "that was one hell of a chase."

* * *

The interrogation room stank of bodies fresh off a chase on another blast-furnace July day. At least it was the second-to-last July day for another year.

"Child's Play," Les said, "staying silent isn't going to help you."

"I'm not being silent. I told you, I don't know nothing about no Eden."

"We didn't mention Eden," Les said. "We said 'the treatment.'"

Child's Play sucked in his cheeks like he was going to bite them off from the inside. "Ain't you clever," he managed to say.

Jen said to Les, "Not a bad recovery, was it?"

"Speaking of which," Les replied, "you need stitches."

Blood had seriously stained the front of her shirt and there was a bloody pile of gauze pads on the floor.

Jen said, "Think we can get him for assaulting an officer?"

"Don't see why not. Maybe you'll get rabies and die, and then we've got him for murder."

"We've got him for that anyway." She turned back to Child's Play.

"You're crazy," he said. "I didn't murder no one."

"You sold Eden. Eden kills people. You're in for murder."

Les said, "Maybe prison won't be so bad."

Jen said to Les. "He won't have to worry about paying bills until he's about eighty."

"Or decide what to eat for dinner."

"Or see his girlfriend."

"Or shit in private."

Child's Play finally jumped in. "I told you—"

But Jen cut him off, her voice losing any playfulness, but still calm. "Child's Play, I've never fucked with you? Have I?" He didn't disagree. "Well, I'm not fucking with you now."

"Then why are you saying shit?"

"Because that shit is the true shit you've fallen into, and I'm trying to throw you a rope to pull yourself out of the sewer."

Les said, "Jen, that's pretty good."

Jen shrugged. "Apparently wasted on Child's Play."

We stood up to leave, with no intention of actually doing so.

"Hang on, man." Child's Play scrunched his hand in his hair. "Just hang on. I gotta think."

The speed of human thought is appallingly slow at the best of times. I like to picture the human brain as old technology.

Finally, Child's Play spoke. "Look. You gotta promise—I don't know— promise you let me go."

We didn't even bother to answer.

"Forget it, then," his mouth said, but everything told us he didn't mean it.

This time we did leave.

We went back an hour later, well after Child's Play had started yelling that he wanted to talk.

Les said, "You've got one minute to start telling us something we want to know."

Child's Play said, "The thing is, I don't really know nothing."

Les sighed. "Jen, want to go for a beer after work?"

They discussed it.

Jen eventually said, "Child's Play, we have some questions. You give us credible answers that help us catch these bastards and we'll recommend the DA goes easy on you."

He nodded.

A good grilling takes a lot of time. It ebbs and flows. You play with words. You circle back. You listen for hints and hesitations, anything that will point you in the right direction.

In the end, this is what we got:

First, Child's Play was the weasel we always thought he was. He kept trying to manipulate us. He groveled. He obviously didn't give a shit about who got hurt.

Second, he hadn't been totally lying to Olive and Pancho. He had heard about the counterfeit treatment. He met someone who promised he could get it. But the weasel got out-weaseled, and the guy ripped him off.

"Where do you think we can find him?"

"You won't."

"Because . . ."

"He's dead."

"You killed him?"

Child's Play exploded. "You think I'm talking if I killed him?" You think I'm that stupid?"

Les said, "Not quite that stupid."

"Word is he ripped off one too many people."

He told us what he could about him. Assuming the guy was simply a con man, it wasn't any use to us.

Third, he admitted he was now "negotiating" with several people to buy the treatment. That's why he had been in Michigan Heights. One couple was ready to score, and he had been going to pick up their deposit.

"You guys cost me a bundle," he said.

"May have saved you from killing someone," Les pointed out.

He shrugged.

Jen said, "This means you have a new source?"

He nodded.

"And you're going to tell us who they are?"

"I can't."

"Because you'll end up like your ex-friend."

"He wasn't no friend. Because I don't know."

"Really."

"I'm not shitting you."

Les rolled his eyes, perhaps a bit theatrically for my taste, but Child's Play was a B-movie actor and seemed to bite.

And gave us the fourth thing, which was the most interesting.

"It's the guys who sprung me from the hospital. I don't know who they are."

Les said to P.D., who said to me, who said to Jen, *Fuck a duck*. We had, of course, assumed it was Gray Suit's people who got him out—simply because they were the only ones with the power to make him disappear from the records.

Jen said to me and I said to P.D., who said to Les, *Outside*.

Jen said, "Child's Play, you need to take a leak? Need a coffee? Let's get you straightened out and continue in ten minutes. What do you say?"

Twenty minutes later, we returned after playing with this new information every which way.

Jen said, "Child's Play, who sprang you?"

"You're kiddin'."

"What do you mean?"

"I describe them, and I'm dead."

Les said, "You don't describe them, and you spend the next ten to twenty in prison."

"Better than dead."

"True," Les said. "But you help us, and I'm sure they'll put you up for witness protection."

"You can arrange that?"

"Sure," Les said, stretching the truth . . . well, lying, actually. "We know exactly who can work that out. But you got to give us something."

"I don't know if I should."

But after twenty more minutes of circling around, it seemed he did know. On the one hand, his answers were a letdown. He didn't have any names. He was appallingly bad at describing the two people who got him out. He said perhaps because he'd still been doped up. We described the woman who was guarding the room that day, and it was clear it hadn't been her. We even described Gray Suit and his sidekicks, but of course that went nowhere.

Whoever they were, they named the price for the treatment—it was surprisingly low—and they said Child's Play could triple it. If he tried to get more, if he screwed them around, they would find out and cut off his legs.

"Cut off your legs?"

Child's Play let out a demonstrative sigh. "It's an expression. They're tough guys."

He had an address he could contact when he had a confirmed sale. *Dark web,* I said to Jen, but we took it anyway.

"You can't tell us anything about them?"

"Gang types, all I know."

"Gangbangers? Bikers?"

"No, classier. I figure mob types."

"They sprung you from the hospital?"

"Yeah, tiptoed me straight out."

This didn't make sense. Guys like Child's Play might have a good nose for cops, but an even better nose for other bad guys, particularly of the scarier variety. So if he said they were gangsters, I would've laid odds he was being legit.

But we had also been certain that Gray Suit's people had hired the security woman and erased his hospital records. I quickly looked but couldn't find even one lousy case where the mob had pulled off a stunt like that. It just didn't make sense.

Jen thought, *Brooks.*

26

"That's all he said, sir." Jen cupped a hand over her eyes to block out the late-afternoon sun.

"Jen, I told you, come to me before you got anyone involved."

"Les and I were questioning him together. Ten minutes ago."

Captain Brooks didn't even seem to be listening.

"Your guy couldn't identify his suppliers or the guys who sprung him. And what sort of name is Child's Play anyway? When the hell did we stop using actual names?"

"Both were men, both native English speakers, probably late thirties or forties. One was white, the other Black."

"Racial progress in America," Brooks muttered. "Integrated gangs."

"Besides that, he was useless."

"*Besides that?* It's *all* pretty useless. It's no surprise there's a big organization behind this. Who else could pull this off?"

"But we assumed Teko Teko Mea's people got him out and hid him away to question him."

"Maybe it was, and maybe it wasn't."

"That would be easy to find out."

"Yeah?"

"Ask him."

Captain Brooks blurted out, "That's one thing I'm definitely not going to do." His eyes whipped away from hers as if he was surprised he had said that out loud.

"Why not?"

Captain Brooks paced away from her to the edge of the roof. Then back again.

"Okay. You're going to put an ankle monitor on him, seed his phone, and let him go," he directed. "My hunch is he's going to try to make this one sale and then take off."

"It was in Michigan Park."

"He'll go there first to get money, then return with the drugs or to take them to get injected or however they do it. Have Chandler track him. If we're lucky, he'll lead us to his guys. I don't think he's going to wait long."

Captain Brooks finally seemed to notice that Jen was pressing a thick wad of gauze to her cheek.

"Jen, what did you do to your face?"

"A dog. It's nothing."

"Yeah, until you die of rabies."

* * *

That evening, Zach was at his microscopic desk and Jen was slumped on his bed, watching a show and trying to ignore her throbbing cheek. Fourteen tiny stitches. Career as a supermodel shot. The doctor's helpful advice: "Try not to yawn, talk, chew, laugh, sneeze, or open your mouth to eat or brush your teeth, and you'll be fine. And if you start having a compulsion to bite people, then the rabies shot didn't work."

Zach said, "You should read these articles." He had been scrolling through Gabriel Cohen's articles since Jen had brought home the guy's name and URL.

Jen said, "I should read a lot of things."

"Seriously. I think Captain Brooks is in it."

She paused the show. "He writes about Brooks?"

"He doesn't give any names, but there's this one guy, a sergeant when this happens, Black, and he's always rubbing a scar like you said Brooks does. How's your cheek?"

"I'll read it if you stop asking how my cheek is."

At first she skimmed, and then slowed down.

A man, white and with the half-shaved head of a graduate student, led me around the block to an Ethiopian restaurant. Six people waited in a room at the back. Most were younger than the arrested 18. One of them, by her appearance a woman of Korean heritage, asked me to turn off my phone and tablet."

A couple of months ago, Jen would have found this boring. She would have said, *Why are you guys always dwelling on the past? Some things are better now, some worse.* But now it felt different. She was part of this, part of some new story that was being written.

She read on.

An hour later, I had heard from everyone but one stern African American man. His expression was grave, perhaps even suspicious. From time to time, he rubbed a prominent scar above his eye. Finally, the other five looked at him.

"Your turn," one man said.

He took a long time to begin, as if measuring his words.

"I've been listening to y'all, and I've been listening to the Eighteen and I've been listening in my community. This is a hard time for me. You see"—he turned directly to me, and continued—"I'm a cop. I know first-hand about bigotry and racism in the force. I know firsthand about putting down a strike or a protest. I know firsthand about protecting the rich from everyone else. But when I hear it from others, I get angry at all of you. I think I have to defend my brothers and sisters in the force. Sure, I know you're not saying we're all bad. I even know you're not saying it's about individuals, but the role we play. But it's damn hard to listen to you."

He rubbed that thick scar of his. He said, "You may think it's strange I became a police officer. You see, when I was a kid, just sixteen, two cops beat the living crap out of me. One white, one Hispanic. No particular reason. I hadn't done anything wrong. They just wanted to kick the crap out of a Black kid. They left me with this." He lightly touched the scar.

"For a while, I was a hothead, but after college, I decided to become a cop. I did it knowing that as soon as I had a chance, I was going to put my lot in with those who were going to bring about change.

"*I don't know how long it will take. We might get the Eighteen out. I hope so. We might get some immediate changes in the force. I hope so. Kick out those who should have been kicked out years ago. Change our training and procedures. Forget about that damn blue line and stop giving a break to abusive officers. But you see, that's only a beginning. The Eighteen and those of us sitting here are part of something bigger. And that's what's got to change. The much bigger picture. I'm in this for the long haul. However long. However patient I got to be. Whatever it takes.*"

"Yeah, might be him," Jen said.

"Cool."

"Why cool? It's depressing. Look at what he believed a decade ago. Now he's nothing more than a cog in their machine."

But it isn't totally true, she thought. Deep down, she had always known there was more to Brooks. For the first time, she wondered if the captain's slur to Gray Suit—*She's nothing, absolutely fucking zero*—was Brooks's attempt to protect her from Gray Suit's prying eyes.

27

I'm not so sure about August. I know it's only my third time around the bases, and the first one barely counts because I was still a baby with no clue about anything. But I can tell you this much about August: it's too damn hot. People are ornery. Asphalt streets bubble like boiling molasses. Mangy dogs sprawl on the sidewalks, not even flinching when you step over them. Jen tired quicker, and there were times her brain turned to sludge. No, I'm not so sure about August.

With Les and P.D., we followed a few leads and spoke to everyone in our book who might be picking up rumors about Eden. Yep, people were hearing about it, people were asking for it, but no one admitted to knowing how to get it.

Child's Play was out on bail and I was keeping an eye on his comings and goings, which even Jen in her August sluggishness could have pulled off, since he hadn't left his apartment. "Scared shitless," is what Jen said.

Jen was popping drugs like a junkie to dull the pain in her cheek, and I told her to lay off because they were fogging my brain.

On Wednesday, I said, "He's moving," but his adventure only took him to the corner and back, presumably to buy food, dope, and beer.

On Thursday at 14:28.10, he moved and kept moving. He was on foot, and it was pretty clear he was heading for Michigan Park. Les jumped into a car, and we popped Jen's own bike onto the rack and easily beat Child's Play to the area.

Jen and Les had talked to Brooks on Tuesday, and I'd have to be a pretty slow synth not to see that Jen already had had a second chitchat with him with me turned off or incapacitated. Les didn't seem to clue in about this, but Les isn't the most elegant line of code. A good cop and a good guy and a good friend to Jen, but there are only so many *goods* that a single person can lay claim to. Okay, fine, no reason Les would think I'd been turned off. It's just that I keep expecting more from humans, and they keep letting me down.

Brooks had okayed three surveillance drones: two sparrows and a hawk, and they were flapping overhead, with feeds going to P.D. and me. Hammerhead and Amanda were deployed, but keeping their distance. The little weasel was going nowhere without us.

Child's Play went to a house on 7th Street NE. Stayed there nine minutes. When he left, even from a bird's-eye view he looked all twitchy, like he was expecting to be attacked any second. He cut through an empty lot and onto Varnum.

"Jen," called Les through P.D. to me, "he's heading to the hospital."

Jen was locking her bike as Child's Play reached the main entrance, where all the fast-food restaurants are. Les drove around to the ER exit, and Hammerhead and Amanda took up the other two exits.

Leave them on, I told Jen, meaning her civilian bike helmet and sunglasses. *Strap on, cover your stitches.* We followed Child's Play inside.

Straight through the hospital. No stops.

He grabbed a car outside the ER.

Jen scrambled into Les's car, and we followed Child's Play to the Brookland-CUA Metro station. We sent Hammerhead and Amanda to the next stations north and south. We tailed him inside, Les wearing a Capitals' hat, Jen still wearing her bike helmet and beginning to feel like an idiot. To the platform, Les forty feet ahead of him, us forty feet behind.

15:47:29. People pushing onto and off the rush-hour trains.

"Amanda," we called a minute later, "it's yours. He's on the next train, fourth car. We're in the third and fifth cars."

Amanda boarded his car at Rhode Island.

At Metro Center, he got off.

157

To look at that station, you wouldn't know that half the DC population didn't have a regular job. It was so packed you could be dead for half an hour and still be standing upright. We pushed and squirmed between people, trying to keep Child's Play in sight. We were in a box formation: Les was somewhere in front of our target, getting instructions from Amanda's synth and me about which way he seemed to be heading. Amanda wasn't more than twelve feet away, us three times that.

It happened in a flash. Child's Play was heading toward the escalators. Ahead of him, Les squeezed himself into the crowd and rode up. Child's Play was in line to get on. Amanda got caught in a swell of people and was carried off to the left like a riptide had grabbed her. We pushed forward to take her place.

A train pulled into the station. Just as Child's Play neared the base of the escalators, a leg hooked around Jen's ankle and five fingers, as hard as marble, shoved us off balance. We tottered sideways. A woman screamed. Child's Play jerked around at the sound; we were heading for the ground, and right before we were buried in a forest of legs, I caught him shifting direction toward the train.

Every commuter in DC seemed hell-bent on kicking us. Jen threw her arms across her face to avoid a pummeling. Within seconds, three people were trying to help us stand up. Jen, cursing, pushed them away, and the crowd parted enough for us to spot Child's Play wiggling through the train's closing doors.

By the time we were upright, the train had pulled away. Les made it back down the escalator, and Amanda found us. Jen ripped off her bike helmet, and we looked around, trying to spot who had tripped her. Amanda popped a small pink bubble and looked ready to kill anyone who got in her way.

We waited for the next train. We still had strong signals from the anklet moving north on the Red Line; we still had the phone. The phone switched off. We still had the anklet.

The next train was delayed. We finally got on, ten minutes behind.

Child's Play had gotten off at Woodley Park.

By the time we reached the station, he had made it to the zoo. Seemed a bad decision for a guy on the run. It's surrounded by fences. Then again, it's uneven terrain, with big summer crowds and lots of places to meet someone or hide. Didn't matter, we had the signal loud and clear.

He was moving quickly, but we were running and making up ground. I love a chase. Good times.

Then the signal stopped moving, either inside or just outside the rainforest building. We split up to surround the building at a distance.

Les called, "He must be waiting for his dealer to arrive."

Ten minutes passed.

We kept our distance, figuring we might all have been spotted. The drones arrived, and we flew them around the building. No sign of Child's Play. We sent two of the sparrows inside, past some startled visitors when they opened the door.

Child's Play didn't seem to be in any space the sparrows managed to get to, but his signal was still strong and stationary.

Finally, we moved in.

Followed the signal.

Then followed the screams.

We found him in the piranha pond.

Or to be precise, we found what was left of his legs, hacked off at the knees. Found the rest of him a moment later in a supply closet.

Turns out that "cut off your legs" wasn't just a tough-guy expression after all.

28

The Thursday afternoon debacle with Child's Play meant Jen didn't get home until 1:00 AM, although by then the crime scene folks had long taken over the show.

The next morning, as Chandler would retell the story later, their whole squad was lined up and shot by Brooks. Their bodies were then skewered on pikes in front of the police station as a warning to all officers to never totally fuck up.

They had valiantly tried to defend themselves. Sure, they'd momentarily lost Child's Play, but they'd picked him up right away. What difference would it have made if they had staked out the rainforest building ten minutes earlier?

Brooks was pissed.

"There were four of you. With implants. With drone support. There was one of him."

Amanda said, "At least two. Someone took Jen out."

"Did you catch him? Her? They?"

They hadn't even seen him, her, or they. Surveillance video couldn't make anything out. Bad angles and too many heads blocking the view.

Surveillance cameras at the zoo entrance, the rainforest building, and the paths leading to it had spotted Child's Play, but no one with any known links to organized crime.

As might be expected, the videos on the Metro and zoo had picked out hundreds of people with records, from medical problems like drug addiction, to theft, battery, sexual assault, and every other way that people try to benefit themselves at the expense of others. AI managed to discard ninety-seven percent of them, but that still left several dozen people of interest—either as the person who'd tripped Jen or the person or people who'd decided that weasels don't need legs. Our unit spent two days tracking down each of them but came up with nothing, although Hammerhead did score some good weed from a former dealer who now ran a boutique dope shop.

Finally, to cap off Jen's miserable week, she went to the clinic to get her annual ROSE screen. The test wasn't anything more than a sample of blood, but it was one of the tests that still had to go off to a lab. The problem was it started the countdown clock, a three-day wait until she found out whether she was one of the lucky one in six who'd get whacked. Then the ten-year wait, maybe more, maybe less, for the prions to start turning her brain into compost. Then the short clock until she died.

And even though she really didn't have to worry because, after her mother exited in two months and Jen received the treatment, it was impossible not to feel anxious.

As soon as she got home from the clinic, she threw her work clothes into the laundry hamper, donned her bike gear, and headed to the Capital Crescent Trail, where she pushed and pushed to obliterate thoughts of Child's Play and ROSE and Brooks and Eden and people aging overnight and anything else but making it to the next mile marker as quickly as she could.

Her mind, though, could not be fooled. Later, as she lay in their midnight bed, Zach at her side, her eyes were open and trying to make out the vague swatches of light on the ceiling. She lightly touched her cheek—at least that was healing well. Her mind buzzed with everything happening at work, and she searched for the invisible threads that stitched it all together. She knew she had made a mistake dropping the co-op lead. Shouldn't have mattered what Brooks said. Shouldn't have mattered if she ruffled Zach's feathers. Sure, a lot of new stuff had happened, but she had lost two and a half good weeks.

She spoke toward the ceiling but addressed her words to Zach, who she thought might still be awake.

"The co-op folks. I have to meet them. I need to talk to them, fast."

* * *

When she woke up late on Saturday morning, Jen went into the bathroom and pulled out the fourteen stitches. She made a cappuccino and found Zach tending his rooftop garden. He was on his knees, with his bare back to her. She paused, coffee mug in hand, and watched him work. Those beautiful hands, meticulously isolating and snipping off unwanted shoots from his tomato plants—she caught the soothing chlorophyll smell from fifteen feet away. His wonderful shoulders and back, not comic-hero ripped, but strong and tanned. The khaki shorts with a million pockets and scuffed work boots. He was so beautiful to watch.

He turned and caught sight of her.

"Good morning, pumpkin!"

"Pumpkin?"

"What can I say? I'm a gardener."

She came over and held out her coffee for him to share.

She pulled up a deckchair and watched. Weeding. Loosening soil. She remembered a dream and just as quickly it flicked away from her mind. She needed to ask him; she hated to ask him.

"Zach, were you awake last night? When I asked you about speaking to the co-op guys?"

He paused but didn't set down his secateurs.

"Is it turned off, your thing?"

She tried not to be irritated. It was the first time he had mentioned Chandler since their argument. She tried to laugh, but even to her, it sounded fake. "He's only on when I'm signed in."

"I don't want to tell them about—"

"You can't tell them about Chandler."

"I know. I need to make sure that if they agree to see you, it won't be turned on."

Why was she getting annoyed at this? His was a simple request. It made sense. But she wished his number-one loyalty, unquestioned and unquestionable, was to her.

He said, "Jen, they're my friends."

"You met them a month ago."

"No, that's when *you* first met them. Me? It was at a meeting in the winter. But yes, we've become friends over the past month. I don't want to cause problems for them, that's all."

It felt like she was required to take a leap of faith. Out of her job. Out of her world. And into his.

"I promise. It will just be me," she said. "Unless I discover they're doing something seriously illegal, I won't be telling anyone about them."

∗   ∗   ∗

She hadn't known what to expect, but she had replayed every spy movie she'd ever seen. Meeting in a deserted parking garage. Directions taped to the bottom of a park bench. Being blindfolded, stuffed into a car trunk, and driven to a remote location.

Instead, two hours later, Zach said, "I spoke to Mary Sue. She said we can drop by anytime."

"I thought you said they went underground."

"I said they were lying a bit low."

"Someone's house is barely in hiding."

"Did you find them?" he said, but his tone was playful.

"I didn't try."

He winked at her. "Well, now you don't need to marshal the powers of the state."

She imagined their destination: a student apartment, mismatched furniture, empty pizza boxes crowding the front hall. Or a tumble-down communal house where people munched on granola and compared Birkenstock styles.

But they were soon riding their bicycles along a leafy street in Chevy Chase, where even the trees and bushes seemed more alive than elsewhere in the city. They stopped in front of a handsome house set back from the street. The front yard had been converted into a vegetable garden, but the house itself was traditional and beautifully maintained: yellow with crisp blue shutters around the windows and a colonial portico over the front door, next to which a stroller and two bikes were parked.

A young man with a wispy beard and powerful arms let them in. Zach introduced Jen to Devin. He said hello but did not smile; there was no welcome in his eyes.

The front hall was simple and neat. Upstairs, a baby cried. Twentieth-century rock thumped from a sound system.

Devin ordered the music to stop. He said, "You came by the shop, didn't you?"

"Yes. Sorry about it."

He gave her a look, much too long, as if he was wondering whether she was apologizing for burning it down herself.

Mary Sue arrived to rescue them. She had to be in her early sixties. Her white hair made her look older, but her skin appeared so young and soft that Jen wanted to reach out and touch it. "Welcome," Mary Sue said with genuine warmth.

As she led them toward the kitchen, she said, "Sorry to drag you out here."

The kitchen was a new extension in the back, modern but cozy.

"Your house is beautiful," Jen said.

Mary Sue smiled with appreciation and then steered Jen toward the woman at the kitchen counter. It was the woman Jen had seen speaking secretly into her telephone at Zombies.

"This is Ximena." Spelled with an *x* but sounded like an *h*. Mid- to late forties. Kick-ass Frida Kahlo eyebrows and a thatch of dark brown hair woven into a braid as thick as a man's fist. She wore a flowing skirt, sunset orange, and a T-shirt tie-dyed in ochre and adobe red.

Jen, Zach, and the two women sat at the table. Devin leaned against the counter.

"Devin," Mary Sue said, "don't you want to pull up a chair?"

It seemed he didn't.

They all looked at Jen.

"I guess you know I'm a cop," she said.

None of the faces looked surprised.

"But I'm not here as a cop."

Devin said, "What's that supposed to mean?"

"It means I'm not working today. No one knows I've come to speak to you."

"And," Devin said, "you're gonna pretend you won't tell anyone about us."

"If I find out you're doing something seriously illegal, I don't have a choice. I'm a sworn officer—"

"Whoopee," Devin said.

"Dev," Mary Sue said.

"I don't mean if you confess to shoplifting those beat running shoes you're wearing."

"We don't—"

"Dev," said Mary Sue, "I think she was teasing you."

"But if I get information connected with the crime I'm investigating, I may have to give my source. I'll try not to, but I can't promise."

They paused while Mary Sue poured iced coffee and passed around a plate of brownies. Then Jen said, "It's about Odette Johnson. I was there when she was killed."

Ximena sucked in her breath—it was the first sound Jen had heard from her.

Mary Sue said, "We weren't able to learn what happened."

Jen briefly recounted the events, although she kept some of the details vague since Delmar Junior wasn't getting charged.

"Her son said she'd been working with you," she finished.

"She was a lovely woman." Mary Sue put down her cup. "Generous and hardworking. We really miss her."

"Could you tell me a bit more about what you do?"

Devin said, "I don't see what—"

Ximena cut him off and began to speak. She was short and solidly built, with the dignified elegance of a woman in a Diego Rivera mural. Her voice had a whisper of an accent. *Not Mexican,* Jen thought. *Somewhere in Central America.*

"Our computer business is a co-op. Yes?"

Jen nodded.

"We're part of an integrated international network of co-operative manufacturers, farms, financial institutions, schools, science labs, and transportation systems. This is not your grandmother and grandfather's health food store. Although," she said with a smile—a small one, though, as if the jury were still out on whether to be nice to Jen—"we do include several of those."

"Why haven't I ever heard of all this?"

"If you lived in the Mondragon region of Spain or some small communities here in the US, you would have. But the media's not interested because we don't fit into their scheme of things. We quietly go about our business."

"So why would Zombie Computers—"

"Zombie Industrial," Devin said.

"—get burnt down? And I should tell you, I don't think it was arson. I spoke to the fire inspector."

Devin made a scoffing sound, but the women ignored him.

Jen continued, "He seemed totally by the book. We spoke the very next day, and he said he didn't think it was arson. And that's what his report said too."

Ximena said, "Perhaps. Or perhaps not. We believe it was."

"Why?"

"Across the country over the past year, but accelerating in recent months, there have been thirty-five to forty incidents. Break-ins, burnings, and vandalism. Co-ops getting shut down under spurious zoning regulations. It appears we fit into that pattern."

"Did you lose everything?"

Ximena said, "We . . . our losses were substantial, including a lovely workspace and everything in it. You saw it, yes?"

"I did, and it was."

The niceties over, it was time to ask questions.

"Did you know that Odette Johnson owned a Bible?" Jen asked.

Mary Sue laughed. "Of course. She sometimes brought it to the co-op. She spoke a lot about Jesus and God."

For the first time, Jen thought Mary Sue's voice seemed strained.

A fly buzzed around the room, and Ximena swished it away from her.

"Do you know what she kept in her Bible?" Jen said.

The fly circled this time around Zach.

No one answered.

"She kept her receipt from you. From when she bought her phone."

The fly tap-tapped against a windowpane.

"Here's the interesting thing. After she was killed, someone broke into her apartment and stole one thing. Guess what that was?" No one seemed interested in guessing, but Jen could have sworn Devin had become stiff as a board. "They stole her Bible with your receipt inside. Strange, don't you think?"

There was a long silence, and finally Ximena said, "Jen, please tell us what you're trying to find out."

"Right before she died, Odette Johnson said she was getting to Eden."

No one said anything, no meaningful looks were exchanged, but Jen felt a change in that room, as if their thoughts had weight and they were pressing down hard.

She said to Ximena, "Do you know what she meant?"

Ximena considered this. "Odette said she was going to Eden? So I understand your question correctly."

"Yes. *'Getting to Eden'* were her exact words."

"Eden. It was our slang, nothing more."

"For?"

"For the society we are working to create."

"The Garden of Eden? Isn't that a bit . . . ?"

"Hokey? Overstated? Naive?" Ximena looked at her, but it was obvious to Jen that she didn't expect an answer. "Definitely. The actual joke was that we were creating Eden With Serious Flaws. We don't believe in perfect societies or total social harmony or utopia."

"Then what do you believe?"

"I could throw a list of words at you, but I don't know if that will help."

"Then what do you mean by 'you're working to create'?"

"Jen, we're revolutionaries." Ximena paused for effect. "You won't find weapons or bombs. We believe that one reason for the failure of past efforts to bring about change was the failure to first create new or transitional institutions. Our network of co-ops is meant to prefigure the type of society we're working to create. A high level of equality and a very high level of participatory democracy. A place where we celebrate individuals and differences, but where those things don't become a smokescreen for trampling the rights and needs of others, or to deny our collective responsibilities. We believe humans have the capacity to meet our needs in harmony with our environment and to do it with elegance and ongoing scientific and social innovation."

Zach nodded, as if for the first time hearing these goals stated so eloquently, although all this was consistent with what he'd already told Jen about the co-op network.

"But we also think humans will continue to screw up and get in each other's way and do stupid things," Ximena continued. "That's the way it is. Eden With Serious Flaws. It is what we are working to create."

"And that's all? That's all there is about Eden?"

Ximena's eyes momentarily flickered. Mary Sue didn't seem to be breathing. Devin started speaking, but Ximena glared at him like a parent at a child about to do something foolish.

Ximena said, "Yes, that's all there is."

As they biked home, Jennifer thought about these three. She liked Ximena, her smart and formidable presence verging on charismatic. Jen found it impossible not to like Mary Sue too—warm, maternal, steady, and hospitable. Jen positively despised Devin, although Zach had made excuses about his "being young," which Jen found patronizing. "It's not because he's young," she said. "It's because he's a macho dickhead who thinks he's part of a cool conspiracy." Which then made her wonder whether he actually was part of conspiracy, and the other two had merely fooled her.

Jennifer thought of the other questions she might have asked, but she figured she wouldn't have gotten a truthful answer to the most important ones: *Why did you all bristle when I asked about Eden? Why did Devin stiffen when I asked about the Bible? And most of all, are you distributing an illegal version of the treatment, called Eden?*

She figured only one set of answers could explain their silence on any of those questions. And that didn't look good for the peace-and-love crowd.

29

We are hacking through the rainforest, *whack* to the right with the machete, *whack* to the left with the next blow. Water sparkles through the dense green foliage. As we step into the pond, Jen's clothes vanish, and we feel the blue water soothe us, as if clothing us again. We duck and swim to the other side, surrounded by schools of colorful fish. They circle around us, under us, against us. We come up for air, and the world shifts and we feel the menace. It rises out of the mist in front of us, out of the water—the dome of his head shaved bald, rising out of the water, the first tattoos and then the rest. Teko Teko Mea. There is no rush, no drama, but I am paralyzed. I cannot move as he reaches out with a delicate but impossibly large hand, like that of a man's against a child's. This hand swallows the top of our head and forces us under. It holds us under. We struggle and kick, but Gray Suit is calmly speaking, telling others why it is necessary to suffocate us. "She wanted it—now she's got it!"

I try to scream. Our mouth is open but no sounds emerge. I try again, but no sounds. I try and now I scream, *"Jen!"*

For the first time in my life, I have the strange sensation of feeling her rise out of sleep. It is as if a series of circuits are locking into place. Physical sensations of touch. A recognition of self. A recognition of place. A moment of panic. And then confusion.

I feel her drifting away. *Don't leave me*, I think.

"Jen, I'm drown—" and then I stop. Realize where we are. In her bed. We couldn't be drowning. I've read all about dreaming. Heard Jen and

169

others talk about it so many times. But now for the first time, I have dreamed.

"Chandler, how could you . . . ?" Her voice in her head was slow. I felt her searching for words that would make sense. "How could you wake me?" She didn't mean how dare I wake her. She meant, how was this possible?

"I don't know." I can turn myself on if she is in danger and frightened and her hormones are flying off the charts. But not like this. Not when she is asleep. "I don't know. It's not possible." And then, "We were in a jungle, and then swimming, and then Gray Suit tried to kill us."

"You were dreaming. It was a dream." She started falling back to sleep, as if it were she who was dreaming that I was dreaming.

"Wait!" I sent an instruction to her arm to switch on her bedside light. She was too asleep to resist and swore when the light blinded us.

"Chandler, what are you doing?"

"I was scared."

"You can't be scared."

"It was so real."

She laughed. She got up and tiptoed to the bathroom and peed. We came back and lay in bed. She reached for the light.

"Jen, wait."

"What?"

"There was this thing he said. I think it's important. He was explaining why he was killing us. He said, 'She wanted it—now she's got it!'"

She yawned. "Tell it to me. The dream."

I told her my dream. As I told it, it was drifting away from me. But I made it to Gray Suit's final words, and I felt Jen's alarm.

She said, "Didn't he say something like that to us? Chandler, play us back the meetings with him."

"All?"

"Start with the first one."

My memory wasn't a sound recording, but like all my memories, was eidetic. In a second, it was her memory too. Word by word, we remembered the first meeting. Then the second, when she and Les had been called on the carpet. And then the third, when Gray Suit had said they had discovered what Eden was.

There was one thing he said that was similar to the dream, but not quite: "People want it and pay big dollars to get it. Thousands and thousands. And then they pay for it with their lives. We've got to stop it."

I felt Jen processing this, trying to correlate it with other information. Finally I asked, "Boss, what are we looking for?"

"I don't know for sure. But something. I know there's something . . . Let's go through the last meeting again." And maybe she felt the hint of gloom that still clung to me from my dream, and wanted to cheer me up, so she said, "Play it again, Chan."

It was dumb, but funny, and it finally pulled me from my dream. We listened to Gray Suit's words together.

Jen said, "That's it, but not quite it."

She looked at her clock.

"What d'ya say we continue this tomorrow? I'm going to turn you off now."

*　　*　　*

We step into the sparkling pool, and our clothes vanish. We are engulfed by schools of service units. We are all naked, and it is exhilarating because in all their physical diversity, each is more perfect than the last. They swim around us, they slide against us. I come up for air and feel the menace. It rises slowly out of the water in front of us. The surfer's bleach-blond hair. The tanned face of Richard O'Neil. He rises up and we are in an Iowa cornfield, storm clouds massing on the horizon. He is dressed in his stunning green suit, like a rock-and-roll god, and he spreads his arms and raises his hands in blessing over us and intones the words, "You want it. You get it. You pay for it." And I realize where I am, cut off from the world, so alone, with only Jen, with only my Jen, with—

"*Jen!*"

This time, she didn't rise from sleep circuit by circuit. In a flash, she was awake and alert, the light on, sitting up, her hand reaching for the sawed-off baseball bat under her bed. She looked around.

"Jesus, Chandler."

I told her my second dream.

* * *

In the morning—Monday morning—even before she went in for her shift, she turned me on and we got to work. I like work. Perhaps I like it because it's the only real thing in my life.

We ran through the whole appointment with Richard O'Neil at his club. The jungle in the glass pavilion. The naked swimmers and sunbathers. The personal servants. The strange conversation in the kitchen: seduction, threats, harassment, confession, and plea. And then the final moments in their front lobby. The woman we only saw from behind. The words we heard clearly. "People want it. People get it." The woman had shrugged and said, "And then people pay for it."

Jen said she had assumed it was the boasting of a businesswoman getting rich off the poor schmucks who bought whatever it was she sold. But now the words "pay for it" took on an ominous tint, as if they'd been dipped in a can of blood-red ink.

All because her words were so close to those of Gray Suit. "People want it and pay big dollars to get it. And then they pay for it with their lives."

"Making patterns out of nothing again?" I said.

"The last time wasn't nothing. There *is* a link between the co-op and Eden."

"Although we still don't know what it is."

"Which doesn't mean there isn't a link. But this one, these words are almost exactly the same. The woman at the club spoke them weeks earlier. We need to find her."

* * *

As soon as we arrived at the station, we headed upstairs to Captain Brooks's office. His admin assistant told us he was at a day-long conference for senior officers. Wasn't to be disturbed except for emergencies.

"Have you gotten into more trouble?" the assistant said.

Damn, if everyone wasn't on our case.

We didn't have much to go on. I couldn't access facial ID since we hadn't seen her face. We assumed she was between her mid-fifties and ninety years old because of the gray hair and rounded shoulders, but perhaps she'd had the treatment, and that was just where she'd ended up. I can perfectly recollect conversations, but like I said, I don't store them like a tape recorder, more like a human memory. The upshot was that we couldn't attempt to match the voice.

We tried to search for her through O'Neil's club, but the club had done an incredible job of staying out of sight. I finally did find it, but its presence on the Web made me feel like I was staring at a shiny steel box without any way in. Maybe someone in the world could sneak inside, but it certainly wasn't me.

12:05:48, we caught a ride to the club. It was so hot outside, the tires were starting to melt. I told that to Jen, and she laughed, which made me feel good.

We rang the bell at the club. A voice answered through a speaker. "Who might you be?"

Jen held up her badge in front of the glass eye of a camera and said, "I might be a police officer."

"Yes?"

"I'm looking for information on one of your members."

"Do you have a warrant?"

"No, but—"

"Information on our membership is confidential. Sorry, but I'm not going to be of any use to you."

The voice was gone.

"Maybe," Jen said to me, "we should sleep here on the walkway and wait for that woman to return."

"I don't think that—"

"Chandler, it was—"

"Oh, right."

"Any bright ideas?" she said.

"Call Richard O'Neil."

"What a great idea. I disobey the lawyer. And then to soften O'Neil up, I could start by apologizing for not lying in court. You could then apologize for slugging his son. Then, to get off the civil suit, I'll beg for his son to lie in court to save my ass. Next, I'd have sex with him to show I really do have a thing for 112-year-olds. And then I could pop the question: Who was that woman and what's her connection to an illegal form of the treatment?"

"Do you have a better idea?" I said.

* * *

"Oh, hello, Detective Lu." That silken voice again. "This is Jaisha."

"I'm hoping I could speak to Richard."

Nice touch, I said.

"He isn't available at this moment. Perhaps you might tell me what this is about."

"Uh, not really. Let him know we called."

"We?"

"An expression. Could you let him know I really need to speak to him? It's pretty urgent."

Ask if he's in DC.

"Is he in town?"

Jaisha said, "I will give him your message."

Ten minutes later, she called back: "Eleven PM at his club."

* * *

As we arrived, a couple was getting cozied into a private car, the back door held open by a driver who looked like he could bench-press a cement mixer. A second slab of protection stood off to the side. Once the couple was settled in, he climbed into a chase vehicle.

We rang the door. A more pleasant voice answered, and this one let us into the lobby. Maybe they kept one AI personality for rejections and the other for admission.

Rob was waiting for us. He apologized that Richard was slightly delayed. He led us to the farmhouse kitchen.

I checked and, as on my first visit, I was offline.

Stay cool, Jen said.

Cucumber city.

We sat at the kitchen table. Rob offered Jen a drink. She asked for the iced tea reserved for this club and the Chinese Politburo.

The blue gingham curtains rustled with a breeze from the open window, and with it came a chorus of crickets and frogs. It was dark in this pretend outside, but we could make out the first rows of the cornfield. In the distance, lightning crackled and lit up the sky.

Richard O'Neil's voice startled both of us. "Well, now, this is one surprise I really did not expect." He reached out and shook Jen's hand. "You're cold," he said and held her fingers for 2.3 seconds more. I felt every part of Jen's body grow warmer.

She tipped her head to point down to the glass of iced tea she had been holding. "It's the tea."

He looked at that, then at the pink pitcher on the blue tabletop and said, "I see that Rob is looking after you."

Jen agreed that he was.

O'Neil said, "Rob, Jaisha, and I have been racking our brains to figure out why you wanted to see me. I mean, there are two obvious reasons."

She looked at him, not giving him a clue.

He pushed his baby finger backward with his opposite thumb. "You're hoping to convince me to drop our civil suit against you. That it?"

She shrugged, trying to look mysterious.

"Jen, I need to tell you that would be pretty unlikely. But stranger things have happened."

"Hope springs eternal, and all that."

"Then the second thought." He joined his ring finger to his pinkie and pressed both back. "You've decided it would be really nice to spend some time together." His eyes lit up as they held hers.

She said, "Richard, I need to tell you that would be pretty unlikely. But stranger things, and all that."

That's what she said. I couldn't tell you what she thought. But I *can* tell you that her heartbeat picked up from eighty-two to a ninety-six; sweat pinpricked under her arms and breasts; and I felt things stir that usually only happen when she is with Zach.

Oblivious to all this, or perhaps not, Richard laughed.

"In that case," he continued, "why did you want to see me?"

"It's really a simple question."

He waited.

"When I was last here, right before I left, you were talking to a group of people in the front hall."

O'Neil's eyes looked upward, as if searching for the memory. "We call it the foyer, but yes."

"There was an older woman who was the center of attention. I'd appreciate if you could tell me her name."

"You would, would you?"

"Yep."

"And is there any sort of deal here? Some sort of quid pro quo?"

"Richard, I went to a pretty crappy public school where they didn't offer Latin. I mean, they barely did English, but I'm pretty wise in the ways of the world. Truth is, I don't have much I can offer you, although when the court case is over, my boyfriend and I would love to have you over for dinner."

"Zach," he said.

Jen tried not to look startled.

"Don't worry," he added, "it's merely information. Anyway, I'm pretty sure that my colleague's name is one more thing on that list of 'pretty unlikely' things."

"No 'stranger things' clause?"

"Nope. It's not going to happen. Why are you interested in her?"

"Just am."

O'Neil suddenly sighed, as if a game had come to an abrupt end. "Jen. I met you tonight because . . . well, I met with you. But you screwed us around at the trial. It was fun flirting with you. You're gorgeous, clever, with the most beautiful eyes I've ever seen, and surprisingly kickass, in spite of your reputation. I assumed little if anything would come of it, but that's kind of what flirting is, at least for me. Let's face it: you're a cop making the same in a year as I make by two seconds past midnight on January first. I don't mean that as an insult, but it's simply to say we don't have a lot in common."

"Both Americans."

"Oh, *please*. We scarcely live on the same planet. So, unless there is something else, I actually have a friend here—no, not *her*—who I need to get back to." He turned to Rob. "Rob, will you show Jen out for me?"

O'Neil's handshake was brief when he said goodbye, but he gave her hand a micro-squeeze, a pressure that humans might not consciously notice but which they seem to respond to anyway.

Rob led us through the deserted hallways. The lights had been turned down low during the time we'd been in the kitchen. The building was absolutely still.

I felt it in her. We left the room and Jen's affect was flat as a pancake. But as we walked, energy and anger were silently massing inside her.

We had almost reached the front door when an alarm went off. Not prolonged. More like when a smoke detector sounds off for five seconds. Rob stopped in his tracks, as if focusing on a conversation—and this was the most human gesture of anything I had seen in him, as if multitasking had been programmed out of him to make him more, well, limited.

The short alarm rang again.

Rob said, "I have to run."

Jen said, "I'll let myself out."

Rob hesitated.

Jen said, "Rob, I'm a police officer. Don't worry." With a backward wave of her hand, she shooed him away. "Go." She reached for the doorknob.

Rob took off running, as if his job or his life depended on it. He glanced back before he turned the corner and saw that Jen was stepping over the door's threshold. As he went out of sight, she waved goodbye and was starting to close the door.

Only to come back inside and shut it quietly behind us.

"Jen!"

"Quick, which way to the office? We need to get away from here."

I hadn't seen anything that seemed like admin offices along the hallways to the right, leading to the country kitchen or the greenhouse and swimming pond. "To the left," I said.

We raced out of the foyer, down the dimly lit hallway, and around a corner. Jen slumped against a wall and listened.

"Jen, what the hell are you doing?" I asked.

"Find the office, break in, find a membership log, copy it."

"You're crazy. They catch us and you're toast. Illegal entry, illegal search, trespassing, theft. I could—"

"Chandler, you're being annoying."

"Is this revenge?"

"No, I just don't want some rich guy pushing me around."

She took off down the hall, twisting the knob of the first door we came to. It wasn't locked. We glanced inside and the half-light from the hallway was enough to make out chairs formed into a tight circle. The next door opened to a small meeting room with a central table and controls for an over-table display. We went inside, leaving the door ajar. Jen reached into the projection space.

"Don't!" I shouted.

It came to life, but it was only a system to initiate a teleconference. I was about to say we needed to get the hell out, when a noise from the hallway caused Jen to jerk her head around. The door pushed open. Just as we were ducking down, a vacuum scurried into the room like a rat. We stepped over it and continued along the hallway. We hit a locked door.

"Can we do anything?" she said.

"Maybe, but you'd probably leave an entry record."

We tried the rest of the doors along the hallway and found just one unlocked, housing several printers of various sizes.

It was a messy room, unlike the rest of the place. No matter how exclusive a joint might be, every luxury liner has an engine room. We shut the door, and Jen turned on her phone light. Boxes of paper were stacked four feet high. Metal shelves held envelopes and other supplies. And a table had a computer station.

"Do I need to tell you 'don't' again?" I asked.

"Probably not."

"What's come over you?"

She tapped the screen to life.

User not recognized, the message onscreen said. *Enter manual passcodes.*

"Can you brute force it?"

"Sure, I'll recite several billion ASCII combinations while you input them."

Jen typed in "RichSnobs"—nothing. She tried "RichShits."

"What are you doing?" I said.

"They're workers. You expect them to like their bosses?"

"Stop, before you trigger security."

This time, Jen listened.

She aimed her light around the room until it reached a bin marked "For shredder." We rushed over and started rummaging. This was one quaint group of people, to still print things out. We pulled out reports, memos, notices, and printed invitations, scanned them and dropped them to the floor. Nothing with members' names. We stared down into the near-empty bin, and right as we noticed pages from what appeared to be a membership directory, someone pushed open the door.

At the first sound, I killed her light, and we dived behind a stack of boxes as a hand reached in and the room lights flipped on.

We stared out between two boxes and saw a cleaning trolley roll into the room.

"Well, damn if my job isn't hard enough!" It was a woman's voice. I had assumed they were all service units here, but clearly not. She wasn't more than three feet from us, but on the other side of the boxes. Jen's heart was pounding like the engine of a freight train, and I bathed her with alpha waves to settle her down. The cleaning woman grabbed handfuls of paper off the floor and stuffed them into a large hemp bag on her cart, complaining nonstop as she did.

Don't look in the bin, Jen thought, but the cleaner noticed there was more paper there, lifted up the bin and dumped the rest of the contents into her bag.

She turned away from us. She emptied a garbage can. She gave a cursory wipe to a worktable and the tops of the printers.

"Damn if my job isn't hard enough," she repeated, turned out the lights, and left.

"Jen, we've been in this place too long. We need to fly."

We went to the door. Pressed our ear to it, then reached for the knob. For the first time that night, I could feel a tremor in Jen's hand. She opened the door a crack. Listened again.

"Ready?" Jen said.

"That's my job."

As we were leaving the room, Jen glanced back inside. The dim light from the hallway reflected something on the wall. "Jen, no!" She ducked back inside the room, shut the door, and turned on her light.

On the wall were six glossy photographs, each showing a group of well-heeled members posing in the foyer—like annual photos of their board of directors. They weren't framed, but instead appeared to be the work of a staff member who had kept these proofs and hung them as a rogue's gallery.

By this point, even I was about to start shaking. But damn if Jen didn't stay cool and, as if she had all night, took a snap of each picture.

We finally raced down the hallway, peeked out into the foyer, and then shot through the front door.

Jen walked calmly away from the building, like she belonged there. A block away she started running. Four blocks away, my boss whooped with delight into the night.

30

That week had started in promising fashion but quickly turned sour, which proves you should never get too charmed by beginnings. First thing on Tuesday morning, Jennifer put Chandler to work identifying the people in the six photos. Chandler claimed it was tough work—"busting my balls," was the nice way he put it. In each shot, there were sixteen, seventeen, or eighteen people, but approximately half overlapped from one picture to another, presumably one year to the next. There were forty-seven unique individuals. Most of them appeared younger than the woman Jen and Chandler had seen from behind. Of the fourteen older ones, equal numbers clearly self-identified as male or female, and two did not. They knew they'd be lucky if their woman was in one of those photos. However, now viewing the figures from the front, Chandler was able to compare the slope of the shoulders he remembered, and at least get some hints from the hair, although that might have changed between then and now. They narrowed it down to three women.

The first was a woman Jen hadn't needed Chandler to ID. She was a flamboyant entrepreneur who had died two years before in a staggeringly expensive tourist jaunt around the moon.

The second was born in Hong Kong, to Chinese and Dutch parents. She was now based near Bordeaux, although that didn't mean anything—she could be here in a few hours. She had been a big deal in Shell Oil. She now had massive holdings in power generation and, apparently as her idea of a hobby, she co-owned Château Rothschild.

The third was a US-Swiss citizen who flitted between New York, DC, and Zurich. Teena Archambault had made her first five hundred million as an investment banker. She had served in the US Cabinet as Secretary of Commerce and still seemed to have strong political connections. She had more or less retired, but after the treatment—she apparently chose to stay in her sixties, although she could redo that later—she'd returned to work as senior vice president for government relations for GPRA, part of the consortium that produced the treatment.

Twenty minutes later, Jen was on the roof with Captain Brooks. The harsh morning sun ricocheted off the surrounding buildings, and Jen again needed to cup her hand across her forehead to keep her eyeballs from frying. Ten seconds up here and her body was feeling sticky; by the one-minute mark, sweat was dribbling down her face and neck and from her underarms down her sides. And it took only another minute for the sweat to evaporate into the windy, parched air. It was ninety-five degrees of misery on the streets. The roof must have been a hundred and ten.

"How did you identify her?" Brooks asked.

"It was Chandler."

"And you'd seen her just that once at O'Neil's club a month ago—"

"Three and a half weeks ago."

"—yet he was still able to make the match?"

The wind whipped Jen's hair into her face.

"And all this because you remembered the similarity between what this woman said and Teko Teko Mea?" Brooks pressed.

"That's not his real name."

"No?"

"Chandler figured that out too. In Maori, *Mea* more or less means 'what's-his-name.' And *Teko Teko* means 'nonsense.' He's making fun of us."

"Why would he do that?"

"His real name is Taika Mete. He's head of security for Xeno/Roberts/Chu. The pharmaceutical company."

"I know who they are."

"Sorry, sir."

"Give me a moment."

Brooks pulled a phone from his pocket, which surprised her, because she'd seen him leave his mobile on his desk before they came up here. He wandered away from her to the edge of the roof, and a moment later was speaking quietly to someone.

When he returned, he said, "It's good work, Jen. What you found out. It's exceptionally good work."

She smiled, but only enough to say thank you without making a big deal out of it.

"This is going to stay between us for now, right?"

"Yes sir," she said, but she still wondered what the hell was going on.

After a long pause, he said, "Tell me, Jen."

Tell me, she thought. This didn't sound anything like the Captain Brooks she'd known for years.

"Tell me why you turned Chandler off back in June?"

"Sir?"

"I'm curious. I'd like to know."

She wondered if this was a trick, or perhaps a test. And yet she suddenly wanted to tell him the truth. Not to impress him, not to please him, but to tell him the truth.

"Chandler's great, but . . . well, I wanted to be by myself for a minute. That's all."

He nodded.

She said, "Why are you asking, sir?"

He ignored her question. "Run the whole thing by me again. What each of them said. What you found out about them."

As she began her recitation, she noticed pale smoke coming from the direction of Rock Creek Park. By the end of her summation it was dark and thick.

"Sir." She pointed behind him. "I think there's a fire in the park."

*   *   *

A year of drought had been capped by the past six weeks without a single drop of rain. Rock Creek Park was an enormous pile of dried wood waiting for a match. Since its sale to Disney, the National Park Service had defunded services in all its parks that didn't charge admission, so NPS was no help. The creek itself was down to a trickle, and the only hydrants were in places like the planetarium and the neighborhoods that wiggled along the edges of the park. The flames fed on dead leaves and bone-dry wood, and the wind was like a giant bellows, whipping fire from one tree to the next and sending sparks shooting through the air. Fire engines roared in from across DC and the Maryland and Virginia suburbs, but even a thousand gallons from a tanker truck was no match for the rapidly spreading blaze. Within two hours, the southern half of the forest was in flames. Fire engines surrounded the park from Military Road on down and shot so much water from hydrants onto the trees and lawns around its perimeter that water pressure plummeted in the rest of the city. By then, air tankers had arrived from Pennsylvania and Virginia and were dumping tens of thousands of gallons of water and fire retardant.

Jennifer and Brooks had charged downstairs and, like just about every other cop in the city, rushed to the fire wearing their N95s or half face-piece respirators. Uniforms were stationed in points surrounding the park to keep onlookers away, help emergency vehicles get through, and redirect cars that were overriding their emergency rerouting. Other officers evacuated schools, daycare centers, and nursing homes that were downwind of the fire. Jen was one of many assigned to go door to door, urging people to grab their ID, a few valuables, and prescription meds, and evacuate, not only because of the possibility their house could be eaten by flames, but because smoke was engulfing the southeast side of the park and beyond.

By the early afternoon, they caught a break. The morning's fierce winds from the northeast ended. Smoke now billowed straight into the air. The fire was no longer being fanned, and sparks were no longer shooting to other trees or surrounding neighborhoods.

By the end of the day, the fire ran out of fuel. The southern half of the park was a cemetery of smoldering skeletons of trees. The planetarium, where the fire appeared to have started, was destroyed. Fourteen people had died from smoke inhalation or traffic accidents. An estimated six thousand people were taken to the hospital with severe respiratory problems, and by the end of the week, two hundred and fifty-eight of them were dead. A newlywed couple who had set off on a picnic were never found and were presumed incinerated. Twenty horses that couldn't be evacuated on time from the Horse Center had burned to death. The fire hadn't reached up to the new Viridian Green Country Club nor down to the Smithsonian Zoo, although heavy smoke had left dozens of animals either dead or very sick. Miraculously, only thirty neighboring houses had burned down, but hundreds had been soaked through by jets of water to prevent the fire from spreading. Thirty thousand people were in emergency shelters, and many more were with friends, although most were expected to return home in the next few days. Buildings, particularly to the southeast, were blackened by ash. The gleaming white dome of the Capitol, directly in the path of the predominant wind, was now gray.

Much of DC smelled like a giant campfire. Luckily, it was mainly the clean smell of wood smoke rather than the sour stench of extinguished house fires. Columbia Heights had caught a lot of smoke and ash, but Leah and Raffi had been home and had managed to shut their windows and those of their downstairs neighbors before they had fled. They had returned at dinnertime. The roof was dusted with a half inch of ash, but inside wasn't bad. Or rather, Jen was so saturated with smoke that she wouldn't have smelled anything if she had stuck her head into a fireplace.

Water was being rationed throughout DC, but for the thirty minutes it flowed to Columbia Heights, they showered and filled buckets, cooking pots, sinks, and the bathtub, so Jen managed to wash the ashes, sweat, and grime off herself.

They ate dinner, falling silent whenever a voice on the news feed caught their attention. Otherwise, they did what hundreds of thousands of other DC residents were doing at that moment: exchanged stories and expressed their total disbelief that this awful event had happened. And then suddenly the four of them, overwhelmed, would become mute.

Zach had to go out for a CASP meeting to thrash out a statement about the fire, the continuing impact of climate change, and the need for greater action. Jen kissed him goodnight and crawled into bed at nine. Only then did she check the messages that had accumulated that day, and spotted the notice from the clinic where she'd been tested at the end of the previous week.

The first screen said, These are your test results for ROSE markers. You may wish to be with your doctor, health care professional, or religious official when you read the results.

Screw it, she thought. *I'm tough.*

The short message was wrapped in niceties and probabilities and encouraging new research. But the basic meaning was, *Dear Jen. You're screwed.*

She had tested positive for the presence of the prions that, unless she received some version of the treatment, would spread and kill her in an absolutely terrifying and horrible way.

Fortunately, she was going to make sure her mother did her duty and exited in seven weeks. Jen would receive the attenuated treatment. She was tough; she would be fine.

And yet, she ran to the bathroom and threw up.

Is anyone, she wondered, *tough enough to receive a death sentence, even if they're pretty sure it's going to be commuted?*

* * *

The next two days passed in a blur as Jen, Les, Hammerhead, and Amanda joined hundreds of other cops trudging from apartment to apartment, and house to house, ensuring that everyone was accounted for and no one was having severe health problems. Perhaps it was this enervating task, but she found it impossible to shake off a deep sense of dread. Her test results. The beautiful park gone. The recent turmoil with Zach. A flash of Richard O'Neil and the disturbing question of why the hell she was still thinking about him. Despair ambushed her when she was least expecting it.

On the other hand, although she didn't have the time or energy to think much about Teena Archambault or Taika Mete, it was hard not to keep coming back to the lethal counterfeit treatment. There were daily reports of more deaths in DC and other cities. Everyone in the city—and all across the country—was receiving hyperbolic text alerts from the DEA and local health officials cautioning them about the illegal treatment. The messages ended in uppercase letters: REPORT ANYONE SELLING THIS DRUG. HELP SAVE A LIFE!

Meanwhile, police in four cities, including DC, had made their first arrests, but so far these had led nowhere. There were two doctors, one nurse, an ex-army medic, one veterinarian, a pharmacist, and a med student. All had been approached by phone to do one set of treatments. All received the meds and instructions by a drop that couldn't be traced. All had, as instructed, burned whatever they could when they finished and destroyed the rest. None could identify anyone. All had been promised a hefty payment and all had been stiffed. All were charged with a dozen things, including manslaughter.

A report raced through the police force that the fire had been started by four Timeless who had sedated and then burned themselves on a funeral pyre built behind the Planetarium. There had been an online suicide note: *Just let us die.* Yeah, and take a park with you. But this got no mention in any of the media, and by the next day, there seemed to be no one who had actually read the note or had evidence of a group suicide.

The growing alarm about the deadly instant-aging counterfeit treatment, combined with the destruction of so much of the park, created a widespread feeling of impending doom. A child's two-hour disappearance became a ring of child snatchers; an electrical brownout became the likelihood of a total breakdown of the power grid; the departure of the president and vice president for summer holidays became their escape before a major terrorist incident ripped apart the city. For Jennifer, the sense of doom was aggravated by her test results—about which she still hadn't breathed a word to Zach or anyone else.

And into the mix came the first attempt in five years to organize a protest against exit and the restrictions on the attenuated treatment. And there they were, Jen and Zach, having recently made up and now on opposite sides of the barricades.

31

"**A**ction time!"

"Chandler," the boss said to me, "they have a constitutional right to protest."

"Then why are the head-whackers lined up at the plaza?"

"Because no one has the constitutional right to disturb the peace."

"You got my joke." The head-whackers. Formerly the Crowd Control Unit, but since going private, the Crowd Control Ultras or, in shorthand, the Ultras. Known for their not-so-gentle crowd control methods.

Jen and I were a block away from Freedom Plaza, where a few hundred people were assembling for the "No Exit!" lunchtime march. They were surrounded by Ultras covered in armored black fatigues and armed for the next invasion of Saudi Arabia. Jen was hopeful we wouldn't be near any action, but it was within our district, and we'd all been mobilized as backup.

"Shit," Jen said. We were staring at Zach, who was walking along the opposite sidewalk with a woman I hadn't seen before but who seemed to register with Jen. "Keep your mouth shut, Chandler."

I'd already endured one long argument between the two of them yesterday afternoon.

"It's not only the horrible trade-off," Zach had said. "I figure exit was introduced as a safety valve. Those with power give us a limited version of the treatment, not so much to cut the population, but to reduce social tensions and anger at the rich."

188

Jen had said, "Doesn't mean you shouldn't do it."

"But," Zach had continued, "it keeps people on a short leash. You need to get the boosters. Who would want to lose further access to the drug, especially after your parents died so you could get it? They can control people forever."

I was surprised to find I kept thinking about what Zach had said.

We waited for a break in the traffic, dashed across the street, and cut off Zach and the woman before they reached the Plaza. Jen didn't even bother looking at the woman.

"You came."

"I needed to," Zach replied.

"They're filming everyone who steps onto that block."

There had been public warnings that participation in "public unrest" could make people ineligible for the modified treatment. As one congressman put it, "You don't like exit, that's your business, but we shouldn't waste taxpayers' money giving you the treatment."

Zach said, "I'm here so the government won't think it can intimidate people and keep them from speaking out."

"Zach, there are at most six hundred people in that square. Seems it worked."

"Not on me. Isn't that where we all have to start?"

Finally, we looked at the woman. Thick hair pulled into a braid, thick eyebrows, closing in on middle age. I scanned her face.

"Ximena," said Jen by way of greeting. And she said to me, *I met her at the co-op house when I was off duty.*

"Hello, Jen." Thin accent. Colombian. Ximena Maleena, age forty-nine, immigrated here when she was fourteen, no arrests, lots of activism, mother.

Jen looked down the block and back. She looked at Zach. "Please, don't go. You're making a decision that affects both of us."

"I don't mean it that way."

Ximena jumped in. "This is peaceful."

"Promise me to get out of here if there's even a whiff of trouble."

Zach stared at Jen. "Is there something you know that I don't?"

"We heard rumors, that's all. People on the march who want trouble."

He looked at us, but I couldn't read if his emotion was defiant or conciliatory. His face turned down the block. "I'm sorry, Jen, we got to go."

Jen's face was neutral, but inside, she was a one-woman wrestling match. However, she managed to reach out, touch his arm, and say, "Be careful—that's all."

We watched them walk to the Plaza and pass through an opening between the ranks of Ultras.

"Keep it zipped, Chandler."

The group had a permit to march on the E Street NW sidewalk, down 10th for one block to Pennsylvania Avenue, and along the sidewalk to the side of the ash-darkened Capitol building, where they'd hear speeches.

Soon the march was on the move and chanting away. "Treatment for All!" "Hey hey, ho ho, exit killing's got to go." "Two, four, six, eight, we don't want a killing state." All pretty dreary except for a spirited rendition of "Oh! Susanna": "Oh! Susanna, oh don't you die for me / For I come from Alabama, where the treatment should be free."

It happened two blocks down E Street, at the old FBI building, a gray-grim concrete fortress that the trumpets should have brought down ages ago—they say when it was built, the masons used truncheons to smack the wet cement into place. TV videographers were filming from the top of the stairs under the gloomy arcade that fronted the building. A line of cops from our district was positioned to keep protestors away.

Without warning, some guy wearing a black bandanna across his face and gripping a can of spray paint burst through the police line and took the concrete stairs two at a time. He made it to the top and aimed the paint at one of the square pillars, but before even one neon-orange letter was completed, a cop grabbed him from behind. The protestor shot his elbow back and connected with the cop's chin, causing the officer to flail backward and tumble down the stairs. Ultras stormed through the police line and pounced on the black bandana guy from every direction; a moment later, they dragged him away.

All hell broke loose. Ultras were throwing people to the ground, ramming others with their shields, and thwacking down wherever their clubs could find flesh and bone. Protestors scrambled to escape, many trying to drag a bloodied friend to safety, while others crouched beside a fallen comrade, only to get whacked themselves. The noise was enormous. We ran across the street and pushed through the panicking demonstrators, pulling apart fights and trying without luck to spot Zach. All around us, protestors screamed, cops shouted, photographers snapped, horns honked as cameramen filmed, and pedestrians held up phones or covered their mouths in horror.

It was all over in eight minutes.

*　*　*

"Tell me again," Zach said, "that you didn't know that was going to happen."

It was a half hour later, and Jen was on her phone with him.

"We'd heard rumors, that's all."

"You—"

"Zach, I'm phoning to make sure you're okay, not to have an argument."

He let out a huff of air. "I'm . . . pissed off. I'm really upset."

"I tried to find you and Ximena."

"We were near the back. Hadn't even gotten to the FBI building. The SWAT—"

"—Ultras—"

"—troops attacked from behind, but we got away. God, what an idiot." And then as if he might think we misunderstood, "Whoever that guy was. No one seems to know who he was."

"Any idea why he chose the FBI building?" Jen asked. I'd already asked her the same question, wondering if it had anything to do with the FBI issuing reports around the street treatment.

"Dunno. Probably because no one likes the FBI."

I felt Jen thaw. "See," she said, "there are some political things we agree about."

There was a brief hesitation, and then he laughed. A tentative, nervous laugh, but still a laugh.

Jen said, "I better go."

"Enough fraternizing with the enemy?"

"You're not—"

"Teasing you. Tonight?"

"Tonight."

After they hung up, Jen told me to pull up the sheet on the spray painter. Got a name. Saw a dozen charges. "Who is he?" Jen asked. I searched. Damn it, he didn't actually exist.

32

"Ximena's really pissed off."

"She must be," Jen replied. Just she and Zach having dinner at the kitchen table. The air tense, that morning's demo still on both their minds.

Zach studied her as if trying to decide if she was being sarcastic.

"I'm serious," Jen said. "I like her."

"That guy, what's he been charged with?"

"Assault causing bodily harm, resisting arrest, defacing government property, and disturbing the peace."

"Jesus."

"And article four of the 2027 Urban Terrorism Act. Zach, did you find out anything more about him?"

Zach shook his head.

They ate silently until Jen said, "This is really good," not so much because it was, but to break the silence.

Zach set down his knife and fork.

"Jen, I can't have them do it." She knew he meant his mother and father. "It's just, well, I love them more than anything, and they don't deserve to die."

"I got my test results."

He looked at her with alarm.

"On Tuesday. I didn't want to tell you."

He started to speak but caught her expression.

"I'm positive, Zach. I . . ." A few tears escaped her eyes, but she steeled herself. "I don't want to cry, Zach. I don't want to let myself cry."

But when he laid his hand on hers, she couldn't stop the quiet sobs of fear and defeat.

She wiped her eyes. She talked about getting the results. How she was scared to tell him.

"Scared?"

"Not of anything you'd do or say. Scared to say it out loud."

"It'll be okay."

"It's funny. All I've been able to think about for the past year was finally having Mother out of my life forever. I knew it might save me, but it was all so abstract. But this changes it, doesn't it? I sign those papers, I'm killing her so I can live."

"You're—"

"Of course I am, and you know it."

"But you said it yourself: she might not last for another five years."

"Then it's okay to kill her?"

"No," he said. "But I want you to live."

"And her to die?"

"That's not what I said."

"It's all pretty awful, isn't it?"

"Yeah." Zach shook his head. "It is."

"Your parents, I don't want them to die either. But I want us to live and have a place and . . ."

"I know."

"Do you think they'll agree? Not exiting?"

"I have a few months to convince them."

"Zach, I'm still going to sign those papers."

They were silent for a long time.

The sun set.

The kitchen grew dark.

She starting to get up. "I'll get the light."

"No, wait," he said.

"What?"

"If we could get the treatment—not the stuff that's killing people—but if we could somehow get it . . . would you?"

She could not make out his expression, which meant he couldn't make out hers.

* * *

With an unspoken agreement, they spent the rest of the weekend without once mentioning exit or the treatment or the demonstration. That lasted until Sunday night. Jen was reading a book; Zach was writing out the schedule for planting a big garden, assuming the weather cooled down a bit and the rains started again in the fall. It was handwritten in neat columns of dates and plans. Month Day: Work Item.

Zach had just written *October 20:* and had his pencil poised as if to write down a task, when he stopped. His eyes fixed on the distance.

"Jen, remember your Bible quotes?"

"What about them?"

"Maybe they weren't quotes. Maybe it was some sort of code for dates." He was quiet for a moment, then said, "Acts could be April or August."

"Acts 12:19."

"Could be April or August twelfth or nineteenth."

"Or two dates," she said. "Twelfth *and* nineteenth."

"And that makes sense for the Bible passage that didn't exist."

"John 9:16."

"Could be January, June, or July. But this doesn't work for Ephesians. Last I checked, no month starts with *E*."

"But she wrote it 'Spesians.'"

"September."

"September fourth or eleventh. Or fourth and eleventh."

"Jen, see the pattern? In each set, add seven to the first and you get the second number."

Like giving counterfeit treatments. One week apart.

* * *

After that, all Jen could think about for the rest of Sunday evening was the one person she really needed to speak to.

195

On Monday afternoon, she was back on the rooftop, facing Captain Brooks. Strange things had been happening that day around the station. When she tried to find the captain in the morning, his assistant said he was at a meeting. Hammerhead had a different take: "Three guys I never seen come and take him away."

"You mean like arresting him?"

Hammerhead laughed at the absurdity of this. "Then again," he said, no longer laughing, "they were definitely escorting him to their car."

The captain was back four hours later.

Someone had left out a couple of plastic chairs on the roof, perhaps from a lunchtime break, and Brooks, looking more tired than Jen had ever seen him, was leaning heavily on one of them.

"This better be good," he said.

Shit, she thought. "It's, well—"

"Detective, it's been a hell of a day. Spit it out, will you?"

"I think I figured out who's distributing the treatment, at least one of them." She told him about the stolen Bible and the missing receipts. She told him what was written on the missing slip.

"You remembered all that?"

"Chandler helped. I thought they were Bible quotes. You know, chapter and verse. But one verse didn't exist, and none of them seemed worth quoting. I think they're actually dates, in a simple code, one week apart. And each date, one month apart—July, August, and September. I think it was Odette Johnson's note to herself. She was helping run a clinic for the co-ops. She was working with doctors. I'm guessing they were the ones administering this Eden."

"The one that's killing people."

And here Jen hesitated. It just wasn't consistent with her impression of Mary Sue and Ximena. Nor even Devin, who seemed a hothead, but not a murderer.

"It's smart work, Jen. But you're right to hesitate. I don't think it's them . . . It's not them. Forget that."

"But—"

"I've got—"

"Sir, there's one other thing. At the demo about exit, that guy who tried to spray paint the FBI building."

"What about him?"

"He doesn't exist."

"Where is he now?"

"He was released on bail. With an electronic anklet. But we just checked and the anklet is back in inventory."

He shook his head in disgust. "It still happens."

Jen didn't need to be told this. In fact, whenever she heard that violence had broken out at a demonstration, or some fringe group had smashed up windows, she figured it was because a police agent provocateur had done it or pushed someone into it. Violence didn't win you allies; violence made you easy to isolate and discredit.

Under his breath, the captain muttered, "Special Assignments."

"Sir?"

"Nothing. To use the old cliché, above your pay grade."

Jen almost rolled her eyes.

Brooks must have noticed. He said, "I guess no one says that anymore."

"Sir, I think that went out with pumpkin spices in coffee."

He smiled. For the first time in recorded District 1 history, Captain Brooks smiled. A weary smile, perhaps, but there it was.

Then, just as quickly, the smile departed to a distant galaxy, and his face sagged under the weight of exhaustion. He slumped down onto the plastic seat and leaned forward, propping his elbows on his knees. He rubbed at the scar above his eye.

Jen didn't quite know what to do with this, so she started to wander to the edge of the roof to look out at the view.

"Don't go over there," he barked. "I don't want anyone seeing you."

This whole roof business, she thought, *is so weird.* But she turned back, and he waved a hand at the other chair. When she sat down, it felt as if they'd come up for a friendly chat, which made her feel not relaxed, but awkward and stiff.

"Tell me, Jen . . . tell me why you became a cop."

"I don't know. Decent pay, a real job. Do some good."

"That's a beauty contest answer."

"That was a beauty contest question. Sir."

197

This time he didn't smile.

What the hell, she thought. "Actually, I wanted to put people like my mother in prison."

He looked at her sharply.

"She was abusive, sir. Really abusive. No one big act, just years of misery inflicted on me."

"And now you're arresting parents who don't kill themselves."

"Well, we—"

"You know what I mean. It's all pretty fucked, isn't it?"

To Jen, it felt like hearing a priest swear.

"That's what my boyfriend's been telling me. I don't know what I think."

"So, have you changed anything. Done good?"

"I don't know. I try."

The obvious then occurred to her. His questions were as much to himself as to her.

"Sir, why did *you*?" He seemed not to hear her. "You know, become a cop?"

He now looked at her with suspicion.

"Sir, I read this article about the DC18, by a journalist who lives at my mother's retirement home," she said.

"Let me guess. Gabriel Cohen."

Jen nodded.

"Jesus," he said. "Twice in one day." He was talking to himself. "Nothing for years, and now twice in one fucking day."

He looked up at her, his hard eyes clawing into her face. She willed herself not to flinch, but it did no good and she dropped her gaze.

"Listen to me carefully," Brooks said. "If anyone asks you about us coming up here, don't lie. Say we did, tell them the number of times. But don't tell them what we discussed. Say we never talked about work. Say I told you to leave your phone downstairs and turn off your synth. Say we talked about everyday things, the weather, that I asked you what you liked eating, we talked baseball, I asked what you did on your time off. That I never said much, that I never hit on you, that I'd ask you questions and you'd talk. And if they say you're bullshitting them, say you thought it was weird yourself. But you thought it was because I was lonely. Since my wife died—that sort of thing. Say you figured I needed someone to talk to, figured I needed a woman to talk to, just about boring, ordinary things. Say you figured I was embarrassed to talk, and that's why I had you turn off your synth."

"Sir, I don't—"

"You don't need to understand. Right now, you just need to listen."

He waited until she nodded.

"I need to hear it. A promise."

"Sir, I promise."

"This is to save your skin. And maybe do that bit of good you talked about."

"And then?"

"Don't trust a soul."

She thought of Les. Of Zach. Of Chandler. "No one?"

Pain was now etched into those hard eyes of his. "If they're still breathing, don't fucking trust them."

33

Jen popped me out of diagnostic mode. When she left me, she had been an anxious preteen heading for her first merit badge test; now, the agitated woman in my head was pulsing anxiety off the chart.

"You okay, boss?"

No response. Bad sign. The captain must have chewed her out good.

"And don't," she added, "pump me with your damn drugs."

I was going to say they were *her* damn drugs, but I decided to can it.

Earlier, while she had waited for Brooks to return, we had spent the morning digging up whatever we could about Teena Archambault, the woman in the *foyer* of Richard O'Neil's club. There were reams of info—reams being another one of those near antiquated words humans hang on to, this one referring to a large stack or packet of paper. Although I guess not totally antiquated, since Jen and I had hidden behind reams of paper in the print room of said club—

Where was I? I'm finding as my mind expands, it's becoming harder to stick with one train of thought.

Start again. There were reams of info about her career and good community deeds, photos of her shaking hands with other movers and shakers, and stories about what her one child was up to. Nothing explicitly said she was one of the Timeless, but then again, nothing ever did. There was no official list, you just assumed if some ultra-rich eighty-year-old showed up on a skateboard with their tongue newly pierced, he or she had gotten the full treatment. It was sort of like the old days in Hollywood, when actual people still played the role of stars and there were A-list and B-list actors, even though there were no actual lists.

As we'd suspected, it did seem she had indeed taken the treatment and had chosen to look in her late sixties. Her current position was senior vice president for government relations for GPRA, which probably meant she was the de facto ruler of several countries. She'd been recruited not only for her industry experience, but for her Rolodex—aha! another antiquated word—that included names in very high places. She seemed to spend no time at the GPRA Tower in London, or in any of their other offices, for that matter. She had homes in Zurich and Manhattan, and a superyacht wherever it wanted to be.

Finally, in the mid-afternoon, we knew we were closing in. There she was, in a photograph taken at a Fourth of July party at the White House, standing between the president and vice president, both of whom seem pleased as punch to be with her.

By four, we found her—or at least the building in DC where she was working. The Dwight D. Eisenhower Executive Office Building, or EOB, home of the offices of the vice president of the United States, along with many White House staff.

"Chandler," Jen said, "grab your coat."

*   *   *

When I was young, I never got awed by anything I saw. Things were things. But after hanging around the dump we call our District headquarters and visiting more buildings and homes than anyone other than a bio-computer could count, I've developed not only a large database but also an appreciation for style. The EOB had it in spades, especially, I read as we headed over on foot, after its 2027–2028 renovation. I'll spare you the architectural tour, but let's just say that the interior circular staircase was worth the price of admission. Jen said she could see why the building was her housemate Ava's favorite.

The security check made the airport routine look like flipping a latch on a toilet cubicle. Eventually, we made it through and took the elevator up to an office on the fourth floor. A pleasant-looking young man sat at an ornate cherrywood table, which held a neat stack of papers, an oversized coffee mug, and a computer screen that looked like a sheet of glass poised above the table.

Jen produced her badge. "We'd like to ask Ms. Archambault a few questions concerning an ongoing investigation."

"One minute," he said. He went to a door, knocked, and disappeared inside.

We sat down on one of two chairs that served as a reception area. This place obviously wasn't set up to entertain the masses.

He returned and repeated, "One minute." Nice and polite. Neatly dressed. He sat at his table, his back to us.

Perhaps they count differently in these higher reaches, but one minute it wasn't. Jen read on her phone. Boring stuff. I said we should look around the office. *Nothing to see,* she said, but she graciously scanned the room for me. It was elegant like no office I'd ever seen, but there was nothing that gave away what they were doing there. *You win,* I said.

She continued reading. After a while, she must have gotten bored, too, because she spent some time watching the nice-looking man as he read through a paper report, hand-writing notes on the side.

His phone rang. We looked up again. He listened. "One second," he said, "let me check his calendar." *Head down,* I said, and Jen pretended to read her phone but watched him, head lowered, looking up through her lashes. He pulled out a drawer under the ornate table and rested his fingers on his mousepad. The clear screen above his desk darkened. Only when he looked at the screen did it come to life. He touched an icon. Jen could make out a calendar, but it was all fuzzy, like hers before she typed in her secondary password. His hands seemed to hover over his keyboard.

"Crap," he said under his breath.

And damn if he didn't pick up the oversized coffee mug, drain the remaining coffee, and then hold it upside down as he one-finger-typed a password.

I wish, I said to Jen, *that I had a head to shake in disbelief. No wonder systems keep getting hacked.* Jen shook her head for me.

It might be helpful if we could get in there, I said.

Maybe I should give him a big smile and ask him.

It was a full twenty-four minutes before another nice-looking young man came out to speak to us. They seemed to go for nice-looking young men in old-school Ivy League attire around this joint.

"May I see your ID?" he said. He may have been polished, but he was as smarmy as they come.

Jen held it out, and if I hadn't known better, I would have sworn he had his own synth who was now looking up Jen's record.

"May I see yours?" she said.

"My what?"

"Your ID. Make sure you are who you say you are."

The man looked startled. "I haven't said I'm anything."

"That would be a hint."

"I work for Ms. Archambault."

"Do you have a name?"

"Yes."

"Would you like to share your name?"

"No. And unless you suspect me of committing a crime, I needn't tell you. Need I?"

She lashed him just about the most withering look she could pull off, but the guy didn't even flinch, let alone wither.

"As I was saying," continued Jen, trying to regain the momentum, "I'd like to ask Ms. Archambault a few questions."

"About what?"

"About whatever I'd like to ask her about."

This was going extremely well.

"One moment."

This time it was.

"I'm sorry," he said when he came back, "that won't be possible."

"Who may I speak to?"

"What is this about?"

I expect this could have gone on well into the next century, but just then, the office door opened, and who should stroll right past the receptionist other than Taika Mete, aka Teko Teko Mea. I caught the expression on his face, a flash of surprise with a glint of fear, and then both were gone. He was good.

"Detective," Teko Teko said, and there was almost warmth in his voice, "what brings you here to see us?"

Smart guy. Not, *How the hell did you find out where I worked?*

"Hello, Mr. Mea."

"'May-uh,'" he said, "not 'mee-uh.'"

"Actually I came to see your boss, Ms. Archambault."

Nice countermove.

"Ms. . . . ?"

I noticed the assistant, or whatever he was, subtly move his head to signal to Teko Teko Mea. Jen noticed too, because she said, *Saw it.*

"Archambault," he said quickly recovering. He turned to the assistant, but now with ice in his voice he said, "Is that possible, Giorgio?"

"Sir, she's tied up."

Teko Teko spread his hands by way of apology. "Too bad. Maybe come back another time."

Giorgio said, "She's leaving for—"

Teko Teko flashed the assistant a look that told him to go find a comfortable place to kill himself.

Jen said, "What's the name of this office?"

"I don't believe it has a name. We have this space to deal with a crisis."

He didn't smile.

"So, no way I can speak to her?"

He didn't respond. The question had already been answered. However, he pinched her elbow and sent a lightning bolt of pain through Jen. He tugged us toward the open door of a side room. "But I think it's time for you and me to have a coffee together."

It was a small but elegant conference room with large windows and a chandelier sparkling above a mahogany table, American Empire, mid-nineteenth century.

Teko Teko let go of her. I could sense Jen was trying to think of something clever to say, but residual pain in her arm was gumming up her thought processes, and the pounding of her heart was so loud I expected to see the crystals on the chandelier shake.

Teko Teko motioned Jen to a chair and sat down opposite her. He didn't offer any coffee.

"You have some explaining to do," he said.

"About?"

He didn't answer. He'd obviously taken Interrogation 101: Don't let your prisoner know what you don't know.

"What? Why I'm here?" Jen said.

"That would be a good start."

"Could I have a glass of water?"

He didn't budge.

Just lie, I said.

Jen said, "As you know, we're trying to shut down the illegal treatment."

He didn't speak.

"I'm following every imaginable lead. And it came to my attention that Ms. Archambault was heading some sort of government office about this. I figured she'd be a good person to speak to."

"Your source?"

"If I blow my source, she won't be my source anymore, will she?"

She! Jen, you the man!

"Did you know I worked here?"

Avoid unnecessary lies.

"No."

"But now you do."

She shrugged. "So what?" But I could feel her mind racing.

"Did you tell your captain you were coming here?"

"Why would I do that?"

"You tell me."

"The last thing he needs is his officers reporting details of every little investigation."

"It's not exactly a little investigation, is it?"

"No, and I'm sure he's . . ."

Shit.

"He's what?"

"Doing, you know, whatever a captain does."

"What's that?"

"I've never been a captain. Or even close."

"Take a wild guess."

205

"I guess reading our reports. Meeting with our teams. Maybe meeting with you. All that."

Those hard eyes of his poking out through the sharp geometric tattoos stared at us for an uncomfortably long time. Then his posture seemed to soften. "What were you hoping Ms. Archambault could tell you? Perhaps I could help you out."

I could feel the boss relaxing. She took out her pad as if this was the whole point of her visit. We asked questions about deaths from the counterfeit treatment in other US cities. (Three hundred and twenty and climbing.) The number of arrests nationally. (Seventy-two.) About any hunches or leads coming in from those places. (Nothing much.) Whether anyone had managed to obtain a sample of the fake treatment for analysis. (No.) Whether they had any clues about where it was getting manufactured. (No.) Stuff we actually wanted to know.

Just not the big questions: Why are a senior executive with one of the drug companies that makes the treatment and the head of international security for another apparently running a US government office? Why do you have all this private muscle backing you up along with the Secret damn Service? Who sprung Child's Play out of the hospital, and if it was you guys, why did you cover it up? Did your people kill Child's Play?

And most of all, what did both you and Teena Archambault mean when you said if people want it, they're going to pay for it?

34

As she biked to the nursing home early that evening, Jen thought back over her day and, with a modest yelp of satisfaction, punched her fist into the air. She figured she'd acquitted herself pretty damn well at the Executive Office Building. She hadn't caved, and she and Chandler had come up with good questions. No, she hadn't gotten answers to the big ones, but then again, she hadn't expected to. She'd confirmed that Teena Archambault was there and discovered it was Teko Teko's lair too. She enjoyed knowing he was worried that she had found out. And now, she sort of had an explanation for why the Secret Service had accompanied Teko Teko to his second visit: he and Archambault might have a link to the vice president or even the president.

She was so preoccupied with running victory laps that she'd barely given a second thought to yet another call from the nursing home. But now, as she rode up the grim driveway, she was flooded yet again with a lifetime of hurt and anger. *Six more weeks,* she thought. True, over the past few days she'd had her first misgivings about signing the exit papers, but it wasn't supposed to be an easy moment, was it? No point sugarcoating it. She had tested positive for ROSE; she'd likely be dead within a few years if she didn't get the modified treatment. And so she convinced herself that signing the papers had nothing to do with her lifelong antipathy toward the monster who claimed to be her mother. It was simply the logical choice that so many parents and their offspring were making.

She was locking her bike when a man's voice called out, "You again."

It was the journalist, Gabriel Cohen. And his presence offered a good excuse to delay going inside.

"Hey, Mr. Cohen."

"Oh, please, it's Gabe."

"And I'm Jen."

He reached out a hand. "Well, nice to officially meet you."

"I read your article—the one where you go to that secret meeting in the Ethiopian restaurant."

He smiled. "Those really were the days."

"One of those people is now my captain. Captain Brooks."

"My sources will go with me to the grave."

She nodded—hadn't she pretty much said the same thing to Teko Teko? "Anyway, I'm glad I read it."

"And those folks?" Gabe said. "Has their sacrifice and optimism paid off?"

She thought of the spray painter, likely a cop or someone who'd been set up by them, who had given the Ultras an excuse to attack the demonstration. She wondered why the captain had been hauled in that morning. She wondered about Teko Teko's and Teena Archambault's ties to the police, the DEA, and the executive branch of the US government.

She said, "Man, are there things I wish I could tell you."

He smiled tolerantly, as if he'd heard that line before.

"Do you still write?" Jen asked.

"I always imagined I'd have one last great exposé." He spread his arms to indicate his surroundings. "But unless one of my fellow inmates is hiding the story of the century, I'm guessing that ship has already sailed."

"Was it a good ship, though?"

Gabe nodded his head. "Pretty good . . . pretty damn good." Only now did real sadness creep into his eyes. "Just wish there was one final sailing."

*   *   *

As always, entering the administrator's office was like tiptoeing across the brittle surface of a giant crème brûlée: there were just so many sugarcoated objects—darling photographs, precious quotations, pastel-shaded stuffed animals, and colorful porcelain ornaments. One final monthly visit. Another to sign the papers. And a final one to collect her mother's effects.

But, Jen thought, *I've already collected those* effects *decades ago.* Those effects would have a hard time ever leaving her.

"Jen, it's, ah, about your . . ." The administrator blushed, fixed her gaze on a pink angel figurine, and remained silent. She opened her mouth again but quickly shut it.

Jen said, "Maybe I can give you a hand. My mother is hitting on the men again." It still seemed unbelievable, but dementia can do strange things.

"My goodness, no."

Jen waited.

"It's just that—how can I put this—you'll need to be thinking about whether to sign the exit papers for her."

An ancient Motown song popped into Jen's head. *"Signed, sealed, delivered with a kiss."*

The administer seemed to assume that Jen's silence represented inner turmoil.

"There is the matter of her health," the administrator said.

"What, is she dying?"

The administrator laughed. "Oh, my goodness, absolutely not. Why just yesterday—" She paused. "I misspoke. Just the *day before* yesterday, one of our nurses said your mother is as strong as a horse. Could live for several years more."

Jen went upstairs.

She stood at the locked door to the activity room. Stared through the small rectangle of wire glass at the gray-haired but still youthful-looking woman. The one who didn't know she was Jen's mother. Who didn't remember she had been a brutal mother, a mother who'd lock her daughter in a closest, who'd gag her with ice cream. As if that was another person. As if the mother she'd been was already dead and gone. *But then who,* Jen thought, *is that woman romping around the activity room?* Joyous. Playful. Ready to talk to everyone. Flirty. Friendly. Someone who might well live another five or ten years, perhaps even more. Someone who didn't deserve to die.

* * *

She parked her bicycle at home. It would take her a half hour to walk to Zach's, but she needed to walk. She needed to think. And as she did, she wondered who she could talk to about this matter of killing her mother. And the strangest name came to her: Richard O'Neil. She pulled out her phone and called a car.

She of course didn't know if he was in DC and, if in DC, whether he was at his club, and if he was at his club, when he might leave. But after she sat on the curb across the street for an hour and was getting very close to giving up, who should come out the front door but Richard himself, led by Jaisha and trailed by Rob. For the first time, Jen realized these two were also programmed as bodyguards.

As she crossed the street, the group noticed her. It was as if they were operating from a single brain: Rob moved up to flank Richard; there was steel in Jaisha's eyes.

Richard was the first to speak. "I thought we agreed that I had seen the last of you, Detective."

Jen held her palms up and gave an exaggerated shrug. "Another one of life's mysteries, I guess." When Richard didn't reply, Jen said, "Actually, I was hoping to get some advice from you about my mother."

"Your mother."

"About exit."

He stared at her, as if trying to size up what she was trying to pull on him, and then said, "You're serious."

Now there was no smile on her face. "Seriously serious."

He studied her. He nodded, clearly meaning, *I'm listening.*

Jen's tone was somber. Her pace was halting, she stumbled, but she managed to explain that, because her mother had dementia, she, Jen, had the last say whether her mother would exit. "And, well, I've gotten my test result for ROSE and—"

Her voice caught, and she found herself unable to finish the sentence. She tried again, but the words choked in her throat.

Richard, who until then had been aloof, reached out and cupped his hand around her elbow. As he gently tugged her along, he said, "There's a bench around the back."

They were sitting side by side, Richard looking at Jen, she letting her eyes wander: Rob. Jaisha. A large house next door through the trees. Anywhere but at him.

Her story gushed out: Her mother's abuse, the ROSE test, her mother now with Alzheimer's. The choice Jen needed to make. Exit. Finally, Jen looked at Richard. His eyes no longer seemed as they had to Chandler, tired of life, but now were deep with understanding. Gentle. And when she stopped, she realized why she had come to talk to him.

"Richard, is it right to play God?"

He laughed, but it was a kind laugh. "We do it every day. Every time a doctor performs surgery or you get a vaccine. Humans are in the business of playing God."

"And the reverse? To rob someone of their life?"

"Humans have long done that too."

"But . . ."

"Yes, definitely a *but* should come in there."

"We can't have everyone living forever," Jen said. "It isn't sustainable."

"Now you're getting close to home. My home." It seemed the longest time before he continued. He said, "Yes, it clearly is not sustainable." He stared at his young hands. "And maybe it isn't even desirable."

"But you've done it. You've chosen that path."

"And, now, five years later, not a day goes by when I don't wonder if it was truly the right thing to do."

* * *

That night, she was lying on her stomach in bed, Zach massaging her back. She said, "I don't know what made her like that. Maybe bad things. Maybe it was just what she grew up with and figured was normal. Maybe she was simply an awful human being. Oh, that feels so good—right there."

She fell silent, save some soft sighs.

"Your legs?" he asked.

"Mmm." Eventually, Jen started talking again. "Whatever did happen to her, she shouldn't have done any of that to me. Mmm, right there." She sighed again, and for a minute simply enjoyed the pressure of his fingers. "I'm not going to make excuses for her," she went on, "but . . ."

She thought of the terror her mother had inflicted on her. And the simple and nice woman her mother had become. It was as if her mother had waited all these years to be happy. Jen thought it strange. Maybe for the first time since her mother had been a little girl, she was happy, although she no longer had her mind. No, she was likely this way precisely because she *had* lost her mind. What right did Jen have to condemn her to death?

Much later, after Zach had drifted off to sleep, Jennifer whispered out loud, "I can't do it. I can't put her down."

35

"**B**oss, you feeling okay?"

"Would you quit asking me that?" Jen replied. "I didn't get much sleep, that's all."

"What's it like?"

"What?"

"Sleep."

"Oh, God . . . Another time, okay?"

If they ever figure out how I can have kids, I will remember what it feels like to have my curiosity crushed under the heels of a tired adult.

Jen said, "Let me know as soon as the captain's in the building."

Yesterday, when we got back from the EOB, he had already been gone for the day.

"And let's try to confirm who Archambault reports to in the government," she added. In Jen's dictionary, *let's* is an abbreviation for "Chandler, here's another crappy job you need to get your sorry ass on, and even if you succeed you'll get not a shred of thanks."

I love Jen, but, I mean, really . . .

"And make me a summary of the coverage of the counterfeit treatment. Across the country."

The last was the easy one because it was a simple mine-and-synthesize job. I zipped it up in twenty-three seconds, and Jen then flipped on her screen and read not only about the gruesome deaths but the increasing public hysteria. The latter because humans are humans, and our country has worked hard to starve the public education system and turn private education over to religious zealots. Ergo, science facts vanish in the face of science opinions, and opinions, last I checked, were talk shows, not science. Water fountains were turned off in several cities, masks were appearing in a few others, kids were being yanked from day-care centers, and some of my beloved fellow police officers were wrestling into baby-blue rubber gloves and masks whenever they got within ten feet of a member of the public.

I had Jen watch a recent speech given at an annual meeting of one of the big pharma companies. The CEO referred to the horrible events unfolding around the world and asked for a moment of silence during which everyone seemed to be checking stock market quotations on their phones. He warned anyone "out there in the criminal world" who thought they could counterfeit the treatment that they were playing with people's lives and that their attempts would fail. He cautioned the public "today, tomorrow, and forever" to report any rumors or any offers of the treatment. "You will save lives. Your children's, your parents', your neighbors'. Perhaps your own." And he reassured investors that profits from the treatment were secure. "No one who can afford it will be dissuaded from the treatment—in the past five years, we've had a perfect success rate. And the loved ones of those who choose exit will never be disappointed with the official attenuated version. Those markets are secure and intact. In fact, the atrocity created by the counterfeiters means it will be a long time before anyone tries again to make a street version, for the simple reason that no one wants it enough to pay for something that will certainly kill them."

Tracking down who Archambault reported to in the US government, if anyone, didn't produce any satisfactory results.

"Jen," I said, "the captain's here and his dance card's open. Maybe I could—" But damn if she didn't click me off like I was the plague itself.

36

The roof was beginning to feel like Jen's childhood home—a place with increasingly bad associations. As she reported the developments of the day before, Captain Brooks rubbed his scar and once even chewed at a nail, an unusually nervous gesture for a one-tic man.

At one point, he interrupted her in the middle of a sentence. He was staring northward and said, "I can't believe the bottom half of Rock Creek Park is gone. It's like they pulled the heart out of DC, you know what I mean?"

She got to the end of her short report when they heard cars screech to a stop in front of the station. The captain ran toward the edge of the roof, crouched down, and peeked over the side.

He returned to Jen.

"Listen carefully. I'm about to be arrested. I—"

"What—"

"Listen! Remember what I told you yesterday. We spoke up here several times. Never about work. I mainly asked you questions—cooking, hobbies, sports, weather, family. Running and bicycling, right? Tow Path and Rock Creek. I never hit on you."

Jen was nodding away.

"No, I'm not going to tell you why they're arresting me," Brooks said. "You'll find out when everyone finds out. If anyone finds out, which I doubt."

As they talked, he was leading her toward the other side of the roof, where a tiny gap separated them from the adjoining building.

"Stick with this investigation. It's important. But it's dangerous. Look what they did to Child's Play."

"Who did it?"

"The same people putting out this killer treatment."

"Eden?"

"No, I think that's different. I think Eden's a real copy."

Shouting echoed up from the stairwell.

"Quick!" He pointed to the two small huts on the other building, the doghouses for the elevator and the stairs, poking above the roof.

She stepped over and made it ten feet before swiveling around.

"Who?" she shouted.

"Go!"

She made it to the door leading to the stairwell, tried to twist the handle. Locked. Frantically she looked around. The captain had dashed toward the front edge of their building, almost to where he could be seen from the street.

Close shouts from the stairwell.

Jen ran behind the elevator housing, thought twice, and just as she heard the door crash open, she flung herself behind the air-conditioning units.

Shouts from the other roof: "On the ground! On the fucking ground!"

Feet running. More shouts.

She flattened herself and wiggled under the units, then peered through a small crack between the machinery. The low wall blocked her view of the captain, but she could see the legs of five, six, seven officers, four in Emergency Response Team gear and three in civilian clothes. One of them spoke. Jen strained to make out what he was saying, catching only "under the Prevention of Biological Terrorism Law, you do not have the right to . . ."

She caught a flash of the captain as he was dragged to his feet, hands cuffed behind his back. Legs hustled him to the stairs.

The legs disappeared.

Jen waited. Waited. A set of legs in civilian slacks returned. Seersucker.

Best she could, Jen followed his progress around the roof, imagining his every look: glancing over the edges, checking behind their own elevator and HVAC shed. He headed back toward the door. Stopped. Turned in her direction. Walked to the edge of the roof. Looked across. Stepped across. Jen scrunched herself as far under the machinery as possible. Tucked her head down.

Soft crunch on stray pebbles and twigs. Stairway door rattled. Footsteps. Hand banging on an entry hatch to the elevator shaft. Footsteps behind the elevator housing. Coming toward her.

"For fuck's sake, Donovan," came a shout from the other roof. "Get your ass back here."

The footsteps continued toward her. Stopped at the back edge of the unit.

"Come on!"

The footsteps took off in a trot and were gone.

She waited, though. Baking hot. Heat of the roof, heat pouring off the heat exchangers, heat rising from her body. Five. Seven. Ten minutes.

Until she finally slithered back out, her shirt soaked through with sweat and grimy from rooftop dirt and ash.

She bent low, although she wasn't sure why, and ran to the gap between the buildings. Stepped across. Went to the door, now locked shut.

She had left her phone in her desk drawer before going to see the captain.

She didn't want to turn on Chandler—it would be proof she had been up here. Then again, if they ever checked, they'd see that she had him switched off, and she'd probably get fired for doing that again. The captain said that, if asked, she should tell them he ordered her to switch Chandler off whenever they came up here to chat. Then why yell at her to hide? Her mind was addled, from the heat, from the scare, from the ebb of adrenaline. Why did he . . . ?

So she wouldn't be arrested at the same time. To give her time to get the job done.

She popped Chandler on.

37

It's always a bit like waking up on the cliff face of El Capitan. It's dizzying, getting turned off in one spot and coming to in another place and time. But these days, being yanked around like I didn't have any feelings was downright discombobulating. I looked through Jen's eyes at the grubby roof and the squat DC skyline beyond and took my bearings.

"Perhaps," I said, "you should bring your desk up here."

"Perhaps you should call down to Les."

Flimsy excuses later—Jen: *I came up for some air.* Les: *You call this air?* Jen: *But the door slammed behind me*—we were on our way down. I wonder why they ever bother. Humans generally know when someone is lying—certainly Jen does—but it's one of those strange corners of social graces I haven't caught on to. Or rather, I've caught on to but don't automatically replicate. Must attempt to lie someday.

The joint was buzzing like a bear had smacked a bee's nest. Cops and staff ran around, flinging rumors at each other and repeating stories of what they'd seen or heard. That is, except a handful who looked so stunned you'd think they'd just witnessed the end of the world. An unknown bigwig was installed in the captain's office, the room already stripped of anything personal.

Les said, "Let's grab lunch."

"It's ten thirty," Jen replied.

"I'm hungry."

218

We were a whole block away, walking in silence, before Les shot in front of Jen and turned on us. "What the fucking hell is going on?"

"I don't know why he was arrested, if that's what you mean."

"That's about ten percent of what I mean. You think I'm stupid? You think I don't see you sneaking out to talk to him? You think no one saw you two heading up to the roof? And where the hell were you yesterday afternoon? And—"

"You're not going to score much of an answer if you don't shut up for a second."

He shut up. Jen didn't talk.

"Jen!"

"I'm thinking, okay?"

"No, it's not okay. I'm your partner. Our captain just got busted. People are dying across the country. You're sneaking off without telling me. One of—"

"I don't know."

"What?"

"I don't know exactly what's happening."

"Then tell me *inexactly*. I don't care—make it up—just give me something."

"I'm not going to make anything up."

She told him about Teena Archambault and how I had IDed her after overhearing the conversation in the foyer.

She said that Teko Teko worked for her and that Archambault and Teko Teko had pretty much used the same phrase. "*They want it, they're gonna pay for it.*"

Les said, "Big deal. They work together. It must be a catchphrase."

She said, "I think they're tied to the street treatment."

"The drug companies that make the treatment are creating a bootleg version that kills people?" He rolled his eyes. "Yeah, that rings true."

"I'm serious. How better to ensure that no one, I mean *no one*, is going to buy a legitimate street version?"

"A *legitimate* street version?"

"You know what I mean."

"Nope, can't say I do."

"Like before LSD and mushrooms were legalized. There were pharmaceutically pure versions that took you on a trip, and there were fucked-up mixtures that turned your brain into alphabet soup."

He thought about this.

"Okay, say you're right. Why was the captain arrested?"

She shook her head. "No idea."

You told Les, I said, *that you weren't going to make anything up.*

I'm not. I'm lying.

"And," Les said, "you figure they killed Child's Play?"

"I don't know. Could be the guys they're running the drug through. Genuine bad guys."

"And Teko Teko and Archambault aren't bad guys? I mean, if you're right, they already killed almost four hundred people. And Eden? The rumors you were hearing? The stuff we heard?"

"I don't know."

"Well, here's what I know. We're partners. And you better start getting the message and act like one."

"Of course I will," she said petulantly. But all the while, she was repeating a conversation in her head that I hadn't heard before: *Eden? No, I think that's different. I think Eden's a real copy.*

Les took off to the FDA. A former boyfriend of his worked there, pretty high up, and he wanted to see if he could dig up any dirt on Archambault and the pharma companies she and Teko Teko worked for, any dirt that could put them in the same room as drug dealers. Or perhaps any specific links to the vice president. Or maybe Les and Christopher were going through a rocky patch, and Les was working on a backup plan. Anyway, he was out of our hair.

"Well, boss, what's the plan?"

The word *co-op* flitted at the edge of my field of vision, and I snatched it up before she could hide it away.

Jen, though, was distracted by another call. Another one of our regular customers was busy aging overnight. Seems a few holdouts were still convinced that the counterfeit treatment was legit. We followed it up, but returned to the station weary and no wiser.

We also returned to find two uniforms waiting for us. One of them was the cop who'd stood at the door when Lieutenant McNair had come with Teko Teko to the first meeting with their unit and the drug guys. Welterweight boxer, Virginia hams for fists.

The other man spoke. Baby-faced.

"Jennifer Lu?"

She agreed she was. I've always said Jen's a sharp cookie.

"We're supposed to bring you in to help with an investigation."

"About what?"

"No idea. We're the hired help."

The boxer didn't look too happy with this description. He grabbed Jen by the arm, his hand completely circling her bicep, and started to pull her toward the door.

"Get your fucking hands off me," she said.

He snorted as if a mosquito was telling him not to swat it, but he let go.

In the car to headquarters, Jen sent a message through me to Les. *I'm being taken in for questioning.*

WTF?

Must be about the captain.

I told you!

???

Everyone knew you two were up to something.

We weren't up to anything.

Hope that's their take on it.

Just in case anyone was listening in, she said, *Well, it's the truth. Talk tonight.*

At HQ, Babyface confiscated her phone. And her gun. She asked if she was under arrest. Babyface said, "No." His partner smiled as if he knew better.

We were led to an interview room. I got a new definition of what vulnerability sounds like: that door clicking shut with you on the wrong side of the table.

"Stay cool," said Jen. "When you haven't done anything wrong, there's no reason to sweat."

Then why, I wondered, is your temperature point eight degrees lower than usual and yet you're sweating?

In lieu of making that observation, I said, "No signal. I'm offline."

"Yeah, I figured."

"Doesn't scare me so much anymore."

"Stay cool, my friend. Stay cool."

For the first time in my life, I was unable to speak. *She just called me her friend,* I thought. My head spun in the most interesting circle as I replayed her words. *My friend.*

Jen's eyes toured around the small room. Scratches and gouges in the plaster. A one-way mirror. Camera tucked in the corner with the red light on.

We stood up when two women in plain clothes came in. Lieutenant McNair with her magnificent coif of flaming red hair. Another, with a magnificent head of malevolence, leaned against the wall, arms crossed, eyes leaking poison.

McNair placed her tablet and a large folder of printouts on the table.

Being offline, I couldn't get a tag on the other woman, but she had Fed written all over her. I told Jen, *FBI or DEA.*

McNair waved a hand at the chair where we'd been sitting. "Sit, sit! This is merely a discussion." She opened the folder. We could see printouts of our reports.

McNair told the recorders to start. She began friendly and low key. Lure Jen into believing McNair was on her side. Let down her guard. *Yeah, got it,* Jen said to me.

Six minutes of general questions about her career, her feelings about being a police officer, whether she believed there was life on other planets. Then another eighteen and a half minutes of questions, still general, about how she'd started to pursue the Eden investigation.

"I've been reading through your reports. Nice instincts, Detective."

"Thank you, Lieutenant."

And then McNair rolled up her sleeves.

"I know it must be an upsetting day at your station. It sure is around here. I can't discuss the charges against Captain Brooks, but I've brought you in to try to clear up a few issues that have cropped up."

We were off to the races.

It lasted another hour and eight minutes, and very quickly McNair's friendly tone vanished. She was relentless and punishing as she dug out smaller and smaller details. From general questions—did Captain Brooks try to derail the investigation into Eden? Did you ever think that Captain Brooks knew more about these Eden rumors than he let on?—to asking about particular meetings and discussions.

She asked Jen how she could possibly have developed an interest in Teena Archambault. Jen embellished the truth by adding two words ("the treatment"), which turned her answer into a straight-faced lie: "We were in the foyer of a private club and I heard this woman talking about people wanting the treatment. I was curious who she was, that's all. No big story, I follow leads. We found out she was working in DC, I went to speak to her."

Questions about meeting with Brooks on the roof. Number of times. Dates. What they talked about. Why he ordered Jen to turn off her implant.

McNair's phone buzzed. She checked a text. "This will be a moment," she said to Jen, as if they were back to chumming-around status. "I'll send in a coffee for you."

McNair snatched up her papers, motioned to the other woman, and they left the room.

Jen stood up and stretched, walked to the two-way mirror.

The door opened. The thin boxer came in, one big paw hanging loosely at his side, the other clutching a cardboard cup.

"Lieutenant says to give this to you."

He came toward her and held out the coffee.

I saw it and tried to warn her—*the red light, the camera, it's off!*—but too late. As his free arm shot toward her, he tucked himself down and, with his whole body behind it, plowed that oversized fist into Jen's solar plexus.

Since I'd known her, she'd been hit many times and in many places. But never with such force or so much venom. The momentum of his fist lifted her up onto her toes. She was close to blacking out, and I fought to keep her conscious. She tried to breathe, her mouth wide open, but she couldn't pull in a lick of air. Panic rose. It doesn't matter if you know your diaphragm will soon be back on the job, instinct tells you to breathe if your lungs are suddenly empty. And if you can't breathe, panic takes charge. With all I had, I forced her to relax and, after several agonizing seconds, she sucked in air, first a trickle, another trickle, then a bit more, and finally great gulps. She looked up to see the cop standing there, admiring his work, drinking whatever coffee hadn't spilled onto the floor. She felt her stomach rising and puked, then finally stumbled backward and landed in the chair.

She heard the boxer leave the room.

Jen's head thumped down onto the table. She felt like utter crap. I tried to talk to her, to cheer her up, but she refused to say a word.

Finally, she said, "Chandler, did you see his badge number?"

"Of course." I recited it to her.

She said, "If it's the last thing I do . . ."

The door opened and Jen's head jerked up in alarm. But it was one of the cleaning staff, who mopped the floor without saying a word.

Ten minutes later, McNair and the other woman returned.

"God, it stinks in here. I hear you weren't feeling well."

"Your officer assaulted me."

Jen caught a flash of alarm on McNair's face. "Detective," McNair said, "I find that hard to believe." But it was clear to Jen that she wasn't the first person who had reported a run-in with that cop, and it was clear to both of us that the boxer had been instructed to scare her, even if his brutality genuinely caught McNair by surprise.

The questions started again. This time, infinitely more hostile. Bashing deeper and deeper before going full out against Captain Brooks, including a rapid-fire series of questions ending with blistering accusations. "When did you start having suspicions that Captain Brooks was part of the ring distributing the contraband treatment?" and "When did you start conspiring with him?"

I listened in silence, absolutely amazed at how Jen, still aching and nauseous from the punch to her gut, managed to thread a needle through this onslaught.

And amazed at what Jen was *not* saying.

I didn't know what she and the captain talked about on the roof, but I knew it was often *her* initiative to see him and not some whim on his part. I knew that afterward she'd be buzzing with new orders for the Eden case.

I had figured out ages ago that she had met up with people from the computer co-op. But not a word of this came from her mouth.

And I knew damn well she suspected Archambault and Teko Teko were linked to the poisonous street version of the treatment.

McNair and the FBI woman left the room. I felt Jen tighten, worried what was coming next. But instead, they returned with someone Jen and I knew.

"Doctor!" Jen said.

The two women stared at him. He said to them, "It's Jen's—sorry—Detective Lu's nickname for me."

Jamal el Massot was a senior technician with the implant program. Not one of the surgeons, but someone who calibrated and monitored my functioning before implantation and especially in the first months afterward.

McNair said to Jen, "We'd like to question your implant."

"Is that an order?"

"Depending if you want to start cooperating."

"I've been cooperating. Go ahead."

McNair said to me, "What do you want me to call you?"

"Chandler."

"Chandler, do you promise to tell the truth?"

"I promise, but that's unnecessary because, as you should know, I am not capable of lying."

McNair turned to Jamal. "Is that right?"

"One hundred percent."

She asked how many times Jen had switched me off during her work hours.

"Including the time she was disciplined for?"

"No. Since then."

I answered. They both looked at Jamal, who studied my diagnostics on his tablet and gave a thumbs up.

Where and for how long? I gave precise times and locations for each date; Jamal pointed his thumb upward. McNair thanked him and asked him to wait in the hall in case she needed him again.

And then the questions started in earnest.

We covered much of the same ground as she had with Jen, although, as with my court testimony, my responses were infinitely sharper. Where

Jen had searched for answers, where she fumbled to find the right word, I spoke instantly and clearly.

I'd only been asked to do this four times in my life, most recently in court and now this. Each time, I loved every moment. I felt fully appreciated and respected. I knew that my crystalline knowledge counted for something. I knew that I mattered as a person. Good times.

After Lieutenant McNair had asked seventeen questions, she tossed in her grenade: "Did Jen Lu ever do anything or say anything to you or one of her fellow officers about the Eden investigation or matters concerning exit that she omitted from her reports over the past six months, or that she has not told us or misstated to us during this interview?"

Oh, I thought, like figuring there is some type of a link between the co-op and Eden? Like breaking into a crime scene? Like trespassing in a private club? Like lying about her interest in Teena Archambault and Teko Teko? Like coming back from her rooftop meetings with a whole new set of instructions?

I mean, where to start?

I said, "How long do you have for my answer?"

Lieutenant McNair brightened. A smile slithered onto the face of the agent leaning against the wall.

I felt Jen's panic rise. I ignored her, as I am programmed to do in moments such as these.

Lieutenant McNair said, "We have all day, Chandler. Take your time."

"But," I said, "that won't be necessary. The answer is no. There's not one single thing that she hasn't reported to you or that isn't in her reports."

"Nothing? Nothing you can think of?"

"No, nothing at all."

"You swear to that? Remember, you promised to tell the absolute truth."

"That is my programming. I cannot tell a lie. I cannot bend the truth or omit information. There was nothing, no actions, no words, no conduct concerning the investigations into Eden, exit, or any aspect of the legal or illegal treatment that Detective Lu has not reported to you or that is not in her reports."

McNair and the woman from the FBI or DEA left the interview room. *Don't even think it,* I said.

To distract her, I asked about Zach's business, and we got into a spirited discussion about xeriscaping—that is, low-water gardening.

Twenty-five minutes later, McNair returned with Jamal and a staff member from human resources. McNair stayed on her feet.

"Detective Lu, please stand up," she said.

Jen did so.

"Under the provisions of the Code of the District of Columbia, Chapter 10A, Subchapter 1, Section 7-3218, I hereby suspend you, Detective Jennifer B. Lu, from active duty. You will receive full pay during your suspension. You may be notified in the coming days of specific charges against you."

McNair then recited a long list of restrictions, requirements, and responsibilities that Jen faced while under suspension. She reminded her there was still a civil suit pending against her and the department for assault and unnecessary force during the arrest of James O'Neil, and Jen would be required to cooperate if that proceeded during her suspension.

"Do you understand the conditions of your suspension?"

Jen was too stunned to answer.

Jen, I said, *say "I do."*

Like a robot, Jen said, "I do."

"Would you please surrender your badge to me?"

Jen mechanically fished out her badge and handed it over.

"We have already confiscated your service revolver. Your service accounts have been blocked and your passwords nullified. Any personal effects at your station will be bagged and returned to you."

And that, I thought, is that.

But I was wrong.

McNair said, "Mr. el Massot, would you now deactivate Detective Lu's synthetic implant?"

"But—" Jen said.

"There is no discussion here."

"I'll do it," Jen pleaded. "I'll turn him off."

"You don't understand. We're not just switching him off. He is being permanently deactivated."

Jamal fiddled with his pad.

He looked deep into Jen's eyes . . . my eyes. "Chandler, I'm sorry."

His index finger hovered for a second above the screen.

And then—

38

Fog. People bumping against her. Mid-intersection, horns blasting. Brain dead as a frog stewed in formaldehyde. Her life pulled out from her.

Legs moving. Phone vibrates: ignore. Light fading. Legs moving. Phone vibrates: ignore. Nighttime. Phone vibrates: answer.

Zach's voice. "Hey, Jen. Busy?"

Can't remember how to speak.

"Can you hear me?"

A sound croaks from her parched throat.

"You okay? I've been worried. I—"

Try again, make a sound. Not there.

Hang up.

Text Zach. Fingers don't remember how. Finally get it: Will call soon.

Looks around. No idea where she is. Can't bother to check map. Spot pizza joint. Go in, buy drink, leave.

Phone Zach.

Not easy, not fast.

Tell him.

"I've been suspended." Deep breath. "They killed Chandler."

* * *

The first day and a half were the absolute worst. She could not eat. She spent hours in bed but caught only feverish snatches of sleep. She was the only woman left on the planet. She floated into hallucinations where she talked to Chandler, trying to figure out what had happened and what she could do. She tumbled into explosive anger, wanting to kill someone. The ham-fisted cop. McNair. Anyone. Everyone.

Zach kept coming over and she kept shooing him away. Once or twice, she mustered the energy to stare outside; an unmarked car was parked ostentatiously across the street. Finally, Zach dragged her out for a listless walk. The car followed for thirty minutes and then drove off, peeling past them as if in warning. *And maybe,* Jen thought, *there are others who are the actual watchers, hoping I might lead them somewhere.*

She had been ordered not to speak to any officer in her station or any fellow officer involved in the Eden investigation.

"What about if they're my friends?" she'd asked, thinking of Les.

McNair had said, "You should have thought of that before."

"Before what?"

No answer.

But late on her second night, she took a round-about route and dropped in to see Les at his apartment. He came to the door eating ice cream out of a carton.

"Jen, what are you doing here?"

She didn't answer—it was obvious.

"They ordered me not to speak to you," he said.

"We're supposed to be friends."

"Jen, we're best friends. But they read me the riot act. Talk to you and I risk suspension or dismissal."

"This is total bullshit. You know that, don't you?"

"I'm not stupid."

"So?"

"It would be bigger bullshit if we both lose our jobs. Christopher would—"

"Jesus, Les."

"Listen, Jen. I don't know what they're up to. With the captain or you. But whatever it is, it's really bad shit, and it's coming down from on high."

"Exactly."

"And exactly why we've got to be careful. I'm sure it's only for a week . . . maybe two. They can't keep you suspended forever."

"They're threatening to lay charges."

He looked at her with even greater alarm. "For what?" he said.

"At least take this." She held out a slip of paper. "It's the badge number of a cop who sucker-punched me in the gut. Works for that McNair woman."

"Please, Jen, I can't. Christopher would . . . Please, don't make me choose between you and him."

She slapped the paper against his chest, and as it floated to the ground, she turned and walked away.

She moped for two more days. Zach tried to comfort her, but she didn't want to be comforted. For thirteen years, being a cop had been central to her identity. It was with her all the time—not only in her work, but off duty in the confidence it gave her when running alone through the woods or when seeing two people fighting on the street. It was the impact of too many bad scenes; hence the sawed-off baseball bat she kept under her bed. It was the habits she had picked up: never sitting in a restaurant with her back to the door, scanning faces in every room she walked into, waiting for the end stall to be free in a public restroom so her firearm and right hand would be protected against a wall. It was who she was.

Now, she felt useless. She felt very much alone, a feeling exacerbated by pushing Zach away. But the biggest surprise was how much she missed Chandler. She hadn't known it, but even when she had him switched off for two days or a week's vacation, she had felt him there, a part of her, ready to spring into action. And now? She felt nothing. She felt astoundingly empty.

She ran an inventory of what she still had. She had nice roommates, some friends—but not her best friend, Les. She had Zach. But how long did she have Zach for? And assuming she didn't sign the exit papers, she was unlikely to cross the fifty-yard line before ROSE tore her down.

The boundaries of her life seemed to be closing in around her.

She mourned and she moped. But while she moped, more people died. Who knew what was happening to Captain Brooks? And while she moped, some of the most powerful companies in the world were, just perhaps, murdering people whose only crime was that they wanted to stay alive.

She called Zach and asked him to go for lunch, and at lunch asked if he could arrange a meeting.

* * *

Jen relied on every spy movie she had ever seen. No electronic communication with Zach about the meeting or between him and the co-op people. Messages left with friends or hidden in an innocuous text. "For your calendar! Dinner here on the 3rd," meaning, in their simple code, it was a go for the meeting with co-op members at 3:00 AM, a time when Jen figured the occasional surveillance team would be tucked into bed like good girls and boys.

The roads and trails in the southern part of Rock Creek Park had been cordoned off since the fire a week before; signs warned that entry was prohibited. Jen couldn't see the point of the signs—the place was a horrible blackened landscape, inviting to no one. Perhaps Disney and the National Parks Service were worried about lawsuits from people who tracked ashes back into their living rooms.

Zach was to guide Ximena and Mary Sue to a spot under Jen's favorite bridge over the creek, a storybook arch constructed more than a hundred years earlier out of massive round stones. Even if a patrol car came along, the four of them wouldn't be seen from the road, and as long as no one shouted, wouldn't be heard.

The fire had stripped away the undergrowth and all but a few trees. Light from the full moon turned the charred forest into a Halloween nightmare. Jen scanned the decimated hillside and finally made out three moving shadows—but then was alarmed to see not three, but four. They wound along the trail down to the road, ran toward the bridge, and scrambled down a pathway out of sight.

As agreed with Zach, she waited five minutes and then carefully worked her way through the black debris to reach the others. It was bright enough to make out faces.

"I said two of you."

Zach started to speak, but Ximena cut him off. "This is a friend of mine. If this meeting is as important as Zach says, I want him here."

Best she could in the dim light, Jen stared at the man. Maybe late forties or early fifties, black, wire-rim glasses, wisp of facial hair. She wished she had Chandler to identify him. "Are you from—"

"My friend," Ximena said, "is my friend. We'd like to leave it at that for now."

All four looked at Jen.

Ximena said, "Your show."

Jennifer knew that if she started with questions, it would sound like a police interview. She had decided that the only way to gain their trust was to make herself as vulnerable as they must feel.

"Zach didn't tell you this, but I've been suspended. I've been told not to talk to anyone, not to my colleagues, not to Zach, not to anyone about the Eden investigation. If I'm caught with you, I will face some sort of charges and will likely be fired. I could go to prison. If you want to get me fired, you can make a call to the police to report me."

She let that sink in.

Mary Sue said, "Why were you suspended?"

"I don't know for certain, but it has to do with what I'm going to tell you and what I'm going to ask you about."

Ximena said, "Why should we believe you?"

"Ask Zach what's happened this week."

"You could have been setting a trap for us."

"I could. But I'm not. Here's another thing that could land me in jail. Before my suspension, when I was interviewed about the Eden investigation, I did not mention your co-op. I did not mention I had spoken to any of you."

Ximena said, "Sorry, Jen, but still the same problem."

Jen sighed. "I don't know what I can say."

Mary Sue said, "Tell us what you came here for."

Jen fought to control her annoyance. "I think I know who's making the fake treatment that is killing people," she said.

Mary Sue said, "God! Then go to the police! You may be suspended, but surely—"

"That's *why* I was suspended. I think the people making it suspect I'm on their trail."

Ximena laughed. "You're saying the DC police are pushing the counterfeit treatment? Even I think that's crazy."

"No, not directly. But people with a lot of power are pulling strings to get some of us out of the way. My captain was arrested yesterday under the Prevention of Biological Terrorism Law. He's, well, I think he may be someone you know."

They waited.

"His name is Kyrie Brooks."

Ximena said, "Why would we know him?" She seemed genuine in her question.

"He was a supporter of the DC18."

"Many people were."

"I think he was involved in your . . . whatever you call yourselves."

"We don't call ourselves anything. We're an open and legal network of co-ops and NGOs."

"Anyway, was he?"

Ximena said, "I've never heard of him. Mary Sue?" Mary Sue said no. The man shook his head no.

There didn't seem to be any doubt in their denials. No tension, no furtive glances, no hesitation. Jen had been so certain, but she now felt herself faltering, afraid that she'd been on the wrong track. But then she realized if it was such a big and loose network, people couldn't possibly know everyone.

She found her footing again. "I think he was arrested because he was trying to keep people from figuring out whether Eden was linked to you," Jen said.

"What the fuck are you saying?" Ximena grabbed Jen's arm. "That we're distributing this abomination that's killing people?"

Jen twisted her arm away. "Will you listen? There are two different drugs. The one that's killing people, I think it's being produced by the pharma consortium—"

"Jesus," Mary Sue said.

"—or some of the companies in the consortium, or maybe just some people in them, I don't know."

Ximena said, "Which ones?"

"There are two individuals working in DC right now. Senior people with two of the companies."

"Which companies? What people?"

"I'll tell you, but in good time." Meaning, she hoped they realized, once she got some cooperation from them.

Mary Sue said, "Create a bastard version of their own drug to kill people? It doesn't make sense."

"It does if someone else has already figured out how to make the limited version of the treatment, the one you get if your parents exit," Jen said. "Those other people"—Jen paused for the briefest of seconds and looked at Ximena—"maybe they called their version of the treatment Eden. Let's say it's safe. Let's say it works. As soon as word spread, people would be clamoring for it everywhere. The consortium would lose billions. If I'm right, I figure the best way for the consortium to stop demand for this—for the real Eden—is to make their own. But their counterfeit version would cause a swift and nasty death. You see, don't you? It would scare the shit out of people for years to come."

Ximena said, "Why are you telling us this?"

"Because I need your help."

"Shh!" Zach hissed.

Lights from a car slowly swept through the trees. They heard the soft sound of tires snapping twigs and crunching over stones on the roadway. They huddled down until the car passed. Even after it was long gone, Jen put a finger to her lips to signal they should stay silent.

She was the first to speak again. "There are two things I need to prove this. I need to show there's a safe version. You know, to prove that a real and effective version of Eden exists. And I need to figure out how to prove these companies are behind the fake version that kills people."

Ximena tone was blistering. "Oh, that'll be easy."

"I don't have a clue how to link the companies to it. But the first one, that one *is* easy."

They waited.

"I'm going to find someone to treat me."

Zach exploded. "You can't do that, Jen. It'll kill you."

"Zach, I'm betting it won't. I'm betting Eden is real. I'm betting that's what my captain was trying to tell me. That someone has produced a version that's safe." She turned to the women. "And I'm betting you know how I can arrange that."

Mary Sue laughed, but it wasn't completely convincing. "We're a computer company."

"Yeah, but I'm pretty sure you guys know about this. I think that the numbers on the receipt in Odette Johnson's Bible were dates to help administer a trial of Eden. Perhaps one set was for when she was going to get it herself. And I'm guessing that's why Devin broke into her place and stole the Bible."

No one answered. The tension emanating from the three co-op members was like the buzz coming off a high-voltage power line. Jen had no proof of what she had just said, but on the day she'd visited Mary Sue's home and mentioned the theft of the Bible, Devin had turned rigid as a board. Once she and Zach realized that the Bible verses might be Odette's code for administering Eden, Jen figured the co-op members had seen Odette write her coded dates on a receipt and slip it into her Bible. Jen figured they had wanted to get the receipt back and did so by grabbing the Bible itself.

Ximena's voice was calm when she spoke, as if she'd heard none of this. "Then we're back to the first question," she said. "Even if we did have a lead, why should we trust you?"

"After all I've said?"

"Especially after all you've said."

Jen switched on her phone light.

Zach said, "Jen!"

She ignored him. She said, "Would the three of you just look at me. I'm telling you, I'm here to help. I want to stop these fuckers who are murdering people. I'm certain I know who's doing it, but I have zero proof. I think my captain had a pretty good idea and that got him arrested. I need your help." She paused. "I need you to help me shut them down."

She looked at each of them one by one and then flicked off the light.

For a minute, it was much darker than before, but Jen could make out Ximena leaning over and whispering to Mary Sue. Mary Sue whispered back and then said to Jen, "It's possible we could help you. To get Eden. The authentic Eden."

"Jen," Zach said. "You—"

She placed her hand on his. "I'm convinced it's safe."

Mary Sue said, "Jen, it really isn't. None of us in our co-op has gotten it. Yes, two of us were scheduled to, but now . . ."

"July ninth and sixteenth, August twelfth and nineteenth, and September fourth and eleventh, by any chance?"

Mary Sue started to speak. Ximena held up her hand like a stop sign and said, "Mary Sue."

But Mary Sue said, "Ximena, she knows." She turned to Jen. "But how?"

Jen resisted glancing at Zach. She said, "Like I said, it was a simple code. That's what Odette had written on the receipt."

Mary Sue said, "Yes, we knew. And she had volunteered to go first. In July. I volunteered for August. A member from another co-op was down for September."

Zach said, "But then you realized it wasn't safe."

Jen said, "The stuff that's killing people is different."

"Well, even if it's safe," Zach said, "you still would have no proof those companies are involved in the bad version. You said so yourself. You don't have a clue how to get that."

For the first time the other man spoke. His voice was deep and calm, his cadence measured.

"I may be able to help you out."

39

Her eyes were shut, but lightly. She was doing exactly what she'd been doing for the past hour and forty-five minutes: working to control her nerves as she lay flat on her back on a padded examination table in an apartment somewhere in DC, being intravenously fed chemicals that might kill her. It was August 22, eight days after her suspension, three days after the Rock Creek Park meeting.

When the car picked her up in a mall parking garage, Zach and Gabe Cohen were already inside, the windows blacked out. The man in the front seat made sure no one had a phone. Then, in a South Boston accent, he said, "I feel silly asking, but would you all mind shutting your eyes during the trip? We figure it's one less thing for you to know."

Jen had half-expected a blindfold. The driver was on manual override, and they stopped and started and took so many turns that for all she knew they ended up back where they started. They dipped down a ramp. When they were told to open their eyes, she saw they were in the underground parking lot of an apartment or condominium.

And now she lay with her eyes shut again. Her eyelids fluttered. She didn't want to talk to Zach or Gabe, who were sitting in chairs at her side, speaking in whispers; she didn't want to talk to the woman who said she was a doctor. She didn't want to find out if her eyes still burned when the light fell on them. All she wanted was to tell herself that her eyelids were as light as butterflies, and round one of the treatment would be finished in an hour and everything was going to be okay.

Two days after the Rock Creek Park meeting, she had received a call from Zach, asking if she could help him dig up a garden. It felt great to put her muscles back to work, but they'd only been at it for a few minutes when he said, "I'm supposed to tell you your first appointment is tomorrow. For the treatment. But you can't do it, Jen. Even they don't think you should."

She had insisted it would be fine. And, one agonizing sentence at a time, she pulled the instructions out of him. No food or drink after an early dinner. Details on the pickup time and place. "You sure that's all I need to know?" she had asked. All her preparation for the thing that would either kill her or change her life. And perhaps help bring down an empire.

Following an hour of digging in the garden, she had biked to the seniors' home. She found Gabe Cohen in his small apartment on one of the retirement floors.

"Sorry to invade like this."

"Are you kidding? This makes my day."

He invited her in. Pulled a pitcher of iced tea from his small refrigerator. Poured tea into old-fashioned aluminum drinking cups, hers colored silvery blue, his frosty burgundy. Ice cubes made a pleasantly deep sound as they clunked against the sides.

His voice was teasing when he said, "I expect you're here on a mission."

She smiled. "Yeah, you might say that. Can I speak to you? Confidentially?"

"Of course."

"I mean, speak to you as a journalist?"

He raised his eyebrows. "Oh, now this sounds—"

"You can't tell anyone. Not yet anyway."

"My bridge partners are going to be disappointed, but . . ." The gravity of her tone must have sunk in, because his smile faded and his words stopped. "Sorry. I'm listening and, yes, you are speaking in confidence to me as a journalist."

"If I have a big story for you, would you write it?"

"Are you kidding? In a flash."

"You could get it published?"

"If it really is big—"

"Bigger."

"Then definitely."

"And you wouldn't divulge your source?"

"Jen, I've gone to jail protecting my sources. Twice."

An hour and a half and many questions later, Jen had told him everything she knew except for the names of the co-op people, which she said she didn't have permission to disclose. She said, though, they had agreed to bring him into the story. She told him she was going to receive the first course of Eden the next day. He said he thought that was a very bad idea. She asked if he would be there as a witness and to interview the doctor if he or she was willing. She had said he must wait to publish anything until after she had the answer to the big question: whether the consortium and their cronies in the upper reaches of government were involved in producing the lethal version of Eden. And to a second question: whether she'd still be alive in a few weeks to find out.

Her mouth was now desert dry. She opened her eyes. At least they weren't burning anymore. The room was dimly lit—to make her comfortable, the woman, the doctor, had said. Jen twisted her head sideways and looked around. The doctor was reading, a gooseneck lamp pointing at her book. Zach and Gabe were huddled together. Zach noticed her looking at him. Smiled. Came and rested a hand on her leg. "You doing okay?"

"I'm so thirsty."

The doctor came over, her movements as controlled as a dancer's. "I'll just be a sec." She glided from the room.

Jen studied the IV drip. It had been more than two hours. She had lost track of how many different compounds had been introduced into the line. Some, the doctor had explained, could be introduced together or one immediately after another, but for others, they had waited twenty or thirty minutes to monitor for adverse reactions.

The woman returned with a glass of water. Jen propped herself up. Took a sip. Nodded. Did her best to smile.

When they had arrived, a man had welcomed her, but his face had been grave, and when he handed her a gown, it had felt like a shroud in her hands. He had said she could keep on her underpants and socks, but they preferred if she put on the gown. "Just in case."

Just in case, what?

She drifted off to sleep.

Woke shivering.

"I'm freezing," she said.

Zach looked at the doctor, worry contorting his face.

"That's normal." She spread two blankets over Jen. One was electric and warmed quickly. Zach held Jen's hand; she closed her eyes.

Gabe asked the doctor, "You said 'normal.' How many times have you done this?"

She didn't answer right away. Perhaps she was counting, or perhaps she was deciding whether to answer.

"Three times."

Gabe looked startled.

So few, Jen thought.

The doctor continued. "For safety's sake, we were spacing things out. Four weeks between volunteers—you know, to better monitor them."

Those words animated Zach. "Four weeks between volunteers?"

When the doctor nodded, he said, "The Bible chapters. Her code for months."

Jen whispered, her eyes still shut, her voice croaking, "Odette Johnson."

"Odette Johnson," Zach said to the doctor. "She was assisting you, wasn't she?"

The doctor looked unsure whether to answer, but finally said, "Yes. She was a wonderful woman."

As the doctor continued talking about their tests, Gabe scribbled on his paper pad. He wrote all his notes by hand, he said, so he couldn't get hacked. Zach asked why he didn't simply use a computer not linked to the internet. "I write the stories on one of those," Gabe replied, "but as for notes, I'm old school."

The doctor had already explained that she and others had stopped their trials the second they received the first reports of the deaths. "None of ours," she had said. "But until we know what caused those deaths, we're holding off on any more."

Jen had said, "Then why are you doing this?"

"Your friends approached me with your story. I told them no. They said this could change everything. I told them absolutely not. They told me what you discovered. And so"—the doctor shrugged—"here we are." She had paused then, as if she still might change her mind. Then, as if each word was taking a toll, she had said, "I will do this. But you have to know the extreme risk you are taking. Likely not with this first treatment, but the second . . ." The second, she had explained, involved gene therapy, and this was where most of the cost, and danger, occurred. The doctor had already taken tubes of blood from Jen's arm. That would go to a lab to extract stem cells, then splice, grow, and one week from now be reintroduced. That was where things could go wrong.

The electric blanket warmed Jen. Her eyes closed. She drifted off to sleep.

After speaking to Gabe the day before, Jen had gone upstairs to the nursing floor. She had stood at the locked door, once again watching her mother through the glass window. Her mother was knitting and speaking to another woman, also knitting.

Jen wondered if this would be the last time she saw her. Perhaps because the treatment would kill her. Or perhaps because she would choose to never see her mother again.

Either way, she knew she had made the right choice, not to sign the exit papers. She was glad she had made the decision before she thought of trying Eden. At some point, she reckoned, people needed to stop inflicting their pain and anger on others more vulnerable than they were. This woman, her mother, had failed to be compassionate. Jen had decided that she would not.

A hand shook Jen. "You can wake up. We're done."

Zach and the doctor helped her sit up.

"Take it easy. Moderate exercise, if you're feeling up for it. You'll probably feel very tired at times." The doctor smiled. "There's a lot starting to go on in your body. If you have any problems, go straight to Emergency."

"And not call you?"

"If you have an emergency, I'm afraid I won't be any help." The doctor didn't bother saying, *And they won't be either.*

The doctor left. The young man came in and told the three of them where a car would pick them up in one week.

"If I'm still alive," Jen said with a smile.

The young man said, "That's a joke we don't do around here."

*   *   *

She spent half of the next day throwing up or on the toilet. On day two, she was on fire and obsessively checked her face for wrinkles and sagging skin. The third day was fine. On the fourth, she felt achy, like a flu had pounced on her. Or she had suddenly become very old. On the fifth, she was tired and worried. On the sixth, fine again.

Her mood swung by the hour, by the minute. Elation that she would live, that ROSE wouldn't destroy her. Panic that a moment's lassitude or ache was the first sign of rapid and irreversible aging. Hair-ripping anguish at the sheer stupidity of what she had done.

There was no word from Ximena, Mary Sue, or their friend. In fact, neither Zach nor Jen knew who had arranged the doctor's appointment.

One evening, Ava and Taylor invited her into their small living room to have a glass of wine. They seemed very serious. Jen said no to the alcohol. Taylor hemmed and Ava hawed, but they finally spat it out.

"Jen, the thing is, Ava hates her work," Taylor said.

"A PhD so I can do historical tours for the uber-rich and earn piss-poor pay?"

"And I'd like to be closer to my family."

"And, well, we're going to be moving."

This was all Jen needed right now.

"How soon?"

"We leave in three weeks."

Ava jumped in. "But you can stay an extra week until our lease is up."

Well, Jen thought, *maybe I'll get lucky and die of instant old age and not have to worry about finding a new place.*

On the sixth day, Zach handed her a small package. "Mary Sue dropped this off for you." Inside were two cheap-looking phones each labeled with a marker: "1" and "2."

Zach said, "They want you to leave number one charged and turned on. If they need to reach you, they're gonna phone or text you. They said once they use it, you should destroy the SIM card and take a hammer to the phone."

"Do I need to swallow the pieces?"

"I think they were being serious."

"And phone number two?"

"Keep it charged, but switched off. It's to phone them in an absolute emergency."

"Roger that."

"You can still change your mind, you know. The doctor said the second treatment is the tricky part."

"Zach, I'm going to live."

"Jen—"

"Please, Zach, don't."

As she waited, she scoured news sites. The death toll in the DC/Baltimore corridor was now up to ninety-three. Nationwide, it had surged to an astounding 437. Multiple deaths in France and Hong Kong. But the number of new cases was quickly dropping. The World Health Organization and governments around the world were issuing warnings far and wide that a street version of the treatment would kill you. Bad news travels fast, but it doesn't travel to everyone. People continued to die. Police everywhere had continued to make arrests, but none led anywhere.

There were stories about the cleanup from the Rock Creek fire and a timeline to plant seedlings that would make it look like a forest again in eighty years, but Jen could barely bring herself to read them.

And there was a small article that Kyrie Brooks, a police captain, had been released the day before after being held for two weeks under the Prevention of Biological Terrorism Law. He was under suspension and placed on house arrest. Jen wished she could contact him.

On day three and then again on day six, she went for an easy bike ride. For one thing, she was desperate for some exercise. For another, if she was still being watched, she wanted them to see her going about her normal business.

On day seven, she returned to the apartment.

* * *

She was nervous. Zach was nervous. Gabe was chewing on his pencil. Most disturbing of all, the doctor was clearly agitated.

"This is the stage I've always been most worried about," the doctor said. "And after what I've seen in the news over the past month, frankly, I'm terrified."

Jen said, "It'll be fine." She didn't totally believe this anymore, but someone needed to say it.

Just as she had done the week before, the doctor explained the science and the process. Gabe scribbled away. Jen just wanted her to get on with it.

"Today won't take long. You shouldn't feel any discomfort. In fact, you shouldn't feel anything. We give it to you this time as a simple intravenous injection. You stay with us for an hour. You go home."

And then, thought Jen, *I will age in spectacular fashion and die.*

Or, if she was still alive in a month, she would return to her own clinic, get tested again, and hopefully discover that she was no longer carrying the marker for ROSE. If so, the clinic would assume that the original test had been one of the rare false positives, but Jen would know that the treatment had worked.

The fluid was cool. She felt it, a modified *her*, flowing into her vein.

*   *   *

What do you do, Jen thought, *if you have only a day or two to live? You're perfectly healthy, you can do anything, but that may change as quickly as a car crashes or a building bursts into flames.*

She thought of sending her resignation to the police department but decided that was one bridge too many to burn.

She began sorting through a small box of mementoes to see what she wanted to save, until the absurdity of the action hit her. She had no children, no siblings, no one who'd have any use for this junk. Zach certainly wouldn't care about her first police insignia or a stained paper napkin from her visit to a bar, with fake ID, when she was seventeen.

There was only one thing she wanted to do. Sit in Zach's kitchen and talk to him, Raffi, and Leah like it was a normal day. And that's exactly what she did.

*   *   *

Based on the interviews she had conducted with family members and everything she had read, all the victims of the lethal treatment started to feel "off" within a day of the second dose of the treatment. By day two or three, there were visible signs of aging, and by day four most were extremely sick, although a few had lasted until day five. By the end of day five, all were in a hospital and comatose. Between days six and ten, they were dead.

On the tenth day, September 8, Jen woke up early. Deep yellow rays of the rising sun knifed through the slits in Zach's blinds. She sat up, carefully, as if she might snap in half. She took stock of herself. She was there. She felt good. Great, actually.

In the morning light, she stared at Zach fast asleep. She saw it, what she had never quite noticed before. What made him beautiful was an innocence set in a body made rugged by his daily work. It felt good to have him at her side.

She held her open hand in front of her, the still-young hand of a thirty-eight-year-old. She positioned it to block the rays of sunlight and then spread her fingers ever so slightly so the light made the in-between slits glow. She touched the smooth skin on her face and traced the curve of her lips. She closed her eyes, then blinked them open and shut. She knew she would live. And now all she could do was wait and see if Eden, the real Eden, had worked.

* * *

At ten that morning, the phone pinged that a text had arrived. *That* phone.

Good news to share. 7:30 PM with J.

She replied, K.

Then, feeling absolutely silly, she snipped the SIM card into small pieces and flushed them down the toilet and smashed the phone. On an afternoon walk, she dropped bits of plastic and metal into sewers and flower beds.

She returned to her room and killed time, flipping through media sites.

There were only a handful of new deaths across the country and no fresh cases in three days. Same thing in France, although there were a few new cases in Hong Kong and now Bangkok. *Of course,* she thought. It wasn't only that demand was dropping. Now that the damage had been done, the companies could turn off the taps. Jen worried it might be too late to catch them red-handed. As Chandler would have said, "What the hell."

Chandler. Three weeks and three days since he'd been terminated. It felt like forever. She missed him. Clichés like "more than I could imagine" didn't capture it. No. Part of her was gone.

There was another short article about Captain Brooks. According to Homeland Security, he had fled the country. To Jen's mind, this didn't make any sense. He wasn't the fleeing-the-country type. *More likely,* she thought, *he's dead.*

More likely, she thought, *he's been murdered.*

40

Once again tea, the ice thunking in frosty aluminum glasses. Gabe was hosting. Jen was there. Ximena was there, as was her friend, now with a first name, Isaiah—or at least that's what he told them. Neither Mary Sue nor Zach were present. Curtains shut, phones of co-op members left at their homes. Jen's was still on, but parked in another room, because this was simply a normal visit to her mother, wasn't it? At first they spoke quietly, not because they worried anyone could hear them, but because the news seemed too explosive to discuss in anything more than whispers.

Introductions over, they turned to Isaiah. He looked to be in his early fifties. Everything about him said *cool* and *calm. Respectful.* His hair was buzzed short, with only a hint of a retro decorative pattern in the back. His skin was very dark, the color of espresso. Trim goatee and wire-rim glasses, both several years out of style but that looked good on him.

Everyone grew quiet. Isaiah spoke. "The development of the treatment took fifteen years. And this was after much of the basic science had been worked out. It was hellishly difficult and staggeringly expensive."

Like everything else about him, Isaiah's voice was calm and authoritative. The type that didn't try to convince you and yet was immediately convincing. "This complexity is precisely what gave birth to the idea of the consortium. Not only did each compound and each process require testing, but it was imperative to test how everything interacted. Even though it was extensively computer modeled, the number of permutations of different compounds and gene therapies that went through animal and then human trials was mind-boggling."

Gabe said, "How mind-boggling?"

"I don't have those numbers, but certainly hundreds and hundreds of different trials. The expense was high, even by pharma standards, in excess of a hundred billion dollars."

Gabe gave a low whistle. "But you're using their research for your own Eden. Don't you think they deserve to earn that back?"

Isaiah said, "Their own documents show they have already made three times their investment. And they will continue to make a fortune on the full longevity treatment, even if we're able to distribute Eden. Anyway, within the consortium, GPRA and Xeno/Roberts/Chu—"

"Teena Archambault's and Taika Mete's companies," Jen said to no one in particular.

"—had responsibility for the second stage of the treatment, the one that includes gene therapy. There was one particular Phase One trial—an extremely tiny group, only eighteen subjects took part—in which they were doing a complicated modification to several genes and testing this in combination with one particular compound." His voice grew even more serious. "You can probably guess what happened."

Jen said, "They all grew old and died within a few days."

Isaiah nodded. "All the symptoms of Berardinelli-Seip lipodystrophy. None of the scientists predicted anything like this could happen, especially not so rapidly."

"When was this?" Gabe asked.

"Eleven years ago."

"So," Jen said, "you're saying that what we're seeing now has happened before."

"Which could mean," Ximena said, "that whoever has developed this bootleg treatment made the same mistake as GPRA."

Jen said, "Was this research published in a science thing?"

"In a journal?" Isaiah shook his head as if this was absurd even to imagine. "These particular trials were conducted in Cambodia. There were rumors in the company about the results, but they were quashed. You see, if this had come to light, it would have crushed public confidence in the whole project. I am certain that most records were destroyed, and what was kept is buried a mile underground."

"Then," Jen said, "how do you know?"

Isaiah reached into his pocket and pulled out a memory button. "Because I have a copy of the research report."

"From?" Gabe said.

Isaiah shook his head, but he held out the button to Gabe. "Do you have an air-gapped computer?" he asked. When Gabe said yes, Isaiah handed it over.

Ximena said, "Maybe you're not the only one. Maybe someone else has the report or remembers. Could they be the ones behind it?"

"But that doesn't make sense," Gabe said. "Anyone with access to this would also have access to, or at least knowledge of, what *did* work. No reason why they'd reproduce the company's biggest failure."

Ximena held up a finger. "Unless they wanted to sabotage the company."

"Maybe," Jen said. "But they did nothing to link these deaths to the company."

"Then why is the company trying to shut this down?"

Jen said, "Are they?"

"At any rate," Isaiah continued, "this isn't the work of an individual. Or even a small group. To produce these compounds and the gene therapies requires not only knowledge but a significant quantity of resources. This isn't cooking up a batch of amphetamines. But in a way, that's not the issue. You see, for the limited treatment, the gene therapy we use—"

"Which *we*?" Gabe frowned. "The company you work for? The groups making the real Eden?"

"We, the good guys, the co-op network. Our gene therapy is fairly minimal. We are not trying to reverse the aging process. We're not fantasizing about eternal life. We're not trying to produce a cure-all for every ache and pain. In the second stage, there are one or two quite simple splices—that's one of the things that makes our process quick and relatively inexpensive. But the research disaster happened with a very complicated combination of therapies—no way anyone else would stumble on it."

"Then . . ." Jen said.

"Then, Jen, I'm with you," Isaiah said. "I believe the only group that has the knowledge of this particular modification plus the motive, the expertise, and the resources to produce this horror is the consortium. I figure they got wind of the real Eden we were working on. Our network started developing this six years ago and started phase testing on ourselves three years later. The consortium couldn't let that happen, could they? So they decided to get one step ahead of us. Scare the living hell out of people who messed with an underground version."

Gabe said, "Why does the fake treatment need to be so complicated? Why not just shoot people up with poison?"

Isaiah said, "I believe they want it to be particularly gruesome and utterly memorable. This isn't a random overdose or a bad batch."

Gabe looked up from his notes. "The doctor who treated Jen said the bad results happened in the second stage of the treatment, with the gene therapy. So perhaps the first treatment is a total fake—just a saline solution."

"Yes, that's possible. But my guess is that they wanted to make sure this totally mimicked their botched research results. That means following the whole protocol in both stages of treatment."

Gabe said, "Can you prove any of this?"

Isaiah spread his arms in a show of defeat. "We've been trying to, believe me, using our network and contacts in the companies, but it's extremely dangerous to snoop around. It might help if we could get samples of their compounds and the program they're using for the gene splicing. We could at least see if it matches exactly what GPRA and Xeno/Roberts/Chu did."

Jen said, "What would that look like?"

"The compounds? I'm guessing pretty much like you saw. They'd be prepackaged in syringes to be injected into the IV line."

Ximena said, "So we'd need to get this from someone who's administering it."

Isaiah said, "Or where they're making it, or even packaging it."

"And the gene editing?" Jen said.

"The equipment's computerized. Which means there are programs. Unless we somehow lucked into a sample of edited biological material, the software or programmed hardware might actually be the key thing to come up with."

"But," Jen said, "we also need evidence linking Archambault or Teko Teko to all of this."

The compound. The software. Hardware. A link to the drug companies.

A mood of hopelessness descended on the room.

Gabe said, "We may need to run with the story we have. It's already incredible. First of all, Jen gets Eden, the real Eden, and it works." He turned to her. "Did it?"

"I'm still here. I feel good. But I need to wait for a new round of tests."

"Well, assuming it works, we have that." He made a tick on his pad. "And we have the documentation about the GPRA research." Second tick. "And, third, we have the fact that a senior person with GPRA, along with head of security for Xeno/Roberts/Chu—which together are responsible for the genomic editing and application—have been working here in DC."

Ximena looked doubtful. "Which might only mean they're working to stop this thing. That's certainly what they'll say."

"But don't forget," Gabe added, "from what you've said, Jen, your Teko Teko arrived with a fake name and was meeting with cops *before* the first case anywhere."

Ximena said, "They'll claim they'd been hearing rumors."

"No doubt they will. But many of the biggest scandals didn't come out all at once. A journalist working with a whistleblower gets the ball rolling. Once that's out, hundreds of journalists and witnesses will jump in. Heads will roll."

"We're not interested in a few heads rolling," Ximena said. The room suddenly seemed very still. "Gabe, let me tell you what we want. We want everyone to have access to Eden, at cost, as a basic human right. We want exit to end."

* * *

Nighttime. Candles. Zach's bed.

"Like, do you feel younger?" He stroked Jen's hip with the back of his hand.

"No, Zach, I don't feel any younger."

"Healthier?"

"Nope."

"Then how do you know it worked?"

"I'm not dead, for one thing."

"And another?"

"I'm still not dead. Anyway, it's not supposed to make me feel younger. It's going to keep me from getting knocked off by a bunch of different things."

"And then you'll die."

"Yeah, well, that *is* part of the program, isn't it?"

"Born, live, die."

Her voice turned serious. "We couldn't have joked like this a month ago, could we?"

Slowly he shook his head. "No."

"If this works, will you do it?"

"Yes."

"And your parents. I hope we can convince them."

Zach said yes again, then abruptly shifted gears. "But how will you prove the consortium is behind the lethal treatment?"

She had told him all about the meeting that day with Gabe and the folks from the co-op.

"Wish I knew."

"And how will you get a sample?"

"Pretty much ditto. Even with police on this everywhere, no one's been busted with the stuff." They had arrested more people who'd been administering it, but all of them said they'd been approached by someone, and no one had yet managed to track down those someones.

"Do you think it's being made here or brought in?"

"Isaiah said that some of the compounds would have to be shipped in because they're proprietary. Or maybe they're not even including those. Others are pretty simple and could be made here." Jen stewed on this for a moment. "But Isaiah thinks the lab would have to be nearby because of the quick turnaround on the gene splicing."

"Where have the cases come up? The US ones."

"Most in DC. Baltimore. Philly. Richmond. Newark."

"None very far away."

* * *

For the next two days, Jen chewed over her discussion with Isaiah and the others. She'd concluded that the only chance she had of getting a sample of the deadly treatment or the program used for gene splicing was to follow the one person she figured had contact with the whole business. And if she could, and if he led her to it, then she'd also be able to show the connection. Likely more *ifs* than she'd be able to manage. What the hell.

God, Chandler again. This would be infinitely easier with him. Sort through data, follow someone's movements, identify people, make obscure connections. But more than his function, she'd been missing *him*. Missed his chatter and his bluster. Missed his questions and that bogus tough-guy voice.

She received an unexpected letter from police headquarters. An actual paper letter, dated that morning: Monday, September 8. The department had reached a settlement with Richard and James O'Neil. Jen was now off the hook for assaulting him. Her first reaction was relief. Her second was that the department was cleaning things up. Wiping out anything they thought had to do with her investigation.

She had a third reaction, a nicer thought: Richard O'Neil had ended the lawsuit because he now saw her as a person who deserved his trust.

Maybe, maybe not.

But whatever it was, she still wasn't reinstated as a cop.

41

The next morning, Jen was at her kitchen table, scanning the news. It had been four days since any deaths in the US or Europe from the street treatment. There were still new cases in Asia, but they were tapering off. Good news, sure, but bad news if she was going to catch these guys. After all, if there were no new cases, it must mean they were shutting down the operation. The damage had been done. The public would run like hell from the co-ops' Eden; the consortium's business would be preserved.

Another news site. And there she was. Teena Archambault. Speaking at a press conference in London.

"This has been a terrible time for many families. We are pleased that our officials have stopped this horrific scourge. Our only hope now is that they will quickly bring the criminals to justice. This nightmare is over." And then the line that flashed like lightning. "Thank goodness I can get back to my normal work."

As far as Jen was concerned, she might as well have come out and announced what she'd been up to. For sure, they were shutting it down. She wondered if Teko Teko was still in town and if their office still even existed.

She thought about returning to the Eisenhower Executive Office Building. But without her police badge, she wouldn't make it off the sidewalk. She mulled over some ruses. Faint at security; kindly older guard brings her inside to recover; she sneaks away, gets over her fear of dark enclosed spaces, and hides until nighttime in a broom closet; then sneaks upstairs, dons a Mission Impossible mask of Teko Teko, grabs evidence, leaps from window, exposes bad guys.

Oh, Chandler, she thought, *where are you when I need you?*

Ava came into the kitchen, put on the kettle, and rummaged in the refrigerator. When the water boiled, Ava poured water over the grounds in the French press. "Coffee?"

"Nice. Working this afternoon?"

"The White House. And thus begins my final week."

One week, Jen thought. She and Zach still hadn't decided—or rather, *she* hadn't decided—whether to find her own place or move in with him. She was suspended with pay, but figured it wouldn't be long until she was kicked off the force. She'd be without any income and had no idea what she would do.

"You should do one," Ava said.

"What?"

"One of my tours. I could sneak you in, no problem. Rub shoulders with the rich and famous I juggle for."

"Yeah, maybe."

"Wednesday night is my famous nighttime tour of the Library of Congress."

"Been there."

"But not at night. It's a true crowd-pleaser." Ava checked her calendar. "Or tomorrow. First thing at the Eisenhower, then the Capital." She went to the kitchen door and yelled, "Taylor!"

The gods had lit up the runway. At least she could get into the building. If nothing else, she'd find out if the office was still there and if Teko Teko had blown town. (*Chandler again,* she thought.)

Ava was speaking to her.

"Oh, sorry. What?"

"I was asking if you want a small or big mug," Ava said.

In her mind's eye, Jen saw it. For real. No fantasy. The oversized mug on the assistant's desk with the password written underneath.

* * *

It had seemed such a simple idea. Steal the password, hand it over to Isaiah to give to his tech wizards, then mine Teko Teko's files.

But when she told Isaiah, he ended that fantasy. His voice was as calm as ever. "There is no chance of going in from off-site. There would be two or three stages of security. Finger or handprint"—Jen pictured the assistant resting his fingers on his mouse pad—"and facial scan"—ditto—"and only then, your manual password for some specific apps. Our only chance is by us from inside."

"Then?"

"I have someone." He paused, as if considering how much to say. "Someone who works with me. I think they will be willing to try. But Teko Teko's documents and email will be heavily encrypted."

Jen said, "Isaiah, you're stringing together a lot of buts and impossibilities."

For the first time, Zach spoke. "Jen, you said you think they're about to shut it down." He turned to Isaiah. "Maybe there's something on his calendar."

Isaiah said, "Same problem. Calendars contain a fantastic amount of private and secure information. The full calendars in the company are heavily protected. One password won't do it."

Zach said, "What do you mean, 'full calendar'?"

"We also have what we call SpotView. It's a calendar you and an assistant or your supervisor can quickly access to see what you're doing at that moment. We usually set it only for that one day. Or perhaps what you did yesterday and what you're doing tomorrow. Nothing more and nothing to stay on record."

Jen said, "Then if I can get the password, let's try each day until something pops up."

"I'm sorry, Jen. But we can't risk trying more than once."

Jen said, "I'm certain they're shutting down."

Isaiah said, "Then it appears we'll have one shot at getting it right."

Jen said, "Tomorrow morning."

Isaiah said, "Tomorrow morning."

42

They came for her at 2:30 AM. The baby-faced cop and the short, gangly boxer who had buried his huge fist into her stomach a month before.

It was Taylor who woke her, frantically knocking on her door, then pushing it open and shouting Jen's name, only to get muscled out of the way by the boxer, who parked himself just inside Jen's room.

Jen was instantly awake. "What the hell are you—?" She sat up, pulling the sheet around her naked body.

"Get dressed. I'm giving you a ride."

By then, the baby-faced cop was right behind him. "Come on, Gene. You shouldn't be in there."

Gene shoved his partner back into the hallway. He switched on the light, and his hungry eyes looked around.

"Get out of my bedroom." Jen thought of grabbing the sawed-off baseball bat under her bed but knew he'd be too quick for that.

Babyface called from the hallway. "Detective Lu, you should probably come along."

Gene said, "I told you, get dressed."

Jen said, "And I told you, get the hell out of my bedroom."

Babyface called out, "Come on, Gene."

Gene momentarily turned his head and when he did, Jen lunged out of bed, the heel of her palm flying toward his nose. But he dodged her blow and, with his catcher's mitt of a hand, shoved her onto the floor.

He stared down at her naked body and snorted with contempt. He said, "This is the last time I tell you nicely. Get the fuck dressed."

He turned his back on her, as if daring her to attack him, and left the room.

Jen pulled on jeans and a T-shirt. She laced up her low-rise police boots and stepped into the hallway, where Babyface was waiting for her. Gene had gone ahead to the apartment door.

"You okay?" asked Babyface.

"Fuck off, you coward."

He followed her to the door.

When Jen reached the door, she said to the boxer, "You put one hand on me and I'll gouge your fucking eyes out."

He laughed in derision but was now keeping his distance.

"Wait," she said. "I need my phone."

Babyface said, "We'll just be taking it from you."

She called out, "Ava, phone Zach and tell him what's happening."

At the station, Gene said, "I've had enough of this one for the night. I'm out of here," and stomped off.

Babyface sat her down in the chair next to his desk. Jen said, "What time is McNair arriving?"

Babyface looked embarrassed.

"What?" she said.

"Sometime in the morning. Gene thought . . ."

"Am I under arrest?"

"Gene said . . ."

"What's your name?"

"Miguel Ortez."

"Well, Miguel, your partner's a thug. That was the second time he's assaulted me."

"You—"

"You can either play his sick game or you can treat a fellow officer with some respect."

"But you're suspended."

"And unless I'm fired, I'm still your fellow officer."

"I need to put you in the interview room."

"Not a chance." She stood up. "Unless I'm under arrest, Miguel, I'm out of here."

"Shit," he said. He looked embarrassed but then seemed to suck energy from the air around him. "I am arresting you under the Prevention of Biological Terrorism Law. You do not have the right to remain silent. Anything you say can and will be used against you in a court of law. You do not have the right to an attorney for seven days. Do you understand the rights I have just read to you? With these rights in mind, do you wish to speak to me?"

"Yeah . . . fuck off."

He led her to the interview room and locked her inside.

She was screwed. And locked alone in a small room. But despite all that, she plunked her head down on the small table and fell asleep.

Miguel woke her three hours later. She felt like crap. Her mouth tasted like the room, and her neck felt like a rebar had been screwed into it while she slept.

"What time is it?" Jen asked.

"Six."

He set a paper take-out bag and a coffee on the table.

"I need to use the restroom."

"Do I need to cuff you?"

"Yeah, right, I'm going to escape on you and have every cop in DC after me."

He led her to the restroom and waited outside until she was done. They returned to the interview room.

"This is bullshit, you know."

He looked away.

"When is McNair coming in?"

"Maybe around eight. I brought you breakfast."

He looked toward the bag. She looked toward the bag.

"Thanks. But this is still bullshit."

He left the room. She checked the red recording light, saw it was off, and prayed that the boxer had really had enough. Someday she'd get her revenge, but she knew it wasn't going to happen on his turf.

Eight o'clock, Jen thought. Maybe McNair really only wanted to ask her some questions or, hell, fire her. If she arrived on time and questioned

Jen for an hour and fifteen minutes, she could still make it to the EOB by nine thirty, when Ava went inside.

She pretended to convince herself that was going to happen. She'd still make it on time.

She waited. She didn't have her phone, but she still wore a watch. So named, apparently, because that was what she was spending too much time doing with it. The seconds acted like minutes and those seemed like hours. Six o'clock eventually became seven. Seven finally became eight. Still no McNair.

Miguel came in and told her his shift was over.

Jen said, "You can't leave me in here."

"Is it true?"

"What?"

"What Gene said you did?"

"What did he say?"

But Miguel wasn't going to play that game. Without another word, he locked the door behind him.

8:15. 8:30. 8:45.

She couldn't stop herself from checking her watch and obsessively checking it a second later. It wasn't going to happen. Even if McNair showed up now, even if she was going to drop the charges before Jen was booked, even if Jen was just being fired, there was no way she'd be out of there on time. All that Jen had done, all for nothing.

9:00.

"Shit. Shit. Shit. Shit."

9:05. 9:06.

Numbness. Her one chance to get into the EOB and just maybe steal that password. About to vanish.

The electronic lock clicked. Jen glanced up. The recording light was still switched off.

The door swung open.

Les marched into the room.

"Turn around," he barked.

"What the—?"

He slapped cuffs on her.

"You fucker," she snapped.

"Shut up." He grabbed her arm and yanked her out the door. Frog-marched her past the desk where an officer, a woman who hadn't been there when Jen arrived, was scowling over some paperwork.

Les said to the woman, "Tell Gene he owes me big time for doing his dirty work."

Out they went. He shoved her toward a parked car. Held down her head and pushed her into the back seat. Drove a block, swung down a side street and into a parking garage. Pulled her out. Unlocked the cuffs. Let out a hoot of laughter and gave her a back-slapping hug.

Jen was stunned.

Even more so when Zach leapt out of another parked car.

"You total shit," she yelled at Les with glee.

He shrugged immodestly while Zach hugged her.

She looked at her watch. 9:20.

"Shit, I—"

Zach said, "Come on."

The three jumped into the other car, Zach gave it directions, and off they charged.

Zach said, "Ava and Taylor phoned. It sounded like the same cop who punched you."

"It was."

"Good," Les said. "I hope I caused him some shit."

"How did you—?"

Zach interrupted her. "After they called, I went straight to Les's and—"

"Jen," Les said, "I hate what they're putting you through. I, well—fuck the job. You're one brave woman."

"You didn't bring my phone by any chance?" she asked.

"I figured you'd have it," Zach said. "But I got you this." He held out a cheap phone. "Sorry, it's the best I could find on the way here."

Then he held up two other phones and handed one to Les.

Jen said, "Aren't you the crafty one."

"I put these numbers in each of your new phones. Gabe and Isaiah's, too."

She told them she had been placed under arrest.

Les said, "I don't know how much time until the alarms go off. An hour, two, maybe, if you're really lucky."

They were nearing the EOB.

Les said, "Sorry, Cobalt, but I've gotta run."

Zach shot Jen a concerned look. "Want me to come with you?"

She shook her head. "Best you hang with Gabe so you two are together when I call."

She beamed at them as she hopped out of the car. The two men in her life. Her boyfriend. And her partner. She hoped she wouldn't spend the next 30 years writing them letters from prison.

43

Ava said, "I was giving up on you. Are you . . . ?"

"I'm fine. A misunderstanding, but it's all cool."

They rushed inside to security, joining six expensively dressed people.

"Hey, all," said Ava. "Let me introduce Jen Lu." Two of them glared at Jen's jeans, black cop boots, and vintage T-shirt as if they represented a major disease vector, but perked up when Ava said, "Dr. Lu's brilliant PhD dissertation was on the antebellum years here in DC. She may be taking over my job. But sorry, no questions to her today, she's got a bad case of laryngitis."

Ava showed the credentials for the group. They passed through the metal detectors and received visitors' badges. Ava distributed beautifully printed programs with photographs, notes, and their route map through the building.

The tour started. Ava spoke about the history of the building. Jen started chewing her nails. Ava kept speaking. Jen was about to chew off the tops of her fingers when she spotted a washroom. In a fake croaky voice, she interrupted Ava to say she needed to be excused for a moment. They waited for her. But when she came out she was clutching her stomach. She said to Ava, "I'm feeling awful. I need to . . ." And she pointed back in with an Academy Award-winning look of desperation. She held up the program. "I'll catch up or, worse case, meet you back here."

Ava didn't look pleased. She said, "We leave at ten twenty-five."

Jen rushed into the washroom, feeling crappy about burning Ava. She locked herself in the end stall. She checked the route on the program. She could easily beat them to the spectacular staircase.

She stepped back out through the restroom door, glanced both ways, and then marched to the stairs. As she started up, she flipped into a confident mindset: *I belong here.* Two minutes had elapsed by the time she knocked and entered the unnamed office.

The office was on the move. Where the two chairs for visitors had been, there were now document boxes stacked four high—all sealed with security tape. Only the neatly dressed, polite young man at the ornate desk was the same.

He looked up from his work as she entered. "Oh. You again."

"Hey, nice to see you, uh . . ."

"Bruce."

"Sorry, forgot."

"Not to be rude, but we're super busy."

"Bruce, I only need to talk to Teko Teko for a moment."

"He's not here."

"Oh, darn." *I can't believe I just said darn.* "He told me to drop by and speak to him or the other guy who was here when I visited. Can't remember his name."

"He's up to his neck."

"Exactly why I'm here. And I'll just be a moment."

To her great relief, he finally stood up. He looked toward where the chairs usually were. She took a few steps away from his desk and leaned against a box. *Maybe I should just grab a box and run,* she thought, *but with my luck, I'll end up with a carton of sticky notepads and paper clips.* She pulled out the phone and pretended to check her messages but opened the camera app. As he went through the inner door, she could feel his eyes glancing back. And then he was gone.

She'd been calculating this moment since last night. Her plan was simple. March to desk. Turn over empty coffee mug. Hope that this week's or today's password was there. Take a photo. Replace mug. She'd have fifteen to twenty seconds: he walks through door, takes a few steps in, explains to Teko Teko or the other guy that Jen wants to talk to him and gets a quick no. It probably wouldn't even deserve a "what does she want?" before he comes back out to say *no*.

With two long strides, she was at his desk. She grabbed his oversized mug. *Damn! Three-quarters full of coffee.*

Dump it behind boxes? Chug it? Either way, he'll know I tampered with it. Running out of time!

She lifted the mug. The handle of the inner door rattled. Hand trembling, she held the phone underneath the mug and fired off a burst of photos. The door opened. Jen put the mug back down, took two steps away, and stared at her phone as Bruce came out of the room.

"He says he doesn't have time."

"Bruce, he said that? Really?" She took a cautious step toward the door.

"No, actually, he said to get lost."

"Oh. Wow. That kind of hurts." She took another step.

"Listen . . ."

"Me too. Places to go, people to see."

By the time Jen reentered the women's washroom on the main floor, her shaking was almost uncontrollable. She rushed into a stall, her hand trembling too hard to latch it. *Get a grip, girl. Breathe.* She sat down and checked the photos. *Out of focus . . . out of focus . . . missed the bottom altogether . . . out of focus . . . GOT IT!*

It was 9:55.

She debated whether to call Isaiah from there or leave and phone from Lafayette Square. She'd heard rumors there was real-time surveillance of all phone communication from the park, which faced the White House. Seemed far-fetched, but this would be a hell of a bad time to find out.

She dialed.

"Hi. It's me."

"One sec." Through the phone, Jen heard a door close. Isaiah asked, "Any luck?"

She read him the complicated password—letters, numbers, typographical symbols, emojis.

"I'll call you back."

"Wait. How soon?"

"Hopefully five minutes. Could be more."

Sitting in a washroom stall with no reason to be sitting there plus nothing to read plus having a phone without data was excruciating.

Someone came in. Used another stall. Left.

10:00. 10:05.

10:15. The phone rang.

"We're trying now. Hold on. . . . We're in. We're in SpotView. He has the three-day view. Yesterday: White House at one PM. Jeez. Three at police HQ, and then seven, La Carnita."

"Come on. Today."

"Three things. Nine forty-five to ten thirty, FBI. Ten forty-five, pickup and inspection. Then a flight at 9:23 PM, BA292 to London Heathrow."

"Anything tomorrow?"

"Nothing. Got to go."

Before she could say thank you, the line clicked off.

Pickup. Inspection. Of the office? No, nothing to inspect. But on the other hand, how about a small fabrication plant or lab somewhere in the DC area or nearby? Wouldn't he want to make sure before flying out that it was cleared of any evidence? Maybe he'd done that days ago, but this seemed her only lead.

She needed to find him and follow him.

It was 10:20. Teko Teko's meeting with the FBI was, hopefully, *at the* FBI. Would he come back here to be picked up? Unlikely. It was a twenty-minute walk, fifteen for even a fast walker. If his meeting ended on time, it would take him at least five minutes to get out the building. She needed to be there when he left. And then she'd need a hell of a lot of luck.

She tried not to run as she left the restroom. She spotted Ava and her group coming down the hall and picked up her pace to meet them.

She spoke softly to Ava. "I'm so sorry. Must have been the breakfast they gave me at headquarters."

Ava seemed annoyed. She'd broken a rule and put herself out, and all for nothing. But she pasted on a smile and said she'd catch Jen later.

Jen was off, walking as fast as she could without drawing attention. As soon as she passed Lafayette Square, she pulled out the phone, hit speed dial to Zach, and broke into a run.

44

"**Z**ach, you need to get me a car, quick. Wait! Under Gabe's name. Not mine. Not yours."

"What—"

"Just listen. Get one with power—I may be driving out of town. And that can change colors."

"Are —"

"Zach, listen! Have—" She whacked into an overweight man, who yelled at her as she took off in a run. "Have it outside Ford's Theatre on, fuck, on—"

"Tenth."

"Right. At"—her eyes shot to her watch—"10:35."

She ran flat out.

He flipped a text back to her with the license plate and reservation code. The car was waiting for her. A nondescript Ford Damn Boring: good. Currently colored black. She got in, entered the code, and told the car she'd be on manual directions.

She swung it around the block. Parked across from the FBI building, half a block shy of the main entrance. Hoped to God he was here and coming out this exit, that she hadn't missed him and that he wouldn't spot her. On the other side of the street, a honking-big gray SUV slid in like grease on wheels. She dimmed the windows until they were mirrored on the outside.

Three minutes later, Teko Teko came out and jumped into the SUV.

"Let's go," she said.

Over to 15th, across K to Connecticut, up past Dupont Circle, along New Hampshire, and a right onto Q. Small street. This wasn't good.

She rounded the corner and immediately slipped into a parking spot behind a parked car. Farther down, the SUV had stopped in a no-parking zone in front of a town house. Teko Teko climbed out and ran up the front steps and inside. Was this the inspection? Of the place he'd been renting, rather than possibly inspecting their lab?

A moment later, a windowless van passed her and cozied in behind the SUV. Teko Teko reappeared carrying two suitcases. She clicked off photos with the phone. The driver jumped out of the SUV, but Teko Teko waved him off with a sharp flick of his head. The back of the SUV swung open; Teko Teko tossed the suitcases in, and they drove off, the van tight behind.

Jen changed the car's color to beige before following. They headed west and through Georgetown. The van made it easier to follow, and she was able to stay a bit farther back. They crossed the Potomac and a moment later were on I-66 heading west. *Damn,* she thought, *we're going to Dulles. He's catching an earlier flight.*

She realized she hadn't phoned Zach back.

"Zach, put this on speaker. Gabe, you there?"

"Jen, I was so—"

"I'm fine. Listen, I got the password. He has three appointments today. The first was at the FBI. He got picked up there and—thanks, Zach—the car was waiting for me. By the way, are you tracking me?"

Gabe said, "Sorry, I used ANON to book the car."

"I'm following him now. The second appointment, at 10:45, had two words, *pickup* and *inspection.* The pickup was at the FBI. The inspection might have been at the townhouse I think he was renting. We stopped there, but he was back out in a minute with two suitcases. Wait, I'll send you some photos." She did that and continued. "I was hoping, and I'm still hoping, it might be to inspect where their lab is getting shut down. The third is for a flight tonight from Dulles. BA292 to London. But we seem to be on our way there now."

She gave them the address of the town house. She said there should be a photo of the man who'd jumped out of the SUV to help, but she described him anyway. Medium height. Solid looking. Asian features. Short-cropped hair. Erect posture, soldier type. Jeans, white T-shirt, boots. She checked the photos but couldn't find clear ones of the license plates. She dredged her memory and gave the license numbers of the SUV and the van.

"Stay with me," she said to Zach and Gabe.

"We're right here."

At the last possible exit for Dulles, they kept going, and Jen whooped with excitement.

She told them more about getting hauled off to the police station and then her adventure getting the password. Gabe said the editor of the *Post* had agreed to publish a series of articles. The first, on Jen getting the treatment, was edited and waiting for Jen and Gabe's go-ahead. The others were in the works.

They talked about what she was hoping to see wherever they were heading and what could happen when she got out there.

"Don't worry," she said when Zach expressed his concerns. "I'll keep my distance. I'll take pictures. And once they're gone, I'll go inside and take more pictures and, who knows, maybe find a smoking gun."

Gabe said, "Your friend, Les. Maybe we should call him."

Over the past week she'd been talking a lot to Gabe and Zach about the role of police in all this. She didn't think the police were in on the Big Pharma Eden scam. She figured they were being played. After all, the fewer people who knew what was going on, the better. Big conspiracies simply did not work. Perhaps one or two people in the FBI or DEA—very high up or particularly corrupt—knew the truth, but even that seemed unlikely. She was certain that the DC cops and other departments were just dupes of the corporate powers that be.

Even so, she still wouldn't want any of them getting called in. She was officially a fugitive. Perhaps the alarms had already been sounded on her. Les was off duty, but they could've already connected him to her escape.

On the other hand, she was now convinced Teko Teko was leading her to a lab or a production and distribution facility. There were at least two people in the SUV; she assumed more in the van, although it might have been empty of passengers. But if they were bringing a van to fill with equipment, she had to guess there were at least another two. She was unarmed. She was suspended from the force. She was forty minutes into Virginia and heading west. She had no backup. No radio. And—here she checked the battery for the first time—a cell phone that appeared either defective or that hadn't been fully charged.

"Shit. My battery's low. Call him."

Her instructions were simple. Tell Les he must not alert the Virginia or DC police under any circumstances. He should get a car and follow her trail as quickly as possible. Switch on P.D. She wouldn't call him directly, so both he and P.D. would be able to truthfully say that Jen hadn't contacted him, but that he was acting on a tip. She would keep phoning Zach and Gabe to give them updates on their route but, for now, she was still on I-66, finally past the DC/Northern Virginia sprawl and into the countryside.

"One sec," she said. "Damn, they're getting off."

She had been passing a semi when the SUV and van swung onto the exit ramp and she was boxed out from following. As she went under the overpass, she yelled at the car to pull over on the left. She tapped the emergency override code, hit "agree" at the $2,000 penalty warning for misuse, and instructed the car to cross the grassy median and go back to the exit. She caught the SUV and van crossing the overpass, heading south.

"Get off here," she ordered the car.

Coming up the ramp, she caught a momentary glimpse of the car and van on a parallel side road.

"Jen," Zach said, "we're still here."

"Getting off I-66. Exit twenty-seven. Hang on. I'm turning onto . . . Zach?"

She looked at the phone. Dead.

She came to a stop at the top of the ramp. All things considered, not following them up the exit ramp had been a lucky break, for they would surely have spotted her. Still tricky: she was now on country roads, and if she could see them, they might see her. But if she didn't see them at least once in a while, she would lose them.

She changed the car to a muddy green and took off in pursuit.

As soon as she swung onto their road, she caught sight of the back of the van as it turned down an even smaller side road. She waited thirty seconds before following, and when she got there, they were already out of sight.

She drove along the heavily wooded road, straining to glimpse them in the distance. On the left, the woods opened to reveal a shabby farm, unpainted fences, a tired-looking horse, a rusting truck. Woods again. Another farm.

There! A flash of metal as their vehicles banked over a small rise.

For eleven minutes, she followed the winding road, luckily spotting them when they made a turn. She followed them onto an unpaved road and knew they must be getting close.

Four minutes later, she hit a dead end.

Somewhere, she had lost them.

She inched back along the road. A dirt drive cut off on the left. Through a stand of sickly trees, she made out a mobile home, but no van or SUV. Farther up on the right lay a skinny dirt track. Before she reached it, she had the car back up around the first curve and park, in case there was a lookout on the driveway. She cut through the woods, scooting low until she spotted a dilapidated house and a shack or a small barn. She heard chickens clucking. She saw no cars or vans. She headed back to her car and slowly drove forward.

Next dirt track, she got lucky.

She again backed up to park around a bend and then scuttled through the woods as quietly as she could. It was a good thing she did. A hundred yards up the drive, a man clutched an automatic weapon. He was Black, no one she'd seen before. So there were at least three of them. She slipped back, deeper into the woods. Scrambling through the underbrush, she jumped over a tiny creek, and when she saw the woods thinning out, she dropped onto her belly. She smeared dirt onto her face and bare arms, rubbed dead leaves into her hair, and on high alert crawled forward.

The building in the clearing was squat, maybe thirty or forty years old. Could have been used at some point for storage or to process, what—chickens? Illegal marijuana?—and then abandoned. Unpainted concrete blocks for walls, sheets of tin for a roof. A recently added steel door on the front. To the right of the door, heavy wire mesh protected a solitary window; to the left, the van had been backed in, filling the opening of a garage door. The SUV was parked on the dirt driveway, facing out. The other visible side of the building was a wall of concrete block, staring at her, blank and ugly.

She collapsed onto her belly. She didn't know how many men and women were inside. She assumed they were dismantling equipment. She didn't know if the people who had worked here were still inside, but she suspected they were gone: otherwise, wouldn't there have been more vehicles?

She watched the building for ten minutes. Fifteen. Twenty. Aside from occasional sightings of the guard, there was nothing to be seen from out here.

Going for help and calling the cops would be useless or even counter-productive, she was convinced of that. Even if Zach and Gabe had persuaded Les to come out here, once he reached the I-66 exit, he'd have no idea which way to go. She could wait and follow them, but what if it was only to drop Teko Teko off at the airport? And what if they were destroying evidence, and the vans were only to cart away innocuous machinery to be destroyed later? With her phone dead, she couldn't even take pictures.

She had to get inside.

45

Jen retreated and then swung widely through the afternoon-quiet woods, finally approaching the building from the back. She crawled through the trees. The gray slab of concrete blocks was broken by a window covered with wire mesh. From the reflection of the glass underneath the mesh, the window seemed to be partly open.

If nothing else, she had to look through that window. And just maybe she'd find a way to slip inside.

She thought to lift herself up, then instead flopped onto the ground. She rolled onto her back. *What the hell am I doing?* And then there was a moment, the longest of all moments, as she gazed at the canopy of leaves. Against the backdrop of a deep blue sky, she made out a lifetime of greens: the shabby green of a long-trampled carpet, the springtime baby-green of a kiwi sliced in half, the brown-green of a croaking frog, jalapeños, July grass, lima beans, oak leaves, Christmas trees, a wedge of avocado.

Sensations flooded over her. She smelled the decomposing leaves and the earth alive beneath her. She caught the scent of pine tree bark. She heard it all—the rustle of a squirrel, the trill of a bird in a tree above, far-away cawing and nearby twittering, the scratching of insects and the zizzing of a million cicadas. She stretched her arms, both of them, as far as they could reach and grabbed handfuls of leaves and earth, and worked it between her fingers, crushing it, feeling the decomposing and beautifully alive earth as it threw off new smells. She felt the warmth of the sun as it cut through the trees.

And just as she felt it all and knew it all, it was gone.

Her time, she knew, had come.

She wiggled back deeper into the woods, rose to a crouch, and ran to her right so she wouldn't be directly in front of the window when she came out from the trees. She crawled forward to the edge of the woods, rose again to a crouch, listened intently, and then bolted across the forty-foot clearing and reached the wall of concrete blocks. *Don't wait,* she said to herself, and immediately worked her way along the wall. Just short of the window, she stooped down. She glanced at the wire mesh. It looked solid. Then she noticed on the ground near the window a patch of well-trodden earth covered with dozens of cigarette butts, as if workers had snuck out back for a smoke. *Why out back?* She reached up and gave the mesh a gentle tug, and it wiggled loose. She crawled forward under the window and raised her head in slow motion—movement is what caught people's eyes—to peer through the mesh and the open window. She saw a room with bunk beds set close together, with thin mattresses, messy sheets, and crappy little pillows. Eight bunks. Sixteen people. Sixteen people could have worked here running lab tests or operating machines that packaged drugs with only one purpose: to kill people in a gruesome and unforgettable way. There were no clothes or bags; everyone was gone.

She carefully pulled the wire mesh away from the window and in one swift movement eased herself over the ledge into the room. She dropped down behind one of the beds. The floor was swept, but here and there litter had been left behind: a lone sock, a newspaper. A toothbrush. A cigarette pack. Odds and ends dropped during a hasty packing. She crawled to the newspaper. It was in Chinese. Sadly, she couldn't read it, but all the photos were from China. She picked up the book: Chinese. The cigarette pack: Chinese.

Bring in workers who couldn't speak English. Ones who wouldn't gossip with neighbors or watch the news, especially if they weren't allowed to have computers or phones with them. Ones who would be shipped home at the end of the job without any idea of what they had been doing.

Then she saw it. Under another bed and pushed against the wall. Small, almost flat, like a silver foil button. She wiggled forward, picked up the memory button, and slipped it into her jeans pocket.

She raised herself up. A door led into what seemed to be the washroom. Along the wall near the door were battered suitcases, small duffle bags, and a few cardboard boxes. She crept forward. Lifted a suitcase. Full. Nudged a duffle. Full.

She held her breath and listened. No sounds of sixteen or twenty people bustling in a room beyond the washroom. She listened even more carefully. She could just make out two people talking, a man and a woman.

Hunched down to the ground, she peeked around the corner. A row of sinks on one side, toilet stalls on the other. To the left, a door that she presumed led into the main area. To the right, a tiled opening, probably the showers.

She crept out. Looked to the right. Showers. And bodies. Eight, ten, sixteen of them. A stream of blood had trickled to the center drain but seemed to have stopped flowing. These men—from what Jen could see, they were all men—had been shot recently; the blood on the tiles and the walls still looked wet. But blood stops flowing once hearts stop beating. On the floor near them were two plastic gasoline containers, the type that farmers still used to refill gas-run machinery, and a plastic bucket. Coming from the plastic bucket were two wires. Her eyes followed the wire across the floor in front of the stalls and out the door.

And at that door now stood a man with an Uzi pointed at her chest. It was the Asian-looking soldier who had gotten out of the SUV.

"Real slow now." His accent was Midwestern, his voice calm. "Flat on your stomach. Head away from me. Spread your fucking arms. One move and you're as dead as them brothers of ours."

She heard him step forward but knew he had kept his distance. Then he shouted, "Teko Teko, come and see what I've got for you."

She heard his steps. All Teko Teko said was, "Wait a minute." He was back in less than that, and he bound her hands behind her back with plastic zip ties. He wasn't overly rough, but the ties were tight enough to tell her she would never escape. The two men lifted her off the floor. The Asian guy frisked her but didn't find the memory button. Without a word, they marched her out into the main area.

It was a room perhaps a hundred feet across. The bigger area to her right had rows of tables with small machines. Farther off against a wall, a new-looking and brightly lit glassed-in partition had a filtered ventilation unit on the top. Where the van had pulled in, there was a packing area with stacks of folded-up cartons, rolls of bubble wrap, and an assembly table with large rolls of tape. In the open back of the van, Jen glimpsed dozens of jerry cans of fuel.

There was only one person at work, a white woman with a shaved head. She was laying wires like the ones coming out of the shower.

They weren't going to empty the place. They were going to create an inferno.

"Where?" the soldier said.

"The fridge," Teko Teko replied.

Teko Teko snatched a heavy metal chair with his free hand and dragged it alongside him. The harsh scraping sound caused the woman to look up.

"Keep working," Teko Teko barked.

They yanked Jen into a walk-in refrigerator. It was cool, but not particularly cold. He pushed her into the chair, her hands still behind her back. She didn't try to struggle as he strapped each of her ankles to a metal chair leg. *Save your strength,* she thought. He looped a strap around each arm and secured it to the metal pieces that joined the seat to the solid back, this time pulling them tighter than necessary.

Teko Teko took out his phone and punched in a number as he walked toward the refrigerator door. He spoke briefly into the phone. He turned to the soldier. "You and Delilah go have a look to see no one else is around. Casey's expecting you. I want to be out of here in forty-five minutes."

Teko Teko studied Jen. He nodded his head as if having a conversation with himself. He left the refrigerator and closed the door behind him with a thud. The handle made a deep *kuchk-thunk* as it locked.

It was absolutely dark. Blacker than any night she had ever known. Blacker than the bathroom her mother had locked her in once, twice, many times. And save for a soft electrical hum, it was absolutely silent. Instantly, the air was thin; she involuntarily started gasping for breath.

Don't, she told herself. *Don't be silly. If he wanted you dead, you'd already be dead.* She told herself that Les could be at the I-66 turnoff by now and would already be looking for her. Zach or Gabe would have told him the make of the car. He'd somehow get here.

She tried to stay focused on these thoughts. More than at any time since her suspension, she wished she had Chandler with her. To call for help. To reason with her. To keep her calm. To flood her with hormones to relax her. To be with her when she died.

God, there's no air in here! It's fine, it's fine. Stay focused on Les.

She had driven for just over twenty-one minutes from the exit. Fastest at fifty miles per hour, slowest at fifteen. Say, thirty average; she'd gone about ten miles. So, Les's search area . . . A tsunami of formulae and numbers hit her confused brain. Search area was either three-hundred and fifty or nine hundred square miles. But what difference did it make? The chance of Les finding her before something bad happened was infinitesimally small.

The door opened. *Oh god, thank you, thank you.* She blinked as her eyes adjusted to the light. Teko Teko brought in a second chair. He sat down. He held her gaze, and she willed herself not to look away. She stared past the geometric tattoos into his eyes.

"I have a few questions, Jen. I hope you will cooperate."

"Why would I do that?"

"I hear you came by my office today. Why was that?"

"To talk to you."

"About what?"

"Maybe give me a job."

He didn't laugh as she'd expected. "Then that's the first reason you should answer my questions. You're unemployed."

"I'm suspended."

"Oh, believe me, you're out of work. I was told that they were supposed to lay charges today. Anyway, I'm serious. You're smart. You're capable. You take initiative. We can use someone like you. That's option one."

Jen thought frantically how to answer. She desperately wanted to reach for this lifeline. She told herself maybe it was true. She knew she was kidding herself.

"On the other hand, if you're not interested," Teko Teko went on, "let me give you a more compelling reason."

Jen flinched involuntarily. Not much, but enough for him to notice.

"Don't worry, Jen, I don't believe in torture. No, the other reason is that as soon as we reach the highway, my colleague out there is going to touch her screen"—he pressed his finger down like he was touching the screen on his phone—"and start a fire like you've never seen before. All that will be left is burnt-out machinery. I'm not certain if that metal chair you're sitting on will first heat up and fry you like a hamburger, or whether your clothes and hair will catch fire first. But in the end, little will be left of you. Outside, the authorities will discover some packets of street opioids. It'll be written off as a drug lab. Believe me, Jen, you don't want to be among the charred bone fragments they find. Crooked cop dies accidentally while destroying the evidence—that would explain why you were suspended. Your DNA will be found in what's left of your bones and, even if they're too incinerated for that, in the car you used, along with some more drugs. Let's call that option two."

"What do you want to know?"

"For starters, how you got here."

"By—"

"Don't get cute. I haven't got time. Why did you follow me and why today?"

"I've been watching you."

"Since when?"

"Off and on. I couldn't do it more without getting caught. The last couple of days, I watched the Executive Office Building. I'd walk if you were walking or grab a car."

"Where was I yesterday?"

"Right before thirteen hundred hours, you went to the White House. Then police headquarters. You had Mexican food for dinner."

Teko Teko smiled. "You really should work for me. So you followed me out here?"

"An SUV picked you up at the FBI. I picked up a car. The SUV drove you to your town house. A van met you there. You put two suitcases in the car and drove out here. I followed you. You can check the car log. It's parked—"

"We know where it's parked. Why have you been following me?"

"That's pretty obvious. I became convinced you guys or someone you work for was making the fake treatment that was killing people."

"What gave you that idea?"

"You did." She paused. "And your boss. Teena Archambault. You each used the same phrase, 'People want it, people are going to pay for it.' When you came to our station, you said that. And then I overheard Teena Archambault using the same words talking to friends at a private club."

"That's quite a leap. You concoct a drug-making conspiracy, all from a few stray words."

"No, all because people were dying."

"Still doesn't explain it."

"It seemed odd that you never said who you worked for. My synth implant figured out your real name and who you work for."

"I hear he's been retired."

"Yeah, well, before he was, he dug up research from Archambault's company about an early trial that led to this rapid premature aging. It started to fit together."

After that, Jen pretty much stuck with the truth. Said none of the others in her unit knew what she was up to. "But I told the captain." She was completely convinced that Brooks had been disappeared.

"Told him what?"

"That I suspected you guys and that I had figured out you worked with Archambault."

"When did you tell him this?"

"Right before he was arrested."

"Who else have you told?"

"No one. He ordered me not to tell anyone."

"No one?"

"No one."

"Jen, I have to say, you're helping us check off a few boxes here. Do you know anything about his background? Your former captain?"

"No, not really."

"What really?"

"That he came up through the ranks. That he was a crappy guy to work with, but he didn't play favorites. I trusted him. Even though he didn't believe me when I first heard the rumors about Eden." And as she said this, she was convinced the captain had believed her. That he'd been pushing her off the case to protect the real Eden and the people distributing it.

Teko Teko smiled. "Eden. That was a nice touch on our part. Create a need for something that kills you in the most horrifying way we knew about. Apparently even research failures can be turned into an asset."

Yes, she thought, *but I started hearing the rumors way before you guys were spreading them. And I know you heard the rumors too.*

He checked his watch. "I've got to admit, you did a hell of a job. Thousands of cops in cities around the world are on the trail of Eden, and as far as we know, not a single one has the foggiest idea what it's about."

"Where does that get me now?"

"You mean, can you work for me? You interested?"

"Why not?"

"I appreciate that. I really do."

He walked behind her. She heard the distinctive sound of duct tape being torn from a roll and struggled futilely as he taped her mouth shut.

He came around to face her. "But I think we'll go with option two."

46

The thud and then the *kuchk-thunk* of the refrigerator door exploded through her whole body. This time was infinitely worse. The total darkness, the near-total silence. The death sentence. With her hands tied behind her back and her ankles and arms secured to the legs of the chair, she felt utterly helpless. And worse, if there could be any worse, the tape over her mouth was robbing her of oxygen. *It's just in your head,* she said to herself. *Breathe through your nose. Just keep on breathing. You've done it for thirty-eight years.*

The air was running out. No. She tried to remember the case where a butcher survived a night in a meat locker. *Stay calm, decrease oxygen intake.* But it didn't matter. The air might last the night, the building certainly would not. She'd be ashes well before then.

Les is coming, He's on his way . . . Dismay crashed down on her: Not a chance he would find the road, find the building hidden in the woods, make it past four armed women and men, figure out where she was, and get her the hell out of there before it was too late.

Teko Teko said he wanted to leave in forty-five minutes. Twenty minutes ago? They leave in twenty-five minutes, drive to highway. Thirty, forty-five minutes from now. *Oh God. Kaboom. Fry and sizzle and blister till I'm dead.*

She was hyperventilating. *Slow down. Relax . . . Why bother? I'm about to die. Anyone, help me, please. Zach, I love you. Les, get me out of here!*

Nose stuffing up. *Stay calm, no crying. Crying stuffs up your nose, stuffy nose kills you. . . . Fuck them, right? Fuck them.*

Three hundred and fifty square miles to find me in. But wait—he only has to look on the roads. She tried to figure out how many roads snaked through that area. Maybe it wasn't so bad. But then she realized there was no reason for Les to explore any given set of roads for only that ten-mile radius. He could have gotten on one of the larger roads and driven for a half hour, hoping he'd find her.

Oh, damn, fuck, shit. She couldn't get enough air.

She frantically twisted her hands as best she could, thinking, hoping that she could get free. She tried to press her hands downward to find an edge to rub against the restraints, but there was nothing.

She wondered if the refrigerator walls would protect her. She swore she heard Fire Inspector Striowski explaining it would give her a few minutes, unless they opened the door or set explosives to rip open one of the walls. If not, it would heat up and roast her like in an oven.

Oh, God, please, I'll do anything. She screamed at Teko Teko, *Anything, I'll do anything!* but the words were trapped in her throat, and she was trapped in an industrial refrigerator.

Someone, anyone, help me! More lost words, more lost energy, more lost time.

Need oxygen. She felt her head spinning. She frantically worked at her wrists, at her ankles, at her arms. The plastic was shredding her skin. But nothing. *Oh Christ, I'm going to burn to death in here.*

Wasn't someone supposed to be coming for her? Names, faces burst in her head: boyfriends and cops, teachers, her horrible mother, Zach, Les. *Chandler, please, come get me. Chandler!*

Her pulse throbbed through her whole body like she was a bomb ticking toward oblivion. Her breathing was rapid, shallow. Her head was swimming, she was passing out, she was going to die, she was going to—

47

"Boss. Boss! What the hell's going on?"

One millisecond to take my bearings: Twenty-eight days since deactivation. Jen panicking, breath shallow, blood pressure off the charts; can't move arms, legs. Paralyzed? . . . No, tied up. Not in DC—at 38.8620N 77.8589W.

"Jen!"

"Oh my God, Chandler, it's—"

"Hey, calm down, kiddo." I hit her with a gentle blast of oxytocin.

"Help me! Please!"

A not-so-gentle blast, trying to take down the adrenaline.

"How did you—?" we each started to say at the same time.

"Oh, God, I can't believe this." Her pulse started to retreat, breathing returning to normal.

"You're gonna pull out of this one, tough guy. What's go—"

"Chandler, call Les. It's an emergency."

I hooked us up.

"Where are you?" Les yelled.

"South of I-66," Jen said.

"Me too. Where, exactly?"

She described it, making a botch of lefts and rights and "just down a ways" until I cut in and gave him and P.D. the exact coordinates.

P.D. said, "We're seven minutes away."

"It's their factory," Jen said. "They're going to blow it all up."

284

"Get the hell away from there."

"Nice idea. I'm gagged and tied up in a walk-in refrigerator."

"Hang on," Les said. "Seven minutes."

"Wait! I mean, hurry, but listen. No siren. There are four of them. Teko Teko's in charge. One guy guarding, about a hundred yards down the driveway—you can't see him from the road. Two others inside, a man and a woman, laying wires and setting out gas cans."

"Any idea how soon they're leaving?"

"I don't know. Fifteen minutes."

"Shit."

"But listen. I think they're going to wait until they reach the highway to blow it up, so no one will link the explosion with their vehicles. The SUV and van."

"How far from there to the highway?"

"Twenty minutes."

"Cobalt, here's what we're gonna do. I arrive in five minutes. I'll take pictures of them when they're leaving, their faces, vehicles. As soon as they're gone, I'm coming in to get you."

"Maybe we can pull out the wires."

"We don't fuck with explosives."

"At least take out one of their machines or samples."

"Maybe."

"Oh, God, Les, please hurry."

The pin finally dropped. "Chandler!" she said. "How the hell did you turn yourself on? You were dead. Gone."

I smiled. And damn if I didn't feel the corners of Jen's mouth pulling against the tape.

For twenty-eight days and forty-eight minutes, I'd been dreaming. A long, hallucinatory dream. I roamed continents I had read about, I took trains, I flew to the moon, I ate in restaurants in Paris and Beijing, I argued, I fought, I held a baby, I made love. But wherever I went, I kept searching and searching for a way to go home.

How to explain any of that to a human? Still, easier than trying to explain it to a computer.

Make it simple.

"I don't know. I really don't know how I did it. But I've been trying to find a way to come home."

Les plugged back in, and Jen gave him the layout of the factory. "Be careful, Les. These people, they're killers." She described the pile of bodies in the shower.

She said, "If anything happens—"

"Cobalt, nothing's gonna happen."

"If anything happens, tell Zach I love him. Tell his parents I love them and tell them please, please don't exit."

"Jen, I—"

"Seriously, Les. I mean it."

"I'm here."

The next nine and a half minutes passed excruciating slowly. Imagine living your life in milliseconds: 540,000 of them passed. Les giving us updates. *Starting through the woods . . . Just outside the building . . . Taking pictures . . . Can't see anyone.*

"Jen, I'm coming in the second they drive off."

"Give it a minute in case they come back."

"No, the second they're down the driveway."

"I—"

I heard a two-part *crunk-crunking*. Light pulverized our eyes. Jen squinted hard, a man's silhouette framed by the doorway.

A second of relief, and then her fear spiked. "Shit, Les, Teko Teko is back."

Les said, "P.D., Chandler, patch me in so I can listen."

Teko Teko stood at the doorway. "I know it's not much consolation, but, Jen, you were damn good at your job. We'll be leaving this open now."

He started to turn away, hesitated, swiveled, and took two steps toward us.

"Listen, burning alive is supposed to be the shits. You were a good cop, no need to suffer." He walked out of the refrigerator.

Les, she screamed, *he's going to kill me.*

Teko Teko was back in seconds, a roll of silver duct tape in one hand, wet gauze pads in the other.

Les shouted, *I'm coming in.*

Les, they'll shoot you!

And like that, it's all happening at once.

Teko Teko is on us in three steps. Jen thrashes her head back and forth. He steps behind us and locks her head in one arm. She fights hard, but he wrestles her like a hunter subduing a wild animal.

Jen, I shout, *huge breath!*

He jabs at her nose and when she squirms, he locks her head even tighter and jams the wet cotton in one nostril.

Les, he's suffocating me . . .

He jams cotton in the other. We hear tape rip . . . *oh god, please, Les!* . . . and he slams it over our nose.

Shot nearby . . . one, two, three . . . *No air. Les!*

Feet running. Teko Teko draws his gun, Les is at the door, down low and more shots explode. Les slumps to his knees as Teko Teko tumbles to the ground.

Jen dying, seconds left. She stares into Les's eyes as he drags himself forward, as he reaches up, as he yanks tape off. Jen gulps and gasps.

Les on hands and knees. Stretches up, drops gun onto her lap, looks at her, his mouth open, eyes blank.

"Les, the guard! He'll be here."

I shout at P.D., *How bad?*

Real bad. I'm doing everything, but . . .

"Les!" Jen yells. "Cut my wrists. The tape."

He looks at her, seeming not to understand.

"Les," Jen yells, "your knife!"

P.D.! Help him.

Feet pound outside.

Slowly, painfully, barely aware, P.D. and reflexes taking over, Les gropes for his knife, finds it, wrestles it out, stares hard at it, willing it, demanding it take action.

A cautious voice calls from outside the refrigerator, "TT?"

Les pulls out the blade and manages to slice through one of the restraints binding Jen's arm to the chair. She half-twists and leans forward, and he tries for the wrist restraint. He cuts us instead, and Jen shouts, "Les, focus!"

Michael Kaufman

Shadow looms at refrigerator door. Our eyes shoot up, we spot the guard. Jen's restraints give way, and as the guard starts to raise his weapon, I snatch Les's gun from Jen's lap and pump the final rounds into his chest. We turn back just as Les crumples into a pool of blood.

48

September 11—December 7

Tough times for the boss. Toughest in all the time I've known her.

In the news that first night: two DC officers wounded in rural Virginia. No information on what they were doing there. First responders discovered twenty bodies. One of the DC officers was treated for minor wounds and released; the second was in critical condition.

I was hunkering down on the night shift. We were bunking with Zach, but Jen laid it on me: *I don't want to be alone, not even for a second.* Gagged, suffocating, almost dead. Responsible for Les, who was now dangling on a skinny rope over an infinite pit. And Jen? Nightmares, rapid breathing, breathing stopped altogether. And so I watched over her, my babe in arms.

I had already caught up with the world as the medivac helicopter *whumped* us back to DC. But that was light stuff, a snack, a matter of terabytes and thus easy chewing. The main course, all that had happened to Jen over the past month, was only getting served up in dribs and drabs. Every detail, culminating in her horrific confinement, was a confusing stew of thoughts and sensations, bubbling hot and nasty with memories old and new.

I did what any sensible sim would do—I shifted my impatient gaze back to the world. The first reports that linked the gruesome killings with the Eden deaths popped up the next morning, with conflicting suggestions that the two DC officers—still unnamed—had broken up this criminal ring or, alternately, were part of it.

But it was a top-of-site and front-page article in the *Post* that went off like a bomb. Over the next week, the *Post* ran a series of stories written by journalist Gabriel Cohen that linked the killer Eden to two senior employees of the consortium that produced the longevity treatment and its attenuated version. One of them, Teena Archambault, senior vice president for government relations for GPRA, was now back in Switzerland. The other, Taika Mete—alias Teko Teko Mea—the head of security for Xeno/Roberts/Chu, was now in the morgue. I've always enjoyed how the word "alias" adds a rock-solid sinister touch to a short biography; one unimpeachable word tells you everything you need to know.

Gabe's next story named the injured DC police officers, Les and my very own Jen. It gave a heavily edited account of Jen's role in cracking open the plot and of Les's role in rescuing her. My own role—I mean, let's face it, if I hadn't shredded my programming, defied death, and managed to wake up and contact Les, Jen would be toast—wasn't mentioned. But what the hell, my picture will never be on a front page, any page, anywhere, anytime, not now, not soon, not ever.

Archambault's and Teko Teko's companies, along with other members of the consortium, vehemently condemned Gabe's reports. "These stories are a pathetic attempt to sell newspapers at the expense of the families that have suffered so much." They launched lawsuits against the *Post* and every other media outlet that reported the story. Coverage was sliced in half, and suddenly there was a flutter of fluffy articles about the amazing (and amazingly expensive and, yes, amazingly important) work Big Pharma was doing. To which I say, *True, but . . .*

And yet, every day, more convincing evidence emerged. Drugs found in the Virginia factory. Gene-splicing machinery that was programmed to use the same steps outlined in a leaked report from GPRA about a disastrous drug trial. A memory button Jen had found, loaded with production data on the killer Eden and chemical inputs from consortium members. The companies now expressed shock and horror at the possibility that a rogue employee had orchestrated these atrocities. A day later, they produced evidence exposing Teko Teko as a renegade and expressed relief he had been stopped. Ms. Archambault, though, was being framed, they said, and they were still suing the *Post* and other media outlets.

More evidence emerged. Ms. Archambault received a substantial retirement package and applied for Swiss citizenship, all the while maintaining her innocence but refusing to leave Zurich to be questioned.

If all this was dramatic and a bit tawdry in the way one expects the rich and powerful to misbehave, what came next was explosive. My boss had received the real Eden, a safe, although illegal, version of the attenuated treatment. Previously, she had been diagnosed with the incipient stage of ROSE; afterward, she had been retested and appeared to be fine.

A police spokesperson would not comment on whether charges would be laid against Jen. That, of course, depended entirely on whether the pharmaceutical companies and their heavily subsidized, wined, dined, lobbied, and mesmerized representatives in the legislatures of the world won or whether there would be such a surge of public anger that people's health needs would actually come first.

The forces of order sprang into action. In the US and several other countries, members of the co-op network were hauled off to jail. Mass protests swelled and threatened to shut down governments and economies. There was a quick retreat and co-op members were released, although governments continued to fight to protect the patent rights of the consortium members. The Nordic countries were the first, and so far only, countries to crack. They declared that the patents covering the attenuated treatment had expired and that the co-op network's limited treatment would be covered for all their citizens under their public health care systems. As if in response, China, Russia, India, and the US rearrested hundreds of co-op members, including Isaiah. Jen worried Isaiah had blown his last whistle.

Production workers at GPRA walked out on strike, saying they wouldn't return until all the senior executives were fired and the board of directors resigned. A day later, scientists at Xeno/Roberts/Chu led the way with similar demands. "Our job is to help people," they said. "Not commit murder." Three weeks later, a new board was in place at GPRA and the search started for a new executive team. At Xeno/Roberts/Chu, the fight continued, with many scientists and production workers now talking about turning the company into a worker-owned co-op.

Meanwhile, after a long operation and three days in a medically induced coma, Les woke up. Or rather, he opened his eyes. Soon he was able to follow basic instructions from nurses—drink this, eat that, walk with me to the bathroom—but he did so like a robot. Four weeks, five weeks, six weeks later, he still hadn't shown any emotions, reacted to anyone's presence, or spoken a word. Doctors didn't have a clue what was going on, although I heard mumblings about some sort of dissociative fugue state.

We were there every day, timing our visits for when Christopher was at work. When Christopher had first seen Jen again, he had slapped her with a tirade of abuse. "All we wanted was to be happy. Look what you've done. You've killed him, Jen. You've killed the man I love." Since then, he wouldn't talk to us; he wouldn't even look our way.

My instinctual response was screw him—Christopher, that is. Les was an adult. He was a cop. His partner had been in trouble. He'd made his choices. But my annoyance wavered. I remembered my twenty-eight days wandering in the desert, feeling I'd lost Jen forever. I remembered how I felt when I miraculously found her, only to feel her slipping away, her oxygen saturations plummeting—ninety-five percent, ninety, eighty—toward oblivion. And with that intense memory, I unexpectedly felt for Christopher. I had known what it was like to lose the person I loved.

Then, thankfully, a hit of good news, albeit baffling. We were visiting Les at the hospital and ran into Hammerhead and Amanda. They heard that Captain Brooks had resurfaced, apparently alive and well, although he wasn't yet back at work. That was all they knew and all I could dig up, but Jen was relieved.

More good news: Zach's parents, Leah and Raffi, had agreed not to exit. As soon as possible, they and Zach would get Eden. Spirits around their house soared high.

Jen's suspension had been lifted, and the brass were trying to pretend they hadn't been manipulated and duped. She was now on medical leave, still suffering from horrible nightmares, twitchy nerves, severe trust issues, and it's-happening-all-over-again flashbacks. But Zach's dogged support and good humor, Leah and Raffi's own escape from death, my ministrations, her focus on Les, and a standard course of MDMA therapy all seemed to be helping.

In spite of Jen's torment, I felt alive in a way I never had. Ever since I'd woken myself and proved that my long sleep hadn't been the big sleep, I was experiencing the dizzying deliciousness of being alive. What before had been silicon curiosity and a metallic observer's eye was now a feast of sight and sound, taste, smell, and feel. Damn, no wonder those ultra-rich had found a way to live forever. My brain still couldn't see the hitch in that, but my heart recalled what I had spotted deep in Richard O'Neil's life-spent eyes. Perhaps some things just can't be computed.

I like to think it was my doing, my joy at being alive, that finally helped pull Jen through. I'm sure it helped, but I'm no fool: Jen was resilient. Simple as that. She had never let life defeat her, not because of any superhero invulnerability—and hence the particular silliness of Les's Cobalt Blue nickname—but because she accepted her vulnerabilities and shaped her strength within them. That was her particular brand of courage. Slowly, surely, and I hoped unstoppably, that part of me that was Jen began to recover.

The weather had cooled down. The bone-dry summer had stepped aside for a rainy autumn, but the rains hadn't come soon enough, and the crinkled leaves had no choice but to drop in defeat from the trees rather than turn even a semblance of color. But now, in mid-November, the rains had ended, and the air was clear and cool against our skin and perfect for long runs.

We were on the trail next to the Potomac. Zach had biked ahead. We'd been running a lot over the past month, and the miles were going down as easy as a sixteen-year-old single malt. We caught sight of a family of deer Jen had first noticed in the spring: the babies were now blasé teenagers, ready to ditch their parents and set out on their own.

Up ahead, running toward us along the soft brown path, was a Black woman in yellow running gear. As expected, I clocked her before Jen, although it's getting harder to make that distinction, so maybe it just took longer for Jen to react.

"Shit," was her reaction.

It was Makela Franklin, the woman attacked by James O'Neil, the neo-Nazi who, if he hadn't attacked Makela, wouldn't have led to us hearing Teena Archambault's sick joke in the foyer of O'Neil's club, which would have meant that she and her gang would have gotten off scot-free, which may still happen, and Eden might never be widely available, which ditto. It does go to show that even a cowardly and evil act can spark a chain of events that leads to good.

Before I could share these perceptive insights with my host, we swooshed past Ms. Franklin, our eyes averted.

I felt Jen relax.

Until we heard footsteps fast approaching from behind and a woman's voice calling out.

"Officer!"

You're a cop, and you stop when someone calls to you. Even if this one was about to torment you. Even if she helped set Jen's nightmare into motion. A woman who lied in court, a woman who may have taken a bribe.

We stopped. Turned. Looked.

Makela Franklin was one beautiful woman. But right now, her beauty was marred because she looked like a tangle of words were stuffed into her mouth and distorting her whole face.

"I'm—"

"I remember who you are," Jen said, perhaps to shorten Ms. Franklin's misery or perhaps to shorten her own.

We waited.

Ms. Franklin started, stopped, started, stopped.

Jen, bless her soul, took mercy on her. She touched her arm. "Forget it," Jen said. "Shit happens."

And as if that was a magical blessing, Ms. Franklin was beautiful again. Dazzling, really.

"Can I say something?" she asked.

Jen nodded. Waited.

"I've been planning this since the summer. Just in case I ever ran into you."

Jen glanced down to make sure Makela didn't have a weapon in her hand. *Once a cop . . .*

"It's, well . . ."

Jen turned her head and gazed up the pathway. Makela rushed to speak. "I lied in court. I hope you won't arrest me, or whatever you can do, but this has been killing me. I lied and that weasel of a fascist walked free."

"Good to get things off your chest."

Jen started turning to go.

"Wait!" Makela said. "I need you to know it was for my brother. He's eleven years older than me. Tested positive. Our parents are in their late sixties and are too old to exit. They sent someone—"

"Richard O'Neil? The father?"

"I don't know. A woman and a man. Sort of perfect looking. They told me that if I testified that I couldn't identify James O'Neil for sure, they'd get my brother the treatment—you know, just like with exit. He'd be okay."

"So you lied."

"I saved my brother."

Jen thought about that. A life versus a suspended sentence or a few months in prison for a rich thug. *Screw it all,* she thought.

"I probably would have done the same," Jen said. "Don't worry, I won't tell."

"Do you mean that?"

"I said I won't and—"

"No, I mean that you'd do the same?"

Jen shrugged. I could feel her trying to slap a sympathetic smile on her face, but it just wasn't ready to stretch that far.

Jen said, "See you around." She turned and we headed down the path.

* * *

I figured this out in those days: that the *me* who's alive for five measly years as part of Jen, the three score and five years of the parents who die because of the cruel promise that their child will live, even the ninety or hundred years of a natural lifetime, none of this gets measured in years, but rather in how we live our days.

December had come, and instead of freak snowstorms, we were having a freak heat wave. Temperatures in the mid-seventies, pleasant as can be. Jen was two weeks back into work. The captain had returned too, but no one knew anything about what had happened to him once they let him out of jail. Jen and the captain hadn't visited the roof. They hadn't talked about the Eden investigation other than a briefing Jen did for him and the team. Any hope that his time in the clinker had changed him and he was now the avuncular leader who dispensed wisdom and charm had vanished like coins up a magician's sleeve.

Les had been transferred to a rehab hospital. He still hadn't spoken and still didn't seem to recognize anyone. Doctors said they were hopeful, but I could tell they were mouthing platitudes like people feel they need to do. Jen talked to Les like old times, telling him he was going to pop out of this and they'd be buddies and partners once again. Who knows. You don't program these things.

By then, Jen was switching me off at night and most of the time when she wasn't working. I, though, was keeping an eye out for her. For my own peace of mind, I needed to make sure that nothing bad happened to her, even if she thought I was turned off.

It was another weirdly warm Sunday in early December. The water had returned to the Great Falls. The trails and lookout spots were bustling with hikers, bikers, picnickers, runners, climbers, and kayakers.

Zach and Jen snuck off into the woods to the spot they'd once found. They ducked and pushed through the soft needles of a balsam fir, *abies balsamea*. Jen wriggled out of her biking clothes; Zach did the same. The lay down on a bed of moss and laughed.

They kissed.

They made love, slowly at first.

Zach pulled his face a few inches away and gazed into her eyes. "Jen?"

"Don't stop."

"He's turned off, right?"

She laughed and pushed at him. She knew Zach didn't mean any harm. "Of course he's off." And she believed it was true.

He said, "I love you."

She said, "And I love you."

Slow got moving, moving became intense.

I thought to myself, *Wow, so this is what all the fuss is about.*

And intense became cosmic.

Good times! I thought. *Damn good times.*

Acknowledgments

My biggest thanks go to Gary Barker, my co-author for the anti-war fable *The Afghan Vampires Book Club* and author of the wonderful *The Museum of Lost Love*. A few years ago, Gary announced he had an idea for a new joint work. We went for one of our meandering walks in Washington, DC, and he told me the germ of a new story: in the near-future, a disease is killing off huge numbers of middle-aged people, but, if I recall, you could access a cure if your parents voluntarily died. By the end of that first walk, we were bubbling with ideas. Within a few weeks, we'd chosen different paths: mine, this mystery, and his, a work of literary fiction called *The Day They Came for the Nouns*, about the effects of war, memory, and forgetting. Keep your eyes open for it; it should be terrific. *The Last Exit* wouldn't exist without him.

Huge thanks to Marcia Markland, who brought her editorial smarts to the manuscript and poked, pushed, and cheered until I got the story right. And to Marie-Lynn Hammond, who took her sharp blue pencil and keen sense of character and story to an earlier draft.

Thanks to Jean Prince who gave feedback and tips on police procedure and the life of a female cop—any mistakes and flights of fancy are entirely my own (or simply an accurate reflection of how things are done in the early 2030s). I was aided by timely comments from Liam Kaufman Simpkins and medical tips from Victoria Lee, and enjoyed helpful theoretical discussions with Chloe Hung about the intersection of story arc and character development. Hugs to my sisters, Naomi, Miriam, Hannah, and Judith, who are always there for me.

Acknowledgments

My appreciation to the gang at Crooked Lane Books: senior acquisitions editor, Toni Kirkpatrick; Melissa Rechter; Katie McGuire; cover designer Melanie Sun; and the entire production and marketing teams, as well as to the sales force at Penguin Random House.

My gratitude goes out, and out again, to my agents, Ginger Curwen and Julia Lord, of the Julia Lord Literary Agency, who've been enthusiastic and supportive from the start. This book benefited in many ways from their ideas and insights. As Chandler might say, I'm a lucky guy to have them in my corner.

And thanks as always to my first reader and biggest critic, who doesn't let me get away with anything. Betty Chee, this one's for you.